BLUE ON BLUE

HEARTACHE IN WARTIME

ROSE CLAYWORTH

SWEETSPIRE LITERATURE
MANAGEMENT

Table of Contents

Glossary

1) **https:dictionary.cambridge.org**

   blue on blue, adjective, military, specialized

   relating to an attack in which soldiers, etc. are injured or killed by their own army or by soldiers on the same side as them.

   Many North Atlantic Treaty Organization (NATO) militaries refer to these incidents as blue on blue, which derives from military exercises where NATO forces were identified by blue pennants and units representing Warsaw Pact forces by red pennants.

2) **https://www.urbandictionary.com**

   Referring to when a police officer testifies against another police officer in a court of law.

3) **https://www.police1.com**

   OR, when one police officer fires on another.

4) Bobby Vinton, 1963, song, 3 weeks in Billboard's popular music charts

   "Blue on blue, heartache on heartache, ..."

Dedication

This book is dedicated to all victims of violence and oppression, especially those who suffered in the invasion of Kuwait, Gulf War 1, *Desert Storm*, and Gulf War 2, *Shock and Awe*, as well as the thousands of casualties in Iraq since 2003, and in particular to my late colleague, Margaret Hassan, Dip.TEFL.

Requiescant omnes in pace.

Wisdom

*"Love never dies a natural death. [...]
It dies of blindness and errors and betrayals.
It dies of illness and wounds; it dies of
weariness, of witherings, of tarnishings."*

Anais Nin

*"I am the master of my fate;
The captain of my soul."
Invictus, W.E. Henley, 1888*

*"Mankind must put an end to war before
war puts an end to mankind."*
John F. Kennedy

Acknowledgements

I am grateful to my family and friends for their encouragement and understanding as I strove to tell this tale. I wanted to record the impact of war on ordinary people and to seek to understand these stages of my life. My story may encourage others to continue their quest for happiness.

For their invaluable editorial help, I thank J. Molland, C.D. Howell and J. Vincent. You boldly went where others feared to go.

For technical and creative assistance with my web page and my own photos to produce the covers, I credit and sincerely thank L.R. Hutt and J.J. Hutt.

Disclaimer

This story is based on personal experiences recollected as memories. All names, some locations and other details have been changed to avoid harming anyone, living or dead. The political and military background described is as reported in the media at the time or in books after the events.

CHAPTER 1

Gulf War 2
Shock and Awe:
The Nightmare
Repeated

21 March 2003

Early morning mist was rising from the Waikato River alongside State Highway 1 as Rose drove north from Farmerston to Auckland on Friday, 21 March. She had set off at 5.30 am to arrive at the University campus in plenty of time for the staff training session. The Breeze Radio was playing a '60s hit song written by Burt Bacharach and Hal David, sung by Bobby Vinton. She was singing along with the familiar refrain, *Blue on blue, heartache on heartache,* while concentrating on the road, as the six o'clock news came on. The news reader announced in serious tones that the combined United States (US)-United Kingdom (UK) *Shock and Awe* campaign had begun in Iraq. The air bombardment of Baghdad had been 'successful' and now the first ground troops had moved into Basra, near the Kuwaiti northern frontier.

The news struck home to Rose as strong and swift as lightning, evoking memories of war, loss and sadness. How apt that refrain was at this moment. Those bombs would certainly bring sadness and heartache to both civilians and combatants. Rose knew that several incidents of friendly fire, or *blue on blue* in army terminology, had occurred in the First Arabian Gulf War in 1991. On four reported occasions UK troops were killed by allied US forces. Nine soldiers had died and 16 were injured. *Blue on blue* was sure to follow the start of the Second Arabian Gulf War thought Rose, gripping the steering wheel more firmly.

United Nations' (UN) discussions had been going on for months about US President George W. Bush's proposal to remove Iraq's leader, President Saddam Hussein. Bush was determined to find and destroy Iraqi Weapons of Mass Destruction (WMD) and establish a 'free', democratic Iraq. These discussions had intensified into bitter recriminations amongst politicians in the USA and the UK and had even led to the resignation of British ministers objecting to George Bush Junior's and Tony Blair's plan. Most recently Britain's Foreign Secretary, Robin Cook, a well-respected statesman with wide experience of Middle Eastern affairs, had left the Government. It was difficult to keep up with all the details in the time zone of distant New Zealand, but Rose had noted that the Chief UN Weapons Inspector Hans Blix wanted more time to search for hidden WMD. The grounds for the war were therefore in doubt. It was all very worrying but Rose was glad to be out of the geographical war zone herself, selfish though that sentiment was.

Rose knew the terror of war and how its aftermath could spread out in concentric circles, affecting all it touched. This

Second Gulf War might involve her friends in Saudi Arabia, Oman and the United Arab Emirates (UAE). In the First Gulf War in 1991 Oman and Bahrein had been spared both invasion and the Scud missiles which the Iraqis had trained on Israel and Saudi Arabia. Israel had long before readied itself against possible Arab missile attack, but the 'friendly' Gulf countries were taken unawares by the Iraqi invasion of Kuwait. Rose recalled how Kuwait radio news announcers prior to August 1990 referred unctuously to their northern neighbour as *Iraq ashaqiqa,* or 'sisterly Iraq'.

On the first day of the invasion of Kuwait, 2 August 1990, no vestige of sisterly affection was in evidence. Iraq's tanks had rolled down Kuwait's broad four-lane highways into Kuwait City to attack both Government buildings and the personal palaces of the Royal Family. The Kuwaiti army was small and unprepared to protect either the indigenous or the expatriate population. Many families were out of the country on long school summer holidays in August but those residents who were able to flee across the desert in four-wheel drive vehicles went to Bahrein or Saudi Arabia which became a safe haven for the Kuwaiti Emir. Those rich enough to travel further fled to Egypt, Lebanon or even London. Rose's husband Nabeel had stayed in Kuwait through the Invasion till November, when he joined her in England. The war of liberation had begun in January 1991.

Rose had left her English teaching position in Oman in January 2003, partly for fear of this Second Gulf War. In 1990 she had been on annual holiday in the UK when the Iraqis invaded Kuwait. That aggression had destroyed her marital home, annulled her job, and ultimately wrecked her marriage. Events had eventually brought her to New

Zealand, to a new job, new friends, and a new life. Rose felt lucky. Her life had not been easy. She had experienced an impoverished childhood in a broken home with a physically disabled mother. She had uprooted herself from her family, her home and her career for married life in Kuwait in 1976. Then she had endured a prolonged and bitter divorce after a 23 year relationship with the man she married. At 55 she felt that the tide had perhaps turned in her favour at last. But the news of war took her thoughts back to the Arabian Gulf where she had lived for nearly 23 years. Her heart ached for the Iraqis and for the Kuwaitis who had waited 12 years for revenge on Saddam Hussein for invading their country.

This time the suspicion was that Saddam had stockpiled chemical, biological and even nuclear weapons so there was fear that the terror could reach further than it had in 1991. Neither Kuwait nor the rest of the Arabian Gulf Cooperation Council countries had missiles to intercept weapons carrying biological warheads. In the *Desert Storm* campaign of 1991 under George Bush Senior the US and UK troops' limited objective was to drive the Iraqis out of occupied Kuwait. Now in 2003 under George Bush Junior, the overt mission of the coalition forces led by US and UK troops was to liberate Iraq and remove its dictatorial leader. But the Western invasion of a sovereign nation could wreak havoc in the complex politics of the Middle East. After World War I and the destruction of the Ottoman Empire the countries created according to the Allies' Sykes-Picot boundary lines (Syria, Lebanon, Iraq, Jordan, and Palestine) had left many Arabs unhappy. Since then Iraq's political history had been chequered with coups but Saddam Hussein had been in power since 1979 thanks to his tactics of oppression. Saddam did not hesitate to torture and kill opponents of his Ba'athist political regime. Freedom was not a word applicable to society in Saddam Hussein's Iraq, but was it the responsibility of international forces to intervene in what had clearly been a national issue until the invasion of Kuwait in August 1990?

Ever since 9/11/2001, G.W. Bush had waged a War on Terror, beginning with the campaign in Afghanistan in 2002. Rose was in Bahrein on that infamous date which commemorates the massacre of more than 2,500 helpless workers in the destruction of New York's twin World Trade Towers, the attack on the Pentagon in Washington, and the thwarted hijack of United Airlines Flight 93 brought down by heroic passengers in a field in Pennsylvania. The perpetrators were Islamic fundamentalists who saw themselves as martyrs in a holy war, a *jihad*, against 'Satan' America. This propaganda was the slogan of a network of Islamist terrorists called *Al Qaeda,* under the leadership of the Saudi-Arabian born dissident and exile, Osama bin Laden. Having failed to find bin Laden's hiding place amongst Afghanistan's Taliban militias, Bush Junior had trained his sights on the Iraqi President Saddam Hussein using the 'axis of evil' rationale to link Iraq to *Al Qaeda.* The UN had not gone along with Bush's push to remove Iraq's legitimate leader since the leaders of some nations, including Russia, France and Germany had dissented. Only the UK's Prime Minister Tony Blair had whole-heartedly adopted the US stance. For this Blair had been denounced and derided in the mass media as Bush's lap dog.

Even in this far corner of the universe where New Zealanders slept while the populations of the Northern Hemisphere woke and went about their business, Rose kept an eye on overseas news. She had been perturbed by media reports of the controversy surrounding the plans to start Gulf War 2. Removing Saddam Hussein in 1991 might have been judged more appropriate while Kuwait's oil wells were burning, causing tremendous environmental and financial damage, and Kuwaiti and other prisoners of war were still being held in Baghdad. But Bush Senior had not dared, or cared, to take that final step, perhaps assuming that the wholesale massacre of Iraqi soldiers fleeing towards home on Highway 80, the 'Highway of Death' as it was dubbed, was sufficient punishment.

Rose understood the rationale that attack is the best form of defence. There was a real fear in the West that other American cities, and even London, Rose's former home, could suffer similar 9/11 tragedies. Rose had seen for herself the havoc wreaked by the Irish Republican Army (IRA) bombs in London in the 1970s, and by Islamist suicide bombers who attacked the American Embassy in Kuwait in 1983. Inside Iraq the Kurds in the north of Iraq and the Marsh Arabs in the south of Iraq had suffered terribly at Saddam's hands. 5000 Kurds had been gassed in Halabja in 1988 while the Marsh Arabs had seen their historic marshland homes at the mouth of the Tigris and the Euphrates, a 20,000 square kilometer area, drained of water. Chemicals such as mustard gas had also been used to poison these Shiite Muslims who Saddam Hussein, a Sunni Muslim, regarded not as his citizens, but his enemies. Didn't these people deserve some outside help? Bush and Blair's motives for the invasion of Iraq were mixed but many different points of view were strongly defended in the media.

As Rose concentrated on the road, mindful of the 100km speed limit and patrolling traffic police, the seven o'clock news bulletin interrupted her thoughts. In Kuwait air raid sirens had prompted reporters and cameramen to run for their gas masks and the public shelters constructed after the State had been freed in 1991. Media folk, including CNN and the BBC had rushed in a feeding frenzy to the imminent war zone, relishing the opportunity to record real war movie scenes more exciting than any in a film script. But this was no fiction. It was real life terror and destruction. G.W. Bush appeared to be trying to achieve what his father twelve years earlier had been unable to do. Rose wondered why George Bush Senior had not felt it necessary to remove the tyrant after *Desert Storm* in February 1991. Had the Americans been supportive of Saddam behind the scenes, as some media reports suggested? Politics is a dark art: Motives for current actions may be hidden in the distant past.

Some commentators had assumed that Saddam's continuation as leader after his outrageous invasion of Kuwait was a concession won from the American Government grateful for his September 1980 attack on Iran. The Iran-Iraq War of 1980-88 was seen by some as third party pressure for the release of 52 US Embassy hostages held by Ayatollah Khomeini's government for 444 days from November 1979 to January 1981. The evidence for this theory was the US support for Saddam's eight year war, which resulted in victory for neither side but thousands of dead and injured for both. The US Embassy hostages in Iran had been freed but the American politicians trusted Saddam more than Iran's Shiite leader Khomeini and his political successors. It was believed that the US feared Iraqi Shiite opposition to Saddam, a

Sunni Muslim from the Sunni minority. If the Shiites could take over the Iraqi Government, their shared religion made a future alliance with the Iranians possible. The USA supported the moderate Sunni Gulf leaders who were willing to invest their oil wealth in the US and Europe and work with Western political leaders. Maintaining the balance of power in the Gulf had been just as important in 1991 as in 2003 but had become even more difficult. The Shiites were a majority in Iraq and the Kurds a sizeable minority, but the Sunnis held the power and under the Baath Party rule of Saddam Hussein it looked as if they were going to keep it.

Rose smiled despite herself as she recalled her own experiences of life in Kuwait with her husband until 1990. The Middle East, a mystical place culturally, a tragedy historically, and a muddle geographically, was still a mystery to most outsiders. Even those who were familiar with the Arab World knew better than to try to explain anything. Living there was a magic carpet ride, which could be fascinating. Egypt had a long tradition as a tourist magnet with its Sphynx, the gigantic Pyramids at Giza and along the Nile, the majesty of the temples at Luxor, the royal tombs in the Valley of the Kings, and the enormous statues and temples at Abu Simbel. Despite the disastrous impact of the ongoing Palestinian-Israeli conflict on its borders Lebanon too had a thriving tourist economy before its long Civil War began in 1975. More recently Bahrein, Oman and Jordan had attracted tourists with their climate, scenery and historic sites.

For resident Western workers the Arabian Gulf countries were not easy to live in, with compulsory Aids testing, strict division in residential areas and restaurants of families from 'bachelors' (male workers living without their families) and strict adherence to Islamic laws such as abstinence from alcohol. In Iraq indigenous Christian sects had been tolerated under Saddam's regime but restrictions on the practice of their religion and reports of misappropriation of property and funds had caused many citizens to leave Iraq over the decades. Saddam had chosen a Christian, Tariq Aziz, original Assyrian name Mikhail Yuhanna, as his Foreign Minister but this positive affirmation had not prevented the decline in numbers of Christians in Iraq from 1,400,000 in 1987 to 1 million in 1991 and only 800,000 in 2003. Rose knew that some had come to New Zealand as refugees or immigrants and now they were reacting to the latest news by calling in to the chat show following the radio news.

Rose listened to the outpouring of emotion against the bombardment. Like Rose's ex-husband Nabeel many Arabs were supporters of unity against the common enemy, Israel and the USA, on account of the loss of Palestine and the suffering of the Palestinian people in the Israeli Occupied Territories. However, within the separate nations of the Arab World no one could agree about the solution to the 'Palestine Problem'. Rose understood that this deep-seated sense of injustice could surface as a call for support for Saddam Hussein. The US/Israel coalition was usually blamed for any affront or injury to the Arab nations. Conspiracy theorists can twist reality any way they want and Rose knew the historical reasons for doing so in the Arab World.

As the traffic slowed on the outskirts of Auckland, New Zealand's largest and most traffic-congested city, Rose empathised with the anti-war emotion of the callers. She had visited Beirut three times between 1973 and 1993 with

Nabeel and witnessed the devastation of warfare on what had previously been a beautiful city, once dubbed the Paris of the Middle East. In 1973 they had stayed first in downtown Hamra Street and heard Israeli jets breaking the sound barrier above the city. Then high up in the mountains above Beirut she had seen sandbags around the French windows of pretty mountain homes. She had heard shells falling in the next valley, frightened dogs barking and cockerels crowing in the middle of the night. Even though New Zealand seemed very far away from the terror of the Middle East, a threat made years ago by her husband could still make her experience a shiver of fear down her spine. She feared for her personal freedom as a woman, her ability to live alone and enjoy her new life. These freedoms were taken for granted by Western women but Rose knew they were not universal. In some cultures, such as in Taliban controlled areas of Afghanistan, women were not even educated, so lowly was their position in society.

On top of that cultural awareness, Rose feared for her life. 'It would be cheaper to have you killed,' Nabeel had said the last time they had spoken on the phone about their impending divorce and division of finances. For her estranged husband, arranging Rose's murder would be easier than agreeing to a divorce settlement. His affidavits showed that he assessed their long relationship in terms of dinars, dirhams, pounds or dollars. He valued the investment in their marriage as wasted time and money. Questions Rose could not easily answer came to mind. Where had the 23 years gone that she had spent with him? Why had she let him take away the best part of her life? *Blue on blue, heartache on heartache,* was a melancholy refrain which resonated from the past with present relevance.

Rose switched off the radio as she spotted signage for the Harbour Bridge. Crossing that would take her to the North Shore, a mistake that would make her seriously late for her appointment at the University. She was heading for the car park of the landmark Sky Tower, the easiest to find and the closest to her destination. Auckland is a beautiful city, with many beaches, sea inlets and coves, but designed with wide streets and modern buildings interspersed with the occasional remnants of nineteenth century architecture. This was the first time Rose had driven here alone. Her line manager had brought her up the previous month to introduce her to her new colleagues. Now she needed to concentrate on finding a parking place.

Fridays were not the best time to drive to Auckland. The city was severely congested at rush hours and especially on Fridays. There had been talk about introducing a rail system, building another bridge or digging a tunnel to better handle the traffic but as yet, commuters had to deal with the problem. Leaving the city at 3.30pm Rose would most likely be stuck in traffic. The average 'Jafa', sometimes interpreted as Just Another Fantastic Aucklander, liked to get out of town early to start the weekend. In her life so far work had always been top priority, but now she hoped to achieve better work-life balance. Meanwhile, on with the new job!

CHAPTER 2

Gulf War 1: Repercussions, Recriminations

20 November 1990

I tied yellow ribbons and balloons painted by my artistic six year old niece Noelle and her three year old brother Rupert onto the front door knocker of my brother's house in London, while Katie, my sister in law, pinned to the door frame the *Welcome Home Nabeel* banner she had designed on the computer. My brother Bill put champagne on ice and Katie prepared dinner while I drove to London's Heathrow Airport to meet Nabeel off the plane from Beirut. I was excited. I'd waited three months for this day.

The journey was slow as usual. I sat in the traffic jam on the North Circular in the second hand Ford Ghia I'd persuaded the bank manager in Mossfield to let me buy. Arabian Gulf residents' UK bank accounts were closed by the British Government within a month of the invasion of Kuwait on 2 August 1990 to prevent Saddam Hussein from accessing donations from supporters with British bank accounts. It was highly unlikely that I would be financing Saddam when my marital home had been trashed after Kuwait's invasion, but precautions were necessary I suppose. This would make Nabeel laugh, I thought. I had so many things to tell him after three months apart. Phone calls had not been possible as the lines were closed on the first day of the Invasion. Since then only short messages had passed between us, through Jordan-based Palestinians who were able to travel to and from Iraqi-occupied Kuwait.

I hoped my husband would appreciate that I'd chosen this car wisely in my distressed state of mind in September. I'd never bought a car on my own before, but this was a bargain, fully automatic, with sunroof, power windows and central locking, just like our cars in the Gulf, if a lot smaller. Our cars in Kuwait had always been American but Nabeel had finally treated himself to his first brand new Mercedes in June, 1990, a mere two months before the invasion of Kuwait. I'd only dared to drive it for a couple of hundred metres, fearful as I was of damaging this expensive purchase. Nabeel deserved this indulgence after years of hard work as a 'middle man', or sales representative, in the supply of hardware to the oil industry. I'd learned from the few messages from friends in Jordan that the car had been stolen from in front of the British Embassy in Kuwait as Nabeel watched from inside the building. I was told that he'd taken shelter in the Embassy on Invasion day. But there was so much I didn't know and I was eager to find out more about what happened to him and to our lovely home. We'd both worked hard since our marriage in 1976 to achieve a level of comfort we both relished. Although non-Kuwaitis could only rent accommodation, our furniture and possessions were status symbols which marked our career achievements.

I wondered how angry Nabeel would be now about the events and aftermath of the Invasion. Already a chain smoker of 80 cigarettes a day, I wondered if he'd increased his cigarette intake as a result of the stress he must have suffered. I knew we'd lost our home to the occupying Republican Guard. I also knew he hadn't been able to go to his office in Kuwait City. He'd spent the past three months at his brothers' apartment in the south of the State. I certainly had no affection for the invaders who had deprived me of my husband, my home and its contents and my job as an English language teacher. Watching the BBC TV coverage of the Invasion in Mossfield with Mum had incensed me. Our home was next to the Emir's private palace, just across the road from the Kuwait Towers, the symbol of modern Kuwait. As the Iraqis had made the Towers their Invasion headquarters, I'd glimpsed my garden on TV. The ping pong table in our garden was visible from the revolving restaurant in the tallest of the three Towers. Although I was keen to know what happened, I was glad that I'd been spared the agony of experiencing the Invasion first-hand. Either I would have been a reckless idiot and put myself at risk from the invading soldiers, or I would have been a coward and not dared to defend my possessions. Like many other wives on overseas summer vacation on the second of August, I had to endure the waiting and wondering. However, I was luckier than those women whose British husbands were picked up by the Iraqis and held as Human Shields. Some British families had dared to escape across the desert to avoid capture but a plane load of passengers in transit had been taken into captivity. My plight was nothing compared to theirs.

I'd kept myself busy in the UK looking after my disabled Mum. I enjoyed being her caregiver as well as doing the garden to save paying the gardener to keep the quarter acre tidy. I'd even converted a vegetable patch to lawn as Mum no longer had family at home to feed. A novice gardener, I'd been the object of a surprise attack from the residents of a wasps' nest in the compost heap at the bottom of the garden. I laughed, recalling Mum's amazement as I ran as fast as I could up to the house. I wondered how our lovely garden in far away Kuwait had fared through the hot summer months with temperatures of 45 degrees C and higher. Like all Kuwait residents and the State Government we spent a lot of money on watering gardens to keep the inhabited areas of the desert green. I visualized the tall multi-coloured hollyhocks at the back of my flower beds, the short sweet-smelling, golden marigolds and the two metre palm tree near the front door, which had sulked for months when we first moved in. Until we took over the apartment no one had cared for the palm and it had only just started to respond to regular, deep drinks of water. My questions would soon be answered, I thought, as I finally reached the Airport and found a space in Heathrow's Terminal 3 multi-storey car park.

I ran to the arrivals hall, afraid that I was late, my eyes frantically scanning the board for MEA 619. It had landed and already passengers carrying distinctive Beirut Airport duty free plastic bags with the Cedars of Lebanon symbol and Arabic lettering were coming through from customs control. Where was Nabeel? Would he have less hair? He was already balding when I last saw him, though he'd had a thick head of hair when I met him twenty years earlier. Would he have grown a moustache? Did he have a moustache when we were in Europe on summer holiday just before the Invasion? Strangely I couldn't remember. He tended to chop and change with the moustache. I didn't like it, so perhaps he'd grown one after the Invasion while I was not there to criticize him. Would I even recognize him? And then, there he was, tall at 6'3", slender at around 95 kilograms, with short dark hair on the back and sides of his bald head, his face distinctive with his long, irregularly shaped nose. Well-dressed always, his height gave him a distinguished appearance, even though he was the least handsome of his brothers and he hadn't aged well.

I had to admit to myself that his smile, with his large, uneven teeth, reminded me of a friendly camel. Although this negativity was unspoken, it was no doubt a subconscious retaliation to his frequent taunts about my appearance, comparing my legs to the Roman pillars still standing in Baalbeck and the size of my mouth to the grotto of Jaita. Both these famous tourist sites in Lebanon had become standing jokes to Nabeel, but permanent 'put-downs' to me. All jokes have seeds of truth in them, but these were unkind, capable of sowing lack of self esteem, although I had not understood this at the time. For now, however, we moved towards each other for the first hug and kiss on the cheek since we had parted at Paris' Charles de Gaulle airport on 21 July, 1990. I'd taken a plane for London on that day, while he'd returned to Kuwait, arriving there just in time for the Invasion.

'Hello darling! How are you *habibi*?' My limited Arabic returned spontaneously as I clutched his shoulders in a hug impeded by his loaded luggage trolley.

'Fine, fine,' he murmured, returning my hug with one arm extended.

His French-accented English and familiar, slightly high-pitched voice were the same as ever. His moustache brushed my cheek. All six feet three of his thin frame seemed to wrap around me, and I felt my anxiety dissipate. Whatever had happened to our home or our possessions was unimportant. We were alive, we were well and we could be happy again. We moved politely aside from the other incoming passengers, pushing his trolley, laden with a large suitcase and brief case, plus two duty free bags with the maximum permissible 400 cigarettes, a single malt whisky for us and a bottle of cognac for Bill I guessed.

'My car's on Level 5. Come on, here's the lift. This way.'

We both knew Heathrow Airport well after living in Kuwait for 14 years after we married and travelling to my home in England once a year. Together we pushed the trolley clumsily towards the car, arms slung loosely around each other.

'How are Asma, Henri, Edouard, Adel, Marie and the children?'

Nabeel's sister Asma and brothers Henri, Edouard and Adel, as well as Nabeel had finally fled Kuwait in November 1990 and gone back to Lebanon, where the Civil War had just ended with the exile of Christian leader Michel Aoun. Other family members, including their sister Marie, her husband Younis, and their children had lived through the Lebanese Civil War which had started in 1975. That war had prevented us from setting up home there. Now war had touched us directly, removing us from our marital home in Kuwait, and depriving us both of our livelihoods. Nabeel's commercial business as an agent for suppliers of technology and hardware for the oil industry had faltered as the Iraqis took over Kuwait's Petroleum Industry. No new hardware had been bought while the country was under Iraqi occupation. If Saddam had his way, Kuwait would be part of a Greater Iraq, the 19th State, and perhaps Nabeel had been tempted to continue his business in Kuwait. But for now, *elhamdulillah,* Thank God, we still had a home in England, and our families to love us. With a sigh of relief I started the car and drove out of the airport, to make our way to my brother's house in London's northern suburbs.

War had been the permanent background to Nabeel's life. His mother and baby sister had both died after childbirth at home in Haifa, in 1942, when Palestine was riven with strife and terror. Nabeel's father had taken his six surviving children into Lebanon for security, leaving the key to his house and his tailor's shop with a relative. Subsequently his home had been sold to house the Jewish refugees flooding in on ships from war torn Europe. Those survivors who fled Europe where they had been hunted down by Hitler's Nazis, came to their new homeland and took over the homes of refugee Palestinian families. Nabeel's family had lived in a Beirut refugee camp for years surviving on rice and tomato soup, with a weekly treat of roasted chicken. Since then Nabeel couldn't stomach tomato soup or chicken.

Nabeel's family were by religion *roumi,* Catholic following Rome, so they had been fortunate enough to obtain Lebanese passports, given the balance of power in Lebanon between the two faiths, Islam and Christianity. Unfortunately, the vast numbers of homeless Muslim Palestinians, who would outnumber the Christians if given Lebanese citizenship, were condemned to remain in homes built of cardboard and corrugated iron in the refugee camps to the present day. Even though the fighting which prefaced the creation of Israel in 1948 was over, all Palestinian refugees from that period were denied the right to return home. Many Palestinians I knew in Kuwait, including one of Nabeel's aunts and uncles, still displayed the key to their former home on a wall of their current residences. Two wrongs and no right had been the *status quo* in Palestine for 70 years. I wondered how this second major displacement and loss had affected Nabeel's mental state, but knowing he would be tired after the ten hour flight, I tried to maintain a positive mood as long as possible.

'How was the journey, darling? Are the Syrians still 'guarding' the airport in Beirut?'

It was well known that the Syrians were interfering in Lebanese politics. They were most visible at the airport where the Syrian Army had assumed the right to check incoming and outgoing travellers' bags for drugs or weapons. At least that was their ostensible *raison d'etre*. As I had experienced for myself, the soldiers tried to intimidate travelers into giving them money or items from their luggage.

'Yes, they tried to take the things I've brought for you. They always want *bakshish* – money or gifts - before they let you through, just like before.'

'You brought me things? There was no need. I'm just glad to see you here safe at last.'

'Safe? I was always safe. No need to worry about that. I was a soldier you know, in Black September. I'm not afraid of those cardboard cutouts.'

I smiled to myself. Nabeel always maintained the pretence that he'd fought in the Palestinian uprising against the Jordanians in 1970 which had ended so badly for the

Palestinian Liberation Organization (PLO). In the Six Day War with Israel, in 1967, the Palestinian people had lost Jerusalem and Transjordan and been confined to Gaza, a small coastal plain. Many Palestinians had found safe haven in Jordan but the Black September uprising of 1970 resulted in the PLO being driven out of Jordan to Tunisia. Despite the ongoing failures of past wars and present uprisings such as the *Intifidas* against Israel, Nabeel entertained dreams of victory. He liked to think of himself as a hero, even as a future leader and saviour of the Palestinians. He used to say about the divided Palestinian people, some supporting *Hamas*, others *Fattah*,

'They need a dictator - a benevolent one - I can do that. I know what they need.'

He'd clearly not changed his political stance despite the impact of Iraq's invasion of Kuwait. Many Palestinians had stayed on in Kuwait while the Iraqis were in charge, which was a convenient but dangerous tactic if the Kuwait Government was eventually reinstated. The Kuwaitis would not take kindly to what amounted to treacherous behaviour, siding with the enemy. Saddam Hussein portrayed himself as the defender of the Palestinian cause, and the enemy of Israel, so the Palestinian workers had been allowed to continue in their jobs during the Iraqi occupation. This meant that the oil and petrochemical industries could continue to function, while the workers needed money to live, given that they would probably not be able to find jobs in Jordan if they left Kuwait.

Nabeel's Lebanese passport showed his date and place of birth in Palestine. He had hung on in Kuwait for three long months, doing exactly what, I wasn't sure, though I'd heard that he had visited Baghdad to renew his travel papers. Avoiding the sensitive topic of the Invasion as I drove, we chatted about his family in Beirut, his sister Marie and her husband Younis, her first cousin, and their children. These nieces and nephew were growing up, studying, working, getting engaged, marrying, with the oldest girls ready to have children of their own now.

Despite my curiosity, it seemed wiser to concentrate on safe topics of conversation rather than the loss of our home and possessions. There would be time for that later I guessed. Tonight was for celebrating the start of a new life, perhaps even a life elsewhere than in Kuwait. We were both tri-lingual, speaking English, French and Arabic, intelligent, hard-working and motivated to make a fresh start. I was more than ready to work again after an enforced, unemployed stay in the UK since 2 August 1990, a date I would never forget since it changed my life so completely. We'd been together since 1970 and knew each other well, I believed.

When I met him I had been intrigued by his romantic, bohemian appearance, French accent and London lifestyle. We both loved travel, dancing, film, music and theatre and had busy work and social lives in London. But Nabeel's life story as a Palestinian refugee had saddened me. I was born the year before Israel was created, so knew nothing of the political history. After six years together and many quarrels, I hadn't been keen to marry and live so far away from home, especially leaving behind my disabled mother. But after much deliberation and with my mother's support I had made that decision. Nabeel and I had had our ups and downs over the years, but war couldn't affect our long relationship, could it?

CHAPTER 3

Gulf War 2: 'A' Day - Aerial Attack

22 March 2003

Rose had slept badly. After leaving the Auckland campus the day before at 3.30pm and getting gridlocked on Symonds Street, the journey south on Highway 1, New Zealand's geothermal route, had been slow and arduous, as drivers jostled for pole position in the lanes. The highway was under construction so it was important to pay attention to the road. There was no chance to relax behind the wheel until she got closer to Farmerston and then she had to turn into her motel at a major road junction. A minor mistake could end in a major accident with unforgiving local drivers.

The motel's owners had offered Rose long term rates at a price she could easily afford on her salary. She was grateful to have the clean, neat serviced room with *en suite* shower room and cooking facilities. She was determined not to waste money on motel fees for longer than necessary so this served her purposes well enough. The only downside was the location, with heavy goods vehicle drivers screeching their brakes as they approached the lights at the junction at night. Rose didn't mind waking early to catch the UK and US news on TV but the weekends were much noisier as night owls drove home from the bars and clubs in the central city. Drivers often skidded as the lights changed and Rose would wake with a start, dreading to hear the follow up thump that signalled a crash. These crazy accidents reminded her of driving to work in Kuwait, where it was not uncommon to find a car crashed on the centre of a roundabout on a Saturday morning, the first day of the working week. Last night as usual she had fallen asleep around 9pm watching the ongoing war reports, anticipating a quite different Saturday morning in this city.

For the first three weeks after Rose's arrival in New Zealand in February the University had paid for a superior motel within five minutes' walk of the downtown campus. She had been in the cheaper motel for only a couple of weeks so far. She could still walk into work but it took almost 30 minutes and in the continuing heat of the Southern Hemisphere summer it was uncomfortable. So she had made buying a car a priority. The purchase of her new home was next on her 'to do' list. Although her stay in the motel was temporary while she searched for a house, she had always enjoyed the bed-sitter life as a student in London. She had often joked that if she ever got the large house with a grand piano in the drawing room which she aspired to, she would still keep one room where she would spend most of her time with her books around her. So living out of two suitcases in one room was a pleasure. It limited the amount of time she spent deciding what to wear each day and reduced housework to personal laundry.

This weekend morning, only the fifth Rose had spent in New Zealand, she woke at 6am as usual despite the lack of sleep occasioned by the noisy highway traffic. As she made her morning cup of Earl Grey tea she still had to remind herself that in New Zealand Saturday is not the first day of the week. She had spent fourteen years in Kuwait and eight in Bahrein where Saturday is the start of the working week. This Saturday she could take her tea back to bed and return to the TV war reporting. It appeared that CNN had just been expelled from Iraq, accused of broadcasting misinformation. The BBC team was still there, and the New Zealand reporter seemed to be enjoying the excitement. He had even slept through two of the air-raids in the night, he happily told his viewers. The strategic bombing must have been pretty accurate, otherwise he wouldn't have been so happy, Rose guessed. There was little mention of collateral damage, but no doubt many Baghdad citizens were hiding in fear for their lives or had fled the terror of bombing over their city.

There had been antiwar protests in the UK, where 'peaceniks' had been proposing to go to Iraq to offer themselves as 'human shields'. Those UK citizens who had suffered as victims of Saddam's 1990 Human Shield Defence had written to the press to protest at this irony. Even in New Zealand, a non-participant in this non-UN approved war, the notion of this UK/US coalition attack was not welcomed. New Zealand's Prime Minister, Helen Clark, could remonstrate with male political leaders that war doesn't get you anywhere, but the ideology of Venus, Goddess of Love, holds no sway while that of Mars, the God of War, is still the accepted dogma of many power hungry nations. In Iraq, Saddam saw himself as a strong man, with an ego the size of the statues of himself he had erected all around his capital city, Baghdad.

The replica statues of Saddam's forearms brandishing a sword thrusting out of the ground on a large traffic roundabout had amazed Rose back in 1988 when she had visited Baghdad to assess two female teachers studying for an English Teaching Diploma at the British Council school. At that time Saddam was seen as a hero in the Arab World, on account of his pro-Arab unity stance. However, his long war with Iran, in which thousands of conscripted soldiers died, proved that he cared little for 'his' people. So important to his continued success was the cult of personality that he forced householders to display his portrait in their homes on pain of punishment. Torture, imprisonment and spying were the tools which kept him in power.

Satellite TV was showing the antiwar demonstrations in the Arab world, in Bahrain, Cairo and Yemen. Saddam was working his 'spin' as the sole Arab hero, accusing his oil rich Arabian Gulf neighbours of siding with the USA, friends of the Arabs' bitter enemy, Israel. Rose recalled how in 1990 Saddam, the great Arab leader, proclaimed the intention of destroying Israel with his Scud missiles. He maintained that was the fourth reason why he had invaded Kuwait, which he regarded as Iraq's 19th province. His first excuse for invading was that Kuwait had stolen Iraq's oil by slant drilling into Iraq's Rumaila oilfield and extracting the oil by means of a secret pipeline under their joint border; his second, that Kuwait had formerly been part of Iraq under the Ottoman Empire; his third, that Kuwait had sold too much oil and reduced the price, negatively affecting Iraq's economy. Saudi Arabia was also to be punished for siding with the USA against him. In 1991 Scud missiles had fallen on Riyadh and in Israel. In several cases the US Patriot missiles launched to destroy the Scuds collided with them over the intended target, causing fatalities and injuries. However, the greater fear was that the Scuds would have chemical or biological loads, causing Israeli and Saudi Arabian citizens to wear gas masks under attack. That dreadful scenario had not eventuated in the First Gulf War, but now residents were again fearful of chemical or biological weapons.

The following radio news item was about Turkey. Having decided initially that they would not participate in the war, the Turkish Government had now realised that as things were going well – perhaps even, Saddam had been wiped out with the first aerial attack – they should get in and control the Kurds in the north of Iraq before the Kurds took advantage of their freedom and struck out for a country of their own. Like the Palestinians, the history of the Kurds was tragic. Rose felt blessed to have been born in Britain, which, though invaded throughout its early history by the Romans, the Vikings, and the Normans, had ultimately established the rule of law and educated a literate population to make change by means of the ballot box, not violence.

Arab and other conspiracy theorists had attributed the US motivation for the invasion of Iraq to gaining control of Iraq's oil industry, which had been given a protection plan. Seven Iraqi oil wells had been set on fire by the fleeing workers but the main outlets for loading petrol onto vessels in the Gulf had been secured by the UK/USA allies. In February 1991 the Iraqis had polluted the Arabian Gulf and almost destroyed Kuwait's oil production system by setting fire to hundreds of oil wells when they were driven from Kuwait. Post war Iraq was on everyone's minds now. The wealth of the oil economy would be needed in the reconstruction of a free Iraq. Even the dissenting politicians in Europe were committed to helping the Iraqis get back on their feet. Unlike Afghanistan's capital, Kabul, which had been virtually destroyed by decades of civil war, Iraq's capital, Baghdad, was still standing, even though Iraq had suffered economically from UN sanctions since the First Gulf War. Saddam had contributed to the dire state of the economy by plundering Iraq's oil economy to increase his own private wealth and possessions, and by making expensive and illicit purchases to fund his desire to create a nuclear bomb. Once he was removed, the general assumption was that it would be possible for Iraqis to live better, peaceful lives in future, even if no one seemed to know exactly how this would come about.

TV was showing Iraqi buses full of old men and women loudly expressing their patriotism and love for their leader. Perhaps they had received a financial inducement to demonstrate for the media and/or had benefited otherwise from the Ba'ath party. Saddam had created a harsh regime with rewards to individuals for loyalty but severe punishment for independence of thought and action. Many Iraqis had gone into exile since Saddam took power in 1979, escaping with only their lives. All citizens were subject to strict laws to prevent the exit of manpower and money from the country. So early in this game of war you could not expect the ordinary person to know how to react except in an indoctrinated way. But in the face of the combined US and UK armies, it was surprising that people continued to shout in Arabic, 'Long live Saddam!' Rose sincerely hoped that the accurate bombing of the Presidential Palace meant that Saddam was dead, like her ex-husband. This new war was bringing back all the old feelings, hidden, suppressed, but not forgotten as she struggled to rebuild her life and reinvent herself after years of putdowns and constraints in her marriage.

Rose glanced at the clock. It was midnight in Iraq and 8am in New Zealand. In the UK, where her mother had died almost a year ago, it would be 8pm. In the past on weekends she would ring Mum for a long catch up. She sadly missed her now but she could distract herself with her favourite leisure activity, shopping! Rose had a container full of furniture and possessions at the docks in Bahrein awaiting shipping to New Zealand, so window shopping was the preferred option. With a break for lunch that would be equally consoling. This was not the first time she had built a life for herself alone in a new country. It was exciting making a fresh start. Above all, she was glad to be far away from the scene of war where so many were suffering.

CHAPTER 4

Conspiracy Theory

21 November 1990

The late rush hour traffic was steady and as dusk fell I turned the car into Landridge Road, where the balloons and ribbons were waving bravely in the autumn breeze. A tiny smile creased the corners of Nabeel's mouth as he noted the decorated front door, but only for an instant. He was preoccupied with finding another cigarette. I recalled how I had to say *cigarette, watch* instead of *turn right, turn left* to give directions when chain-smoker Nabeel was driving. He always had a cigarette in his right hand, and he wore his watch on his left hand. Using these words I could be sure he wouldn't make a wrong turn. I noted that he wasn't using his expensive Dunhill navy blue enamel and 22k gold lighter. His pride and joy had perhaps been lost in the post Invasion looting. I wondered when he would talk about the things that had been taken and what exactly had happened. He'd not said much as I drove.

Now Bill was opening the door, with Katie and the children welcoming us. Kisses, in the Lebanese way, three for each person, left cheek, right cheek, left again. It was a ritual we always observed, joking about the Lebanese greeting.

Nabeel's family was Palestinian by birth but also Christian, fortunate to acquire Lebanese passports as refugees in Beirut. He had been educated in French and spoke French fluently, as well as excellent English, though his mother tongue was Arabic. Anyone meeting him would think he was French. Lebanon had been a French colony, while their country of birth, Palestine, to which they could never return, had been under the control of the British Mandate, as a so-called Protectorate. With friends like those to protect you, who needs enemies? But now, I had to concentrate on making Nabeel feel welcome, after our 100 day absence from each other.

Within minutes we were sitting in the lounge, the pale pine furniture and flowery chintz upholstery offering comfort far removed from what Nabeel had seen in Kuwait where our beautiful home was torn apart and trashed. The champagne cork popped. Bill was as ever the attentive host with a good cellar ready for the appropriate occasion. We drank Mumm's, our champagne of choice throughout our married life, in honour of my Mum who, disabled with rheumatoid arthritis (RA), was unable to travel independently. We'd be talking to her on the phone soon, and driving up to Mossfield to stay with her after a couple of days in London. Meanwhile, we all wanted to hear what had happened to Nabeel in Kuwait on and after 2 August 1990.

I'd only had the briefest of messages from Nabeel since the frantic final phone calls I had made to him on Invasion day. These short communications had been passed along by friends on the phone from Jordan. Palestinians had been free to travel to and from Kuwait during the Iraqi occupation, though it was my understanding that Nabeel had stayed in

Kuwait from August to November. Our friends Ronda and Mark were staying with Nabeel on the night prior to the Invasion. They were on the point of leaving Kuwait after residing there for several years for their new home in Spain. I had had no news from them until Ronda contacted me by phone in September and we had met in London for lunch. She told me how she and Mark had left our home on the morning of the Invasion, thinking they could get away across the desert in their four wheel drive vehicle and keep to their plan to drive back across Saudi Arabia to Europe. Instead, they had been stopped by a Republican Guard tank commander, and compelled to take out their luggage. They had had to open their suitcases for searching, and in the confusion some of Ronda's Marks and Spencer (M&S) knickers had ended up under the wheels of the tank.

Once home in the UK, Ronda, a consummate marketing expert, had contacted M&S with the story. They'd presented her with a gift voucher to replace a few pairs of knickers and written the event up in their staff magazine. It was even more amusing since M&S is a Jewish-owned company whose goods were black-listed in the Arab World. If the Israeli boycott office in Kuwait had known about Ronda's predilection for M&S lingerie, she could have been in trouble, though most often a blind eye was turned at Kuwait Customs on Westerners' luggage contents. In my life in Kuwait I was far more discriminating on account of Nabeel's background. I never bought anything Israeli made on trips home to the UK, though I'd once committed a serious *faux pas* when writing some material for English language teaching. I'd used the Ford car as an example of mechanical invention, but Ford cars were banned in Kuwait in the 1970s because of the Arab

League boycott of US companies which traded with Israel. Fortunately I was able to apologise to my students and avert complaints.

According to Ronda their last days in occupied Kuwait had been very frightening. After initially being stopped and their luggage checked, they had been ordered to go to the beach, leaving their vehicle and its contents near our house. The beach was thronged with people who had been travelling into the City to work that morning, but had been intercepted and commanded to sit on the beach. This was hazardous as shells fired by the Kuwaiti defenders inland, were falling onto the invading army on the Beach Road. By sheer luck the couple had encountered Nabeel on the beach, and together they had gone to the British Embassy. They'd sheltered there for a few days, but when things quietened down and the supply of food became an issue for the Embassy staff, they were asked to leave. So they'd all headed back to our house, which was well stocked with my home-made beer and wine. After a few days the Red Berets, or the Iraqi Special Forces, had come to the house and told Nabeel that it would be wiser to vacate the premises. It seemed that a rag, tag and bobtail people's army was descending on Kuwait from Basra, a small town on the Iraqi border. The elite Republican Guard Brigade were perplexed, but they knew that once an armed rabble was in Kuwait, their ability to maintain law and order would be compromised.

So Mark and Ronda had gone with Nabeel to his brothers' flat in Salahiyah, further south and away from the City. There Ronda had cooked meals with Asma, Nabeel's unmarried sister, who looked after her bachelor brothers and had been glad of the female company. There could have been problems for Mark though, since all British men were being rounded up, and taken to Iraq, to be part of Saddam's Human Shield, his defense against allied Western attack. Although Ronda hated to leave her husband behind, especially as he'd been operated on for cancer in Kuwait's excellent oncology centre only two months earlier, she'd had to admit that participating in the evacuation of women and children was preferable to being imprisoned in Iraq. She'd been able to leave Kuwait with Australian and New Zealand women on a specially chartered bus which travelled to Baghdad by road. From there, Ronda had flown to London and rejoined her sister and Mark's parents. Meanwhile, her husband had been obliged to hide in the false ceiling of friends' apartments to avoid being picked up by the soldiers and transferred to Iraq. He'd only been able to move out of the ceiling to use the bathroom at night and was being fed by Palestinian friends like Nabeel. It had seemed unbelievable to me then but now we could sit back and hear the details of the Invasion, blow by terrible blow. I wondered what would happen to Mark trapped in Kuwait.

'Now, darling, tell us what happened from the moment you put the phone down on me that terrible morning last August.'

'You know, it's been more than three months since then. A lot of water under the bridge as you say.'

'Yes, but surely you remember the first day?'

'Of course, how could I forget? I thought I was going to die.'

'Oh dear. Ronda said they were stopped by the Red Berets and made to go onto the beach where they met you. Then you all went to the British Embassy.'

'Yes, that's right. As Ronda and Mark were British, I was allowed to go with them. But before I saw them, I was trying to dig a hole for myself in the sand, to protect me from the shells Sheikh Jaber's men were firing from his palace. They were trying to defend the Emir's Palace, and kill the Iraqi soldiers. Every time they missed the Iraqi tanks on the *Corniche* they almost killed the workers they'd made leave their cars and go and sit on the beach. I felt sure I was going to die with the others.'

'Oh my God! How awful. Thank goodness you found Ronda and Mark.'

'Yes, we met up on the beach near our house and went to the British Embassy. We were allowed in by the Ambassador and that's when I was able to make that short call to you.'

'Yes, I was so relieved to hear from you that day. Mum and I didn't know what to think as we watched the Invasion on the TV. So what happened after that?'

'Well, there wasn't much food or drinking water in the Embassy, so after a couple of nights, when the fighting had died down, I went back to our house and asked permission of the Red Berets to go inside.'

'Hadn't they already looted the place?'

'No, the soldiers were good people. They didn't loot. In fact, they were guarding our house.'

'What do you mean?'

'They asked me to prove it was my house. So I took them inside and showed them my photo on the piano.'

'So that photo of you with the big cigar in the silver frame was still there? That's surprising. So what did you do then?'

'Well, first I just took some water back to the Embassy, but the Ambassador asked if Ronda and Mark could leave with me because they couldn't accommodate them any longer. So they came back to the house. I gave some water and some food to the Iraqi soldiers because they didn't have anything. No supplies at all. They thought they were coming to get the Emir, and then they were going home.'

'Oh? What happened to the Emir?'

'He got away. The head of the snake, that's what they called him. They even wrote it on our house wall, just outside our front door. But they were unlucky. He ran away as soon as the Iraqis began driving down the four lane highways from the northern border into the City.'

'Well, I don't blame him. Had he done anything to deserve being captured?'

'You don't know half of it.'

'I agree. I don't know any of it. You told me there was no problem when I spoke to you on the phone the night before the Invasion. I had the shock of my life when you rang the next day and said it had happened.'

'OK, OK, I made a big mistake. No-one in Kuwait was prepared for it really. It seems they had been taking oil from the pipeline, and lying about it.'

'But that seems so weird. Why on earth would they do that?'

'The Americans are behind it. You'll find out soon enough. That ambassador, April what's her name, she gave Saddam permission to invade. She knew what was going on.'

'Oh, my God! Is this possible?'

'I know you won't believe anything I say against the USA.'

'That's not true and you know it. I'm just amazed. We've heard nothing about that here.'

'OK, OK. Just listen though if you want to know what happened.'

'Well, just one more question for now, where's Mark? What happened to him? I saw Ronda. She was trying to get him out by petitioning the UK government but you know how slow to react the bureaucrats are.'

'Well, I took food to him at least twice a week, after dark, and he seemed to be OK. He didn't want to be taken prisoner so that was the only way to survive.'

'How did he manage to avoid being captured?'

'He hid in the false ceiling of an apartment during the day, and came out at night. There were others like him who did that. Anything rather than be caught by the Iraqi soldiers.'

'Oh, my God! So was he still there when you left?'

'Yes. I couldn't take him with us. He'd have been caught at the border. I stayed in Kuwait as long as I could, but everyone is convinced there'll be a war now.'

'I see.'

We all sat in silence. I was horrified by the thought of Mark, alone in a hot apartment. Even in November, the daytime heat of Kuwait would be hard to bear without air conditioning.

'Can I smoke?'

That plaintive cry broke the silence and made my stomach churn with anxiety. My addicted smoker husband was still keen to get his own way, refusing to understand that secondhand smoke was dangerous to others, even if he chose to live his life in a toxic cloud. Katie went to find an ashtray, but I pointed to the kitchen door.

'It's not cold, darling. Could you please smoke in the conservatory or outside?'

Grudgingly he left, and Bill, kind, though not sympathetic about having his young children surrounded by smoke, followed him in there, making conversation. I heard Nabeel's voice, excited and fast. Clearly he'd found his tongue. Could he be talking about business and money, his favourite topic? I thought he'd be depressed about not being able to conduct his affairs as usual. What could be happening?

Katie and I put the food on the table. I'm a vegetarian and Nabeel a meat-eater, but uninterested in food. To cater for all tastes, Katie had prepared a buffet with broccoli quiche, smoked salmon, pork sausages, warm boiled potatoes, boiled ham and hot English mustard, with green salad. Pork products were *haraam*, forbidden, in Moslem Kuwait, so Nabeel, a Roman Catholic, and I, an Anglican Protestant, always enjoyed sampling the forbidden dishes when we came to the UK. 'I'm the only vegetarian who enjoys a ham sandwich,' I would joke. Bill opened up a special bottle of Nuits St Georges, one of our favourite red wines, filled our glasses and the meal became a feast. We ate, drank, and soon the stress of the past few months began to tell on me as deep fatigue.

'I'm ready for bed. Are you coming, Nabeel?' I asked pointedly.

As so often before, he failed, or pretended to fail to understand my implicit meaning. I was asking him to come to bed with me, so that we could talk, perhaps make love, and have some private time together. He never got the message and perhaps it was my fault, since I never learned to ask directly for fear of rejection. There was always the need for just another cigarette, another story, another wrestling match to watch on TV on Friday night, whatever the excuse to stay up later than me and avoid being together as a couple. I looked at my brother pleadingly.

'Well, we are all tired, Nabeel, and I've got work tomorrow so why don't we call it a night?' Bill suggested.

'OK, OK, let's see if we can remember how to sleep together!'

Taken at face value the words were crude, naïve or simply a sign of embarrassment. The comment was unnecessary in any case as I hadn't found him gifted in the arts of love. I hadn't had a point of comparison as I was a virgin when I met him, intending to keep myself for my husband, as my mother and religion expected me to do. Nabeel had been my first and only lover till the day I decided my inhibitions were old-fashioned. Ignoring his comment we all said goodnight and went upstairs. For once the kids were fast asleep. The late night had brought them oblivion. But for me and my partner of 20 years, the night brought trauma as we undressed for bed. Alone at last I opened up the topic of the Invasion again.

'How are you really feeling, darling? Are you sad at losing our home? That bastard Saddam has a lot to answer for.'

'Bastard? Saddam? What do you mean? It's the Americans who did it.'

'Americans? What do you mean?'

'Don't you know it was a plot? ... another Western plot like the one that lost Palestine, that destroyed my home when I was a child, and that has nearly ruined us all again.'

'Don't you blame Saddam at all?'

'No, it was an American plot. The American ambassador in Baghdad set it up: She said she didn't care what the Iraqis did, the USA wouldn't interfere.'

'But Iraq and Kuwait were friendly, you know, *Iraq ashaqiqa,* as they used to say on the news all the time! If they were so friendly how could Saddam invade? And what about the way he treated the Kuwaitis? The torture, kidnap and rape of girls? The premature babies snatched from the incubators in Jahra hospital?'

'That's all lies, just another conspiracy to discredit a strong man, an Arab hero.'

'A hero? What do you mean?'

'A real hero, the only Arab leader strong enough to stand up to the USA, the policemen of the world, that's who they think they are, and yet they are rotten, they are behind all the troubles, they and *Mosaad,* the Israeli secret police. The CIA does everything bad, then blames their enemies.'

I was stunned into silence. My stomach churned. Who was I talking to? Where had this logic come from? It was the reasoning of a dyed in the wool anti-Western Arab. Yet this was my husband of 15 years, my lover of 20 years, a Christian, French educated, trilingual, versed in French philosophy and literature, now expressing the limited, naïve and biased views of the average Arab in the street. I could hardly believe my ears. I'd had no notion of this in the few messages we'd exchanged, but could this be the reason why Nabeel had delayed so long in leaving Kuwait? I'd sent several messages warning of the attack by the Western allies, threatening divorce if he didn't get himself out of danger and come to the West. Had he been convinced by the posturing of the madman, Saddam? Had his family come round to the same way of thinking and brainwashed him? Or was this the result of being traumatized by the loss of his business and home, built up with such effort after his tragic childhood? I didn't know what to think, but I tried to change the subject.

'Darling, never mind all that now. Let's talk about our house. I've been longing to ask you. Do you mind?'

'Go ahead – it was all gone, everything. Anything we could save, we took to Beirut. You'll see it when you come over.'

'Oh, that's great, so some things were saved. I'm so glad. All our lovely things.'

'Not much, I warn you. In fact, it was quite funny really. We dragged our big fridge all the way to Lebanon, only to find out that the stupid folk who'd trashed the house had cut out the transformer! So all we have now is a big metal cupboard.'

'Oh, my God – so they weren't that intelligent, the Iraqi soldiers!'

'Iraqi soldiers? What have they got to do with it?'

'Didn't they trash our house? They were living there. They took it over, didn't they?'

'Yes, but they were great guys – the elite, National Guard, the Red Berets, I got on well with them.'

'So what happened? Can you tell me? For example, what happened to my books and my study?'

'What? Is that all you care about? You love your books more than you love me. That's the truth.' Nabeel's voice was raised in anger suddenly.

'What do you mean? What are you saying?' I could hardly believe my ears.

'You just want to know if your precious books are all right. You don't care about me.'

'Why do you think that? Didn't I beg you to come out, even threaten you with divorce if you didn't? Didn't you get those messages from our Jordanian friends? I was terrified for your safety. Why are you here now with me if you think that?'

Nabeel couldn't answer. Emotionally fraught, probably traumatized by losing his home and possessions for the second time in his life, he was not using logic. There was something hidden, I felt, which had triggered this reaction. Although he spoke proudly to others of my teaching and leadership work, of my achieving a second B.A. as well as a Master's degree while working in Kuwait, deep down at some primeval male or cultural level I suspected that he had always resented my career, knowing that the language teaching profession gave me my independence, the power to leave him, and an identity with which to exist apart from him. I guessed that he could not bear that thought, or face the fear that I might leave him one day. I wondered if he had forgotten that it took me six months to consider his proposal of marriage before accepting it. When I said 'yes', all those years ago, I hadn't realised that the wife of a Christian Arab must be obedient to her husband. I certainly had not promised to obey him in our marriage ceremony. But for now the wine from earlier had its effect and we both fell asleep without further discussion of this touchy subject.

CHAPTER 5

A New Home in New Zealand

13 April 2003

Rose turned the TV off abruptly. She had been watching in amazement as the Iraqi people, 'liberated' by the UK and US coalition, and aided by US soldiers, pulled down a huge statue of Saddam Hussein in Baghdad's *Firdos* (Paradise) Square on 9 April, the date when the capital was formally 'secured' by the US forces. To show his disgust at Saddam, one man slapped the statue with a sandal. On the following day the Kurdish forces had captured the northern oil city of Kirkuk. Saddam himself had disappeared. Rose was engrossed in the war reporting. Disaster reported in an unfamiliar country has a completely different effect than that in one known to the observer. Her heart beating wildly after witnessing more details of the Western allies' invasion of Iraq, Rose realized she only had ten minutes to get to the real estate office in town. She would be late and for property sales agents time is money!

New Zealand was experiencing a property boom. Houses were increasing in price by 10,000 dollars a month. Rose had purchased two homes in the UK, the first in the 1980s for her mother and younger brother and the second in 1999 as a base for her doctoral studies. The property balloon in the UK was also high in the sky and she was hoping to experience the euphoria of profit-taking when Mum's home was eventually sold. Accustomed to the solid brick and tile construction of UK houses, Rose found some New Zealand homes flimsy with their wooden frames and builder's paper walls. But she had found a building surveyor who could be trusted to help her play the property game. University colleagues had advised her to take house purchasing slowly as there was a serious problem with poorly built houses on the market. Even a motel guest had warned her of what was known as 'leaky building syndrome'. Rose had gone online to look it up in the *New Zealand Herald* archive and had grasped the key details: The roof must have satisfactory eaves to protect the building from rain as well as substantial cladding for the exterior to be weatherproof. But to her way of thinking, why not buy as fast as possible, when paying rent and waiting around for prices to go higher wouldn't get her anywhere? Her budget was limited and her shipping was waiting at the shipping company to sail to its destination.

As she raced off into the city in her nearly new Mitsubishi, Rose reflected on the choice of colour she'd made. The saloon was white with a grey interior, the reverse of Nabeel's new Mercedes stolen by the Iraqis in 1990. She'd only been in that car a few times, but she'd enjoyed its luxurious white leather interior. Now she'd had to settle for fabric upholstery, but the soothing dove grey inside and the bright white exterior were still a delight. This was an outward and visible sign that at last she'd begun to build her new life, and soon she expected to have a new house to go with her new job and her car. As she pulled into the parking lot of the agent's office, Miranda was waiting for her.

'Hi – sorry I'm late.'

'No worries. Let's go. Get in mine. It will be quicker.'

Rose jumped into the saleswoman's truck. Miranda was wearing a smart cotton dress, with bare legs for what was still summer weather in late March, but she also had bare feet! Rose had noticed this with other Kiwis and been amazed at their ability to endure walking on hot tarmac or concrete. Was it a physical test, an economy drive, or a health practice? She didn't feel bold enough to ask. Miranda was working on a Sunday to take Rose to some houses which did not have 'open homes', fixed public viewing times. These viewings were by appointment only.

'Now, I've got a nice house to show you by the river.'

'OK, fine. I like being near water. I wanted to live in the Bay of Plenty at the seaside, did I tell you?'

'That would be too far for commuting to work, wouldn't it?'

'Yes, for sure. In fact, I've agreed to live here in Farmerston for a couple of years, but I'm going to buy a plot of land in the Bay of Plenty so as to be ready to build my retirement house over there. That's why I've come to New Zealand. To die, but not today.' Rose mimicked the Ozzie accent with her little joke.

'Retirement? You don't look nearly old enough for that.'

'I'm not yet. But I am 55. I just scraped in at the age limit for permanent residents. Lucky for me!'

'Wow. So you've got some years of work ahead of you then. We can't retire here till at least 65, and even then some of us have to continue working, like me!'

'Oh, really? Have you been in real estate long?'

'A few years, but it's only a sideline. It keeps the pot boiling. My main interest is horse breeding. I breed trotters.'

'Pigs?'

'No, trotters are horses which pull carriages, like Prince Philip's.'

'Gosh. I had no idea. Where do you do that?'

'In Cambridge, a lovely country town near here. You should come along one day. It's very enjoyable.'

'I hope I'll be able to when I'm settled, but I'm determined to get a house and get my job under control first.'

'You know, you could live in Raglan, on the West Coast, if you want to be by the sea.'

'I've thought of that, but it's still a bit far to drive and the road is very winding. It can't be easy to drive in the winter.'

'Too true. We get a fair amount of fog then. Well, here we are. The Waikato River is visible from the first floor of this house.'

Rose and Miranda made the tour of the house, Rose taking off her shoes as she entered the front door. She smiled as she noted that the soles of Miranda's feet were probably dirtier than any pair of shoe soles. But the dark fitted carpet didn't show any traces of dust. The house was presented immaculately but the corner plot and big picture windows looking out onto the street were not for Rose. Twenty two years' residence in the Middle East had accustomed her to seclusion behind high walls. Then there was the threat on her life that Nabeel had made. Rose was looking for privacy and security. A fence or a hedge and a gate were high on her list of criteria.

'Sorry Miranda, that won't do. Too exposed, too public.'

'OK. I've got one more. It's billed as 'different', so it might suit you!'

'OK, I agree I am different! I don't want to be seen by everyone while I'm in my own home. Let's hit it.'

As they drove to the next house Miranda chatted about her trotters but Rose's mind was elsewhere. She was thinking about the different homes she had shared with Nabeel over the 22 years they'd spent together. First they had lived in bedsitters in London's Gloucester Road area, known as Kangaroo Valley on account of the large number of Ozzies and Kiwis who lived there. Then they had rented a flat near Queen's Court Gardens, another popular 'antipodean' area of London. They had got married there after knowing each other for six years. Their courtship had hardly been idyllic. After meeting Nabeel by chance at her postgraduate college in October and beginning a platonic relationship, Nabeel had been prevented from returning to London by his siblings when he went to Lebanon in December for an older brother's wedding. Afterwards he said he had been compelled to work in the family company in Kuwait. Three months later he had managed to get his passport from the office safe with the help of a trusted friend. On returning to England in April he encouraged Rose to abandon her principles and begin her first sexual relationship outside marriage. After working in London for four years he had gone back to Kuwait, set up his own business with his brothers, and then asked her to marry him. She had taken six months to consider his unexpected proposal. Marriage was not in her life plan.

After their marriage in London they had left for Kuwait, Rose to take up an English teaching job and Nabeel expecting his family to offer them a home. Instead, they had been thrown out, literally shown the door, though Edouard had taken pity on them and driven them to a cheap hotel. Nabeel had no money and neither had Rose. She had expected him to look after the financial side of their lives but there went the first of her hopes and dreams. She was to be the sensible one in the marriage it seemed, though she was a stranger in a new land. Fortunately, a waiter in the hotel had befriended them and had found them a cheap, ground floor flat which was available immediately. They needed to move out of the hotel since they could not afford to pay the bill for more than two nights. The rent on the flat was supposed to be paid one month in advance but Rose had a letter from her employer confirming her salary was to be paid retrospectively, so the landlord had agreed to take them on.

Rose soon found out why ground floor flats were cheap. Peeping Toms lurked around them. One evening, preparing a meal in her underwear on account of the extreme heat she sensed someone watching her. As she turned to the window and screamed at the figure she saw, the man disappeared into the darkness. She had berated Nabeel for not warning her about snoopers, but he appeared more naive than she was about the surroundings. That flat had been their home for only a few months. At Christmas the ice between the brothers had thawed and eventually the hatchet had been buried.

Their next home had been much more secure. They rented a first floor flat in a Kuwaiti landlord's house close to the English Centre where Rose worked. They had stayed there for several years while Rose continued her studies to complete her second BA and then her Master's degree. Once she had her postgraduate degree she was able to work at the University which provided staff apartments in modern tower blocks. Nabeel hadn't wanted to suffer the ignominy of living in his wife's flat, but finally Rose had insisted that they move to the 'free' accommodation, rather than paying rent. She had been able to bring her disabled mother out to stay with them for three months as the University apartment had lifts. After putting up with the University accommodation for a while, Nabeel had found first a villa, then a huge rental apartment with a garden in a large house near Kuwait Towers. This was their lovely home which had been destroyed during the Iraqi occupation of Kuwait.

Rose, single again, though still fearful, didn't want to think about the past. She turned her eyes back to the road. They were approaching a one storey house in a small *cul de sac* off a quiet road. In the bright sunshine the house looked clean and inviting, and there were no picture windows giving onto the street. Rose realized she could be almost home. The houses she'd viewed in the last two months had been disappointing in the main, most of them in need of renovation or at least redecoration, but this one was a new build, with a modern update on the traditional weather board cladding which Rose preferred. She'd looked at some vintage Californian bungalows with exposed wooden floors, freshly stained and varnished, but in the end, the upkeep of an older home was not appealing to a woman with no liking for Do It Yourself.

Suddenly the perfect compromise was in front of her: the indoor-outdoor flow was excellent on two sides of the modern, multi-functional main space, encompassing kitchen, lounge and dining area. There were three bedrooms, with a family bathroom as well as a master with *en suite* shower facility. One bedroom could be the study, where Rose planned to finish her doctorate and then write her novels. The garden wrapped right around the house and was given over mainly to lawn, but with pretty flowerbeds, a water feature in a rock garden and even a *ponga* tree and rambling rose climbing the wooden fences around the property. It was manageable and exactly to Rose's taste. Even the name of the street and the number were appealing: 3 Lavender Place. Three was her lucky number, and lavender her favourite fragrance. Rose decided to place an offer straight away. Within the hour, she was the new owner to be, with legal papers to be finalized on Monday, the next working day. Miranda was delighted. She would receive a big slice of the hefty commission the agents charged.

Back at her motel, Rose sighed with relief. Next, she'd send for her shipping. She opened a bottle of New Zealand *sauvignon blanc* to celebrate. With tears in her eyes, she raised her glass. Thanks to Mum's focus on further education as a way of escape from factory work in the UK's industrial heartlands, Rose had been able to find a lucrative professional position wherever she went. In this new country, she was grateful to the person who had been her driving force and inspiration. *You are the wind beneath my wings,* was the song her disabled Mum sang for Rose, but really, it was the other way round, Rose felt. As she sipped her wine she recalled Mum's words: 'What will be, will be. You can't change the past. Only the present is in your hands. Do your best every day and count your blessings.' Rose raised her eyes to heaven. 'Cheers, Mum. This one's for you.'

CHAPTER 6

Making Plans

November 1990

The next day Nabeel seemed in a different mood, no longer emotional, with business on his mind. He unlocked the heavy suitcase he'd hauled upstairs to our bedroom and showed me what he'd brought over from Beirut: delicious salted and unsalted pistachio nuts, rose, lemon and vanilla squares of luscious Turkish delight, different types of nougat stuffed with peanuts, cashews and pistachios and dark fragrant *bunn,* roasted, ground coffee, with cardamom and without, for what was traditionally called Turkish coffee. The Arab tradition of drinking small, strong cups of coffee was a legacy from the Ottoman Empire which had ruled the Arab World for 600 years.

After revealing the gifts, Nabeel opened up his Samsonite briefcase and began making his usual stream of business phone calls. I hesitated to interrupt and spoil his mood, so went downstairs to talk to Katie and Bill, taking their share of the oriental goodies with me. Bill had already left for work. He was a senior accountant at a major supermarket chain with headquarters in North London. Katie was in the kitchen.

'How are you today, Rose? Is Nabeel OK?'

'Yes, he's fine. I'm afraid he's making a lot of calls at prime time…you know he never notices things like that. I'll let you have some cash for the phone bill.'

'Oh forget it. It's not a problem. What do you think he'd like for dinner tonight? Would you like to go out?' Katie asked.

'Well, that depends on you, Katie. It's easier to go out but on the other hand, Nabeel will probably only eat steak, and that's quite simple to cook here. I'll just have a baked potato and salad.'

'OK – we'll eat at home then. I've got a few things to do today. What time for dinner? We usually eat around 6.30pm.'

'Fine, thanks. We'll probably go into the city, or at least take a walk to a bank. We have to organize our finances now and make some plans for the next few months. We can't go back to Kuwait, so we are stranded here now.'

'You know you can stay with us as long as you like, Rose.'

'Thanks so much. But I need to get to Mum. In fact, she'll be upset because we didn't call her last night. Gosh, I'll have to tell Nabeel to get off the phone for a few minutes.'

'OK. Give Mary my love.'

'Will do. Nabeel, *ya* Nabeel!' I called upstairs.

'Naam?'

'We need to talk to Mum. Can we do that now? When shall we tell her we'll be arriving?'

'Oh, let's go tomorrow shall we? It'll be great to see her.' He seemed in quite a different, much calmer mood now, the dark mood of the previous night forgotten.

Nabeel had always loved Mary and he persisted in calling her Mum though she wasn't old enough to be his mother, at only 20 years older than me and a mere 12 years older than him. She was the same age as Nabeel's older, unmarried sister, Asma, who had acted as little mother to the family since their mother died. All Nabeel's siblings had met Mum when she came to Kuwait to stay with us for extended periods. They admired her fortitude in suffering her painful disability. RA had begun to cripple her while she was in her 30s. In her 60s now, she needed a wheelchair to leave the house and someone to bathe her and open her medicine bottles. Apart from a small amount of help from Social Services, she still managed to look after herself at home alone in Mossfield, eating frozen meals heated in the microwave and with daily support from our kind and caring next door neighbour, Betty.

'Fine. That's great. Just give me a moment on the phone when you can, please.'

As soon as the phone was free I called Mum and apologized for not calling the previous night, with all the excitement. I left out the confusing issues Nabeel and I had discussed, just confirmed that we'd arrive the next day, with shopping and food for our stay. She didn't have to prepare anything. She was a little hurt at our not being in touch earlier, but she stoically accepted the situation and was looking forward to our arrival. Inevitably she had to accept what was happening to her and around her. She never complained but that didn't stop me from feeling guilty about living in the Middle East so far away from her. Out of the bad news of the Invasion in August came the good news, the chance for us to be together for longer than had been possible since my marriage when I left London for Kuwait.

The rest of the day in London went quickly with a visit to the local branch of Barclays Bank, more phone calls, and then some time spent discussing the future. Nabeel had made contact with the UK companies he represented in the Middle East, but there was no point in visiting them right now, as there was no chance of placing any new orders while Kuwait was occupied by Iraq. One of his major client steel companies had had to recall an order for parts which was already on the high seas, and they'd lost money on the deal. Lloyds of London refused to pay compensation as acts of war are regarded as outside the normal parameters of insurance claims. To make up for the loss of petroleum business, Nabeel, ever the entrepreneur, had made contact with friends who were dealing in manpower recruitment. It transpired that he wanted to go to the Philippines to set up a contract to recruit male technicians for the oil companies in Kuwait and female maids for the domestic market. This dealing in people who needed jobs, but often suffered poor working conditions and minimum wages, was a sad and shameful business, in my opinion. Nabeel only saw the business side of it, and a chance to 'wheeler deal'. Profit was king in his book.

'You know, I might have to go to the Philippines to seal this deal,' he told me excitedly.

'Oh really? Straight away? But what about our plans for Europe? Remember I bought the land we saw and liked in Spain last summer, just before the Invasion. I thought we could go over there and make some plans for our castle! Wouldn't you like to repeat our drive to the Continent? We could enjoy some warmer weather than here.'

'Of course I'm talking about the future. Let's see what happens to Kuwait.'

'Well, the allies are talking about waging war on Saddam. But the Human Shield is still working as a deterrent. He's using one of my teachers as part of his defence, you know. George, my summer school teacher, is still there. He was taken prisoner and moved to Basra, but Sinead, who was working on the Medical English summer school, came out on one of the special buses provided for women. She came and stayed with me for my birthday in September. You know, my 43rd birthday, the one you missed! She gave me a lovely black leather Filofax. It will come in very useful to keep track of all these changes in our lives, and new addresses of friends.'

Nabeel didn't comment on that piece of information. We'd celebrated his birthday in June 1990 while travelling round Italy, France and Spain for business and pleasure. We'd enjoyed some happy times with his business associates, though I'd brought back a peacock's feather from Italy which Katie told me presaged bad luck. She'd been right I suddenly realised. My missed birthday didn't merit a comment from Nabeel, but he seemed surprised by the news of Sinead, my Irish friend, a lovely young woman, one of the language team in the Health Sciences English Centre.

'What happened to Sinead?'

'Well, do you remember she was dating a British guy who worked at the Doha power station? She was teaching summer school when the Iraqis came in. She stayed in her apartment and intended to lie low for a while, but her boyfriend was picked up by the Iraqis on his way to work. He was captured and was so worried about her that he told the Iraqis where she was and they came and got her. Can you believe the stupidity? They put the two of them in the Sheikh's Palace near the Hotel where they imprisoned a lot of other Brits. I think it was the Messilah Beach Palace.'

'Really? I didn't hear about that.'

'Yes, well, the Iraqis couldn't look after them properly. There was no bedding or towels and food was a huge problem. They put the passengers from the BA plane that landed in Kuwait just after the Invasion there too. There was so little to eat it was a very difficult time. Sinead told me they found some paint and painted a Union Jack on the roof to identify them, in case there were any bombing attacks or rescue attempts.'

'So how did she get out?'

'Well, the Iraqis received petitions from the British Embassy, so they finally decided they'd better let the women go. The Embassy organized evacuation buses out through Baghdad. And do you remember my friend Jack? The Supervisor for English at the Central Language School? He was captured. They kept him in a camp in the city. Then they moved all the Western men to prison camps in Iraq. Sinead's been back in Ireland for a while but I'm rather afraid that the trauma of captivity might affect her negatively in the end. I do hope not. She's a great teacher and bound to find another job soon. I've spent some time since August writing references for colleagues looking for new jobs. The University cancelled our contracts as of the date of the Invasion, apparently.'

'Well, I looked after some of the Brits who were hiding in flats in Kuwait, taking them food and water, but in the end, I'm here and I guess they are still stuck there.'

'Yes, I'm glad you are here! You were so quiet over there I thought you'd never make it before the fighting started. I'm very proud of you for helping the guys in hiding. I do hope Mark will be able to get out. His cancer is a serious problem in such a stressful situation.'

'True. It's hard to think of him living in hiding for so long over there. What's Sinead doing now?'

'Like all the rest of our teams, looking for a job and wondering if there'll be any compensation for losing our jobs and our homes. I don't suppose there'll be any chance of that if Saddam keeps his grip on Kuwait.'

'Let's not go there. Who knows the future? Time will tell. And isn't it time for a drink?'

Nabeel was obviously not going to spill the whole beans about his delay in departing from Iraq. I wondered what lay behind it.

It was, however, the cocktail hour. Bill would be home soon, and I poured stiff drinks of scotch, ice and soda before we sat down to watch the news, while Katie fed the children. It seemed that Lebanon, Nabeel's country of citizenship, but not his natal home, was finally emerging from the grips of civil war, while Saddam was using the Human Shield to defend himself against the threat of allied invasion in Kuwait to drive the Iraqi Army out. It was hard to know what to expect, fear or hope for. I thanked God Nabeel was safe at last. At least I wasn't a widow as I'd expected to be every day while he was still in Kuwait. Thankfully he had left for Lebanon just as the Christian Army leader General Aoun had accepted to go into exile, ending the civil war. That civil war had raged for 15 years, destroying much of Beirut. So many people killed, and so many children had been orphaned.

Now at last we could plan possible alternatives for our own future. Perhaps we could include one of those poor orphans in our lives as we hadn't been fortunate enough to have our own children. I mused on the possibility. That would be a good outcome to our problems, I felt, though

Nabeel had been adamant that he would not adopt 'other people's children' when his own fertility issues had been discovered two years after our marriage. I had been blamed for the lack of reproduction and the true facts had never been revealed to Nabeel's family. I had put up with the situation as I did not want to be disloyal. Infertility is not something easy to explain or understand and especially in the Arab World is considered very private. However, now that our lives had been turned upside down by the Invasion, I hoped that we could revisit the options of creating our own family. I wondered if Nabeel realised that I simply had to work when I had no children at home to look after. I had married with the expectation of having children, but in the event, my work and my desire to gain higher qualifications had taken their place. Despite my own wishes I knew I would not be able to force a change on him. It would have to come from within. I would have to accept whatever fate decreed.

'*Inshallah*, God willing,' I murmured to myself. 'What will be, will be.'

CHAPTER 7

Moving In

14 April 2003

'Good morning, Jane. I've put some muffins in the tea room. Blueberry, apple, white chocolate and raspberry, all healthy ones! Can you pass the message round, please. There's plenty for everyone.'

'Oh, Rose, thanks. What's this for?'

'Well, I found the right house at last. I'm signing the papers later today! It's an Arabic tradition to offer food in thanks for happy events.'

'Gosh. You found a new home fast. Where is it?'

'In one of the new subdivisions in the north east of the city. It's clean and quiet up there and I can get out into the countryside to explore at the weekends.'

'Cool. It sounds lovely. You wouldn't believe how the city has grown. That area used to be in the country ten years ago. I hope you'll enjoy being in your new home. Thanks again for the muffins and have a good day.'

'You too. See you later'.

Rose wasn't surprised that others had no time to chat and needed to get on with their work. She had had a relatively easy start up period in her new job in these first two months. She had been given a first floor office in the downtown building where the school operated, with windows which looked out onto Farmerston's test cricket ground. With any luck, she'd have a front seat for any future test or international matches – perhaps even with England. Colin would like that. Involuntarily her thoughts turned to Colin, who had stolen, then broken her heart. As if replaying a video she could see him in whites batting for the Gulf Polytechnic College (GPC) cricket team. They had met in Bahrein. Rose had been bowled over by his blue eyes and physical grace. In his 50s, he focussed on maintaining his fitness.

She smiled as she recalled watching unobserved from a tenth floor window of Bahrein's tallest hotel on their first Valentine's Day, as Colin ran down the street to meet her. He was so downright attractive that watching him run was a pleasure. This had been their first such small celebration. She had invited him to lunch downtown to spoil him and he had been a little late arriving. Her plan for an intimate lunch had fallen flat, as they were the only ones eating in the restaurant and as a result they had both felt rather embarrassed with too many waiters in attendance on them. Since then they had had many fun, uninhibited occasions at home, often just dressing up and dancing around the sitting room after a lovely dinner and a bottle of Mumm's champagne. With a sigh Rose realized those happy times were over. She had travelled half way round the world to make a new start and such melancholic sentimental thoughts were not going to help her settle in. She should not indulge in them as they only made her feel sad at first, then angry later when she recalled the down sides of their relationship.

Turning to her computer she checked for emails. Yes, Colin had written to her over the weekend. She did not have internet connection at the motel, though she would soon install it in her new house. She refused to read the message immediately, sticking rigorously to her self-imposed rule. Work came before personal life in working hours. Some would think her mad. She had been told often enough that Kiwis strove for work-life balance. Rose had never experienced such a phenomenon, but now at 55 she was ten years away from New Zealand's retirement age, so she rather hoped she might get to taste it soon. All her jobs to date had demanded 150% commitment and energy from her and she had never hesitated to give it in the past. She had been amply rewarded by steady progress along her career path and excellent salaries. Her driving ambition here in New Zealand was to complete her doctorate in the spare time which her new work schedule should allow. After all, she had taken a drastic reduction in salary and made a sideways step in her career progress to come to New Zealand as a teacher developer. She anticipated achieving her lifetime's ambition in this new context. For now, though, she needed to deal with the other messages related to work.

With three English language teaching centres within her responsibility for teacher training and professional development, she had a long job list even at this early stage in her new job. There was plenty of work to do both in teacher training and in curriculum and assessment development. Several improvements could be made if she was given the opportunity to lead the way collegially. She was a team player, not an autocrat and despite having worked in many different countries with teachers of various nationalities, here in this English-speaking former UK colony English Rose felt her 'foreign status' more keenly than elsewhere. She did not want to appear patronizing. She looked forward to getting to know her colleagues but change is always difficult to effect and innovating it is more so. She sincerely hoped she would be able to initiate a new learning curve for herself as well as for others.

At lunchtime she left the office to sign the sales contract for the new house with the real estate agent. Dates for exchanging final contracts were agreed and a moving in date was decided on. Back in the office, Rose wrote an email to the shipping company, attention of the manager in charge of her consignment. He had been waiting patiently for six months without charging her an additional amount for storage to deliver her shipping container. When she left Bahrein she hadn't been able to tell him where to send it. At that time she had begun a primary English language teaching job in Oman, thinking it would be a change from teaching young adults at the GPC and yet still keep her close to her friends in Bahrein. The job was challenging, working as a primary school English language inspector and teaching and curriculum advisor, but the perks included a white Landrover Freelander, and a spacious walled and gated villa right on the beach. Since she loved the sea this was especially attractive. However, she had found the working and living conditions challenging. She expected better after eight years in Bahrein in purpose built colleges with the latest facilities for technology in teaching and learning, and staff accommodation in modern apartment buildings containing gyms and swimming pools.

Living in Oman was like going back in time. Rose could not do it happily, but she had given it her best shot. In her middle age she was too aware of her own identity and too independent-minded to get used to wearing the Islamic female apparel, the *abbaya* and *shayla* (flowing robe and headscarf) for work and in public. But if she didn't do so, muttered prayers could be heard from the men she passed: 'Protect us from evil, oh God.' She had had to accept that the simplest way to a peaceful life was the 'when in Rome' policy. But even though she disliked wearing the black, cover-all cloak, known as the *abbaya*, she hated wearing a headscarf more.

To make matters worse, the youths of the area had been amazed that a single woman was living alone in a large house by the sea. They seemed to think she was running a brothel, and took every opportunity to climb the high walls to get a glimpse of her. Although they were only children and teenagers, it was hard to comprehend such avid curiosity and it made Rose feel vulnerable. Failing to sight her when they clambered on the walls, the youths began throwing stones at the walls of the house, which had been even more terrifying. She had complained to her landlord who lived in a similar house nearby and he had taken her straight round to see the parents of these local kids. Rose had worn her *abbaya* for the visit and used her limited Gulf Arabic to speak to the parents but felt both embarrassed and guilty when she realized the children and youths would be beaten severely on account of her complaint. She had hoped to live in a friendly environment, getting to know her neighbours, not alienating them.

Even being able to use Arabic to communicate in social circumstances was becoming a liability rather than an asset. One youth appeared to have fallen in love with her and began stalking her on her newly purchased mobile phone. She couldn't recall at this distance of time how he had got her phone number. Giving it out had been a big mistake obviously. Her phone had both English and Arabic script but Rose couldn't always decipher the messages he sent in both languages. Her young suitor also designed and sent picture templates which were quite touching. But when the young man began to leave presents near her compound gate, such as plates of homemade biscuits, Rose felt she had to change her erstwhile friendly behaviour. She spoke firmly to the boy and asked him not to leave anything else outside her gate. Eventually he desisted but nevertheless, Rose felt uncomfortable. No-one could visit her without being in the public eye. Just going to work and coming home again involved running the gauntlet of curious eyes and risking further stones. Her close friend and former colleague, Hinewai, visited with her daughters and was instrumental in getting her out of the place. 'You are not staying here,' she declared. Rose was glad to have a friend who knew her own mind so well. She could learn more than a thing or two from her direct approach to life.

> *Dear Sir, Please prepare shipping documents for Auckland, New Zealand and invoice me for storage and final costs.*

Rose typed out her work address and sent the email message off. There should be some financial support from the University for her shipping expenses from Bahrein, where she had been recruited, though she was not sure of the details as the process of recruitment had been swift. She had been diagnosed with a serious dental abscess at the end of the previous year. Treatment for this was not available in Oman so she had travelled to the Emirates for an endodontal operation. Afterwards she had recuperated at her friend's house. Concerned for Rose's wellbeing, Hinewai had told her about a job at the university in New Zealand where she had completed her own postgraduate studies.

Rose's video interview had been so successful that she had been offered a higher level job than the one she applied for. The only problem was that the new job was based at the main campus in Farmerston, whereas Rose had expressed her preference to work at the seaside campus in the Bay of Plenty. She had been promised that her future base would indeed be in the Bay. But on arrival she had been persuaded by her line manager to stay in the rural location of Farmerston for a year or two until the job became familiar. Consequently she had purchased her new house with half of the budget she had set aside from her Gulf savings. The other half was for a second house near the sea, which would be Rose's main home in retirement. In her ten year plan, she would use the first house for rental income as accommodation for students and staff was always in demand in the University city.

Rose intended to search for her permanent seaside home in the tranquil Bay of Plenty, as named by Captain Cook, the famous seafarer, after his first visit in 1769 on account of its wealth of fish and other seafood. She needed to get on with the search on the East Coast as soon as possible. The property balloon was steadily rising, and even though she had secured her first home at a reasonable price, she wanted to get a second property while her budget allowed it. The sea with its immense power and inspiring natural beauty held an inescapable attraction for her. Rose had lived near the sea for more than 25 years since she went to Kuwait to live and work as a married woman but her response to the call would have to wait for a while. For now she still had a lot to learn in her new job, country and home.

Almost as an afterthought at the end of the day Rose read the email from Colin. Despite leaving the UK after discovering yet another infidelity which had finally made Rose break up with him, Colin was still in charge of her penthouse flat on the UK's South Coast. Rose adored the flat with its sea views. She had intended to live there with Mum in her retirement but Mum had never seen it. It now contained all her UK possessions. The second bedroom was stuffed with boxes but the master was comfortable enough for her brother, Bill, to stay there with Katie. Colin held a set of keys and liaised with the building management company for her. She was grateful for that. As usual, some communication from management needed handling at her end, but he was making things easier for her and she thanked him in her response, updating him with the latest development in her new life. She didn't know if he would be missing her or simply moving on with the 'other' girl. She wished him luck. She needed to cast her net wider in the hope of catching one of those other fish in the sea. She enjoyed sharing her life after being married for many years, but only with someone she could trust implicitly.

CHAPTER 8

Rural Bliss in Mossfield

25 November 1990

'Cigarette. Watch. Cigarette.'

We were back to the old driving routine. Cigarette in the right hand. Watch on the left hand. I remembered Nabeel's driving had always irritated me. As well as his erratic use of the accelerator and brake, there was the way he flicked his cigarette ash into the car. He could never be persuaded to smoke with his left hand and use the ash tray in the central console. 'You can't teach an old dog new tricks,' he maintained. He drove as if he was in a left hand drive car, flicking ash towards the driver's door, which did not contain an ash tray. Sometimes I made a joke of it, recalling our Greek Cypriot friend Theo who lived in our bedsitter house in Central London in the '70s. Theo was a heavy, messy smoker. His motto was: 'My car is an ashtray.' Why we should have found that acceptable, I fail to understand, but it made us laugh as it was so obviously true.

I tried to relax, opening the magazine on my knee. I was able to read in the car even if I couldn't doze since Nabeel needed directions all the time. Only if there was a stretch of 100 km on a motorway could I trust him to keep going without my help. He could drive the wrong way into a petrol station if I didn't keep an eye open. But we would soon be in Mossfield where Mum was waiting for us. A few days at Bill's had been enough for everyone. Living with a person who smokes 80 cigarettes a day isn't easy and Nabeel was not the type to change his habits. If he wasn't talking about money, that is making money, wheeler-dealing, then he was smoking outside on his own, no doubt dreaming of such deals and planning his next move to make money. Of course, he would drag Bill out with him if he could, but Bill was a health freak. Whenever Nabeel went out for a smoke, Bill headed off for a jog, or to the squash court. Bill was too polite to comment, but I sometimes wondered what he really thought. I knew that I was beginning to tire of such habits after twenty years together and had started to wonder how much longer I would be able to put up with them. Still I hoped that the trauma of loss would eventually recede and give Nabeel new impetus for change so that we could move on into a new future, with new ways of life.

Even though the Mossfield house was tiny, with Mum confined to her bed for most of the day Nabeel and I would be able to go through some of the issues in private which had still not been resolved. I knew better than to raise any of these while driving. The slightest mention of Kuwait drove Nabeel into a tantrum or a sulk. I'd had to accept that the subject was off limits but I was still confused. My mind turned over the events and facts that had emerged over the last four days. I hadn't been able to work out why Nabeel had stayed in Kuwait for three whole months between the Invasion and his final departure with his family in November. A suspicion crossed my mind. Had he intended to get back into the supply of hardware for the petrochemical industry by hook or crook? If the Iraqis were running the oil industry in Kuwait, had he planned to take his cut as usual? Surely even Nabeel had some scruples?

Sometimes I wondered about that. My life was based on a code of ethics and a set of values. Commerce is not necessarily antithetical to ethics, but profit ruled Nabeel's code of conduct in his material world. Professing to despise computers, which in itself suggested the narrowness of his world view, this assiduous marketing man would slave over a manual spreadsheet for hours, calculating the smallest increase in price per item which might be tolerated by the client. Fixed prices were only applicable in terms of the lowest price acceptable to the 'principal', i.e. the producer. Nabeel imported quality materials for use in the petrochemical industry. He didn't want to stock products as he had no warehouse and stock gave no liquidity or flexibility. On top of the principal's cost price, he could fix his middle man's commission as he liked to secure the deal. Gifts for individuals who could help smooth the path of profitable sales were common place and expected, not illegal.

Once I had understood this I asked Nabeel never to discuss it again. I preferred not to know how he was managing his commercial deals. Even though ignorance of crime is not a defence, it was necessary. I felt justified in turning a blind eye to the possible corruption occurring on both sides of the middleman's fence. I was working and earning my own money, although my salary went into a joint-account for which I had no cheque book. Nabeel's profits were going into the family company which paid him a salary. I had no say in how family money was earned or spent. Even more galling when I took time out to consider Nabeel's business was that should he drop dead from smoking 80 plus cigarettes a day, I would be entitled to only half of his property. Since we had no children, the other half would pass to his brothers and sisters. This was a slightly bitter pill, because we had no children as a result of Nabeel's infertility and his decision not to have children by any other means, including adoption. Such thoughts were recurring concerns for me, but for now we were escaping to the English countryside which would provide some respite from both world politics and our personal problems. Perhaps he would change his mind about adoption now our lives had been so drastically altered by the Invasion.

'Is this the bush?' Nabeel's voice broke into my thoughts. I realized with a start that Nabeel had managed to find his way through Mossfield's one way street system without asking me for directions and we were already on the private road on which Mum's home stood, approaching the house with its large, distinctive flowering hydrangea at the bottom of the long front lawn. The bungalow's façade was typical of a child's drawing of a house: square, with a tall chimney in the middle of the roof. There was no visible door, however, as the front and back entrances were on opposite sides of the house. Mum's bedroom gave onto the patio and back garden, so that she could enjoy the views from her bed. The façade of the house had first attracted me to the small, simple house, which had been my very first self-owned property, funded, of course, by my loving husband, into whose bank account everything I earned was always deposited. I had never seen a bank statement in all my years in Kuwait.

'Yes, well done, that's it. Look, Mum's standing at the front window.'

We'd let Mary know that we were on our way, and she'd been listening for the sound of the car all afternoon. I'd warned Mum not to raise the issue of Kuwait until Nabeel did. She'd visited us there at least three times for extended periods, so was concerned to know how things were back home for us. She had her own room in our house in Kuwait, with her own specially made high chair and high bed, and her own wardrobe and clothes, as well some crochet and knitting so that she could occupy her time and be comfortable once she'd survived the eight hour plane ride. She had to dehydrate herself by drinking nothing both for a few hours before and during the journey as she could not get into the tiny airplane bathroom, but it was a sacrifice she was prepared to make.

As soon as we were able to afford it, we'd purchased this little house in Mossfield as our family home in the UK. I can still recall the proud feeling of ownership as I gazed at the snow on our own apple trees when we'd visited during our first winter as owners of the house. We'd taken photos of the occasion. Mum had invested a lot of time redesigning the kitchen so that it would be both more modern and suitable for her while using a walking frame. My parents had never been able to afford to buy a house, so I was pleased to be able to give Mum a home where she could live comfortably despite her disability. She would be financially secure too. She was brought up to live within her means, to buy something only when she had saved up for it and to sacrifice her own wants to the needs of others. How she managed to do it, no one knew. Friends, neighbours and family all were amazed at her thriftiness and generosity. She always had a joint of meat in the freezer, or cakes and tinned goods in the pantry, when others had run out of something and the shops were shut. She had sweet treats hidden in her wardrobe for whenever the grandchildren came by. Friends could help themselves to apples and pears from our trees and raspberries and blackberries from our canes. She never stinted on giving, yet seemed to have received so very little from the universe, in terms of health, wealth and happiness.

'Hello darling. How are you?' Mum asked as she limped forward unsteadily on her walking frame, reaching out with permanently crooked arms to hug me.

'Hi Mum. Are you OK?'

I reached out my arms to her but I held her delicate frame with care. We'd not been able to touch Mum without being supremely careful since we were teenagers. We had to treat her as if she was made of china, as any rough movement would cause her the greatest pain, which would not pass until the next dose of painkillers was due.

Mum settled into her high-legged invalid chair with its self-help push up cushion, in the sitting room observing us from a safe distance as we unloaded the car with Nabeel's cases and my overnight bag.

'I've put the kettle on. Shall I make the tea?' she called out when she could see we'd almost finished installing ourselves.

'No, I'll do it. Thanks. One for you?'

'Yes, please. Not too much sugar though.'

Mum always watched her diet, avoiding acidic foods such as strawberries and tomatoes though her arthritis had not responded to dietary change. The bookshelves were full of naturopathic recipes and remedies, some of them tried and some not tested, but none of them brought the slightest respite or relief. From the very early days I'd dreaded the attacks of pain which had wrought Mum's limbs into deformed shapes. Sometimes I feared for myself, in case this immune system disease was inherited. I knew that Bill felt the same, and we surreptitiously checked each other out whenever we met for signs of deformed fingers or enlarged knees. So far we'd been lucky, but I always put my hands together as if in prayer and placed them flat under my pillow before I slept each night, in the hope that they wouldn't start to go crooked overnight.

For me, this would be the worst deformity to bear as I loved wearing rings more than any other type of jewellery. We hadn't been able to afford much when we were first married, but a Jewish jeweller in Hatton Garden, London had made our matching 18 carat gold wedding bands at Nabeel's last minute request. Years later, after much teasing from his wealthy friends, Nabeel had given me a 1.25 carat brilliant cut solitaire diamond in a Tiffany setting for my fortieth birthday. I was 43 years old, and so far I'd kept my slim, straight fingers, though I did not take it for granted that they would always be so. I still delighted in being able to play the piano for Mum, who had scrimped and saved to pay for lessons when I was only six. I was grateful to her for the sacrifices she had made for me as a young mother and felt guilty not being able to do more for her in her old age as I lived so far away. At least we were together again now and had been since the invasion of Kuwait in August 1990.

'Here's your tea, Mum.'

Mary nodded her approval of the hot drink, holding her melamine mug, the only cup she could lift for herself once it was heavy with liquid, with her thumb stuck into the handle.

'How've you been? Any problems while I was in London?'

'No, my bath nurse, Celia, came as usual yesterday, and Betty has been in each evening before bed. I'm fine. Don't worry.'

Celia and our neighbor Betty had been constant supports since Mum had moved into the little house. She needed friends she could rely on as I'd left home at 19 to study at University, then moved to London for postgraduate studies and later work. I'd visited her regularly and twice taken her and my kid brother on holiday to the warmer climate of Spain, but since my marriage and departure for my new life in Kuwait she'd had to wait for my annual visits. Of course, she hadn't been totally disabled until the early '80s. She'd managed to bring up John, my younger brother, alone and also held down a job at the Singer Sewing Machine Company shop. She'd even retrained for an office job when Singer dispassionately sacked her for being unable to carry the heavy knitting and sewing machines on which she was an expert trainer. Her office job hadn't lasted long because she had become unable to climb on board a bus to travel to work. Her wages weren't enough to pay for a taxi and even getting into a car was difficult without someone to lift her in and out. Now she could get around outside only with someone pushing her wheelchair. It would be good having Nabeel here to help for a while. We could take her out while we were waiting to see what happened to Kuwait.

'Well, you know what I always ask as soon as you get here: When will you be off?'

'OK, Mum, we know that old joke. We're here for a while if you can put up with us. Nabeel's got some plans for the future in Kuwait, but we'll have to get Saddam out of there first.'

'I've got a plan for that – I'll tell you later!' She giggled. She'd been watching the news as obsessively as we had. She hated the invasion of Kuwait and its effects, as well as the perpetrator. But that was a topic Nabeel and I and the rest of the world did not agree on. He interrupted the conversation so as to end it, I guessed.

'Can I smoke?' he asked as petulantly as a child.

'Outside darling – it's not cold really, but if you like, you can stand in the porch.'

'That's nice – I can't even smoke in my own home.'

His joke was pointed, and Mum was eager to please her son in law.

'Well, if you really want to…' she demurred.

'No, Mum. Don't give in to him. Your chest is no good, and I'm not spoiling the whole house and our health with smoke.'

I was certain that smoking was no good for Nabeel, nor for us secondary smokers.

'OK, OK. I get the message. I'm not wanted here,' Nabeel retaliated.

'You know you are, but your cigarettes aren't!' I riposted. He wasn't going to get away with emotional blackmail.

He went outside, unwilling to explore the garden and enjoy the tranquility as dusk fell, only focusing on not being allowed to smoke inside, feeling disgruntled. He had his own theory about smoking: 'It kills germs.' At least I hadn't heard that refrain for a while. There had been some positive aspects to our enforced separation I began to realise. I'd worried about Nabeel for months, but he seemed to have survived intact. I checked on Mum's needs before organising our evening meal. I knew that she enjoyed a hot soak as much as I did.

'Would you like a bath, Mum?'

'Not now, dear, but perhaps in the morning, if you have time.'

'Of course. We're here now indefinitely. We have to do some planning.'

A hot bubble bath was Mum's only physical pleasure, which she could indulge only once a week. Celia, the Social Services bath nurse, had become a friend. She fitted in extra visits whenever she could. Mum always made it worth her while. On winter mornings the coffee after the bath would have a dash of rum or whisky in it, to cheer the cold dark days along. Celia was able to fill in some of the gaps an absentee daughter left in my mother's life. I knew that even if I lived at home Mum would need some friends to balance our relationship, but guilt always overwhelmed me when I came home on leave. At least I'd been a comfort to her during this 'Invasion' holiday. I was sure she was dreading my eventual departure.

'OK then sweetie. We'll go and get fish and chips for tea. Will you have some?'

'Yes, please. Just some fish and mushy peas, no chips.'

'OK, back soon.'

We drove down to the Barracuda Fish Bar at the bottom of our road. Nabeel stayed outside, smoking, while I went into the small shop, with the old-fashioned white ceramic wall tiles and wide zinc counter on which stood the large metal salt shaker and the glass vinegar bottle. The huge, live barracuda fish was still in its glass tank, looking lonely and old now but as scary as ever. I had never looked too closely at it before and I didn't do so now. As a vegetarian, I liked the small amount of fish I ate to be minus eyes and any sign of life. That was the only way I could stomach it but Nabeel enjoyed fish and chips as much as any other food. He would even eat mushy peas, the local Northern delicacy. I took our white paper wrapped and strongly malt vinegar scented packages out to the car in a plastic bag.

'Where's the newspaper?' Nabeel showed some interest in the plain paper wrapping.

'Oh, that's old-fashioned now. It's too messy as well. The ink comes off on your fingers. This is cleaner and nicer. The fish and chips taste just the same.'

We drove back in silence, looking forward to some TV, a glass of wine and the food eaten on coffee tables in the living room. I gave Mum her small portion which she ate in her bedroom with her own wall-mounted TV switched on.

'There's news of the war to liberate Kuwait from Saddam. It looks as if it'll be next year now,' Mum told us as we stood in her bedroom doorway to say good night. Unaware of Nabeel's attitude towards Saddam, she added gleefully,

'We were working on a plan to go and see him, you know, when he was holding those British families hostage. It was disgusting, the way he used that young boy on TV, pretending to be kind, when the hostages were his shield.'

Nabeel was silent. I covered his lack of response. I wondered if he'd even seen that footage of the British boy, Stuart, and his family and if so, what he really thought about it.

'OK, Mum. Nabeel's tired after driving. We'll just relax now in the sitting room. I'll collect your plate later. Have you got some water for your painkillers?'

She nodded. I closed the door between her room and the living room so that she could go to the bathroom and then to sleep when she was ready. Nabeel and I watched some

TV and got more news of Kuwait which was, of course, still under Iraqi occupation. I said nothing as I did not want to start another argument, but I was thinking of the TV program Mum and I had seen in late August, when Saddam had released a film of himself talking to his British hostages, including young Stuart Lockwood. In the glory of Saddam's gold-trimmed palace, the seven year old boy and his parents looked on uncomfortably while Saddam pontificated in Arabic. They had become prisoners, or 'guests' of Saddam during the invasion of Kuwait and used as his *Desert Shield* to deter the allies from unleashing the threatened onslaught of *Desert Storm*. This masquerade of hospitality had been a dirty defensive weapon in the political/military fight to remove him from the Presidency of Iraq. Mum and I had been so incensed we concocted a plan to visit Saddam and assassinate him with a gun hidden in Mum's wheelchair. It was a wild dream we could never have carried out of course.

Before too long all three of us were in our beds and asleep, comforted by the warm, filling food. At least one of us dreamed of Kuwait, where our home was controlled by forces working under the orders of Saddam Hussein. But who would remove him, I wondered? Certainly not Mum and me!

CHAPTER 9

Easter in Paloa Beach

18 - 20 April 2003

Rose spent her first Easter break in New Zealand in Tauranga. The first two months in her new job had flown by. It was strange, packing her car to go over to what the locals call the Mount for the holiday weekend. Mount Maunganui at 232 metres is not really a mountain, but it stands out from the surrounding plains for miles around and serves as a landmark on the East Coast. Known as *Mauo* in *te reo*, the Maori language, it is sacred to the Maori people whose legends tell its history. Rose had first seen the Mount with Hinewai, her Kiwi friend. She'd come over to New Zealand in February with Rose to 'butter her paws', as Rose liked to say. Her trip was intended to give Rose a chance to meet Hinewai's aunt, uncle and cousins, so that she would have a support force to fall back on, should she feel isolated or be in need of help. That extremely kind gesture had been very much appreciated. Hinewai had stayed ten days and it had been fun to discover the beautiful Bay of Plenty with friends rather than alone as Rose was now. She had grown used to being alone since she separated from her husband. In fact she normally preferred her own company in her free time, especially when her teaching and training job was so demanding and full of people. Being alone all weekend was just the antidote she needed to being surrounded by students and teachers all week.

This long weekend break was Rose's first paid holiday since starting work, and she was looking forward to choosing a piece of land at the beach now that she had settled into her job and house in Farmerston. She had booked into a small motel, and taken just a few things over on Good Friday morning, preferring not to drive on Thursday night, when colleagues had warned her that the traffic would be atrocious. The road to the Bay of Plenty from Farmerston passed over a mountain range, the Kaimais, which could be challenging in wet, windy and foggy weather. When planning her weekend trip Rose hadn't packed any food or wine, because it seemed like carrying coals to Newcastle. That was her first mistake, assuming New Zealand culture matched that of the UK. Speaking the same language was not the same as sharing the same culture. Arriving at the beach on the afternoon of Good Friday she found that she couldn't buy a bottle of wine on account of New Zealand's licensing laws! On seeing the bottles of wine in the 'dairy' – a corner shop - covered with a white cloth, Rose wondered whether she'd strayed into an outpost of the Islamic world. Having had the legal situation explained to her by the young shop assistant, and as her motel didn't have a bar, rather than go out alone to a pub or bar she decided to abstain from drinking that night in memory of her Mum, who had passed away almost a year earlier.

Rose's mother's death had been sudden though not unexpected, given Mary's long history of illness and disability. The suddenness was caused by septicaemia. The bacteria which had been surrounding a replacement knee joint had finally and overwhelmingly won the battle over Mary's immune system. Rose had been distraught at the loss of her dear mother. One year had not been enough to complete the grieving process since she was guilt-ridden too. Rose had not been able to be with her Mum when she died as her work in the Middle East was at its busiest in the summer exam period and also Colin was on holiday with her for two weeks. The previous summer, Mum had spent six weeks in hospital fighting and eventually recovering from the same infection. Rose had been with her in the UK then and was hopeful that Mum would overcome the infection again. Uncertain what to do Rose had hesitated until it was too late to reach Mum's death bed. She had completed her work and flown to the UK to help with the funeral and then to close up Mum's house and put it up for sale, following Bill's 'good accountant' advice, before returning to work in Bahrein.

Rose consoled herself to a certain extent with happy memories of past times with Mum. She and Mary had spent the previous Easter at Bill and Katie's house in London. Rose recalled how ill Mum had been on Good Friday. It had been exceptional for Rose to be in the UK at Easter, but she'd been recruiting for the GPC system at the annual International ESOL Teacher conference which started just after Easter. Bill had driven Mum down to his house so that they could all be together and Rose had shared Mum's bed so that she could help her get up in the night to use the toilet. Despite the serious pain Mum was experiencing at that time, a sign that the antibiotics she was taking were beginning to lose their efficacy, Rose had pushed Mum in her wheelchair into a local church on Easter Sunday morning and they had taken

Holy Communion together. The morning walk was warm and sunny, the church was gaily decorated with daffodils and irises, and the music had been delightful. It had been an uplifting church service. It was the last memory of a happy time spent together because Rose's next summer holiday had been spent mainly visiting the Medical Centre. During that awful 2001 summer Rose had asked a priest to come to give Mum a blessing at her hospital bedside. Mary was a Christian and a firm believer, but only had limited access to formal church services because of her homebound invalid status. At least Rose felt she'd done her best to give Mum support in her faith in her final year of life.

Although Rose questioned her own faith, which she now regarded as a cherished tradition, she decided that this Easter Sunday she would find a congenial church and take Communion there, in memory of Mum. Perhaps it would become her parish church in future when she moved to the beach. For now, she tied ribbons onto the basket of chocolate eggs, rabbits and chickens she'd selected to take along to say 'hello' to Hinewai's aunt. The elderly lady was a wonderful artist. She had had a full life and was still energetic and full of fun. Rose hardly ever had free time to spend with the rest of the family, friendly, talented and interesting though they all were. In the past eight weeks there'd been no earlier opportunity to visit the Bay of Plenty, despite Rose's plan to buy a second house there before the property boom made such a purchase impossibly expensive for her budget.

However exhausted she felt after working hard and doing so many new things in a new environment, in Rose's quiet times, such as this Easter weekend holiday, her lifelong learning study ethic was gradually re-awakening and the unfinished doctorate which she'd started back in Bahrein in 1999 was beginning to trouble her. She'd started the doctoral study programme when life seemed relatively sweet, after the protracted divorce from Nabeel had been finalized, and her life with Colin had been experiencing some vicissitudes. A doctorate had been on Rose's to do list for a long time. After a lifetime spent on her English-language teaching career, she felt the urge to affirm her knowledge and confirm her commitment to the profession. Not many language teachers could afford to study for a doctorate in terms of both available time and money, but as Rose had never had the children she had wanted, she felt she owed it to herself and to her Mum to achieve this lifetime ambition. This weekend she felt strong enough to follow up on her enrolment status with the University. It would be cheaper to continue her studies in New Zealand, but on the other hand, she'd completed half of her requirement already with a UK University. She needed to sort out her priorities and check her study options.

Thinking about her new job, her new home and her abandoned study program had fully occupied Rose's time over the past months but she had also kept a close watch on the progress of the Second Gulf War since that day in March when the Western allies had started their two pronged attack with a land invasion through Kuwait and aerial bombardment on Baghdad. Saddam had been given 48 hours to leave Baghdad but had now disappeared. In early April the US forces had secured Baghdad, then the allied Kurdish forces had gained control of the northern city of Kirkuk. In mid-April the US had control of Tikrit, Saddam's birthplace and home town, but Saddam was not found there. A former US Lt. General, Jay Garner, had taken charge of the Office for Reconstruction and Humanitarian Assistance in Iraq but despite the appointment of this civil administrator there was a collapse of law and order. Saddam's personal palace had been pillaged, looting was rife and the capital's museum director was complaining bitterly about the state of chaos which had followed the invasion, with antiquities looted. The situation looked bleak for all concerned.

Rose was horrified by the destruction of these historic cities, famed in ancient Mesopotamia and now in modern day Iraq. In 1988 she had marvelled at the reconstruction of Babylon when she had visited Baghdad for a couple of days as an ESOL Teaching Diploma assessor. No one knew where Saddam had escaped to, but there were graphic reports of the gold plated taps and other extravagant luxury items found in his personal palace. Unlike the deprived Iraqi population Rose had all the creature comforts she wanted. After a hot shower she got into bed to watch Sky TV channels. CNN and BBC reporters still appeared to be revelling in the fighting in Iraq. She couldn't bear to watch for long, the news was so depressing.

She looked out of the windows of her room. This motel did not have sea views, but the sight of the Mount changing colour under the rosy glow of the setting sun's rays was compensation. One day, perhaps, Rose would enjoy views of the coast from her own home. She would have a security system to allay her fears, and perhaps a dog or two. For now she had her weekend schedule planned. Over breakfast she would scour the local papers for information in preparation for Easter Saturday's property hunt. On Easter Sunday she would go to church then take the Easter gifts to her new 'family'. With pleasant plans in mind, even with no alcoholic bedtime drink she drifted off to peaceful sleep easily.

CHAPTER 10

Viva Espana

November 1990

When Nabeel and I awoke in Mossfield the next morning, the birds were singing in the garden despite the slight autumn frost and my view on life seemed much simpler and more relaxed than it had been in London. I slipped out of bed and made us all a cup of tea, taking Mum's into her room, then sitting back in bed against my pillows to drink mine. Nabeel was lying on his back, staring at the ceiling, deep in thought.

'Good morning, darling. Your tea's on the bedside table. How are you feeling today? Can we talk?'

'Yes, as long as it's not about your books,' he grumbled.

'Please, sweetheart, let's not fight about that. Do you remember how we spent our summer vacation in Italy, France and Spain?'

'Yes, of course. I'm not senile, you know. I've been in touch with Pietro in Milano, you remember his company? Well, they are waiting for me to go back to Kuwait so that I can place some orders for their product.'

'I loved Pietro and his wife. They seemed to like my stories in Italian too. But you won't be able to get back to Kuwait for quite a while, will you?'

'No, of course not. I'm just telling you I remember our holiday perfectly.'

'Well, the big thing that happened while you were in Kuwait, which was worrying me a lot was the contract we had set up in Spain to buy that piece of land. I mentioned it to you in London but you didn't say anything, you didn't react.'

'Are you talking about the land that Miles found for us?'

'Yes, that's it. I didn't know what to do about it.'

'So what did you do?'

'Well, I went ahead and bought it.'

You bought it? Really? What with?'

'With our money, of course. The joint account money in the Isle of Man. I got special permission from the Bank of England to move some to Spain. Our accounts were closed in case we were Saddam sympathizers, sending money overseas to support him. As if!'

'Good for you. Very nice. Well done.'

'So, shall we go and look at it?'

'What for?'

'Well, we had decided to buy it so as to build our 'halfway house' between Lebanon and England, hadn't we? You know, so that we'd have a home in both our home countries and then another one which belonged to both of us.'

'Yes, but things are a bit different now, aren't they?'

'You know, I wasn't sure about that. Although you stayed over there instead of coming home to me in the UK, I thought things were still the same between us. Aren't they?'

'You tell me. You're the clever one, buying bits of land all over the place. In your name I suppose?'

'Hang on a minute! That's a bit much. We searched for a house in Spain together and you didn't like anything we saw, so in the end we decided to buy this land. It was a bargain, which was why you went for it.'

'Yes, but I didn't know you'd go ahead without me.'

'That's why you should have come out of Kuwait before now,' I reminded him crossly.

'I needed you to help me make decisions about our life. I kept sending messages to you through our friends in Jordan, you know. I really wasn't sure what to do. If you had died, I'd like to remind you, our money in the Isle of Man is the only money I would inherit.'

'I see. Nice thought, hey? Things like that didn't cross my mind. I wasn't having a picnic over there after all.'

Obviously Nabeel was still in an unforgiving mood.

'OK. Well, I'm sorry if you didn't want me to go ahead, but what's done is done. We could always sell it on if you don't want to keep it. But if we do, then we've got Miles over there who could build something for us. Remember he drew an outline plan with a budget for us. I've got it here. Do you want to take a look?'

'OK. Let's not rush things though. Shall we go down there to have another look at it?'

'Yes, let's. I'd love that. We can go in the car. By the way, you haven't said whether you approve of that purchase either. It's automatic so that we can both drive.'

'Yes, I know. That's good. We needed a car for sure and it drives well. I know you are good with money. You spent wisely. We might as well get out of here for a while.'

'Yes, we should set off before the winter comes in here. We often get snow in January, so perhaps we could make the journey before Xmas? It'll still be warm in southern Spain.'

'OK. Let's get the map out and make some plans.'

'That's great. I'll tell Mum.'

The rest of the day passed quickly with the AA map of Spain we had used that summer on our vacation trip to southern Europe spread out on the dining table to help us plan our itinerary. I also retrieved the outline plan that Miles had drawn with his cost estimates for a two storey house on the foundations already in place. The land had belonged to a couple of young British men who had started to rebuild a *finca*, or Spanish farmhouse within the legal requirements, i.e. on the foundations of an original farm house. They were not very practical it seemed. They had planted a pomegranate tree in a corner of the house, not grasping the fact that the inevitable growth of the tree and its roots would damage the integrity of the walls and foundations. We had their plans for the use of the extensive land for various fruits, including figs, apples and almonds, and I had already paid for an electricity pole, wires and supply which my neighbours had begun to use. Miles and Sheila's house was across the valley from our land, so we would be able to wave to each other across the distance, we had joked the previous summer. Miles had been in charge of building a large villa with swimming pool for our mutual friends from Kuwait, Mark and Ronda, so we envisaged a small, friendly community in the future.

Before Nabeel's return from Lebanon I'd made some apple cider, or at least, I'd put the must down to ferment. The apples had ripened before Nabeel came out of Kuwait in November. The must was now bubbling gently in a bin in the corner of the warm dining alcove, like Macbeth's witches' brew. It would have to wait for me to come back from Spain to bottle it. My hopes of being economical and using everything we had in the garden were going to be sabotaged by the cost of the trip to Spain, but if we were careful we could afford the petrol for the journey and the cost of cheap roadside motels. In Spain the weather would be warm and I hoped it would give us a chance to recapture the past summer's holiday spirit and rid us of our disagreements about Saddam Hussein and the issue of who invaded Kuwait, Iraq or America. Of course, Mum was disappointed we weren't staying longer, especially after we'd spent more than three months together since that fateful day, the second of August. But I think she was secretly relieved to have the tension in the house removed, as well as Nabeel's constant complaints about having to smoke outside.

Before we could set off both Nabeel and I had some tasks to complete. I had to finish writing references for my team in Kuwait, as all of us had been left high and dry by Kuwait University. There had been no salary for expatriate employees after the invasion, although workers still in Kuwait had been summoned to their positions by the Iraqi authorities. Most members of my team were looking for new jobs elsewhere, apart from those who were detained, courtesy of Saddam Hussein in either Kuwait or Iraq. My friend Beatrice had found a good job in the Emirates Polytechnic Colleges (EPC). I was busy helping everyone else, while I myself was in limbo. I was not able to apply for new positions in other countries while my husband was still in Kuwait. Now it was clear that Nabeel was looking forward to re-establishing himself there. He'd been contacting his 'suppliers' since his arrival in the UK, so his intentions were clear to me. I wasn't sure how I felt about that, but for now, with his principals all alerted to our plan, we were free to roam while Kuwait was still under Iraqi occupation.

After a few days we were ready to leave, with our international driving licences, our European travel insurance, and 200 cigarettes on the back seat of the car which Nabeel would smoke within four days I predicted. Duty free shopping as we crossed the English Channel would allow him to replenish his stock. I'd also stockpiled frozen meals for Mum as well as dry goods and cans. John would be visiting and assisting her as he used to before the Invasion and my enforced stay at home. I'd enjoyed being in Mossfield and seeing John and his children as well as my Dad and his family. But now I was ready for a trip to Spain, a country whose culture and climate I loved. It would keep us busy while the politics surrounding the Invasion of Kuwait worked its slow way out. There would be a war, it seemed, but I wondered about the outcome. Nothing seemed certain any more. Being away from the war zone was a blessing.

'Bye, Mum. Take care of yourself. See you in a month. We'll be home before Xmas.'

'Bye darlings. Drive safely. I'll be fine. Don't worry about me.'

Mum's sad face belied her unselfish words, but we were off.

'*Hasta la vista*, Mama. See you soon.'

Mary watched us drive away, standing at the window, waving a little as she always did, despite the pain and suffering she had in those crooked hands and arms which would not straighten. When she had waved us off, she would be going back to her room, to lie on her large, but unconsoling bed, unable to turn over or move her limbs while prone on account of her disabling RA. If friends or nurse visits were expected she would sit in the sitting room for a while, on her specially adapted high chair with elevating seat cushion. Both the sitting room and her bedroom had pleasant views, but she could not go outside without someone to assist her. Even inside she needed to use a walker to move around safely.

Mum was in a trap, no matter how comfortable in appearance the trap was. '*A creaking gate swings forever*' was her frequent saying, but sometimes, she told me, she wished that RA would kill her to take her from her suffering. It broke my heart that I could do nothing to help other than providing her with the home she enjoyed. Despite the current political misunderstandings Nabeel and I were having I wasn't ready as yet to stay in the UK permanently. I had made a huge sacrifice by deciding to marry him and to leave Mum and my excellent career prospects in London. But I had always imagined that she would live with us later, either in Lebanon, or Spain which we had considered a half way house, with a climate warm enough to ease her pain to some extent. Mum was a bold traveller despite her disability. She had enjoyed being in Spain on holiday with me and John a couple of times in the '70s when she was younger and at the beginning of her disability. Also, she had travelled solo to Kuwait three times and spent three months each visit with us. I envisaged us building a home in Spain for both sides of the family. I certainly anticipated taking care of Mum till the end of her life.

CHAPTER 11

Memories of Easter Past

April 2003

After an undisturbed and alcohol free Good Friday night Rose awoke to a beautiful Easter Saturday morning and the sound of children splashing in the small motel pool. She had bought some croissants at the dairy where she had not been allowed to buy wine the previous day, so she made herself a filter coffee and warmed a croissant for breakfast. She recalled how Nabeel had never enjoyed eating breakfast, but drank around ten cups of coffee loaded with sugar over the course of each day. Small things like this came unbidden to her mind, but she pushed them away without any sadness. Not living with cigarette smoke surrounding her was something she appreciated every day away from him. It was a pity that he had threatened her life when they finally broke up. Now she hated these sneaky memories when they crept up on her. She wanted to be completely free of him. Perhaps when she had her dream home at the beach she would be. A new environment would bring a new mindset, she hoped.

With that in mind she took her coffee over to the bed where she could spread out the newspaper and check on the location of the open homes she was planning to visit that day. The property press was remarkably well-organised, with maps, addresses and even small photos of homes for sale. She was also going to visit some show homes set up by the different building developers. But she had a definite list of priorities. Her house by the beach must have double glazing, solar water heating, insect screens and no open fire or gas heaters. She was aiming for a complete rejection of all the bugbears from her childhood. Coal fires, grates, ash and coal dust were not on her future agenda. Even the smell of burning wood was enough to take her back to those early days in her father's mining village house.

Having circled half a dozen adverts, Rose got ready to go out and find the properties. She would enjoy investigating the area in depth. Aware of the ongoing property boom she was keen to buy as soon as possible in hope of still getting good value for money. Paying too much for a property during a boom meant there would be almost no chance for increase in your investment over the long term. Buyers could well end up with negative equity. Armed with a street map book and the papers, she headed south towards the Paloa Beach area, which, though decidedly down market compared to the more obviously prosperous Mount, could offer the chance to get a bargain from among both newer subdivisions and older houses which needed doing up. Rose knew she wouldn't be able to handle a complete renovation, but refurbishing a property seemed within her reach. After all, her Mum's house in Mossfield had needed some repairs before resale and Rose had met the challenge headon.

Paloa Beach had undergone extensive redevelopment Rose found as she drove along the Beach Road and parked in the Fashion Island shopping area. There was a large mall with the popular 'Red Shed' bargain department store and a Countdown Supermarket, as well as numerous small shops and various amenities for beach dwellers as well as visitors. She had noted several motels as well as holiday parks with camping facilities and purpose built chalets for holiday makers on her drive along the road parallel with the beach. The beach extended from Mount Maunganui, behind her, as far as the Maketu spit, which jutted out on the far horizon. Walking the beach would probably be more than a day's trek, but it offered a tantalising scenario for Rose's dream home. She mused on the possibility of owning a seafront house. She knew from past experience in Kuwait the damage the wind and salt could do to a building and to plants and trees. And, of course, a sea front house would be exposed to the passing public. Something more secluded would be best.

With this in mind Rose checked out the properties she was keen to see and enjoyed noting their strengths and weaknesses. It was clear that she could learn a lot from viewing these homes, since there was a much greater range of new properties here than she had found in Farmerston. She was particularly intrigued by the idea of building to her own design. It seemed that this was not an exclusive right of rich people, as it was in the UK. Architectural design was needed for tricky plots, such as slopes, or grand plans, but the more modest 'design and build' option was popular with ordinary people with ordinary budgets. Rose had been a careful saver in her prestigious full time position in Bahrein. She had managed to build up a small nest egg in only eight years, as well as spending money on holidays in exotic destinations with Colin.

After her 23 year relationship with Nabeel she had come out of her divorce without a penny, only awarded the costs she had incurred by using an expensive international solicitor to try to get fair treatment at the hands of the law. She had learned a lot of lessons in the process, however. Rose had been defrauded by Nabeel and still smarted at her stupidity in falling into his trap by giving him several blank A4 sheets of paper with her signature at the bottom of each. Supposedly for her new husband to obtain visas to Lebanon for her, these had been used to retrieve the lump sum of a quarter of a million sterling which she thought she had put out of his reach until a divorce settlement was achieved legally. Little did she know to what extent he would be prepared to go in revenge for her leaving him. Still, she could salve her wounds by reminding herself that everything she now owned was the result of her own efforts and hers alone. This was a healing thought. She owed her ex nothing.

Hunger pangs reminded Rose that is was time for some lunch, or perhaps, some ice cream. New Zealand dairy ice cream is delicious and Rose was always on the lookout for a new flavour to try. It was hard to choose from the wide variety, but boysenberry sounded healthy. A single cone was enough. As she looked at the various tubs in the shop's freezer display she couldn't help recalling that Colin loved rum and raisin ice cream. On the other hand, Nabeel would have preferred a cigarette to ice cream, that was sure. She ate her ice cream as she strolled along the beach, enjoying the sunshine and the sea air. None of the properties she had viewed were ideal for her. She needed lots of storage and bookshelves too. Perhaps a design and build plan would be best. Design and build was an option which customised the 'off the shelf' plans to suit the clients and their piece of land, without going to the expense of hiring an architect. She'd go into that in more detail back in Farmerston, using the booklets she'd been given. A trip to the cinema would round off today's 'to do' list. She'd noted that a new film, *The Whale Rider*, was showing at the Mount, which was convenient for her motel, so off she went to get a ticket for the afternoon session.

The film was a perfect antidote to the chill Rose always felt when thoughts of Nabeel crossed her mind. The negativity left behind after what she had always believed was an honest relationship, often crushed her with sadness. How could he call himself a Christian after treating her as he had? Defrauding her, leaving her with nothing, as he thought, and threatening to have her killed rather than coming to an amicable divorce settlement. The film she was watching about the Maori people's beliefs in ancestors and in spirituality was soothing to Rose's spirit and a reminder that personal relationships can be the source of sadness and grief. Cross-cultural relationships are challenging in their complexity and Rose had definitely injured Nabeel's self esteem. But was revenge the right reaction, she wondered? He was the one who had pushed for the marriage, and she had given in. It was hardly surprising that the marriage had not withstood the absence of children and his continual putdowns. Then came the ultimate blow, the Iraqi invasion of their home in Kuwait and the subsequent war which had divided them not just physically but mentally, politically and emotionally.

'The past is the past,' Rose told herself firmly. But a still, small voice in her head said, 'but it's the foundation of the future, and don't forget it. Learn from it.'

After the film Rose picked up fish and chips, as well as a bottle of wine, now readily available in the dairy, and enjoyed her evening meal in front of the TV in the motel. She had had a very different day from her usual working routine, so was able to congratulate herself on how far she'd come from those dark days of the divorce. The TV screen reminded her how much people in Iraq were suffering, and the soldiers and news reporters too. News was filtering out about a British reporter for ITN, Terry Lloyd, who had been killed in March by what was originally reported as crossfire during fighting in Basra, but turned out on investigation to have been US friendly fire, *blue on blue* again. Rose's heart went out to the families of all those killed. She knew Basra, having driven up to the northern border of Kuwait in the happy days of peace. The lovely old Red Fort at Jahra was a tourist attraction well worth a visit, and the camel farms in the area were interesting too. Mum had enjoyed her time there even though a camel had tried to eat her straw-coloured hair as she stood by its pen for a photo, immobile and unable to move away without Rose's help. They had laughed about the event often since then. It was unbelievable that the silent desert and the small quiet town should be riven by gunshots and worse. Why had Saddam taken that violent step of invasion back in 1990 she wondered yet again and where was he now, as so many people paid the price belatedly for his actions?

The next day, Easter Sunday, Rose was glad to be able to walk to the nearest church for Holy Communion. The priest was female, which was a first for Rose, whose faith had begun to fade as she grew older. By the time she was married she no longer believed in the Christ story, and was sure there was no 'imaginary friend' in the sky, but in times of need she still found herself crying for her Mum, and for God, to help her. Old traditions and cherished beliefs die hard. The service was simple but moving, the Gospel saga of the Resurrection giving Rose pause for thought as always. She had been a regular churchgoer as a child, thanks to Mum's insistence, but her father did not support religious views, and so she had always suspected there was something amiss with the challenging tales, for example, of the Virgin Birth. The tragedy of the Crucifixion, she knew, was real, and it brought tears to her eyes. The memory of Mum's sudden death, when Rose had not been able to get to her bedside, reduced her to floods of tears. In the small congregation the priest noticed her crying and gave her a concerned glance. Rose attempted to smile a reassurance, as she mopped at her eyes with yet another tissue.

After the service ended, the priest came over and asked if she needed any help. Rose explained her recent bereavement and distance from her home country. The priest nodded in commiseration, urging her to come back again whenever she was in the area. Rose was surprised at the sudden intensity of her grief. 'Better in than out,' she murmured to herself. She hadn't been to a church service since Mum's funeral a year earlier. Her breakdown was completely understandable.

From the church Rose drove to Hinewai's Aunt's house. She had prepared a basket with chocolate eggs, flowers and ribbons, as several grandchildren might be visiting that day. Indeed, there was a small group of adults and children when Rose rang the bell, and she was invited in for coffee. It was a pleasant gathering and Rose felt happy to be included. She appreciated the sense of not being completely alone in a completely new country. She was very impressed by the family's talents. There were three accomplished artists in the family as the many pictures on the walls bore witness to. There was an easy air of kinship in the house, which was pleasant to experience given Rose's current solo status.

Hinewai's cousin reminded her: 'Don't forget, we're here if you need us. Your Kiwi family.'

'Thank you. I'm so grateful,' she told him sincerely.

After a short while Rose made her excuses and left. She was heading back to Farmerston that day. Although the University had both Monday and Tuesday as Easter holidays, she needed to get ready to leave the motel on Monday morning. She was moving into her new home and had already been informed that her container was on the high seas. It was amazing how her belongings had multiplied since she had moved into the motel. Despite determining to limit shopping she had given in to temptation a few times in Farmerston. She was glad she'd made the effort to come over to the beach for Easter. All was well with her new world, if not with her old one.

CHAPTER 12

Spanish Interlude

November - December 1990

The bronze metallic paintwork of the Ford saloon glistened in the pale wintry sun as we sped away from the house, on the correct side of the road for the UK, i.e. the left hand side.

'Well done, darling!'

'What do you mean? I know how to drive, you know.'

'Yes, I know you do. But you've made mistakes before when the road is empty, so you've done well to remember which side to drive on this time.'

I veered away from this touchy subject and tried another.

'I've got all the paperwork - passports, ferry tickets, maps and the mapbook Mum gave me. I'll keep a note of our mileage in that. It'll be interesting to record our long drive.'

'It's not that long. I drove to Baghdad last month you know. Then we drove to Lebanon. I like driving. I'll be fine. Go to sleep if you like.'

This was the first I had heard from Nabeel about his visit to Baghdad. I was surprised, but decided to keep quiet about it. My earlier suspicion about his motive for lingering in Kuwait was reawakened. Why had he gone to Baghdad, I wondered? Dare I ask? I didn't want to upset him while he was driving, so put away the thought.

I was tired after staying up late to finish both our packing and the preparations that Mum needed. Her food supplies in the pantry had to be placed for easy reach when standing supported by her walking frame. Her medicine also needed to be in the fridge at the right level for her to grasp in her crippled hands. She had to balance food and drinks in the basket of her walking frame to take them back to her room to consume. I was worried about her, especially as we'd enjoyed the months from August to October together. Now I needed to worry about the driver beside me.

'Careful, darling. This is a 40mph limit.'

'I know, I know, I can see, you know. I'm not blind.'

'OK. Do you remember where the motorway is?'

'No. Just tell me as we go.'

After negotiating the local roads calling out 'watch/cigarette', the simplicity of the motorway driving was a welcome relief. I could relax, read or doze and wake up again ready to give directions once we reached the exit junction for North London, the turn off for Bill and Katie's house where we were spending the night. The next day we had car ferry tickets from Dover. It was good to see my brother and sister-in-law and their kids again. We had a good meal, some fine wine, as my brother's refined tastes required, and a reasonable but short night's sleep. I made sure we had two alarm clocks primed to wake us.

Just before dawn the next day we were weaving our way through London's dark, empty central city streets towards the Kent road to the Dover Ferry Terminal. The unfamiliar journey wasn't easy, with little light to read the map book by, and the fear of missing the ferry in the back of our minds, but we did it. The ferry trip itself was fun. Neither of us had taken a car ferry before, so we enjoyed the novelty despite our tiredness. Our first night was spent in Boulogne at a small hotel. The sea breeze was fresh and invigorating, and we could laugh again in this new environment. As we both spoke French fluently, it was as if we were on honeymoon again. In fact, it was better than our original honeymoon as this time I could speak the language, whereas in 1976 I had very little Arabic to cope with a holiday in Egypt. There had been linguistic challenges in that situation, which had amazed me. I had realised that Nabeel had lost his communicative skill with Arabic after several years in the UK as a student, first of English, then of Business, and ultimately as an employee.

The following day after breakfast in Boulogne we started a marathon drive through France and Spain to the little *finca* property between Fuengirola and Mijas on Spain's south eastern coast. We'd chosen it and begun the purchase procedure together while on holiday in July just before the Invasion. I hoped Nabeel would still be enthusiastic about it. The property had cost nearly fifty thousand sterling pounds and included a small farmhouse under renovation, terraces for growing fruit trees and a stream, but no electricity. I'd obtained Bank of England permission to send the currency equivalent to Spain during the wartime period of financial control. The remainder of the permitted money had been spent on installing a power pylon but there was enough left for our expenses on this short trip. At least we had some pesetas in the bank to look forward to when we arrived. Meanwhile, my record of the drive illustrated Nabeel's obsessive nature. Each day he wanted to beat his own record by driving more kilometers than the day before. On average we drove 500 each day, or at least he did. I wasn't allowed to drive.

My mind became a blur as we raced through the beautiful but unappreciated countryside. When compelled by exhaustion to stop, we checked into small roadside motels and ate the basic food available there. Fortunately Europe's *routier* restaurants are much better than the norm in the UK, so my palate was satisfied. For Nabeel, only cigarettes mattered. A little duty free whisky for a nightcap and a carafe of *vin de table* with our meal was all we drank so our budget was not stretched. Petrol, of course, was another thing but overall our trip was not expensive. I think Nabeel's need to drive was caused by the desire to occupy his mind. After all, he'd lost one home when Israel was created in Palestine, the land where he was born. Now he'd lost his home in Kuwait and perhaps more importantly to him, his business, which he had built up single-handedly. I didn't complain about the haste. I wanted to get back to Mum in time for Xmas but the journey would have been more pleasant if less rushed. I was reminded of Lamartine's poem: *But at my back I always hear time's winged chariot drawing near.* There was no chance that chariot would catch us on this swift journey through France and Spain.

As we drove further and further south the weather got warmer. England's autumn had been pleasant, but Spain's was much more so. Fuengirola is a popular vacation place for locals and expatriates with a Spanish atmosphere. We had not seen our old friends Sheila and Miles since they helped us select the land in summer. They were building a villa for Mark and Ronda who had been with Nabeel on the night of the Invasion. We checked into a small hotel in the middle of

Fuengirola where we could enjoy the local restaurants and met up with Sheila and Miles the next day. They were longing to hear details about the Invasion but once again, Nabeel would not be drawn on that topic. When they enquired about our mutual friends he was similarly reticent. When we left London Mark was in Iraq as a captive, although Ted Heath, a former UK Prime Minister, had begun negotiations with Saddam Hussein to release the hostages. Ronda was staying with Mark's parents, who were helping out financially with their villa building project by buying Mark and Ronda's small flat in southern Spain. Both parents and wife were in London awaiting Mark's hoped for release.

Sheila and Miles had their own adventure to relate, so Nabeel's reluctance to speak about the invasion of Kuwait wasn't so noticeable. After living in Kuwait and enjoying the easy life of a childless couple, in Spain they had unexpectedly conceived their son, now a primary school child. I felt a pang of emotion, given my childless status, as I saw how happy they were. In Spain they had managed to build their own bungalow while constructing Mark and Ronda's palatial villa. When we built our own home on the site we had chosen in July, we would all be neighbours. Ronda had told me about her villa's location when we were still in Kuwait.

'I'll be able to wave to you from my house. We can signal where and when we will meet for coffee!'

All the dreams we had shared in Kuwait had encountered a different reality now. We commiserated with each other and passed the *Rioja* round. The only way now was up! Building our new home in Spain on our land would be the way forward. It would provide us with a home which was neither the UK nor the Lebanon, a neutral ground, where politics did not intervene. Palestine and Kuwait could be forgotten for a while, with all the sadness attached thereto.

Miles had submitted a draft plan to us for our house and was keen to go ahead with construction. But before we reached the final house design stage we needed to tie up any loose legal ends. One important issue for me was making a will. Inheritance laws around the world differ dramatically. In Lebanon I had already been advised that as we had no children, in the case of Nabeel's death I would only be entitled to inherit half of his and our joint wealth, including properties. The other half would pass to his family members. In Spain, tax was payable on property which was inherited by non-family members. I wanted to make sure that my brother was named as my heir for this property, while Nabeel wanted to name one of his brothers. So a visit to the lawyer with our real estate agent, Carmen, was urgent. We needed Carmen's assistance as she spoke reasonable English, whereas my Spanish was halting at best. The lawyer spoke only Spanish, but the details were not complex. This kind of work was normal in Fuengirola, which many British and Scandinavians had adopted as their own seaside home. Having completed the legal requirements, we could relax a little and think about the new house. I wondered if we could still afford to build after the impact of the Invasion on our finances. Over lunch I started a discussion about matters I was still unsure of, but hardly dared raise.

'What happened to your business and our private bank accounts when the Iraqis invaded, darling? I heard that they tried to get their hands on the gold reserves in the National Bank of Kuwait?'

'Don't worry about that. They couldn't do it. And the Bank has promised to reimburse all those who lost money while the bank was under Iraqi control. I'm working on that now.'

'That's wonderful news. Did you have any goods in transit in August? Were they stolen?'

'I had one shipment on the high seas in July, but fortunately I could alert them and the ship turned around. There are issues I have to sort out with regard to that. I'm surprised you're thinking about the Invasion from my point of view now.'

The old argument had begun again.

'That's not fair. I know you suffered emotionally as well as physically on that terrible first day. Running around on the beach, trying to avoid shells must have been awful.'

'Yea, I tried to dig a trench and got some others to help me - we jumped into it when we heard a shell coming over.'

'I'm so glad you got to the Embassy and the British allowed you to shelter there.'

'Well, they do know me, so that helped.'

'I'm sure all this makes you think of when you had to leave Palestine.'

'You're right. It was terrible. I was only a small child and Menachim Begin was as much as terrorist then as Saddam Hussein now.'

'I know. Why Margaret Thatcher was able to talk to him but refused to talk to Yasser Arafat still makes me wild. One man's politician is another man's terrorist, hey?'

'Yea. People forget history.'

'So they are condemned to repeat it... that's how the saying goes. Anyway, did you know that Ronda and Mark's household effects were at the port on 1st August?'

'Yes. What happened to their container?'

'They told me they haven't heard where it is yet. Meanwhile they have to make a United Nations claim like us for our home.'

'Mm. I want YOU to submit a claim for our home to the British Government. I'll handle the business claims.'

'Really? In my name? Are you sure?'

'Yes. They'll handle it better than the Lebanese Government I'm sure.'

'OK. There's a new group which is supporting people like us, who have lost their homes and are in limbo. It's called the Gulf Support Group. We will have to wait and see if we can go back before we submit any claims. After all, I don't really know what is there and what has gone.'

'Don't start that again. You and your books. That's all you care about.'

'Sorry. I didn't mean it like that. Let's not argue about the same thing over and over.'

'Why not, if that's all you have to talk about?'

'Well, let's talk about the future. What about planning our new house in Spain?'

'No. It's too soon. I want to see what happens in Kuwait first.'

'OK. Well, what shall we do between now and then? After all, we don't know when we'll be able to go back, though the USA and the UK keep talking about using direct force to oust Saddam.'

'I don't think they will go that far. After all, the Kuwaitis deserved it.'

'What on earth do you mean? How did they deserve it?'

'They had been stealing the oil for years.'

'What? How?'

'The Kuwaitis had drilled into Iraq's oilfields at an angle under the border, taking Iraqi oil into Kuwait.'

'Really? Is that possible?'

'You don't know anything about the Middle East. Anything is possible. Kuwait was originally part of Iraq and the British drew the borders again after the war. It's just the same as Palestine - interfering imperialists creating huge problems.'

'Is that why Sheikh Saad went to Baghdad at the end of July? To say sorry for stealing oil?'

'Yea. But he didn't go to Baghdad, he went to Jeddah. The Saudis were trying to sort out the quarrel. But the US was in on it.'

'You're crazy. What do you mean?'

'It's the truth. The Americans wanted Saddam to invade. The US Ambassador in Baghdad, April Glaspie, okayed it. She told Saddam that the Americans wouldn't interfere in the quarrel. She went on holiday on 31st July, she was so relaxed!'

'Well, that's a different thing, from our point of view. Not interfering doesn't mean agreeing to an invasion, does it?'

'It depends.'

'On what?'

'On what the USA would get out of it.'

'What would they get out of it?'

'They wouldn't have to deal with the Kuwaitis separately. It was all about the Soviet connection. The Americans had been supporting Saddam for eight years through the Iran-Iraq war so they preferred to stay out of his quarrels with his neighbours.'

'But the invasion of Kuwait nearly caused problems with Israel, the US ally. Why would they agree to an armed invasion which brought him within reach of Israel with his rockets?'

'You'll see. It'll all come out one day.'

'Oh yea, so who looted our house?'

'Not the Iraqis. I met some of the Republican Guard. They were nice guys.'

'Really? I've heard that Iraqis looted the University. They were throwing computers carelessly into a truck, that's how clever they are. They didn't realise they would break them and they would be useless.'

'Maybe. But even people living in Kuwait started looting.'

'Who? The Kuwaitis?'

'No. The Pakistanis and Indians who were working in Kuwait.'

'Not the Palestinians?'

'Shut up. *Hash tahki.* I need a cigarette. Let's get out of here.'

We left the seafood restaurant and walked by the sea while Nabeel smoked. Though he could have smoked in the restaurant he was considerate enough to avoid smoking at the table. I felt confused, sad and angry at the same time. Could what he had said be true? Of course not? Maybe? Whatever the truth of the invasion of Kuwait, we had to find a way to move forward, or else this would tear us apart. Perhaps it was a good thing we were going home to Mossfield without delay. We could do no more here until we had sorted our finances out. Looking after Mum at home would occupy my mind, and Nabeel could contact his suppliers to make his business plans. That would keep him busy and away from politics, I hoped.

Nabeel certainly had several more bees in his bonnet than previously and there had always been plenty of justifiable bees there, given the Palestinian situation, though politics wasn't something we discussed often in Kuwait. Nabeel's family had never talked much about Israel in my presence, but that could have been because I was considered the enemy, being British. The UK and the US had given Palestine to the Zionists. I was not to be trusted, nor truly welcomed into the family, though I had done my best to integrate. *Blue on blue*, friendly fire, heartache on heartache. I pushed the bitter thought away. I could only deal with the present, I sighed to myself. The rest would have to wait.

CHAPTER 13

Karl and Oman

April 2003

Easter Monday and Tuesday were statutory university holidays when Rose could move into her new house in Farmerston. She had found her house just in time for the change of seasons from summer to fall. March had been warm though wet, April began to turn chilly and after moving in on Easter Monday, Rose realised that the real estate description of her new home held a hidden meaning. This 'uniquely different' house was not very well insulated! The two spare bedrooms and bathroom had a flat roof through which the winter cold crept insistently. The main bedroom, *en suite* bathroom and open-plan kitchen, living, and dining room were better protected with a more traditional tiled, sloping roof but Rose still needed to buy electric heaters as the house was not centrally heated. At night she wore a 'beanie', a woolen hat, as she slept because of the cold air coming through the window above the bed. In the UK central heating, double glazing, brick walls, tiled roofs and thick insulation were standard. But Rose knew she had nothing serious to complain about. These differences were part and parcel of living in another country. However, after almost 23 years she had got used to living in the Arabian Gulf, a much warmer climate.

Rose moved in with just two suitcases and the fruits of her shopping expeditions in Farmerston. Her household effects were still on the high seas from Bahrein. Over the past two months Rose had enjoyed buying immediate essentials to help her through till her container arrived. She had also bought some summer outdoor furniture to use indoors as winter approached. She loved sitting on the swing after work and on weekends, reading a book or a magazine, or just daydreaming, making lists of things to do and buy. It was good to find time to relax after the hectic months of packing and leaving first Bahrein, then Oman, and finally the UK all within the last nine months.

Watching her tiny TV Rose noted that in Iraq on April 23 the battle for the control of Fallujah began, and fierce fighting was taking place. Coincidentally, on 25 April in New Zealand and Australia Anzac Commemorations of the WW1 Battle of Gallipoli took place. Anzac ceremonies were new to her though the bright red poppy was a familiar symbol of the tragedy of war. In the UK the two World Wars were remembered on 11 November, the day of the WW1 Armistice, with the poppy as their symbol. Soon after the timely reminder of those historic tragedies, the US Secretary of Defense Donald Rumsfeld visited Iraq on 1 May, the same day that Bush announced that 'combat operations have ended'. After only one month in charge of the Office for Reconstruction and Humanitarian Assistance Lt. General Jay Garner was replaced by Paul Bremer as head of the Coalition Provisional Authority. Garner had prior experience in Kuwait after the First Gulf War, whereas Bremer was a civilian. Garner had plans to bring back 150,000 to 250,000 solders of the Iraqi Army to stop looting in Baghdad and maintain security, but Bremer disbanded the army in a process of De-Baathification, and dismissed the officers, leaving them without income and creating a huge number of angry Sunni Arab Iraqi fighters.

Media reports from the grass roots indicated that planning for the takeover of Iraq had been inadequate. Looting of precious historical and archaeological items in the museums was going on unchecked. Saddam's palaces were open access and the President had disappeared. There was lack of security and basic services for the citizens. It was obvious that winning the battle had not meant winning the war. Victory over Saddam did not look so good as Iraq began to disintegrate under the US invasion and occupation. American soldiers could not speak Arabic so clashed with non-English speaking civilians. Soldiers who were scared and suspicious mistreated Iraqis, misunderstanding their words and their intentions while neglecting to try to appreciate how they felt as their homeland became a living hell.

Rose's thoughts turned to how she had set up her house on the beach in Sohar, Oman. Why had she left Oman? The smart white Landrover Freelander 4x4 had been a luxury perk, but the special registration plate made it a target for terrorist attacks, should anyone be planning them. Another perk in Oman, was that Christians could obtain liquor with a special licence. She'd done her best to settle in, and her new friend Josephine had been a great comfort in the early days of orientation in the capital, Muscat. They'd attended staff induction sessions together, then gone out in the evenings. The cold pints of beer and heart to heart chat in different beachside hotels and bars had been a source of comfort as well as a great pleasure.

Work had been satisfying too. The young women she taught were novice or more experienced primary school teachers who aspired to be English language teachers. Their classes involved theory of education in English and they all tried hard to master the language and the 'western' principles of education endorsing democratic rather than autocratic classrooms with equal roles of teacher and students in the process of the social construction of knowledge, rather than its monopoly by the all powerful teacher filling students' empty heads with rote learned information. Sharing ideas and experiences, though new to them, was intriguing. The classes were fun, with the young women relating theory to practice by discussing and drawing scenes of their experiences in the classroom.

Rose had chosen to live in a large house in its own walled compound. She had worked hard to clean the dirty interior because she loved its proximity to the sea. However, she had not anticipated the struggles she faced with the local youths who couldn't comprehend why she was living alone in such a big house. They weren't to know she had a living area, and a separate guest area, as well as an office with a huge photocopier. The stones thrown by the local children had taken the shine off the beautiful geographic location, but she had been determined to stick it out. At work she had had to wear the *abbaya*, though she drew the line at the *shayla* over her hair. As an Omani colleague explained, it saved a lot of muttering 'God protect us!' from her male co-workers. Her civilian clothes had to cover her entire torso, front and back, so Rose had ordered some tailor-made man's shirts to wear over long skirts, to satisfy the stringent requirements for female attire. Despite these constraints and various setbacks, such as the local blind and curtain maker taking the wrong measurements and providing giant size blinds, Rose had expected to last out her contract for at least one year, if not the full three!

But a sudden, serious dental problem had required appointments at the American dental clinic in the UAE. Rose could not take the Landrover out of Oman until her residence visa was processed so transport over the border was difficult. She had to take the bus or ask friends for a lift. At Xmas she had visited her new Kiwi boyfriend, Norman in Dubai. They had hooked up in the UAE at a professional development meeting while Rose was still grieving her Mum. Their relationship showed signs of future success. Norman's villa full of antique souvenirs reminded Rose of her home in Kuwait. They had prepared Xmas lunch at his house and spent the day with a couple of old friends. But Norman inexplicably turned moody on Boxing Day. Unwilling to stay with him if she was not wanted, Rose hired a car the same day and drove to Abu Dhabi to stay with Hinewai and attend her planned dental appointment.

The endodontist confirmed Rose had a serious dental abscess, caused by a failed root canal filling when she was 21 in London! It had to be operated on as soon as possible in the New Year, and would entail follow up treatments. Since her contract with the Omani Education Ministry had not been finalised after three months at post, it seemed that the job she enjoyed was not meant to be. Coincidentally, Hinewai pointed her to a new job opportunity in New Zealand at her old university. It seemed a heaven sent opportunity:

She would be able to continue her career progression and be within easy reach of top class health facilities should she need them for her upper jaw. Rose completed her application and sent off her CV by email at once.

Despite the perceived rejection Rose still hoped Norman would invite her out for New Year's Eve. Instead she spent the day shopping at the Dubai Italianate Mall, and lunching at the Lemon Tree Cafe, then passed a solitary New Year's Eve at her Dubai hotel in front of the TV. On New Year's Day she returned her rental car and took the daily bus to Oman. Back in her seaside house she felt unusually lonely after the inexplicable rejection. No wonder she had fallen straight into the arms of University teacher Karl when he invited her out at a University party a week later. It was a classic case of the rebound as she had learned from Kyle years earlier, but she hoped Karl's buoyant good nature and constant high spirits would be the perfect antidote to her low mood. She certainly needed a hero at this point in her nomadic life.

Soon after meeting the two had made a road trip to visit Josephine. The scenery on the way to Sur, where the famous Green Turtle Beach is located, was magnificent. They'd visited some beautiful spots as they drove south parallel with the majestic cliffs of the Hajar Mountains. They had swum at a deserted cove, enjoying the privacy and the turquoise sea, and had also found a *wadi*, a mountain valley with crystal clear fresh water for swimming. However, they had also argued a fair bit, since they were both strong-minded, but overall, the new friendship boded well. Certainly Karl was handsome, helpful, athletic and fun to be with. He also knew some fabulous places to hang out - in particular, his high mountain spot for viewing the sunset with a cold thermos of wine! Rose loved his resourceful nature but, mindful of her experience with Norman, she knew that a hasty beginning wasn't necessarily the basis for a long term relationship. Karl had driven her over the border back to the UAE as often as needed for the dental appointments, and when Rose finally resigned from her job, having been successful with the application in New Zealand, he had been her saviour once again.

Rose had completed the course she was teaching with 31 young female primary teachers and had enjoyed a wonderful leaving party with them. The girls insisted that she take off her *abbaya,* which provoked a discussion as to why the girls wore them. Rose might not have dared to instigate this discussion if she hadn't been leaving the country the very same day. Demonstrating their ingenuity, the girls had arranged a visual spectacle for her, with juice cartons lined up to fall in a domino sequence. The teachers and School Inspector had bought her beautiful Omani silver farewell gifts. Then the staff had eaten lunch together at the local branch of Kentucky Fried Chicken, which vegetarian Rose discovered was delicious! Immediately after lunch Karl had driven her and her suitcases over the border to Dubai where they spent the weekend at a five star beach hotel before Karl drove back to Sohar to finish the semester at his university. They had had fun together, and Rose had promised Karl could visit her in New Zealand when she was settled into her new life. She owed him some good times for all that he'd done for her and he cheered her up.

Rose mused over the tricks of fate. In 2002 she had known nothing about New Zealand. For example, she assumed New Zealand was as close to Australia as France is to England. It was ironic that she and Kiwi Norman were no longer together since she was now working in his home country. However, Karl had taken up his invitation and was arriving in July. Rose wondered how the visit would go, since it seemed in retrospect they had been forced together by circumstance more than choice. She sincerely hoped it would not be a case of *blue on blue* again.

CHAPTER 14

Planning for Australia

December 1990 - January 1991

Our drive back from Spain's Costa del Sol to the UK was as speedy as our outward trip. Nabeel enjoyed the challenge of increasing his daily mileage. I hated the rush, but suffered in silence as we'd be home soon. After a calm ferry trip we stopped at Bill and Katie's for a couple of nights before driving to Mossfield. The UK weather had begun to turn much colder, which we felt more acutely after being in the south of Spain.

'How is everything with the *finca*? Is it OK? Still yours?' Bill asked in his laconic fashion, hinting that it might have been stolen from me as my home in Kuwait had been.

'Yes, and we've got electricity now. There's a pylon on one piece of the property which the neighbours can hook on to. We are paying for it as no one else seems to have enough money to do so. And if we die, half of it will be yours! We've made wills over there in your favour.'

'Wow!' Bill was truly surprised by this news. 'But just don't die, hey! We'll have to go and look for it next time we are down there on our summer holidays. We've gradually been moving our regular house stays from the south of France to Spain as it's so much warmer there.'

'You'll love it! The land has a great view of the Mediterranean - more than 180 degree views. It's fine for camping or perhaps just a picnic under the pomegranate tree built into the corner of the house! There isn't a bathroom or sewage on site yet though. There's a stream, but it appears to dry up in the summer, so water is another problem. So don't expect too much.'

We kept our conversation to our Spanish property, chatting about our friends in Spain whom we had known in Kuwait. There was good news about Mark. On account of his cancer treatment he was one of the first hundred hostages to be released on 10 December, 1990. He was staying at his parents' home, so we took the opportunity to visit him in London on our second day back. He was pale and tired but in good spirits after spending August and September in hiding. After his inevitable capture he had spent two months as Saddam Hussein's 'guest' in Iraq. Ronda was relieved to have Mark back with her but like myself while Nabeel was still in Kuwait, she had not known what was happening until quite close to the release date. I put the tension between them down to living in Mark's parents' small apartment after the long, enforced separation. We said our goodbyes, expecting to see each other again in Spain sometime in the future.

The following day we set off for Mossfield, stopping at Tesco's on the way to pick up provisions and fish and chips from the Barracuda Fish Bar for an early supper. On our arrival, Mum was upset with me.

'Do you know what happened while you were away?'
'No, what happened?'

'The apples you left in the bin in the dining area started fermenting like crazy. They were bubbling like mad and then they spilled right over the top of the bin and stained the carpet.'

'Oh, dear. I'm very sorry, Mum. How did you manage to sort that out?'

'I got John to come over and clean it up.'

'Oh, that's good. Sorry about that. Did you keep the brew?'

'No, we threw it out. It smelled bad and it's ruined that corner of the carpet.'

'OK, never mind. I'm sorry it caused you so much trouble.'

I knew Mum took pride in the beige shag pile fitted carpet she had chosen for the house only six years earlier, but I also thought sadly of the hours it had taken me to chop up the small apples from our old orchard's trees. Yet another economy which had turned out to be a false one! It seemed that bad luck was coming at me from all quarters and in small and big amounts - from losing my entire possessions in my Kuwait home, to quarrelling with my husband about US politics, to staining the carpet and more importantly, causing stress for my disabled mother. I hadn't realised the central heating in the bungalow would cause violent fermentation in the apple brew!

'Is John coming over tomorrow or is he at work?'

As a toddler John had been angelic, with blonde curls and laughing charm, but he had had difficulties when he reached puberty. Now he was married things were worse, with financial problems which overwhelmed him. At only 20 years old himself he had married a pretty blonde with a three year old daughter. They had then added a boy and a girl to their family, so money was always in short supply, and ultimately the marriage had broken down. John shared custody of the three kids. To help them out, Mum assisted them from her disability pension in exchange for additional care on an *ad hoc* basis. The arrangement suited them all and made up for my absence.

'Yes,' Mum confirmed, 'John and the children will come up for lunch as usual. I've got sausages, chips and peas in the freezer, the kids' favourites.'

'Or we could go out for lunch? Perhaps they'd like McDonalds? Anyway, let's eat our supper now, shall we? Would you like a bath before you go to bed?'

'No, not tonight. Perhaps in the morning, if you don't mind?'

'Fine. No problem.'

Giving Mum a bath was the best treat I could offer her as the hot water relieved her joint pain to some extent. I resumed my role as caregiver and wrote more references for former colleagues from Kuwait University. Most of them were desperately looking for jobs. My counterpart supervisor Beatrice had been fortunate enough to find one in the UAE and would be moving her family in July, 1991, while her Syrian husband Salman was looking for a job, still regretting the loss of his professorship at Kuwait University. The Kuwaitis had replaced expatriates with their own nationals in key University positions. I wondered what would happen to my supervisory position in the University when liberation finally came, as I hoped it would.

Nabeel spent hours on the phone with his 'principals', or suppliers. He hadn't lost his workaholic nature, or his smoking habit. Occasionally we caught up with my father and his wife and my much younger sister. Janet enjoyed talking to Nabeel as she was studying for a Marketing Diploma similar to the one he had completed in London. Despite the disparity in their ages the two of them enjoyed their discussions and I left them to it. I was glad they had struck up a friendship but the business world did not interest me. I'd met Nabeel in London at the College where I took a one year full-time secretary/linguist post-graduate course. I had thought about taking up some kind of commercial career at the time, but I found the business world, with the notion of making the maximum amount of money circulate around the maximum number of people for the maximum length of time, empty and sterile. Instead I trained to teach French and English. I had started teaching my brother Bill to read when I was four and he was two. Then the poor boy had to learn to play piano when I was six and he was four! It seems I was born to the teaching profession.

Once Nabeel and I had caught up with everyone and made the necessary Xmas preparations, we began to wonder what to do next. Iraq was still occupying Kuwait and it seemed that the situation could go on for at least a year. During our marriage we'd been to the Far East, including Japan, Thailand, the Philippines and China, and to Mexico, the Bahamas and the east and west coasts of the USA. We had not been 'down under', however, as we felt the long journey merited more than the one month vacation allowed by Kuwait University. Now we had no time constraints we applied for visas and began to plan our itinerary for the months of January and February to travel around Australia.

Nabeel added in a business trip to the Philippines with some cronies from Kuwait Oil Company before the Australian tour. He was interested in going into the manpower industry when we eventually returned to Kuwait. I was not keen on it at all as I'd heard many tragic stories about women working as maids in Kuwait. My opinion didn't count of course. While Nabeel was away on this project I planned to visit a former colleague who had made a new start in the Sultanate of Brunei after escaping from Kuwait. Magnus and Lily were sincere, kind people, and I knew I would enjoy staying with them and their two young children. Nabeel and I made arrangements to meet up again in Kota Kinabalu. From there we would fly to Kuching for some more sightseeing and then on to Sydney for our big Oz trip. Malaysia was our mutual starting point, where we'd meet up with Nabeel's friends. I felt upbeat about our plans. I hoped that these new experiences would give us a chance to refresh our relationship and cease the emotional hostilities about the Invasion.

After Xmas we drove with Mum down to London to pick up our Australian visas and spend New Year with Bill and Katie. There was snow on the road so I took the wheel, while Mum sat in the passenger seat for comfort with her replacement knees and hips. Nabeel settled himself in the back seat. As I came to the Service Station at Junction 13 on the M1, driving steadily at 70 mph in the middle lane, I noticed a snow plough in the slow lane. As I approached to pass it I saw a spinning object fly off the heavy vehicle towards me. I couldn't move out of my lane as there were faster vehicles in the lane on my right, and the plough itself was now blocking my access to the slow lane. I braked, and as the car began to slow we heard and felt the thud as the object bounced directly in front of my car, and came up under the bonnet, bouncing up under the automatic gear console in the centre of the car between the two front passenger seats.

I looked down in horror and could see the ground between myself and Mum. The car was still slowing so using my indicator I moved safely into the slow lane behind the snow plough, then flashing my emergency lights, came to rest on the hard shoulder just behind the plough vehicle.

The driver was slow getting out. I don't know if he even realised that something had happened, but I was out of my car, banging hard on the left-hand-side driver's cab door to get his information. He told me his name was Pratt.

'For real?'

'Yea.'

'A good name for you, hey?'

'Look, it wasn't my fault. The disc just flew off.'

'Is that what health and safety would say? Is that what the police would say? We could have been killed.'

'OK. OK. You're insured, aren't you?'

'Yes, but this is coming off your insurance, not mine. You caused the accident. And right now, my disabled mother is in shock in the car. She needs to get warm.'

'Well, look, you take her into the service station.'

'I'll have to use her wheel chair. I need a hand.'

'OK. Then your husband can stay with the car and make the police report. They are on their way now. I've called them.'

'Is that OK, Nabeel? Can you cope?'

'Yea, go ahead. Get Mum out of here - it's dangerous.'

I carefully got Mum out of the car and into the wheel chair. Once inside the service station, having ordered a cup of hot, sweet tea for us both, I rang Bill in London and told him what had happened.

'That's unbelievable! How is Mum?'

'Well, she's OK, but she's shaken as we all are. We won't be able to come down now.'

'No, get home and talk to me again. Will you be able to manage?'

'Yes, I reckon so. We did it before, remember? When your car broke down on the way home from Cornwall after Noelle's christening ceremony?'

'Oh, yes. You had to ride in the car on the low-loader, if I recall correctly.'

That 1985 breakdown had at least been in summer. This time it was winter and the accident could have killed us all. As Mum could not be lifted into the cab of the rescue lorry, she and I stayed in the car and were winched onto the low loader while Nabeel rode in the cab with the driver. We tucked a blanket around our legs to keep warm. Back at home I warmed canned soup and made toast for supper. The next day I rang my insurer and the local Ford garage. Neither of them seemed impressed by our narrow escape. The insurers couldn't promise when the issue of fault would be resolved, but as the car was comprehensively insured the repairs could go ahead. We had to put the episode behind us given our imminent travel plans, which would be costly to change. After a quiet New Year's Eve celebration and Mum's New Year's Day birthday at home we took the coach to London. After a couple of days with Bill and Katie so as to collect our visas and tickets we took a taxi to Heathrow, hoping to get away from the snow, road accidents and further arguments. As for the impending war of liberation, on 3 January all Iraqi diplomats were expelled from Britain. Like the Iraqis, little did we know that our *blue on blue* had only just begun.

CHAPTER 15

Karl's Visit

July 2003

American Karl's visit to New Zealand began on US Independence Day. June had been hectic. Rose had bought a bedroom suite and her shipping had also arrived. The huge 40 foot container had almost blocked the *cul de sac* and the removal men had had difficulty fitting all her furniture and packing cases into the four bedroom house. As each bedroom had a fitted wardrobe, and the master had a walk-in wardrobe, Rose had given the movers a two door pine wardrobe for free to take away immediately. A work colleague had space for the six door mirrored wardrobe from Rose's bedroom in Bahrein. There was scarcely room to move around the boxes in the garage. Rose was emptying one box a week, enjoying the surprise of finding things she had almost forgotten about. She folded the white packing paper, keeping it ready for a future move to the beach. The house was bursting at the seams with possessions. She wondered what Karl would make of her new home. July in New Zealand is winter. Rose hoped he would be warm enough in her surprisingly cold new house!

Rose drove up to Auckland Airport after work on Friday afternoon to collect Karl. Sociable and friendly as he seemed, he had not been a success with her close friend Hinewai when he transited in the UAE before taking the plane to New Zealand. She had had an uncomfortable dinner date with him. Rose was surprised that he had upset her friend so much. She had to admit to herself that she didn't know him well, so she was rather concerned about his stay. She did not need additional stress as her new job had turned out to be very busy. In addition, she had started her doctoral research again, so she needed a quiet life. Putting her doubts behind her for the moment, Rose pulled into the Arrivals Car Park and went to look for her house guest in Arrivals.

'Hi Karl - over here!'

He was immediately recognisable for his fair hair and good looks. In his board shorts and desert boots with his unstinting energy he reminded her of the Duracell Bunny. Although Rose had put a little weight on during the six months since they parted, Karl spotted her in the waiting crowd.

'Hey. How are you doing?' he asked her brightly.

They hugged briefly and hurried off to the car park. Karl was travelling light, which was a good thing, Rose thought, given the limited space in her new home now.

'Are you tired? Do you need a coffee? It'll take us about two hours max to get home.'

'Nah. I'm fine. I got plenty of booze on the plane, so I'll sleep it off while you drive, OK?'

'No problem. I'll concentrate on driving. I'm still not familiar with the highways here.'

The motorway was relatively quiet at the end of the day. Rose was thankful she didn't have to battle the usual traffic jams. The journey back to Farmerston went quickly.

'Hey, Karl. We're here.'

Rose nudged Karl gently. He had slept all the way. Now he needed to get out of the car before Rose parked it in her garage next to a smart, red, two door coupe. At work, Rose had replaced a colleague who had just returned to London without selling her hatchback Mazda. To help her out, aware that a second car might be useful, Rose had bought the sporty little number. Karl commented on it immediately.

'Woo - what's this little beauty?'

'Well, it's yours for the duration. Have you got your International Driving Licence as I mentioned?'

'Yeah. Cool. But I'll be hanging with you, won't I?'

'Well, you know I'm working fulltime. I thought you might want to take a week or so and visit the South Island. Come on in and let's have some supper.'

Rose closed the main and the internal garage doors and followed Karl into her house.

'Cool - I love the furniture! Is it oriental?'

'Yes, I got it in Hong Kong. I worked there after the invasion of Kuwait. This was all in Bahrein, but you never saw my flat there, did you? It was in a container at the docks, waiting for its destination to be known.'

'No. Mm. It's classy. Now, where's your cocktail cabinet?'

'What would you like? Beer and white wine in the fridge. Red in the wine rack and spirits in the cupboard.'

'A gin and tonic would be good.'

'How about some bubbles? This New Zealand Lindauer is pretty easy on the palate. Refreshing too.'

'OK. Fine. I'd love to try it.'

'What about some food?'

'Anything you've got will be fine.'

'Some cheese and biscuits, OK? It's so late now, I don't feel like cooking anything.'

'That's great. Have you got that wormy blue English cheese? What do you call it? Stilton?'

'Yes, I've got that,' Rose said, laughing at his description. She remembered how much fun they'd had in Oman. He was a cheerful person to have around.

They sat down at the dining table and enjoyed their impromptu meal. Then came the next move. Where would Karl prefer to sleep, Rose wondered? She wasn't sure of the status of their relationship after an absence of six months. Had he found someone else, she wondered? Had Karl kept the candle burning for her alone, she wondered? She did not expect monogamy after her experiences with Colin.

'I've got two spare bedrooms and I set up one for you, with your own bathroom and tub. The master is in here, with a shower.'

'Are you really asking me? Come over here. I'll show you.'

There was no more discussion that night as Karl worked his magic.

The next morning Rose was woken by the sound of clinking cups.

'Good morning sweetheart. This is the best I could do. Earl Grey and some fruit, OK?'

Rose remembered that Karl was quite a health freak. 'That looks great - I love it when someone peels an orange for me! But hey, aren't I supposed to feed you 'tea and oranges that come all the way from China'?'

Karl laughed at the allusion to the Bob Dylan song and went off to take a shower.

Rose plumped up the pillows against the headboard and sat up to enjoy her cup of tea. This bedroom suite was a new purchase. She needed the extra storage. She had already filled every piece of furniture from the container as well as all the fitted cupboards and walk in wardrobe. Was she a hoarder? She guessed that it was a reaction from the Invasion. She had lost nearly everything except for three small items - a small jade lion, and a single *cloisonne* chopstick, both purchased in China and both sole survivors from their pair, and a modern perspex photo frame containing a photo of herself and Nabeel wearing winter hats, standing under a snow-laden apple branch in the tiny Mossfield orchard.

Nabeel had retrieved that photo from their trashed home in Kuwait and taken it to his brother's apartment in Lebanon. When Rose visited from Hong Kong at Xmas, 1991, she had enjoyed seeing it on the bedside table. It had reminded her of the craziness of life when people could be so happy one moment, and so sad the next. Shockingly, one morning the photo frame had fallen on its face. Although it had happened so many years ago, Rose could still recall her physical reaction when she saw the back of the photo. Whoever had trashed their Kuwait home, going through every intimate detail of Rose and Nabeel's life, had made a special effort to remove the photo and write in English on the back: *I know you, but I do not love you.* That person had then returned the photo to its frame. The callous words chilled her blood. It was a rape of her emotions, of her privacy and sense of security. What had the writer done in their house? What had he seen in the couple's personal possessions? Why did he want to lash out at her personally? Was the trigger the sight of the *Koran al Karim* and the Bible next to each other on the bedhead? Was it the obvious nature of their mixed marriage, her British nationality and her husband's Arab ethnicity? Was it because she was a woman who had to be put down at all costs, as her place was below that of her husband, her superior? Nabeel had been shocked too. He had not noticed the words till the photo was overturned.

Rose no longer knew where that photo was. She supposed it was still in Beirut, but Nabeel would probably have destroyed it after she left him. When the *decree nisi* had come through a few years later he had returned clothes that had survived the looting process via her friend Beatrice. During the extended divorce proceedings she had asked about an heirloom piece of Wedgwood which a deceased American friend had left her. Nabeel had insisted that he did not have it. She had been sure it was one of the things he had taken from Kuwait to Beirut but he denied it. So many items from her past were now gone. She didn't regret them for their material value, but for their sentimental connection to the past, to the people who gave them to her or to when or why she had bought the items for herself. She missed her photos most, especially the baby photos her mother had sent to Nabeel at the start of their marriage and residence in Kuwait. So many things had gone forever.

Coming back from her reverie to the present moment, she heard Karl asking about breakfast.

'Shall I make us some scrambled eggs and toast?'

'Yes, that would be great. But can you manage that in my kitchen on your own? I'll take a shower and be with you in five minutes.'

'Great. I'll do it. No problem.'

Like the Duracell Bunny he raced off, eager to please her. Rose smiled. She was tired after work the previous day and the two hour drive to and from the airport. She didn't like driving in the dark. She didn't like driving much at all, but she realised after her time in the Middle East, that she should be grateful for the freedom to drive. Some women, such as Saudis, were treated like children, and forbidden to drive on the pretext of being looked after like princesses. Princesses in chains, more like prisoners, it seemed to Rose.

As they ate breakfast, Rose outlined her plans for Karl's stay. She explained that she had only one week of holiday due to her, and they could take that together, probably travelling north of Auckland, to the beautiful Bay of Islands, which could be covered in one week. During the working week Karl would have to amuse himself. She explained that the second car in the garage was his to use but warned him about the strict speed regulations and told him he'd have to pay any fines he incurred. If he wanted to, he could take himself off for a couple of weeks to the South Island or to other parts of the country he wished to visit. That would suit her fine.

Karl was clearly a little disappointed at the suggestion that he would be alone for a slice of his stay, but the insatiable traveller within him responded to the offer of the car and the challenge of discovery. The coming weeks would be either fun or a fiasco for the two of them. It would also be interesting to see if their political views coincided or collided. The previous week Rose had been stunned by the news of six

British soldiers being killed by a mob in *Al Majar al Kabir* in southern Iraq. The British had a more sensitive approach than the Americans as occupation forces, but on this occasion they had angered the residents of the town by using dogs in their house searches for weapons. Rose knew how mistreatment of women and children in their own homes would anger the population, and using dogs would be *haraam,* or forbidden.

Whether she and Karl would discuss such issues which affected Rose deeply, only time would tell. The two of them had been thrown together by fate. They were both risk-takers, alone in a strange land when they first met. The only question lurking in the back of Rose's mind: Were they really strangers to each other? Would this be another case of *blue on blue*?

CHAPTER 16

Brunei, Oz and Kuwait

Jan - April 1991

Our overseas trip started at Heathrow, flying Malaysian Airways to Kuala Lumpur. We spent a week in KL meeting Nabeel's Egyptian engineer friends, staying in smart hotels, eating at night markets, viewing the amazing twin Petronas Towers and visiting the Highlands to see the wonderful landscapes in mainland Malaysia. Then we split up for our separate side trips. I flew to Bandar Seri Begawan, the capital of Brunei, while Nabeel and his friends took off for Manila and their business dealings with manpower agencies. We were to meet up in two weeks in Kota Kina Balu.

My time with my friends Lily and Magnus and their two children in tropical Brunei was very peaceful and quiet, which was just what I needed after the chaos of the motorway accident and the cold snowy winter weather in the UK. I saw handmade prawn crackers drying in huge quantities on roof tops around the village, looking like fallen autumn leaves. I learned how to plant a pineapple in the garden, using the top of the fruit so as to generate another one in a few months in the warm wet climate. I watched my hostess, a wonderful cook, making delicious Pinoy noodles, full of tasty morsels of pork or prawn and chicken, and lots of finely shredded vegetables. Lily's homemade desserts were equally delicious, made with tropical fruits, sago balls and coconut milk. I played piano and sang nursery songs with the children and read several novels. My time with my hosts was an idyllic interlude in what had been an extremely stressful period of my life.

One morning Magnus and I visited the College where he worked and I met his Director and teaching colleagues. It was interesting to see the curriculum for both pre-service and in-service nurses as I had written a curriculum and teaching materials for in-service nurses in Kuwait. With my friend and colleague Patricia we'd trialled the materials and attempted to market them, but we were not hard-nosed enough to sell our work in the small English for Specific Purposes market. Magnus had previously been the Supervisor of our English language courses for nurses and four other paramedical professions (Radiography, including nuclear medicine and radiotherapy, Med.Lab Technology, Medical Records and Physiotherapy) in the Faculty of Allied Health Sciences and Nursing in Kuwait University. When he left to complete his doctorate in the UK I was appointed Supervisor in his stead. I'd enjoyed the step up, and had continued the work developing communicative tests for our students, as well as contextually appropriate teaching and learning materials.

Unfortunately Magnus had just returned to work in Kuwait with his young children and wife when the Invasion happened. They'd had to flee across the desert like so many others, and were thankful to be alive despite the loss of all their possessions. Like me, Magnus and Lily were still struggling to come to terms with the past. It was good to remember the old days when Kuwait was peaceful and no one suspected that sisterly Iraq would become an aggressor. My two weeks in Brunei passed quickly but I felt rested when I left for my *rendezvous* with my husband in Eastern Malaysia. It was good to meet up with Nabeel again in Kota Kina Balu after our short separation. The old adage was true, absence made our hearts grow fonder. Even Nabeel's incessant smoking didn't seem so obnoxious to me after a short break away with non-smokers.

We'd planned to make the most of our time on the island of Borneo. In Kota Kina Balu we took a trip up the famous mountain though we didn't achieve the summit nor were we able to visit the orangutans as we'd pre-booked to travel to Sarawak. Our time there was exciting learning about the tribes of headhunting Iban who still lived in long houses deep in the jungle. We stayed in a lovely old colonial hotel, with carved wooden colonnades painted white, cool and inviting in the lush green tropical jungle. We took a river trip and enjoyed swimming in the delightful hotel pool, walking in the gardens, and eating and drinking in the royal style of the White Rajahs.

We had only one week to enjoy this beautiful area before we were to fly to Sydney. On the plane I looked up the address of Carol, an old friend from Kuwait. She and Haithem had left Kuwait for Australia with their two young daughters some years before the Invasion. I found an address for her parents and decided to give them a ring to see where our friends were now. We'd booked a bus tour of East and Central Australia but were to spend a couple of days sight-seeing in Sydney first. When I spoke to Carol's parents they told me she was living in Sydney! Within the half hour we were talking on the phone and planning to meet up in the hotel for drinks that evening. It was good to see old friends again from what had been peaceful Kuwait. Together we discussed politics and surprisingly didn't have any disagreement on the subject, in English at least. Haithem was Palestinian too, so perhaps I didn't catch any disagreement in their conversation in Arabic. Both Carol and I had some Arabic, but we were busy talking about mutual friends from our professional world of English language teaching. To my surprise and pleasure Carol and Haithem invited us to stay with them, rather than in the hotel. We pointed out that we would be leaving on Bus Australia almost immediately but that we'd love to visit them on our return. Our round trip tickets would terminate in Sydney in about three weeks. Having agreed upon a plan, we said our farewells. We enjoyed a day's sightseeing in Central Sydney before getting on the bus with our backpacks.

Our trip was fascinating both for the famous landmarks we saw, including the Sydney Opera House, Uluru, or Ayer's Rock, sacred to the aboriginal people, the endless roads, the oases with kangaroos living in family groups, as well as the many cultural insights we gained. Our bus drivers wore a uniform of short shorts and long socks. They'd evidently suffered at the hands of previous passengers, so were very hard on anyone eating hot food and/or drinking alcohol on board. I felt slightly guilty on finding an empty bottle of booze in the seat pocket in front of me. 'It wasn't me,' I wanted to shout out loud. Instead, I made sure to remove it at the first bus stop!

We progressed in a clockwise direction from Sydney to Canberra, Ballarat, Coober Peedy, the Red Centre and Alice

Springs, then Katherine, Darwin, Mount Isa, Townsville, Cairns, Brisbane and finally back to Sydney, travelling mostly by night and arriving in a city, paying for a motel room and sleeping during the day, with an extra day for visiting the place if it seemed to merit it. It was intriguing to observe other passengers, mostly young, staying in backpackers, or sleeping on the bus so as to keep moving onwards. We enjoyed the flexibility as well as the economical price of the round trip bus pass. We were thoroughly engaged in the trip. There was plenty to read and discover, so there was no time for politics or even business, which was amazing for workaholic Nabeel. We avoided discussing the invasion of Kuwait, and it was not possible to keep up with the news, travelling overnight in the bus.

After three full and tiring weeks of travel our sleek, shiny bus pulled into Sydney. We were met by Haithem who took us back to the Areesh's lovely home near the sea. We met their two teenage daughters, who were causing a lot of fatherly *angst* with boyfriends on the horizon. When I knew them in Kuwait they were still toddlers. I thought our wonderful trip would have a perfect ending, but as soon as we got into this lovely family home, the bubble burst. The two Arab men appeared to have bought into the conspiracy theory and so endless discussion centred on the USA's role in the invasion of Kuwait. I was more affected by the total loss of my home and my possessions. In my view, whether the US had conspired with Saddam or not, it wasn't Americans who had looted and trashed my house, it was Iraqis. For me, there was no room for discussion, and my frustration at Nabeel's opinion, blaming others rather than the agent of destruction, made me angry.

Just as in the very early days of our relationship his bloody-mindedness in arguments made me feel like resorting to violence. I'd thrown an empty bottle at him in our first years in Kuwait, when he'd refused to admit that he'd been wrong in his dealings with his family with regard to me. Now I didn't throw things, but I did want to punch him, and I gave in to the urge once. I had to sleep in the same room with him, but I avoided touching him and sometimes even refused to talk to him. It can't have been easy for our hosts having our conflicted selves around. Fortunately, our flight date was near and our attempts to be sociable and normal came to an end as we left their home. I think they breathed a sigh of relief almost as big as mine.

As we boarded the plane for the UK, I wondered if my application to Hong Kong University had been received. While staying with our friends I had seen an advertisement in the Sydney Morning Post for a Senior Instructor in the Language Centre and I had applied. I knew my friend Neil had gone there from Kuwait a few years earlier. I thought for the first time how grateful I would be to get away from Nabeel and this endless arguing about Saddam Hussein if my application was successful. Would he allow me to take the post though? According to Nabeel we didn't need my income in Kuwait. In fact, he'd often asked me to give up my job at the University. My salary may have been unimportant to him, but I loved what I did. From the date of our marriage my salary had always disappeared into a bank account in his name for which I never saw statements, nor did I have a cheque book.

Ostrich-like with my head in the sand, trusting and stupid, I never thought to question Nabeel about 'our' bank account. I suppose I was a child of my time. My Mum never saw my Dad's pay packet. She accepted her 'housekeeping' money without discussion and had to pay for any luxuries, such as my weekly piano lessons from age 6 to 11 out of it. Despite Nabeel's attitude to my job, my income was a source of my own self-esteem, so I clung to it. After Mum had left Dad and moved to Mossfield I had started working at the age of twelve, doing a Saturday job in a 'milk bar', as coffee shops were called in the 1950s. I took pleasure in the work, especially making hot milky Horlicks drinks in the specially shaped mug with the unusual solid pottery handle. The money from my job went on my clothes, mostly made by Mum. She worked in the milk bar too. It was her first job in Mossfield, but she quickly moved on to the Singer Sewing Machine shop, where she could use her craft skills. She was a good money manager herself and passed on her skills to me.

The job in Hong Kong University I'd applied for had a much better salary than the one I was getting as Supervisor in Kuwait University, and there was furnished accommodation attached to the job. The issue of accommodation had been a bone of contention - another one - between Nabeel and myself in Kuwait. Although my University job offered accommodation in a new, purpose-built apartment block, with lifts and landscaped gardens, Nabeel felt it was beneath his dignity to accept accommodation in his wife's name. So we had continued to live in a small apartment in a Kuwaiti landlord's house with stairs which my mother couldn't access so she was not able to visit us. Finally I'd threatened to take the apartment anyway, without him, so that my mother could visit for a couple of months. Reluctantly Nabeel had agreed on a temporary basis. We had moved for a brief six months during which Mum came to stay, but Nabeel's ego compelled him to search for somewhere he could rent which I would accept. In the end we found a house with wheel chair access which we rented at an exorbitant rate, rather than accept a 'free' flat in my name.

'Chicken or beef, Madam?'

I returned to the present with a jolt.

'Vegetarian, please. I made a request with my booking.'

'Oh, sorry. I'll check the seat number.'

It wasn't a surprise that my vegetarian meal order was not presented to me. It often happened in those days. Being vegetarian was a big deal then. People thought you were trying to get attention, rather than simply trying to digest a palatable meal.

Nabeel knew better than to comment. Lebanese food offered a wide variety of vegetarian dishes, all of which I loved. I wasn't picky, I just couldn't eat meat, or at least, I couldn't digest it. Many friends were not aware of this, even my own brothers.

'Sorry, Madam. Your order didn't come through. I'll make you up a plate from the First Class menu, all right?'

'Yes, thanks very much. That's fine.'

That was the worst thing that happened *en route* home. Back in Mossfield the damaged car had been fixed but the question of liability for insurance was not yet finalised. I put the matter aside despite my irritation as another letter with a Kuwait stamp awaited me. It was from the Dean of the Faculty where I worked, Dr Fawzia. She was inviting me back to the country, to set up the English Language Teaching Unit again. I was excited by the news and so was Nabeel, but the media had reported that Palestinians were no longer welcome in Kuwait because some had openly sided with the Iraqis. I'd had my own doubts about Nabeel. He'd eventually told me he visited Baghdad to get permission to use money in the Kuwait bank accounts and to register the cars they intended to drive across Iraq to Lebanon.

Knowing Nabeel's attitude towards money, I believed that he'd intended to continue his business working with the Iraqis who were then running the oil fields. Ethical considerations were less important to him than financial ones. He certainly had some psychological issues as a result of being a refugee from the age of seven, from his Type A personality, and from being the youngest sibling in a large, parentless family. By chronological age he was not the youngest child in his family but he was treated as the baby. As an adult he was not taken seriously, partly perhaps because he had married me and partly because he had failed at school because of his revolutionary attitude. At school with the *Freres Maristes* he had refused to kiss the Bishop's ring. He had also rejected some of his teachers' ideas and had almost illegible handwriting, so had not passed his 'baccalaureus', the school leaving exam. I felt his smoking habit was caused by inner insecurity, as well as physical addiction. In any case, he needed to smoke to focus on his work, and to succeed for his own self-esteem.

We both needed visas to return to liberated Kuwait, so I contacted the Embassy in London to obtain permits. While we were waiting for the necessary letters to arrive I heard from my friend and colleague Beatrice. She and her husband and two small boys were staying with her father. She too had been asked to return to Kuwait, but her husband had not received a return to work invitation. Like me she had been on summer vacation at the time of the Invasion with her husband and sons. We decided to travel together to give each other support. I felt that if Nabeel was stopped at Passport Control in Kuwait I would have someone to help me. I was extremely psychologically affected by the stress of the upcoming return. Worrying about cluster bombs which had been liberally scattered around the country, many of them still unexploded, was augmented by worrying about Nabeel. Would his outspokenness get him into trouble with the Kuwaitis even if his entry was not prevented? I warned him about my concerns, but he laughed them off.

Such was my suppressed distress that on the day of travel to London, I woke with a stiff, painful knee which made it impossible to walk without support. I rushed to Casualty at the local hospital, but X-rays revealed no distinct cause for the trauma. I was told to take painkillers and rest as it could be the onset of RA, the immune system disorder which had crippled my mother from her mid-thirties, the exact age I was then. The fear of lifelong illness increased my worries, but there was no choice but to soldier on. We had to leave the car in the garage in Mossfield as we were uncertain how long we would be away. We were potentially going back home, but our status and visas as expatriate workers were not clear at that moment, so our planning for the future and farewells were difficult.

'See you soon, Mum. I hope I'll be given some summer holidays after we do the clearing up.'

'Just be careful, darling, that's all that matters. Don't walk anywhere bombs might be.'

I declined to tell her that no-one knew where the bombs had fallen. Ordnance teams were already in Kuwait, employed 24x7 to defuse the cluster bombs but it was reported that children were picking up bombs in the desert and consequently losing limbs in explosions. I reassured her that I would take the greatest care of myself. I didn't know what would happen to Nabeel given the negative press reports but I didn't want to mention that. She was worried enough already. We set off for London by bus to Heathrow Airport to meet Beatrice, who was travelling alone. The good news was that the first of the approximately 650 burning oil wells had been capped, and specialist teams were working on the rest. I wondered what the atmosphere would be like in Kuwait on our arrival. Not only would I have to breathe Nabeel's cigarette smoke, but probably burning oil fumes too. The prospect was not attractive. I took some aspirin tablets once we were seated and drifted off to sleep as we took off on the eight hour flight.

CHAPTER 17

Downfall and Departure

3 July to 22 August 2003

Rose's new job was becoming more demanding while she was hosting her American boyfriend but she still watched TV when she could to track developments in the Middle East. The search for Saddam Hussein was ongoing. At the start of July Bush had defiantly challenged the insurgents attacking the coalition troops with improvised explosive devices (IEDs). 'My answer is, bring 'em on.' In late July Paul Bremer appointed an Interim Governing Council with members selected from different regions and sectors of Iraqi society. Rose wondered how that would work.

For the first week while Rose was at work Karl occupied himself discovering Farmerston, but as soon as Rose could take time off they made a trip to Northland, where the weather promised to be warmer. They headed over the Auckland Harbour Bridge to Dargaville, where they climbed a hill to see the mast of the Rainbow Warrior, the environmental activist Greenpeace ship bombed by French spies in 1985 in Auckland Harbour. They walked into the Waipoua Forest to see *Tane Mahuta*, the great kauri tree spared by the early settlers in their greedy quest for kauri timber which made excellent ships, furniture, houses and other possessions.

In the motels where Rose had spent her first six weeks in New Zealand the hosts had been exceptionally kind. However, as a tourist she found that motel keepers were strict and unforgiving of minor infringements on their list of rules. On one occasion they were chided for bringing their sandy shoes into the room, rather than leaving them outside. Karl and Rose couldn't help laughing at being treated like children, but put their hands to the broom and dustpan to make amends before they left. They sampled Kiwi takeaways rather than eating in restaurants, indulging in delicious Oyster Bay *sauvignon blanc*, or Ozzie *shiraz*, with their 'fast' food. The trip was proceeding pleasantly, until Rose opened the guidebook she had lent to Karl to read before the trip. She hadn't had time to read the new book herself.

'Hey! What's all this underlining here? And in PEN, not even pencil.'

'Oh, I thought this stuff was important.'

'Don't you know you shouldn't write in other people's books? That's so rude. I hate to see books marked like this. How dare you?'

'Sorry. It's only a book.'

'Yes, but it's my book, not yours, so keep your pen off it, please.'

This was the first time Rose flew off the handle at Karl. It signalled a change in her attitude towards him. He was invading her space and desecrating her new books. The second argument came soon afterwards, when she found out that Karl had spilled coffee on her AA map book, which contained pictures of local flora and fauna. She wasn't happy at this difference in attitude. She had started reading at the age of three and the two children had been severely punished for reading in bed by torchlight. She and her brother regretted Mum giving away their Rupert the Bear books and other childhood Christmas presents. Treating Rose's books negligently was tantamount to treating her badly. Nabeel had accused her of putting her books before him. That wasn't so, but in the case of Karl, her books definitely came first.

Trying to be fair, Rose pushed these negatives aside as they drove further north to the Bay of Islands. They stayed in Paihia and visited the famous Duke of Marlborough hotel, restaurant and bar. As they enjoyed their lunch and drinks, Rose softened again towards Karl. It was fun to be sightseeing in a new part of New Zealand but sometimes Rose felt Karl manipulated her and her mood changed as fast as the New Zealand weather. They drove to Bethel's Beach on the West Coast and walked in the dunes enjoying the wind in their hair. It was perfect weather. 90 Mile Beach was not suitable for saloon cars and the road up to Cape Reinga, the northernmost point of New Zealand, where Maori believe the spirits of the dead take flight, was 'metal', i.e. not paved, so the driving was rough. She made a promise to herself to come back one day and they turned southward to Auckland where they spent a couple of days exploring the stylish cafes and shops in Parnell before returning to Farmerston and work again for Rose.

After a few days it became clear that Karl was bored. Rose was pleased that she could now play her winning card - the red car.

'Why don't you go off now and do your solo trip? It's a pity to waste your time here. I'm sorry I don't have more leave, but we only have four weeks per year and I've already used up my entitlement to date.'

'OK. I'll do that.'

Rose breathed a sigh of relief. She was getting tired of having to cook dinner in the evening. On Karl's return he would only have another few days before leaving. He came back with lots of photos of his trip. He had managed to see much more than Rose herself had done to date but she didn't regret that. It had been a relief to be on her own again in her home. No sooner was he back than they began bickering again, to such an extent that Karl slept in the spare bedroom from then on. As the cold winter weather continued, Karl left the heater on all night causing Rose concerns over her electricity bill. Nevertheless, she put such petty thoughts behind her as she recalled how helpful Karl had been to her in Oman.

Before Karl was due to fly back to his own place of work, Rose took him over to Gisborne where she was searching for a permanent place to live by the sea. The trip to Gisborne triggered more arguments. Finally, the trip to the Airport sealed the fate of their relationship. Furious at being manipulated to spend a night in a motel, when she had expected to deliver him to the airport and leave him there, Rose issued her decree. 'I'm sorry. I think we have to end this relationship. We are just not good together. We argue far too much and it just won't work.'

As Rose drove back to Farmerston, she felt relieved that the relationship was over. Perhaps now she might find one which would bring her true happiness? A reminder of how short life could be came within the month. Bill in the UK was operated on successfully for a brain aneurysm.

Rose had to live life to the full. What was she going to do about it? She was far away from her family, but she still felt her decision to emigrate was justified. There were still too many bad memories for her to consider returning to the UK, but had she been too hard on Colin? Should she give him another chance? Was she risking *blue on blue, heartache on heartache* again?

CHAPTER 18

Kuwait Recovery

April 1991

The eight hour flight to Kuwait did my swollen, painful knee no good. By the time we landed I could not flex it, and needed both Beatrice and Nabeel to help me walk. I wondered how I'd cope in the days to come. Fortunately Customs and Passport were easier to get through than usual. Not many people were yet allowed to return to Kuwait, so there weren't long lines. Dr Fawzia had sent a driver to the airport to take us to our accommodation. We were given Holiday Inn Hotel rooms for our first night, but the next day we needed to establish ourselves for the rest of our stay. It was assumed we'd be able to look after ourselves. Beatrice was able to return to her apartment but our rented home had been trashed.

Neither of our cars was in Kuwait. Nabeel's Mercedes 300SE had been stolen on the first day of the Invasion and my two-tone blue Buick Grand Prix coupe had been driven to Beirut when the family left Kuwait in November. Edouard and Adel had left one car in their apartment building's underground parking lot in Salahiyah, which they found still intact. We had asked some English teacher friends if we could stay in their

University apartment in Shuweikh. We promised to handle their packing and shipping if we found their possessions in good condition. We breathed a sigh of relief when we saw that the apartment was habitable. Nothing had been touched. However, the summer vacation period of 1990 had lasted until April 1991 when the liberation of Kuwait was completed, so the coat of dust was much thicker than usual after summer vacation. The fridge freezer was another challenge. Electricity had been cut off for some time during the Invasion, so any frozen food had deteriorated badly then been refrozen. Nabeel tackled the smelly job of cleaning it out. There were sad stories of dead pets, birds and fish, left behind in locked apartments. There was a lugubrious atmosphere in the University's residential tower blocks overall.

The completion of the Liberation was to be understood in military terms only. It did not mean that things were back to normal. On meeting up with Dr Fawzia and other friends and acquaintances we learned what had happened since 2 August 1990. The Invasion, the Liberation, as well as the interim period of Iraqi rule had left a huge toll on Kuwait. First, were the 'martyrs', those who had died in the initial attacks on 2 August, 1990. These included Kuwaiti military personnel as well as ordinary citizens. Our neighbour, Sheikh Fahd, the Emir's brother, had taken up arms on the morning of the Invasion and been killed within a few hours. The Emir had fled as soon as the Iraqi tanks had been detected crossing the northern border in the early hours of the morning. The Iraqi Special Forces had come to catch the 'head of the snake' and had daubed this phrase in Arabic on our front porch.

Many Kuwaitis had been taken in for questioning, tortured and then transported to Baghdad to be held hostage for future negotiations or against reprisals. There were many tales of women being taken into the University housing complex in Shuweikh, with one block in particular described as the psychological and sexual torture centre. We shuddered to hear of the tales, but we hoped some might be exaggerated. The stories of newborn and premature or ill babies being snatched out of incubators in the Jahra Hospital were probably true though. Their parents probably preferred to take their sick babies home rather than leave them to the mercy of an invading army.

Other Kuwaitis managed to endure the Occupation by being tight-lipped. 'Keep calm and carry on' has to be the slogan of any occupied nation. Our first landlord had sat it out with his family. Other nationalities had either fled, as Magnus and Lily did, some in disguise with their skin painted dark and wearing Pakistani *shalwar khameez*, or been captured, as my friend Jack had been, and George, from my own teaching team. George had been teaching summer school planned for July and August. At the mid-semester point, he woke on the weekend to find the beach occupied by soldiers, whom he assumed to be Kuwaitis conducting military exercises. He wandered over to a group and asked them in his best Arabic what they were doing *'Leish intu huna?'* In brisk response he was immediately taken into custody, with only the briefest stop at his flat to pick up a few personal possessions. George had been released before the Liberation and had written to me to apologise for not marking the mid-semester exam papers, which he had had to leave in his flat. He received my sincere assurances that there was no problem with that. I was delighted that he had survived his ordeal.

It was not known at this point if expatriates had perished, but it became known that one man had been killed while helping a Kuwait family stuck in the desert. In the UK the Gulf Support Group had been set up by Josie Brooks and Tim Lewis to help citizens who had problems, and those who had been trying to find missing family or friends. We visited the Messilah Beach Palace where expatriate civilians were held. We drove on to Ahmadi to witness the environmental damage that the fleeing Iraqis had caused by igniting around 650 oil wells, creating oil lakes and allowing oil to flood into the pristine Persian (Arabian) Gulf waters. These scorched earth tactics had two motives: to delay or hinder the attacking Western forces on land and by sea, and also to destroy Kuwait's economy. My yellow cotton top and trousers were permanently stained with soot from the pollution we saw. The process of putting out the fires had just begun in April and the last fire was put out in November.

On arrival Beatrice discovered that her apartment had been looted, and some treasured oil portraits of Salman's family members removed. Even more poignantly, Beatrice's late mother's jewellery had been stolen. Her car was still there but the tyres had been removed, as from many other vehicles across the city. However, there were still items that could be salvaged and furniture which could be moved to Beatrice's new home and job in Dubai. It was difficult for Beatrice to sleep in her looted home, so for companionship she moved into the loaned apartment with us.

In the mornings she and I would go to our respective Faculty buildings to find, sort through and try to organise whatever teaching materials we found. Working in my Faculty had special benefits. Despite the loss of all the modern technology and equipment, there were two or three old wooden shoulder crutches remaining. The Sudanese physiotherapy teachers who had stayed throughout the Occupation were happy to supply me with an ill-assorted pair. In addition to staggering around on mismatched crutches, I had to wear a headscarf folded as an improvised face mask since the trashed papers I found in my English Language Department were filthy. I managed to keep going thanks to very early nights and large doses of aspirin. Vivid images of the early days of my mother's crippling illness recurred in my dreams, but I had a job to do, and I did it.

My Department was housed in a single storey pre-fabricated building which held offices and classrooms. There were around 22 four drawer metal filing cabinets in the shared offices of our 18 teachers, the secretary and office boy, and my own office as Supervisor. Every one of those cabinets had been broken into, with every drawer pulled out and its contents spewed over the office floors. Owing to the windows and doors being left open since the allied bombardment, many files and papers had blown outside onto the surrounding gardens and lawns. I forgot the danger of cluster bombs as I searched around outside to retrieve every page I could find of our custom-designed curriculum and teaching materials. Only at night did I recall the risks I had taken during the day but I could also smile wryly at some of the things I found. Apparently my office had become a barber's salon: There were hair clippings all over the room but my coat-hanger was still behind the door. For some reason the window above my office door had been blacked out with paper. I deduced that someone had been living in the office as there were dark rings from Turkish coffee cups placed on papers, and remains of breakfast items such as *manaeesh*, flat bread baked with olive oil and *zaatar* and *sumac* spices, discarded on the desk.

At lunchtime Beatrice and I would meet up in the Faculty Club which was being cleaned up and was offering a simple menu for staff like us who had returned to work. Nabeel was cleaning up his office premises down town, so he stayed in the City for lunch. In the afternoons I would rest, while Beatrice worked on her family apartment. In the evenings we would put together a simple meal. As more Faculty colleagues returned we shared the occasional weekend meal. Nabeel and I baked a huge snapper stuffed with fennel, garlic, onions and lemon. It was a dish to cheer the hearts of the returned victims of an Invasion, all of whom had lost money and possessions to a greater or lesser extent. The atmosphere was surreal, to say the least. The premises were the same, but post invasion Kuwait was extremely depressing. We fought to keep our spirits high without alcohol, a difficult task for me.

One evening Beatrice arrived at 'our' flat with a small pile of books.

'Perhaps you'd like these, Rose?'

I recognised one of them immediately from its distinctive cover.

'Oh, yes, *Kiss Kiss*, by Roald Dahl. That's excellent. And it's also mine! See, it's got my name in it. Thanks for returning it at last!'

We laughed. It was small fry in the big pond of possessions we had lost. In fact the life we were living just then might have come from a Roald Dahl story!

After putting it off for some time, Nabeel and I gained permission to visit our former home, a large ground floor apartment with a huge garden situated between Sheikh Fahd's palace and the Emir's private guest house close to Kuwait Towers. I had no idea what I would find, but the truth was stranger and more horrific than fiction. The lush garden had dried up though the palm tree had survived. Inside the house nearly everything that could be moved had been taken, but what was left included a few kitchen items and some clothes, such as items of my underwear found on the entrance stairs, and almost all my books and papers, to my secret delight. I hardly dared say I was pleased to see my books were still there, given Nabeel's violent reaction previously. But the remains of our possessions had been soaked with various liquids, such as bath essences, shampoo, bleach, cleaning fluids as well as excreta and urine, which had dried into the fabric and paper. The place had been thoroughly ransacked. Wooden bed frames had been smashed. Even the false ceiling had been torn down in several places by looters checking if we had hidden valuables up there. Some pieces of furniture specially made for Mum, such as her high chair and her wheelchair had been taken. The heavy hardwood cupboards where I had stored my jewellery were still there, but the drawers were empty. Nabeel caught my gaze.

'Oh, I forgot to tell you. When I left the house I took all your gold jewellery with me. It's in Beirut at Adel's flat.'

'That's wonderful, darling. Great news. I had no idea you'd done that. I look forward to seeing it in the future.'

'Yes, we'll go to Beirut and get everything there soon. I carried the gold in my camera bag in case it was taken away from me at the borders.'

'What about those lovely gemstone necklaces we bought in California when we were on holiday there? You know, the green tourmaline, the rose quartz, the lapis lazuli and the jasper necklaces? They all had matching ear rings and were stored in your old cigar boxes, remember?'

'Oh, damn - I forgot about those - I noticed the boxes but I thought they contained costume jewellery. I couldn't carry everything safely.'

'It's OK - don't worry about it. We've done well if you've got the gold! There was quite a lot of that.'

'Yes, and your silver too. I know you love it.'

'That's great. My silver is part of my memory bank - the bangles from our holiday in Mexico, the 21st birthday present from Mum. I'd hate to lose those items with so much sentimental value as poor Beatrice has.'

Later on I realised that I had not queried the gold when Nabeel came to London, only my books. I had assumed that the gold would be gone. I thought it strange that it hadn't been mentioned before, especially when Nabeel took my question about the books so badly. There was a lack of logic in this process of loss and discovery. Why had he reacted so badly to my question about my books? Why had he not mentioned the gold previously? Had he planned to keep it or sell it? Suspicious though I was, there was no point in dwelling on the subject. The house was to be cleared and prepared for new occupants. As expatriates we were not allowed to return to live so close to the Emir's private home, the Dasman Palace.

Nabeel was particularly patient at picking up the trashed photos strewn all over the floor. There were no digital photos in those days. He went through the prints and the negatives he had picked up each afternoon cleaning them meticulously each evening. I planned to put them into an album, even though they were in such disorder that it would take hours to sort out the chronological sequence of events they portrayed. Our videos had been trashed irretrievably, but for that I was grateful. I felt afraid that some of our homemade film might end up on Iraqi TV as an example of the sinful lives of Kuwait residents, drinking alcohol and belly dancing at parties.

By the end of the two weeks we closed the door and garden gate on what had been a happy home, and the site of many large parties with friends and acquaintances, with our large brick built BBQ in the garden, and two cane swing seats hanging from the huge old trees. It was time to look for somewhere else to live as Nabeel was committed to returning to his business with his brothers. We discussed other possibilities, such as returning to Lebanon, or moving to Canada, where our bilingual status would be useful in setting up a new life. But Nabeel wouldn't hear of leaving Kuwait. He was keen to re-establish his contacts and get back to the successful business he had built up for himself from scratch. He had already lost his native country as well as his mother, in Palestine. Getting his business back was important for his sense of self.

As for myself, the Dean of the Faculty told me she would not be able to give me my Supervisor's job as it had been decided that only Kuwaitis could hold supervisory positions. This change to my status was something of a shock. I had been a victim of the Invasion as had all my colleagues. The University had cancelled all expatriate contracts as of the date of the Invasion and we were unemployed and unpaid as of August 1990. The United Nations compensation process allowed claims for lost income, but no one knew how long it would take for Iraq to be made to pay up and settle the claims.

I began to realise that returning to Kuwait for me would be a step backwards. My status at work would be different, our lovely home was gone, and my relationship with my husband was showing more than just signs of cracks after all the arguments. I felt I should try to keep our relationship of 20 years and our marriage of 15 years going, but was concerned that any more pressure would mean that we would certainly split up. I held my tongue and refrained from discussing my own situation with Nabeel as he was busy re-establishing his business, while I was asked to go to London in June to recruit new teachers for the next semester in September 1991. I flew first class on 'dry' Kuwait Airways alongside one of the Emir's black clad wives. The flight was another surreal experience but it was fun to be back in London and I fitted in a brief visit to Mum in Mossfield to discuss the future with her.

'I really don't know what to do, Mum. Staying in Kuwait seems unbearable on both home and work fronts. But what else could I do?'

'You could come home and stay here with me. I'd love that.'

'I know, darling, but Nabeel would have to agree to that. And I need to work after losing nearly everything.'

Then fate took a hand. While still with Mum I received a letter from the University of Hong Kong offering me the position as Senior Instructor in their English Centre which I had applied for in Sydney. For me it was an obvious choice, but I had Nabeel to contend with first. He had refused to entertain other possibilities for us both. Speaking to him on the phone about the new job, I suggested a move for us both to Hong Kong from where he could do petrochemical business with China and the Gulf. He refused to consider the suggestion. He was adamant about staying in Kuwait. But he agreed that I could take up the new post, given the new lack of status in my job at Kuwait University, and perhaps in his heart of hearts he too wanted a period of separation after all the arguing. After all, absence makes the heart grow fonder. So a new door opened for me on an island in the South China Sea. I felt a thrill of excitement at what the future might hold.

CHAPTER 19

Invitation

August 2003

After the dramatic finale to Karl's visit Rose was convinced she had made the right decision in shutting down the relationship. Like the earlier experience with Norman, this episode began to fade from her consciousness as work increased in intensity, she finally got her research studies started again and only occasionally could she keep up with the news of Iraq's development. In late July there had been some progress in the elimination of the supporters of Saddam when his two sons, Uday and Qusay were killed during a three hour firefight in Mosul. Saddam still evaded capture.

Although Rose was busy her new life seemed rather sterile. She was not lonely but she missed having someone to laugh with in after work hours. Almost inevitably her thoughts began to turn back to the passion she had known with Colin, a colleague she had met in her new job after separating from Nabeel. This British man had surprised and delighted her with his love-making and she had fallen fast and heavily for him. Despite all the warnings from her friends and the tears and the heartbreak she had experienced in their eight year relationship he was still the focus of her nighttime dreams and daytime fantasies. Should she make one last effort to see if their relationship could begin again and this time endure?

Rose had drawn the final line under their love affair when Colin's current girlfriend rang him in Mossfield while he was visiting after the death of Mum. During Tillie's phone call Colin had sat transfixed on the sofa. Rose had been so furious she had almost thrown him out. Instead, given the lateness of the hour, she had slept on her Mum's bed next to the container of her ashes and left him to stew in the juice he had concocted. The next day they had talked it through. Tillie, according to Colin, knew that Rose was the love of his life but Tillie had been his stop gap while Rose was still working in the Middle East. Tillie was just trying to spoil things for him. Rose had to admit that Tillie was something of an emotional basket case because she admitted phone stalking Rose in Bahrein. But Rose couldn't blame Tillie. It was Colin who had ruined things by cheating on her. Apparently their values were different. Rose was a serial monogamist while Colin seemed to adhere to the pop song premise 'If you can't be with the one you love, love the one you are with.'

Rose had let Colin stay on for another day as she needed support while she scattered Mum's ashes in the ruins of her old farm cottage home and on her own mother's grave in a nearby rural town. They had visited Rose's grandmother's old home near the historic castle and coincidentally, the Angel pub. Mum had borne her suffering like an angel in her lifetime. The next day Rose had watched Colin drive away. Tillie then began a new campaign of telephone stalking in the UK, wanting to discuss Colin. Rose reassured Tillie that she was not in competition with her. She could have Colin if she could put up with his infidelity. For Rose it was a second time around and this time she had had enough. The Tillie incident was a repeat of what had happened a few years earlier when Colin left Bahrein. Soon afterwards another girlfriend had called Rose blaming her for Colin's cheating. Rose had simply put the phone down. Despite being stricken at his duplicity she felt so deeply for him that she forgave him. But when it happened a second time, that was the end of their relationship for Rose.

After the Tillie revelation Colin had sent flowers, but Rose had left the UK in despair at both losing her Mum and breaking up with Colin. Although she felt there was little hope of establishing a permanent liaison with him they had kept in touch as friends. Rose realised that if she wanted to continue this amicable relationship with Colin she must be careful not to fall under his romantic spell again, unless he intended to change. Rose considered her situation. She had already taken a few days annual leave to travel in Northland with Karl, but with statutory holidays due for Xmas and New Year and the remainder of her annual leave due, she could easily get away and visit the South Island to witness the more dramatic geography of that part of New Zealand. She loved travelling and felt the need to get out and explore after a long period of hard work, but who would she go with? She couldn't contemplate travelling alone. Would Colin be willing to take up the challenge again? She wrote to him with her plan. He would have a week to settle in before the Xmas holiday when the two of them would set off on a sightseeing trip.

Colin accepted the invitation with alacrity. He would arrive in early December and leave early January. He had probably decided to put Tillie on the back-burner for this festive season. Rose did not feel she had scored a point. She was simply in need of a travelling companion and she had not yet got Colin out of her system. Was bringing him to New Zealand his Herculean trial? He would not have to turn out the Augean stables, but turn over a new leaf. If their time together went badly, then the end of the holiday would be the end of the affair. If it went well, then Rose would ask Colin to commit to her alone. If he couldn't do so, then it would be over. She couldn't go on with love the way Colin lived it, like turning a tap on and off. Perhaps she was being naive in hoping he would change, but she felt she was ensuring her decision to cut him out of her life was a logical choice not an emotional reaction.

Now that the decision was made, Rose could look forward to Xmas. She began to look at Interisland ferry sailings as her Kiwi friend, Heather, advised her that prime time holiday bookings might be unavailable at the last minute. Once the ferry trips were booked, the rest could wait till Colin arrived. However, the long range weather forecast began to concern her. Summer could be unpredictable. Rose knew Colin loved warmth as much as she did, so throwing her budget to the four winds she booked an eight day holiday in Tonga for the week after they returned from the South Island. It was intended as Colin's Xmas present. He was paying for his own expensive air ticket to New Zealand and Rose wanted him to have a good time. A new country would offer the pair a level playing field. They could relax and try to revive the flame which Rose still felt burning, despite her better judgment. Mum had not liked Colin and friends had warned her off him. Despite the *blue on blue* of their long relationship, Rose was obviously still hooked.

That first winter in New Zealand was far colder and longer than Rose had expected. Despite the arrival and unpacking of her shipping, she needed more winter clothes. Warm pyjamas and a fleecy dressing gown were top of the shopping list. With Colin due to arrive in three months' time Rose settled into work, which was increasingly busy, and in the evenings caught up on the news from Iraq in front of the TV. The new regime was not making the progress needed to return the country to good order, using a process of 'De-Ba'athification'. This was problematic, since it meant that Army officers, all of necessity former members of the Baath party, lost their jobs. They wanted revenge for their marginalisation. Rose could see trouble brewing.

On 19 August a truck bomb exploded against the UN building in Baghdad and the UN representative, Sergio Viera de Mello and 21 staff were killed. Clearly their security precautions were not effective against the insurgents. Ten days later another huge suicide bomb was exploded in the Shi'ite Imam Ali Mosque which killed a Shiite leader and around 100 worshippers. In September Aquila al Hashimi, a female member of the Interim Governing Council was shot and died five days later. During October matters worsened when the soldiers who had been dismissed no longer received wages. This left hundreds of families without an income and on 5 October these former soldiers staged a demonstration that developed into a riot. More attacks were reported during November, the only light news being a visit to the US troops by Bush and Condoleeza Rice, his Secretary of State, for a Thanksgiving dinner. The Iraqis had very little to give thanks for, Rose thought.

Meanwhile New Zealand's winter weather had started brightening into spring. Finally, the cool spring turned to summer almost exactly on the day of Colin's arrival on 15 December. Leaving work late as usual Rose drove as fast as legally possible on the busy motorway to get to Auckland Airport, then had to wait a while for him to come through Customs. She was pleased about that. She would have hated him to arrive without being there to welcome him. At last a familiar blue shirt could be glimpsed as Colin pushed his trolley past the final Customs officer. The flashing blue eyes had more wrinkles than before, but his good looks were as appealing as ever. She signalled to him to push through the waiting folk before reaching out to hug him.

'Mm. It's good to see you,' he murmured, wrapping one arm around her.

'And you too. Thanks for coming over. How was the flight? It's huge, isn't it?'

'Well, it wasn't too bad, but I'm glad it's over. The flight attendants were very good.'

'Great. Well, let's go and get the car, shall we?'

Linking arms they pushed the trolley outside and loaded Colin's case into Rose's Mitsubishi.

'Hey - you've got a Mitsi - like me!'

'Not exactly - it's just a saloon. I wish I had bought a four wheel drive actually. When I tried to change it, they told me it was only worth 13k. That was only three months after paying 18k for it!'

'Car dealers! They're the same the world over.'

'Yes, no culture shock there I suppose. Anyway, this goes well and it's easy to drive. Do you need a coffee or a cold drink before we set off?'

'No, I'm fine.'

'Let's go then. It'll take us about three hours to get to the East Coast if the road is clear. Accidents aren't as common as in Bahrein, but they are more frequent it seems to me than in the UK. Most Kiwi drivers are rather arrogant, forget to signal or use the wrong signal and drive too fast in the slow lane or too slow in the fast lane!'

'I'll keep my fingers crossed then. Sorry I'm too tired to drive.'

'Did you bring your international licence, or at least your UK one?'

'Yes.'

'That's good. You can drive whenever you are ready to. I don't know this road but don't worry.'

Those words were soon taken back. Rose's nerves were frazzled, whether from tiredness, excitement or nervousness. She had decided to spend their first weekend in Paloa Beach at the motel where she often stayed when she was hunting for her seaside property. She had never taken State Highway 2 so made several wrong exits, having to back track at least three times. Colin wisely didn't show his nerves, though he chuckled as he realised what was happening. He was surprisingly uncritical, which made her feel better.

'I know, I know. This is a first for me. Sorry.'

'No worries. I'm cool as a cucumber.'

'That's good. I'm not!'

'Hey, settle down. We have plenty of time. Take it easy.'

As dusk was falling and the setting sun was turning the blue sky pink, deep purple and orange, Rose and Colin pulled into their motel. It had a small pool and was in a central position for them to go out and enjoy the small city centre. It was a buzzing little place, which brimmed over with holidaymakers in the summer. As schools hadn't closed for Xmas yet, there was a quiet, peaceful atmosphere in the streets.

'Would you like to unpack or just go out and find some dinner?'

'Well, I'm not that hungry. What about you?'

'Mm. I haven't eaten since lunchtime, so I do need something. But a snack would be fine. I've got some wine here in my chilly bin. Do you still love bubbles as I do?'

'Yes, that's fine.'

'Let's have a drink then decide what to do. This is New Zealand's own bubbles - Lindauer - there are a few different types, but I like the *Brut*.'

Rose pulled out the champagne flutes she'd brought with the bottle. They toasted each other, then settled on the bed for a first, long kiss. At the touch of his lips, Rose melted. She had no appetite for food now. 'Here I go again,' she thought. The old magic still worked.

CHAPTER 20

Hong Kong Via Dubai

September 1991

In the UK my University recruitment duties were challenging. I had to inspire others to work in a Department and live in a society that I had decided to leave. In addition the country was recovering from the Invasion and War of Liberation. On my return to Kuwait I made an appointment to see the Dean to explain my position. Dr. Fawzia was visibly disappointed but understood my situation. She was unable to change University policy. She wished me well in my new job in Hong Kong and thanked me for my dedication to my work. I felt sorry to be leaving her side as she was an excellent leader. As an unmarried female academic she was exceptional in Kuwait society. She was no mere figurehead. She had achieved two PhDs in scientific research, one in the USA and one in the UK. I still had hopes of gaining my own PhD. Hong Kong would certainly offer me more opportunities for that. Nabeel and I would be able to stay in the University flat for the month of July, then I would leave in August to say goodbye to Mum in the UK. Meanwhile, Nabeel would have to find a flat, or move in with his brothers who were back in Kuwait. He had already purchased a new car for his new life. When he had met me at the airport I was astonished to see he was driving a huge Jeep Cherokee.

'*Ya Nabeel*, no Mercedes? I thought you would replace it. You loved it so much and you had it for such a short time.'

'No, the Jeep is better. Everyone is buying 4-wheel drive vehicles in case they have to escape across the desert to Saudi again.'

'I don't think that is likely, do you?'

'You never know. Better to be safe than sorry. The Israelis probably have missiles that can reach us here in Kuwait.'

'Well, it's an amazing car.'

'Would you like to drive it?'

'No, thanks. It's a bit big for me - remember I'd only driven your beautiful Merc for about 500 metres!'

'Yea. Did I tell you I parked it outside the British Embassy when I sheltered there?'

'No? So what happened to it?'

'I watched the Iraqis hardwiring it. They drove all the best cars back to Iraq.'

'Really? The Iraqis? Not the Americans? Or the Indians and Pakistanis?'

Nabeel glared at me. I said no more. I knew the loss of his longed for Mercedes had hurt him. He'd patiently waited till he'd built up his bank account before indulging himself. I had been indulged too, as he consolidated his wealth. I'd received a beautiful 1.25 karat diamond solitaire for my 40th birthday. I hoped it was in Beirut with the rest of my jewellery. I never travelled with expensive items in case of loss so I had considered all those items casualties of the

Invasion. We were fortunate in relative terms in only losing material possessions.

Beatrice, my friend and colleague, had already broken the news by mail to her Dean about her new position at the Emirates Polytechnic Colleges, a new educational institution offering vocational and professional training for Emirati men and women. I envied her to some extent because she would be living with her family and working with Arab students. Like me she was married to an Arab and spoke Arabic so the language, religion and culture in her new job posed few problems.

I, on the other hand, was moving alone to a country whose culture and language were unfamiliar. I would have to set up a new home, make new friends and settle into a new job with students whose background was new to me. In tertiary education the students' previous learning experience is extremely important as it influences how tertiary English language and study skills teachers work. In the Arab World compulsory studies in English, the language of the political betrayers, were de-motivating for some. I sympathised with their plight but English was essential for medical studies. In Hong Kong, too, University English was a passport to a good career in law, medicine, engineering or business. I wondered how motivated Hong Kong Chinese students were as I packed a few unscathed teaching books and materials from my former library for the journey.

I booked a return trip to the UK for August so that I could buy some clothes in the summer sales and say goodbye to my mother. In Kuwait, my clothes had been looted or trashed, or taken to Beirut by Nabeel. Although I always kept some clothes in Mossfield they were mainly for cold weather, not for the tropics, and the few summer clothes I had now hung off me. I had lost weight with the physical work of retrieving trashed papers in the high summer heat of Kuwait. Happily my August trip to the UK was enlivened by my old friend Neil's wedding to Alice in Edinburgh. In Scotland I was able to stay with some old friends from Kuwait. Neil had also invited some friends from Hong Kong so it was good to break the ice with people who would become my colleagues in September. Mum was getting used to me dashing in and out for flying visits, but this time it would be a whole year before I saw her again.

Back in Kuwait Nabeel had moved in with his brothers so after obtaining letters of recommendation from the University, and saying my farewells, I cinched my belt tightly to hold up an old but respectable skirt and boarded the plane to Dubai. Nabeel had decided that Beatrice and Salman should buy my ticket to Hong Kong on Emirates, the new UAE airline, to repay him for having their car repaired in Kuwait and shipped with their remaining possessions to Dubai. He was determined that they would pay him back. Although I felt it was ungenerous, given the fact that he had lost none of his money in the National Bank of Kuwait, I couldn't object to this as I left our financial affairs entirely to him.

I hoped the financial issue wouldn't upset Beatrice as I was looking forward to seeing her again and hearing her news, especially about her new job. She met me at Dubai International Airport, a much smaller building in those days. We called in at her office and she described her new job. She was happy in her new environment. She drove me home to the lovely villa she rented for her husband and two young boys, both of whom had been born in Kuwait.

'The boys are already enrolled in a sailing club. They love the after school activities here. They can play football, tennis, swim and go to the beach every afternoon if they want to.'

'That's great. It sounds much more varied than our lives in Kuwait.'

'Yes,' responded Salman, 'but we still miss our old way of life. Kuwait University offered so many professional opportunities for me, like the Faculty Journal I edited.'

I nodded in agreement. 'I know just how you feel about that. I had to abandon the *English for Specific Purposes Newsletter* which Neil had started. We had a circulation of 500 around the world, all receiving our *Newsletter* from the University Press, free of charge! Mum enjoyed doing some typing for the Abstracts section when she was over in Kuwait with us.'

'I think the rulers of Kuwait have always been very philanthropic. The situation now is not deserved by any means,' Salman continued.

Smiling my assent and reassured by his attitude, I began to see that Nabeel's reaction was not universal. 'I agree with you. But Nabeel doesn't think the same.'

'You know, Rose, some Arabs can't see beyond the end of their own noses.'

'It's a relief to hear you say that. We've been fighting since he got to London in November. I'm so tired of it. I'm looking forward to getting away.'

Salman explained that he was looking for work in the UAE, but he preferred to return to Kuwait if at all possible. We discussed events and considered what the future might hold for Kuwait. It made a pleasant change for me to discuss politics without arguments. After a delicious evening meal,

I went to bed early to prepare for the next day's early flight to Hong Kong. However, I was soon disturbed by Beatrice. She was distraught: She couldn't find the air ticket she had bought for me. She'd been searching for it everywhere in the house, her bag and her car. I questioned her gently.

'When did you get the ticket?'

'Only today.'

'Where did you put it?'

'I can't remember. I don't know. It's all a blur.'

'Relax. You're tired and you've been very busy with work, the family and now me. Let's ring the Emirates ticket office at the airport and ask them to reissue the ticket in the morning. Or, if the office isn't open in the morning, let's go there now and get a new ticket.'

'Oh, my God! I've just remembered. I must have left the ticket on the counter in their office.'

'There you are - they will have no problem reissuing it to us.'

After a short phone call the problem was solved. We could indeed claim a new ticket at the airport, but we needed to arrive very early to do so. I went to sleep laughing at the situation. After collecting my ticket, the next day's flight on Emirates Airways was long with one stop in Bangkok, but smooth, with excellent service. I especially appreciated the sophisticated beverage list. Over a few glasses of bubbles, even in Economy class, I had time and leisure to think about events of the past year and wonder about the future. Tears welled in my eyes, whether of sadness, happiness, or just self-pity for the change that I and so many others were experiencing on account of the greed of one man, Saddam Hussein. I could console myself that my losses had been material, while others had been tortured or lost their lives. None of this should have happened, whatever the conspiracy theorists said.

I turned my attention to my co-passengers. The majority were men on their way to the fleshpots of Thailand for a little Rest and Relaxation, or Sex and Relaxation more likely. New employees in the Gulf countries were required to take an AIDS test on arrival, but not the Gulf's citizens returning from holiday. As I could speak moderately fluent Arabic I could detect a Gulf Arab by the thicker, harsher accent and the dialect, such as *shunhoo?* instead of the Arabic of Palestine, and Lebanon, *shuu?* or Egyptian *eesh?* Clothing was another ethnic identifier. The long white summer kaftan worn by men had a distinctive neckline and embroidery with or without a tassle, indicating whether the man was Omani, Saudi, Kuwaiti, or Emirati. The head dress, or *ghutra*, was similarly differentiated by the style imposed by the wearer.

A large minority of passengers were young women. These were the maids, the itinerant workers who kept the large Gulf households going with their cleaning, cooking and child-care. They had boarded the plane giggling and happy, because they were on their way home to the Philippines for holidays or perhaps returning home forever. Although some maids suffered bad experiences, the majority had reasonably happy lives in their host families and usually took home funds to keep their families going while they were away working.

I felt grateful that I had the education and work experience to lead a professional life which made me independent from my husband. According to my friends, he bragged about me when I wasn't there, but to my face he was negative about my relatively low paid job as a language teacher. He also put me down physically at every opportunity. I had been anorexic when I met him in London so he knew I was sensitive about gaining weight. He would sing to one of his favourite jazz records: 'She's a heavy, hippy, Mamma, she's got big fat legs.' He often called me *immishqurdum* or 'mother of monkeys'. Since we couldn't have children on account of Nabeel's proven infertility, this seemed a rather backhanded 'joke' but Nabeel didn't see it that way. He would only laugh if his brothers or sister remonstrated with him. I'd put up with his schoolboy sense of humour for years but perhaps the jibes were intended to lower my self-confidence. However, I knew I could do a good job as a teacher, and as a teacher-trainer, so his putdowns could not affect my professional identity.

Disembarking in Hong Kong I felt like the emotionally wounded, war-weary victim that I had become. My old friend Neil and Alice, his wife of only two months, met me and took me home for my first night. Once I had accepted the job in Hong Kong, I had managed to attend their wedding in Edinburgh, staying with old friends, and meeting future colleagues too. It was such a pleasure to see the newly married couple again and I felt so comfortable in their lovely apartment, which reminded me of my previously lovely home in Kuwait with its Arab interior decor features which Neil had brought along from Kuwait, where I had worked with him.

'I haven't invited anyone around for dinner, tonight, Rose. I thought you might prefer not to have to go over things with too many people at once.'

'You're right. It's still so unbelievable for me, and recounting it over and over is very wearing. I am so lucky to have a home in the UK, a loving family and good friends but the loss of everything in my Kuwait home is hard to bear.'

'Well, I feel lucky that I got out in time,' Neil admitted. 'You can see all my coffee pots, cushions and weavings - I suppose you've lost all yours?'

'Yes, or at least, I think so. Nabeel has taken some things to Beirut, and we found one or two souvenirs in the trashed house from a visit to China in 1985.'

'Wow - that was before Tiananmen Square, wasn't it?'

'Yes. It was. I suppose the events of 1989 in Beijing were as shocking and disastrous to people here as the invasion of Kuwait to us.'

'Indeed. Some people here have horrific tales to tell. The politics is all around us still. Hong Kong Chinese have concerns about their status. Hong Kong will be returning to China's rule in 1997 so we are trying to prepare the people for a new legal system. The basic law posits one law, for two peoples.'

'Gosh. That sounds interesting. I hope I am going to fit in here. Everything is so different.'

'Don't worry about that. You are a good teacher. That's why we chose you.'

'I suppose the language may be a challenge to me.'

'You know we don't use the language in our work, and culturally you'll soon get used to it. All the road signs are in two languages anyway. The lifestyle is good. The Chinese are very private. They keep themselves to themselves, rather like the English. But I warn you, it is a bit like living in a goldfish bowl as a University teacher. There is a lot of gossip among the expats.'

'I don't think I'll be the subject of gossip. I'm used to a quiet life in Kuwait,' I told him confidently.

Despite my brave facade I wept silently in my bed that night, wondering if I would be able to cope with this new life, or if I had made a stupid mistake, reacting to the post-war situation in such a drastic manner. Was I risk-taking? Should I have stayed in Kuwait with my husband and tried to rebuild my life in the new *status quo*? Then I recalled our endless quarrelling around Australia and admitted to myself for the first time that I could not be sure that rebuilding our personal lives would be as straightforward as rebuilding Kuwait, or would even be possible at all. I promised myself I would put my heart and soul into this job and hope for a good outcome for my efforts. It was a chance for a fresh start and I felt I deserved it after trying for fourteen years to be an obedient Arab wife. I had no children and Nabeel was still unwilling to adopt any. I had never seriously envisioned a future dedicated to rolling vine leaves in Beirut. Would this new scenario be another case of *blue on blue*? Or perhaps fate had taken a turn in the right direction for me.

CHAPTER 21

Weekend at the Beach

December 2003

Neither Rose nor Colin woke during the night. They were tired after the journey and the excitement of their renewed love affair. They smiled at each other as they opened their eyes just after first light to the sound of *kakariki*, bright green parrots, in the cabbage trees in the hotel garden. The bedroom curtains were open, revealing blue skies dotted with fluffy white clouds, and the canopy of cabbage trees in the hotel garden with some bright pink bougainvillea climbing up to the windows.

'It's a lovely day. Ready for a cup of tea?' Rose whispered. 'There's some Earl Grey here. Still your favourite?'

'Mm. With milk though.'

Colin was relaxed. They drank their tea in bed and took their time getting up. The schedule was open for the day, though Rose wanted to show Colin the piece of land she had finally bought on a new housing development site near the beach. Over coffee and eggs Benedict in the hotel dining room, Colin scanned the sports pages of the Saturday New Zealand Herald while Rose looked at the Open Homes section, still wondering if she'd made the right choice of property. She'd found her budget insufficient for the kind of house she wanted for the rest of her life, so had decided to build her own. It was a popular choice, giving house buyers the home they really wanted, and at a lower cost. Rose brought Colin up to speed with her plan.

'We can do the Kaiti Hill walk. There's a fine statue of Captain Cook here, then after our walk we can have lunch in one of the cafes in town - there's a good choice.'

'I won't need much after this, you know. Are we checking out of the hotel after breakfast?'

'Yes. We'll go and look at some show homes after lunch, then make our way back to Farmerston. I'd like to spend Sunday at home as I have to work on Monday, you know.'

'Are you taking some time off while I'm here?'

'Of course, I've got ferry tickets for the South Island trip, and I've got a surprise for you too.'

'Really? What is it?'

'Well, everyone tells me that good weather isn't guaranteed over Xmas and New Year, so I've booked a one week package holiday to Tonga.'

'Wow! The South Pacific, great. Thanks for doing that. I'll pay for my ticket,' Colin offered spontaneously.

''We'll see. I meant it as your Xmas present!'

'OK, well thanks. We'll see about that.'

After checking out Rose took the wheel again.

'Do you want to look at the map as we go?'

'No, thanks. I get travel sick if I read in the car.'

'Really? I hadn't realised that. I suppose you were usually the driver when we did things together in the old days.'

Rose recalled the holiday they had spent in Spain where they had hired a manual drive car which she had not been able to drive. Manual cars were cheaper than automatics and Colin always watched the budget carefully. But Rose had learned to drive in Kuwait with a French-speaking Tunisian driving teacher. She had mastered the manual gear system and passed her test on her teacher's car, but her own first car had been a 'yank tank', a huge white Chrysler *New Yorker* automatic, so her gear changing skills had deteriorated. She didn't trust herself to drive a manual transmission again.

Pulling into a parking area they set off on their Hill walk. From the summit the views of the vivid blue sea were amazing. Rose pointed out the sights and the blooming *pohutukawa* trees, New Zealand's own delightful red and gold Xmas trees. She couldn't yet pronounce the name fluently, though she had been practising the word for a week. Colin laughed as he struggled with it too.

'So, are you ready for lunch now or will an ice cream suffice?'

'Ice will be nice after that walk. I'm ready for it.'

Refreshed after a cool dairy treat, they got back in the car and began the drive towards Paloa Beach. On the way, Rose pointed out the Kaimai range and the Paloa Hills running parallel with the beach road. They first visited the section Rose had purchased in a new development next to a picturesque winding creek, inhabited by several different species of water birds, paradise ducks, mallards, heron, ibis/egrets enjoying the water and *pukeko* with their bright red legs and blue feathers paddling around in the weeds and rushes. It was quiet and seemed an idyllic setting to build a new home but Rose had some concerns.

'I'm worried about mosquitoes here, near the water, but the advantage is that no one can build directly in front of me. The banks of this little river are reservation areas, so there will always be creek views, with the wild life interest.'

'Yes, but also you will get members of the public walking in front of your house night and day, weekend or weekday. It could be noisy as well as annoying.'

'True. And then there's that huge pylon over there. The manager of the subdivision said that would be moved in future. But I don't know whether to believe it or not.'

'Mm. At best it could cause interference in your electrical equipment, at worst it might cause cancer.'

'Oh, my word. I think I'd better sell up and find another place! Let's go and look at a show home, if you are interested?'

'Yes, that would be great. They do that in the UK too now, but brand new homes are so small over there, I never thought of getting one.'

Rose suddenly remembered that Colin had bought a modern two storey home with rural views in a small seaside town on the south coast of England on his return from Bahrein. She hadn't meant to criticise his purchase.

'Your house is lovely,' Rose assured him, 'but here you get more choice with your own design and build as they call it. I'm thinking of building with a national franchisee as they have a good reputation. But I'm scared of getting cheated as a single woman.'

'Surely the Kiwis aren't like that? After all, they were the first to respect women and give them the vote.'

'Yes, but the women had to fight for it! I think it's a global phenomenon that building tradesmen have a reputation as bad as garage mechanics. They're well known for ripping people off - men AND women.'

'I see. I suppose you are right. Where's the show home we're going to see?'

'I want to see the latest Splendid Homes show home. It's on a rather more palatial and therefore more costly, fully developed sub-division, one of the first new ones over here. This area is growing so fast because it's cheaper here. Also it's a haven for retirees, which I hope to be in 10 years' time, like you.'

Colin didn't mind the teasing. He retaliated in kind.

'Yes, but I'm a young retiree, while you'll be old, retiring at 65, not 60 as in the UK!'

'But the UK Government can't afford that luxury any longer. Isn't the retirement age being extended gradually?'

'Indeed. You win! So long as you have a good pension and good health, retirement is a wonderful thing, I find.'

'OK. I agree. Now, look at this map: The coast is here and the main trunk road is parallel, with the major sub-divisions a little more distant from the sea. Then the creek runs parallel with the sea and the road. But none of the houses between the road and this creek are more than a ten minutes' walk from the sea. It's ideal really.'

They drove off through the local shopping zone to the show home. From outside it appeared large, light and airy. Two mock-Greek pillars graced the facade, and wide double doors stood open for visitors.

'Shoes off, Colin. That's a Kiwi rule when visiting show homes.'

Unperturbed he unlaced his sneakers, while Rose kicked off her jandals.

'I always wear jandals for this reason - it's so much easier to deshoe and reshoe!'

'Jandals? Do you mean flip flops? Righty O,' Colin laughed.

'Good afternooon!'

The two greeted the short, stocky, casually dressed, young man who came to meet them at the entrance.

'Welcome to the Splendid Homes show home.'

'Thanks. Can we look round?'

'Yes, go ahead but shout out if you need me.'

The entrance hall was lit by an elaborate chandelier which set the tone for the elegant, spacious single storey home. Three bedrooms shared a family bathroom, while the master had its own *en suite* facilities. There was also a 'half bathroom', a toilet and washbasin for guests in the entrance hall. The living room was open plan dining and sitting combined, although a pair of cleverly designed sliding doors could be closed to isolate the sitting room. The kitchen was well designed with both an island and a breakfast bar. The rear of the property looked onto lawns giving onto the same waterway which Rose's section faced further east. Here, however, the waterway was much wider, more lavishly landscaped and therefore more attractive. There was a wealth of wildlife here too, including many more species of exotic waterfowl.

Colin was visibly impressed, as was Rose.

'This is just delightful. How much is this specification and design?'

The agent referred her to the New Build brochures, with their comparative prices and specifications.

'The plot I have is similar to this, with a waterfront setting, on the Golden Sands subdivision,' Rose told him.

'OK. Did you have this size in mind? Do you want four bedrooms? There are various sizes in our brochure. You can, of course, design and build to your own specification, but it costs slightly more. Not as much as an architect would cost, mind you.'

'Well, right now I am just considering the options available. This certainly seems just what I want.'

'We try to make your dreams come true here at Splendid Homes.'

'Well, that's one of my problems. I've never really thought of building a house before, so working out my dream is a new challenge.'

'What I suggest is that you read as many house and garden magazines as possible, and pull out the pages of pictures you like.'

'That's another problem - I don't get a lot of time for reading magazines. But I take your point, and as I've got Xmas holidays coming up, I'll apply myself to the task.'

'Have you any other questions?'

'No, that's fine. Thanks for your time.'

'Well, here's my card. Get in touch if you have any questions. Bye for now.'

'That was a beautiful house,' Colin commented as they got back into the car.

'Yes, I love the sliding doors. I don't think I'll go for Doric Columns though!'

'Right! A bit much, perhaps,' Colin laughed. 'I'm looking forward to seeing your house in Farmerston.'

As she drove home Rose wondered if Colin would indeed like her house.

'A penny for your thoughts?' he asked.

'Oh, just thinking about our 'tea' as the locals call it. Shall I make a cheese omelette? Or what about a takeaway pizza with French fries? I've got salad in the fridge.'

'Mm. Whatever is easiest. No worries.'

Rose switched on the radio and they lapsed into the companionable silence of old friends. They stopped briefly on the Kaimais to take in the view of the Thames valley as it was a clear evening.

'Wow - there's so much to see. It's very interesting here. I'm enjoying myself already. I'm glad you invited me over.'

'That's good. I'm happy too,' Rose told him. 'Come on, let's get home and find the gin and tonic.'

Colin laughed. 'Yes, gin o'clock is coming up.'

Rose breathed a gentle sigh of relief. This visit had started well.

CHAPTER 22

New Friends in Hong Kong

September 1991

In the morning I woke refreshed despite, or on account of, the tears I had shed. Sheer exhaustion had given me energising sleep and as the sun's rays shone through the huge windows in Neil and Alice's spare bedroom, I felt happiness begin to grow like a seed planted but long forgotten deep inside me. I was the mistress of my own destiny again. I had always been independent. In the '60s I had gone to live in France alone as a 20 year old, in the '70s I had gone to live in Kuwait with a husband I thought I knew well, and now, in the '90s once again here I was, a blend of the two in a new country: a married woman on single status, with no husband to care for me or to worry about.

I looked around at the pretty guest room. I love having beautiful things around me. I wondered what my new flat would be like. I knew the scenario: The University provided hard furniture for dining, sitting and bedrooms as well as kitchen cupboards, a cooker and fridge, but the resident/worker was to provide soft furnishings and other household goods, including a washing machine if desired. I would receive a hospitality package provided by the University for the first two weeks including sheets, towels, some crockery, cutlery and some cooking utensils. Today Neil was taking me shopping to the local supermarket to get some provisions which we would then take to the flat. I checked the bathroom was free, had a quick shower, dressed and went into the kitchen for breakfast. Alice had already left for work, but Neil was reading the paper over a cup of filter coffee.

'Coffee for you?'

'No, thanks. Too early. Could I make a cup of tea?'

'Of course. Earl Grey? Lapsang Soochong?'

'Earl Grey would be terrific.'

'The kettle's just boiled. Cup or mug?'

'Mug, please.'

'Here you are.'

The tea was wonderfully refreshing but I felt too anxious to eat anything, though there were *croissants* and *petit pains au chocolat* in a basket on the table. Their aroma was tantalising. Neil followed my gaze.

'We can get just about anything here that you find in Europe. The Chinese bakeries are wonderful.'

'That's great. I adore fresh bread and *croissants* are a real treat.'

'Wait till you try the Portuguese custard tarts here. They are a traditional specialty.'

'It all sounds amazing. I'm so pleased to be here. Thanks again for all your help.'

'No problem. It's great to see you here. Kuwait must seem a long way away, hey?'

'Yes, indeed. And I'm very grateful for that. I feel I have a chance for a fresh start here.'

We set off to the local branch of the Wellcome food chain in Neil's car and I bought tea bags, milk, bread, butter, eggs and marmalade, some packets of instant soup and a few cans of tuna so I could make a simple breakfast for myself in the morning and an easy supper in the evening. Neil told me I could get a good, cheap, cooked lunch each day in the Staff Dining Room. In addition, there was a Senior Staff Common Room which served bar food from lunchtime until evening. It all sounded far more exotic than the simple life I had grown accustomed to in Kuwait over the last fourteen years. Although Nabeel and I had travelled to many exotic destinations and stayed in five star hotels often, our daily life was restricted to work and most of our weekends too.

After the brief shopping experience I was excited as we drove to my allocated flat in Hong Kong Towers. As we approached the buildings I could see they were positioned high up on steep hillsides with views of the sea. I had lived close to the sea since arriving in Kuwait in 1976 so I was thrilled. The vivid blue of the sea relaxed me and gave me peace of mind. How amazing was it that I should have such a wonderful vista from my new home! We took the lift to the seventh floor and I was relieved not to have to go higher. Neil showed me round the three bedrooms, open plan living and dining area, one bathroom with bath, large tiled kitchen and additional small maid's room with a shower room. The place seemed airy and light with one whole wall of folding glass doors looking out to sea. I was intrigued by the long, heavy iron bars I found outside on the balcony.

Neil explained, 'Those are your typhoon bars.'

'Typhoon bars?'

'Yes, if there's a typhoon warning you must put these on the folding glass doors so that they resist the wind better. Oh and here's your typhoon shelter.'

He took me to what appeared to be a walk in wardrobe, but there was no hanging or shelf space inside.

'In case of a typhoon alert, you can put a single mattress in here and there's an electrical point for a radio. You stay in here listening to the radio until the warning has lifted.'

'Wow. That's a surprise. And a bit scary.'

'Don't worry. There's hardly ever a serious alert. But you need to know, just in case.'

'Thanks!'

'Right, here's the key to the door. Be sure to lock the back door too.'

'OK.'

'Now, how about lunch in the Senior Common Room? I select the wine for the bar so I usually have lunch there. I don't always have wine though!'

'Lunch sounds good - I'm hungry now - but no wine for me today either!'

Neil drove the short distance to the University, pointing out the bus stop I could use to get to work the next day. I could see that the journey to work was downhill, which would mean it might be easy to walk to work. However, the humidity of the weather suggested that I might arrive drenched in sweat if I did that. It might be easier to walk home uphill in the evening when I could take a shower afterwards. As Neil parked in one of the limited spaces available for staff with cars I realised that I probably would not be driving myself around this small island.

'Do you need a car here, Neil?'

'Not really. But I've been here long enough to enjoy getting out on weekends, and when I'm running around town collecting wine for wine tastings, it's easier for me to transport stuff.'

Neil led me through the walkways, staircases and many buildings which made up the campus to the modern tower block which housed the English Centre where I was to work.

'We actually work in various buildings, depending on the faculty we are 'servicing'.'

'Right.'

'But we have our own Self Access Centre in this building. It serves all faculties and all language groups. Students can practise English, French, German, Japanese and so on here.'

'That sounds great.'

'We are starting some research into independent learning if you are interested?'

'For sure. This will be a great opportunity for me to start some real research. I've made lots of presentations in the past, but not had any serious publications.'

'Good. Our academic leader will be pleased to hear that. Meanwhile, here we are in the Administrative Office. Here are the most important people.'

I shook hands and said 'hello' to the pleasant, smiling office staff. Then it was time to meet the big boss, the Director. We stepped into her office and she greeted me warmly. She explained I would have an office to myself for as long as possible as a Senior Instructor, but if things got tight I might have to share. I reassured her that that would be no problem. Neil then took me up to the tenth floor and showed me my office. My desk was close to the large window, with views across Hong Kong Island. I already had a computer installed, and Neil gave me the log on, user name and password I needed to get going.

Neil looked at his watch and declared, 'But now lunch! Come on, it's 12 o'clock. Food is served punctually here!'

We took the stairs up to the 12th floor and walked into a huge, rectangular dining hall with wide windows down the far side, serving tables laden with chafing dishes and hot food at one end, trolleys for collecting used plates at the opposite end, and on the wall where we had entered, I could see two huge tureens, one of steamed rice and the other of rice porage, or *congee*. These formed the basis for the meal, with the other dishes, vegetable curry, sweet and sour pork, chicken and cashew nuts, and so on, to be selected from the changing daily menu as the diner wished. There was an air of calm, quiet and purposeful eating. Colleagues sat together but there was a minimum of chatter, with the focus on eating and getting back to work. I realised I would not need to cook for myself at home with such a wonderful variety of cooked food available to me on weekdays, and at a very reasonable price.

After looking around for a moment, Neil led me to a table where some other staff from the English Centre were seated. He introduced me to a vivacious and attractive redhead, who was wearing an armful of silver bracelets, like my own, which Nabeel had told me he retrieved after the invasion of Kuwait, before focussing my attention back on my new colleagues. There was the academic leader of the Centre, a quiet, reserved intellectual, and then, rising to hug me, my old friend and former colleague in Kuwait, Vicky. We had worked together in the '80s with Neil at Kuwait

University. Coincidentally all of us originated in the UK, so our conversation focussed on 'home', though of course we were all now at home in Hong Kong. I felt comfortable and reassured by the familiarity of the conversation. There was hopefully going to be no jealousy although I was coming in at Senior Instructor level.

After a very pleasant lunch, with our choice of English or Chinese tea or American coffee served to us at our table, Neil and I said our goodbyes and went back to my office. Here he showed me how to access emails, timetables, and shared documents for work. I was free for a couple of days, but there would be workshops for staff induction and preparation the following Monday, so I would need to familiarise myself with the curriculum, testing and administration so as to be ready to start work the following week with testing the students. For the rest of the day, however, I needed to simply find my feet and get myself back to my flat under my own steam.

On the main road Neil showed me the double decker buses which plied the route back to my flat, and were numbered and named in English, so should gave me no problem. More difficult to use were the small green minibuses I had seen while driving with Neil, which plied the hillier areas of Hong Kong. Their drivers and their signage were in Chinese. I would need some assistance to use them. As we stood at the bus stop I realised that I didn't have any change to buy my ticket later on, so we retraced our steps to the bank nearest the campus. I needed to open an account in which to receive my salary, so having done that, and with some change in my pocket and dollar notes in my wallet, I braved the minibus ride for the first time. 'Hong Kong Towers, *ngoy!*'

It was easy to recognise the stop to get off at in the bright sunshine, and I climbed the steep stairs to my building feeling a sense of familiarity growing inside me. But on entering the apartment tiredness and emotion overwhelmed me. Looking at the two suitcases standing in the hall which I'd brought with me, I sat down on the sofa and cried again. Those cases were the chains to my past and to my husband but they were also my security, my memories of my previous life. They were the things I knew and loved but had nearly lost in the invasion of Kuwait. Would I be strong enough to make a new life? And would that new life be one I could share with Nabeel or not?

I quickly dried my eyes and got up to make a cup of tea. I'd bought some Earl Grey tea bags. The English staple, a cup of tea would cheer me up for sure. Opening the emergency hospitality kit I found institutional green china cups and saucers, which made me laugh out loud: They were identical to the cups we had had in our Adult Education Institute in London, back in the 1970s. A gap of 20 years was bridged in a Proustian instant. I sat down with my fragrant, steaming hot beverage, basking in the warm late afternoon sunshine from the window and looked around me again. This flat would be a lovely home when I'd given it some soft furnishing personal touches. What could stop me? I had a good job, with an excellent salary - much better than the one I'd had in Kuwait, even as Supervisor - so shopping could be the way for me to cheer myself up by replacing all those things I had lost in the invasion. I had to remember that Thursday and Friday would be work here in Hong Kong, unlike in Kuwait, but Saturday would be shopping and Sunday would be relaxing! Housework would have to be fitted in too, but I made an instant decision to have the wooden floors sanded and sealed, which would make them easier to clean.

The tea had lifted my spirits. I took the cup into the kitchen and searched for my suitcase keys. I had so far only opened my carry on cabin bag for my first night at Neil's apartment, but now I had to tackle the two suitcases I'd been allowed to carry by Emirates Air. The cases were old, as our newer Samsonites had been taken by the looters, but they were serviceable: a large, grey Delsey, and a black American Tourister purchased when Nabeel and I had visited Florida for a company conference in the late '80s. Both the bags suggested years of classy travel experience. Inside was a different story: my clothes were dated ('80s shoulder pads!) and most were too big for me now, but they were smart enough for work with the pads carefully cut out. I found a few hangers in the fitted wardrobes in each of the two bedrooms and noted the electric sockets they had near the floor for a wardrobe heater. I had heard from Alice that Hong Kong's humidity wrecked clothes stored in wardrobes. I would have a good excuse to start shopping as soon as possible to buy these special wardrobe heaters which stopped mould forming. Meanwhile, the choice of bedroom was easy. The three rooms were graduated in size, but the largest looked over the gardens on the front of the estate which sloped down to the road, and from there the views were splendid. Broad sea vistas spread out to 180 degrees, and there were several islands in view, some large, some small. I could see a ferry boat sailing towards the largest. I wondered which island that was. My heart soared: There was so much to explore and enjoy ahead of me but for now, on with the unpacking.

My two suitcases were soon emptied, and I turned my attention to the kitchen. There was a small mains gas stove with four burners, which seemed easy enough to operate, and a large butcher's sink overlooking the paved areas between my building and the other two which made up the estate. The fridge was half size, with a tiny freezer section just big enough for ice. It reminded me of my childhood home, when a fridge like this was the norm in the UK. I'd always admired the higher American standard of living which I'd experienced briefly when I did Summer Camp in the USA in 1970. Our fridge in Kuwait had of necessity in that climate been huge, with plenty of space for my home made beer, which tended to blow up if not kept cold. In future perhaps I'd get my dream, Whirlpool red enamel refrigerator! I certainly didn't have enough food to fill the fridge right now, nor the cupboards. But sufficient unto the day was my little food hoard. I made some toast with the old fashioned eye level grill, taking care not to burn it and set off the smoke alarm, and boiled up half a packet of Knorr asparagus soup. That made a satisfying vegetarian supper after my large lunch in the University dining room.

I'd also got one bottle of duty free whisky left, after giving the other to my hosts on the first night. So, after making up the bed with the sheets and blankets on loan and putting on pajamas, I poured myself a nightcap of scotch and water. From my bedroom window I could see the lights of apartment tower blocks on the opposite side of the road, all the way down to the sea. It was like looking at a Disney World lighting display. Many flats had no blinds or curtains, like mine, but I was well aware that if I had my light on I could be seen as clearly as the occupants of those flats were. So, I sat in the dark, except for the illumination from the window. I couldn't see the moon, which had been a notable part of the night skyscape in Kuwait. But I knew it was there, and that it was looking down on Nabeel as well. I wondered how he was coping without me. He was probably just smoking more, if he had any reaction at all. I was tired after all the novelty and emotions of the first day here. I had no home phone as yet. Tomorrow I would ring him from the office and find out how he was faring. I did not feel any sense of home sickness as I had so much to occupy my mind. In fact, I felt exhilarated. My life was beginning again.

CHAPTER 23

Home in Farmerston

13 December 2003

Sunday was warm and sunny, so Rose and Colin could enjoy getting to know Farmerston, a long established garden city with almost 127,000 inhabitants, noted for its University, huge dairy processing plant and beautiful riverside Gardens. Although as yet only a permanent resident of New Zealand, Rose felt a sense of patriotic pride in her new home as she showed Colin around. They had a sandwich for lunch in the Farmerston Gardens cafeteria. It was wonderful to feel the first strong summer sun on their backs as they ate. Rose felt genuinely happy, putting the vicissitudes of her relationship with Colin to the back of her mind. She explained to Colin the vagaries of New Zealand's climate as she understood them.

'You see, the weather is changing. This feels like summer at last. When I got here it was really hot in February, but then the rain started in March and never stopped. I felt like leaving really, but where to go? Australia? Back to the Gulf?'

Colin shrugged as if it was not a problem.

'You could have come home, you know.'

Rose wondered if this was a personal offer of a home, or just a statement of fact with regard to the UK. She chose the latter interpretation.

'Yes, I could look for work at Exeter Uni, I suppose, and live in my flat in Exmouth. But it would be hard staying in the UK, for various reasons, as I think you know.'

She looked at him meaningfully, wondering if he was really mindful of why she had left the UK but he kept his gaze focussed on his sandwich. He was never one to talk very much, which previously Rose had attributed to his being the strong, silent type. She now believed that his reticence had other causes. Perhaps he was afraid of unwittingly revealing some secrets. Or maybe he was a commitment-phobe. If Rose reflected honestly on her past with Colin, she knew his double life had been a consistent factor in their troubles. She dragged her mind away from the negatives. There was no point in inviting him to New Zealand to go over old ground. If there was to be any discussion about the future it had to be initiated by Colin. Rose opened up the day for Colin to choose their activities.

'Right, what would you like to do now? We could go to the cinema or just go home and sit in the garden as it's warm and read the Sunday papers.'

'Mm. That sounds like a good idea. Have you got something for dinner tonight, or shall we go out?'

'I thought we could pick up some shopping as we go home. We'll be eating out a lot when we take our trips.'

'Fine. It'll be like old times.'

Rose noted that his mind was on the past as was hers. In fact Colin and Rose had not lived together during their relationship. For the first three years in Bahrein they had

had apartments in the same building, but only got together on the weekends. Both their jobs were demanding, so at weekends they ate take away pizza, Chinese or Indian food or Rose's specialty, the full English brunch. Although she had had a fulltime job in Kuwait Rose had cooked on a daily basis throughout her married life. Her repertoire included Italian, Arabic, Chinese or Indian dishes. But in Bahrein work had taken first place and she had only cooked for Colin occasionally.

In the store she picked out aubergines and tomatoes for a vegetarian lasagne with salad. Neither of them had a sweet tooth, so dessert wasn't necessary but wine was essential. They both enjoyed a cold, lemony gin and tonic before dinner and a liqueur after dinner occasionally. Living in Bahrein had presented no problems to this alcohol-tinged lifestyle. In fact, that's how Colin had made his first move on Rose. He had come to her apartment door to ask if she wanted to go to the liquor shop with him. Not having a car was a problem for booze shoppers, as taxi drivers refused to carry the devil's beverages. The Muslim drivers knew their passengers were bearing alcohol from the heavy, large and lurid plastic bags which contained it. The name of the chain of liquor stores printed on the bags was enough to make a driver speed up as they passed the discreetly shuttered shop.

Back in Lavender Place Rose put the meal together while Colin read the paper in the still sunny garden, where the garden furniture had finally come into its own. After a while he came inside.

'Smells good.'

'Mm. Won't be long now. Have a look round. Do you recognize my stuff from Bahrein?'

'Of course I do. There's a lot of it too. You haven't opened all your packing cases yet, I see. Do you remember you didn't have anything much in your flat when we first met?'

'Yes. I was waiting for my container to arrive from London. It hadn't been anywhere except the docks, as I'd split up with my husband after sending it from Hong Kong in 1993. That seems like a hundred years ago now, but it's only been ten years. Thank God it's all over. Nearly.'

'What do you mean?' Colin asked, intrigued.

'Well, you remember I was fighting for my rights in the divorce when I first met you? I only got my solicitor's costs but I also am entitled to any proceeds from the United Nations claim. I'm still hoping that the United Nations claim for compensation for our losses in the Invasion will come through. I completed the claim when I was in Hong Kong. Nabeel wanted the claim to be in my name. It would make a huge difference to my future financial security.'

Business-like with regard to finances as usual, Colin picked up on the reference to security but focussed on Rose's future self sufficiency rather than their future together as Rose had hoped.

'Mm. You're still paying self-employed National Insurance Contributions in the UK, aren't you?'

'Yes, that's thanks to you.' Rose gave Colin his due. It was his financial advice that she had taken soon after she'd first met him ten years earlier.

'I got it all sorted out. I can keep paying to cover the lost years for a while, then they will calculate how much UK retirement pension I can claim. I've no idea what the pension situation is here. Sometimes I don't think I'll be staying very long, given the wet weather and the cold winter. I had expected more of a tropical climate. Anyway, I'm still too young for retirement, so I don't need to think about it too much as yet.'

Rose tired quickly of the subject, raising as it did the spectres of the past. She changed the subject. 'Why don't you make us a gin and tonic? Lemons and tonic in the fridge. Ice in the freezer.'

Colin willingly complied, and they sipped their drinks as he set the table and she made the salad. They enjoyed their meal with a delicious Australian Shiraz, then moved to the bedroom to watch the evening news, lying comfortably propped upon pillows on the bed. Her only sitting room furniture was hard backed Chinese formal chairs, sofas and coffee tables, which were not at all suitable for lounging.

Rose had to work the next day, Monday, so she needed an early night. She had sketched out a rough itinerary and set out the map and guidebooks for Colin to plan their trip in more detail. On the Friday they would be heading off for Taupo, where they would spend the night, then drive on to the ferry in Wellington on Saturday. The rest was as yet to be decided by him. Before she fell asleep she checked the agenda with Colin, mindful of Karl's boredom when he was left alone in Farmerston.

'About tomorrow. I hope you'll be OK at home, planning our trip? I'm sorry I had to get rid of my second car. It was taking up so much room in the garage, and then of course there was the expense of registering two cars. Public transport isn't too good around here as it's a new sub-division. But there are buses if you get cabin fever.'

'Don't worry, I'll be fine. You were right to get rid of it. You must try to live within your budget or at least your income! I have to be careful not to spend too much, you know, even with my two pensions. By the way, I'll try and make a bit more room in your garage for you, if you like, by moving some boxes around.'

Surprised both at Colin's sudden focus on money and his offer of help Rose was reluctant to load him with jobs on his 'holiday'. She hadn't brought him out for that purpose. She wanted them to focus on their future together.

'That would be great, but it's not a major concern. Some of the boxes are very heavy with books and I don't have enough shelves as yet to put them on. I've been unpacking on a daily basis, unwrapping things and stashing them or displaying them as you see. But it's almost a lifetime's work, I reckon. You should have seen the container - it was huge. I had to get a police permit for them to park it outside.'

'Wow. Well, you had a lot of stuff in Bahrein, you know.'

'Absolutely. Once I'd lost everything in the Invasion I never thought I'd put so much effort into replacing it. Stupid really, but I enjoy my stuff.'

'Yes, you're a material girl all right. By the way, I like this bedroom furniture - did you get that here?'

'Yes. I was inspired by the design. It seemed rather Chinese and I thought it would fit in with the rest of my furniture from Hong Kong. Also, I needed more storage, as you can see. I still don't have enough really, but I guess I'll be sorting and selling on Trade Me when I'm a bit more settled.'

Rose declined to ask any reciprocal questions about Colin's house. He had bought it after he left his job in Bahrein and when she visited during his first two years there she had given him a Tiffany-style lampshade and two identical luxurious bath robes. But whenever Rose had visited Colin's house she felt as if she was stepping into someone else's shoes. Now that she knew about Tillie her suspicions were confirmed, so questions about Colin's home and life style were out of bounds. It was best to operate on a 'need to know' basis.

'Well, sweetheart, there doesn't seem to be much news tonight. They are still searching for my good friend Saddam in Iraq. They are calling the campaign *Red Dawn*. I'm going to switch off the light. Ready?'

'Mm. Come here.'

After a while Rose enjoyed a deep peaceful sleep for about four hours. At around 2am she awoke and switched on BBC World, muting the volume so as not to wake Colin. She stared, bemused, at the screen where an unshaven, wild-haired, half-naked Saddam Hussein wearing only white Y-fronts was displayed ignominiously on the front page of the UK's tabloid newspaper, *The Sun*. As Colin was slightly deaf, she could turn up the volume slightly to hear how Saddam had been captured by American soldiers while hiding in a tunnel in Tikrit, his home town. Strangely, despite herself, she couldn't help feeling sorry for the man she had wished dead so many times. He was now in captivity, reduced to a pathetic state after living in an underground 'bunker' for months since his disappearance during *Shock and Awe*, the allied attack on Baghdad.

Rose looked at Colin sleeping peacefully beside her. Handsome as ever despite hair greying now at the temples she wished that their past had been less turbulent. She contemplated how emotionally damaged by her failed marriage she had been during those early years, and wondered how much that had affected the course of their relationship. On the other hand, had it been her feminine instinct that had given her 'the nose' for the deceit that Colin had been practising since the very first day they got together? Looking back it was easy to see that she had been jealous and he had been self-righteously indignant about that. What had he said on their first big date, at Xmas time, when they'd gone to a ball together? 'Go home and play with your toys!' The words still stung in her memory. He had been the one toying with her emotions, ruining a lovely evening by talking at length to a younger woman she did not know, ignoring Rose. In retrospect she wondered if this showed a lack of social competence or a lack of sensitivity. Perhaps she had been at fault, for being too sensitive?

However she tried to rationalise that first date she felt they both could have handled the issue differently and perhaps it was indicative of their future ups and downs. She could have been more forthright and introduced herself, instead of leaving. They almost split up right then, but Colin had called to apologise, then come round to her apartment to sweet talk the situation back. This pattern had been typical of their relationship right up to Tillie's call. *Blue on blue, heartache on heartache.* This time it was Rose who had mended the breech and got them together again, but would she rue the day, she wondered? Sighing, she turned the TV off and settled down to sleep again so as to be ready for another day in her new life. At least Saddam Hussein was in captivity now. He was responsible for so much, including her broken marriage.

CHAPTER 24

A Whole New World

October 1991

The next morning I woke to bright sunshine. After a cup of tea in bed I established that there was hot water in the bathroom, had a shower and dressed quickly. Today I was adventuring. I was glad that it was dry, warm and sunny as I walked down the steps to the road and the bus stop. At the bus stop there was another Western woman, with pure white, thick, short hair and a contrastingly young face. She greeted me with a smile.

'Hi. Are you going to the Uni?'

'Yes. You too?'

'Indeed. I work in the Law Library.'

'Wow. I've just started in the English Centre. This is my second day here.'

'Cool. My name's Lucy.'

'I'm Rose.'

'Do you live in Hong Kong Towers?'

'Yes, Block 3.'

'I'm in Block 2.'

'Great. Hi neighbour! Here's the bus!'

We climbed onto the crowded bus and Lucy helped me find the right change for the fare. I felt so relieved. What a stroke of luck meeting someone who could help me with my first bus ride!

'What are you doing for lunch?' my new friend asked.

'Well, I intended going along to the Chinese Dining Room. I had a lovely meal there yesterday.'

'That's where I go too. Shall we meet up and have a chat?'

'Wonderful. What time suits you?'

'12 noon is best as the food is fresh then and there's lots of choice. Is that OK?'

'Perfect. See you there.'

After ten minutes bumping around on the swaying double decker we got off and crossed the road to the main entrance of the University.

'I go this way to the Law Library. Can you find your way?'

'I think so. But I'd better follow my rat track from yesterday.'

'OK. See you at lunch time.'

'See you later, Lucy. Bye.'

I made my way to the English Centre following the path I'd taken the day before with Neil. Once there I greeted the office girls and asked about phones and overseas calls. Having established that I could be billed for an overseas call I made my way to my own office. Nabeel didn't have a home phone as yet and Hong Kong was five hours ahead so I had to wait until after lunch to call the office. Meanwhile I switched on my computer and opened up my email. It seemed that Nabeel wasn't worrying about me. He hadn't rung or faxed me since I arrived in Hong Kong. He hated computers and never did email. I wrote Beatrice in Dubai a short thank you email then began downloading documents for work. I was quickly engrossed in the details. At 10.30am I had a call from the General Office.

'Hi Rose. Would you like to meet Samantha for coffee?' asked Jennie.

'Yes, that would be great. Whereabouts?'

'Come down to the Office and she'll meet you.'

'Right. See you in a moment.'

On entering the office I saw a familiar petite, dark-haired, olive-skinned, pretty young woman, smiling a greeting.

'Samantha! It's you!'

'Rose! Wonderful to see you again!'

We had done our Master's degrees in the UK in the mid '80s. We went off to the Senior Common Room for coffee and a good chat.

'So, how are you?' I asked. 'It's wonderful to see you again.'

'Well, I've got two small boys now, so I'm busy.'

'Wow. Amazing. And you work fulltime?'

'Yes, but I haven't been able to continue with my studies. Have you?'

We had both been recommended to continue with doctoral programs after our MAs.

'I hope one day I'll be able to start mine, but the Invasion rather put paid to those ideas. I did ask at Brum about continuing in language testing, but they didn't have anyone to supervise me.'

'Oh, you must talk to June then. She's doing her Ph.D. in language testing. Did you meet her at Neil's wedding in Edinburgh?'

'Yes, I did. We had a short chat over lunch. It was a lovely day, with so much happening.'

'Well, she lives near us so why not come over for dinner at the weekend and meet her again?'

'That would be great. I'll need full directions though. I'm only just getting used to moving around here.'

'No worries. It's not too far from where you are in Hong Kong Towers. How would Saturday night be?'

'Great. What can I bring?'

'Just a smile!'

'Thanks - it will be exciting to go out at night!'

As we went back to our offices, I wondered if I would be able to find my way down to the lower levels of the steep hill I lived on. Those small green buses caused me some trepidation! Perhaps I would get a taxi instead?

I worked till lunchtime then joined Lucy in the Chinese Dining Room. The meal we ate was as delicious as the day before. Over our food we exchanged key details of our former lives and Lucy introduced me to some of her colleagues, one of whom was completing her Ph.D. in law. We chatted about the upcoming weekend.

'What are you planning to do?'

'Well, I guess I'll be cleaning and perhaps doing some more preparation for teaching on Saturday, then I'm invited out for dinner.'

'So, what about going to the Stanley market on Sunday?'

'That sounds like fun. How do we go there?'

'It's a bus ride of about an hour. We can have lunch over there, and spend the whole day shopping. There's lots to see.'

'Terrific. What time shall I meet you?'

'I'll come over and get you at around 9.30, OK?'

'Cool. See you then.'

We finished our coffee and I returned to my office for the afternoon. At 2pm I rang the Kuwait office number.

'Good morning, UNETL', said a female voice in Arabic.

'Hi, Hanaan. It's Rose.'

Hanaan was Edouard's Egyptian secretary. She spoke excellent English.

'Hi, Rose. How are you?'

'Fine, thanks. Is Nabeel there?'

'No, he's gone to Ahmadi, to the oil company.'

'Never mind. Just tell him I'm fine and I'll ring again.'

'Right. How are you, Rose?'

'I'm fine. How are things going in Kuwait now?'

'*Y'ani*, getting better all the time. Bye, Rose.'

'Goodbye.'

From her non-committal response I guessed that Hanaan was busy though I suspected that she might be 'short' with me because I had left Nabeel alone in Kuwait. Or perhaps there were things she preferred not to tell me.

The dinner at Samantha's on Saturday night was relaxed. I chose the easy transport option, taxi. Meeting June again, she and I soon became firm friends. With a shared interest in language testing, she introduced me to a part-time job in test-writing for the Hong Kong Exams Authority, adding another string to my bow.

'You've got to be careful here, living as a single woman, you know,' she confided.

'It can't be worse than in Kuwait, I reckon,' I replied laughing, remembering a male shoe shop assistant stroking my ankles.

'Believe me,' she urged, 'it's not the Chinese, they couldn't care less what Western women do, it's the Westerners! Living in the University Blocks is like living in a goldfish bowl. Every move you make is observed.'

'You know, I believe you. Neil mentioned the same thing, and I really appreciate the warning, but I've lived in a cage since 1976 so this is life on the range. For the first time in a long time, at last I feel free, though I don't intend to be the subject of gossip.'

'Well, just be careful.'

'Thanks, it's good to be aware of prying eyes.'

I felt I would have little to fear, given my marital status and my inhibitions created by all those years living in Kuwait. There had been so many constraints on female behaviour that I had become inhibited in mixed society. Even walking alone into the Chinese Dining Room at the Uni was an ordeal for me at first.

Other dinner guests, the Foleys, were eager to speak to me. I had met Philip in London before going to Kuwait in 1976. I asked him about this quirk of fate that had brought us all to Hong Kong.

'Hi! What happened to you? I thought I was coming to work with you in Kuwait?'

'Hello, Rose. I was whisked away to higher things! I was made BC Rep in Baghdad. I think they wanted to make sure the new Rep and his wife had a pleasant posting. So I was shunted off to riskier climes. How did you get on with them?'

'Fine. I worked with the boss on materials writing using his Communicative Syllabus Design and with his wife on teacher training. Then I moved to the Uni when I completed my Master's degree.'

'So it all turned out OK for you. That's good.'

Maria had been listening and interjected, 'It wasn't so good for us though. We got caught up in the First Gulf War. We're lucky to be here now! We had to get out fast and left everything behind. The only good news is that I've got a much better job.'

'I'm following in your footsteps then. Lucky me!'

Our chat reminded me to seek some part-time evening work with the British Council, Hong Kong. If I returned to Kuwait, it would be important to continue to work with the British Council there. On top of my extra British Council teaching, 'A' level exam work, and personal research project, Neil had an independent learning materials project going on. I joined him in the preparation and filming for this and also joined his team in the Extra Mural Department teaching Master's students in evening classes.

As I completed my sociology class preparation I realized that Peter Berger's notion that 'We build our own Alcatraz.' was true about my life in Kuwait. The life of a woman there was like that of a precious bird in a cage, well cared for and protected, but restricted and untenable for a woman like me. In contrast, despite the dangers of visibility in this expatriate society, Hong Kong allowed me to spread my wings professionally. I felt myself to be very fortunate indeed, working in an exotic location, fulfilling my research ambitions, and enriching my academic career beyond my wildest dreams. The notion of returning to Kuwait was far from my mind. I hoped I could persuade my husband to seek pastures new so that we could put the past behind us.

However, before I could put Kuwait behind me I needed to complete our application to the UK Government for compensation for our losses. Taking a fresh exercise book

I drew a plan of our home, then of each room, and itemised everything I could recall. Establishing values and completing the application forms was more challenging, but I got it done and sent it off to the UK by the required deadline. However, for days, weeks, months and even years afterwards, I would see something I had owned, or similar to what I had owned, in shops or in other people's homes, and realise I had not claimed for that item. Even if I had claimed for the item, I felt pangs of regret for the loss. *Blue on blue,* repeated time after time, *heartache on heartache.*

CHAPTER 25

Touring New Zealand

December 2003

The final week of work for 2003 sped by with Rose clearing her desk ready for the Christmas and New Year holiday and Colin planning for the road trip around the South Island. They enjoyed a pleasant domestic routine in the evenings, cooking at home or buying takeaways. Rose introduced Colin to fresh, succulent New Zealand fish and chips. On other evenings Rose cooked Colin's favourite dishes, such as *Pad Thai,* which they'd enjoyed on many occasions on holiday in Thailand. Frequent overseas holidays were one of the perks of the GPC. Teachers had eight weeks' annual leave during the summer but there were also several national and Islamic holidays throughout the year. Holidays in exotic locations had provided some of their happiest memories, though these were now tainted. Sue's shocking phone call to Rose after Colin had left Bahrein for the UK had revealed that their holiday photos were no longer private and that Colin had an established girlfriend of 15 years. Like the photo discovery in Lebanon the episode generated a searing and still raw sense of violation. But Rose knew it was important to focus on the present and the future if she wanted a fresh start.

By Friday Colin had worked out a fairly detailed itinerary and they had two small bags packed for their trip. As soon as Rose got back from work they set off for the long drive to Taupo where they were booked into a lakeside motel. To fortify them on the journey Heather had given Rose a tin of Danish butter cookies, a popular brand in Bahrein, which made them smile. The journey from Farmerston to Taupo took them through Rotorua, famous for its hot water geysers. They stopped for a quick look around the former Government House, now a museum and park. After driving on through dense pine forests, Lake Taupo was glinting in the evening sunlight when they finally pulled into their motel.

Colin exclaimed, 'Whew. I'm a bit stiff, aren't you?'

'Yes, it's been quite a drive.'

'Let's check in then and go for a walk before we have a drink, hey?'

'Great idea.'

Their room was attractive, with lake views and pictures of local beauty spots on the walls.

'We'll have to come back here and see the sights properly,' said Rose.

'Mm. Time is going to be a constraint for us.'

'Yes, I'm wondering why I bothered with the Tonga trip. We could have spent longer here.'

'Never mind. If it does rain cats and dogs while we are in the South Island, we can look forward to the tropical beaches over there.'

'I know. Come on, let's get outside.'

The evening air was cool and refreshing after the warm sunshine during the daytime. People were sitting out having drinks in the last of the daylight. Ducks and black swans as well as a few small fishing and sailing boats still dotted the water.

'It's so good to stretch my legs. I think they've swollen from sitting in the car.'

'It's good that we can share the driving. Tomorrow will be huge.'

'Yes, we need to be on the road again by 8am. The ferry leaves at 2.30pm. We should have enough time to get there safely.'

'You mean without breaking the speed limit?'

'Yes, Kiwi police are hot to trot on fining speeding drivers. So please watch the speedometer! My salary is too small for fines.'

'Actually, what is your salary like? Are you able to live on it?'

'Well, you know me. I like to be comfortable and it's always expensive settling in. I wasted a lot of money setting up the house I rented in Oman, but it's just something you have to do. I never thought I'd be leaving there after only three months.'

'OK, but you have to get a proper budget going you know. It's important to think forward and plan for your retirement.'

'I'm only 56 you know! Not over the hill yet.'

'What, like me you mean?'

'Not at all. You don't show your age. You look like the proverbial playboy of the Western World.'

'But I am careful. I keep my principal tucked away and make sure I only live on the interest and my pensions.'

'You are the perfect financial role model. But right now I have to do whatever it takes. And that means enjoying our holiday. Right?'

Rose never enjoyed talking about money. After the experience of being defrauded by Nabeel, she always felt emotional discussing finances. Her neck flushed in reaction to the bitter memory and she changed the subject.

'Right. You hungry now?'

The pair turned back toward the motel. They perused the menu over a gin and tonic, then opted for trout, fresh from the lake, with their shared weakness, French fries, balanced by a delicious green salad, garnished with large chunks of creamy avocado and long, tender spears of asparagus, both readily available in New Zealand.

'Is asparagus really an aphrodisiac, I wonder?'

'I don't know. If you want to test it out, let's go.'

'Mm. Let's finish this *sauvignon blanc* up in the room.'

The bed was huge, the power shower revitalising and the night was blissful. As she fell asleep, Rose wondered why their lives couldn't stay like this always. In the morning, bird call awoke them before the alarm, and with an aromatic cup of filter coffee inside them, they set off for Wellington and the Interisland ferry.

The high altitude Desert Road from Taupo south through the mountain peaks of Tongariro and Ruapehu reminded Rose of driving over Exmoor in the UK. The landscape was wild and desolate, but the wind was not cold at this time of year. Their journey took them through small towns, villages and hamlets reminiscent of the USA countryside with their wooden architecture and one-horse narrow streets. But they couldn't afford the time to stop as their ferry schedule was tight. They shared the driving, breaking their journey at Bulls where they enjoyed a cup of Milo made with milk, a popular Kiwi children's drink which they both recalled was equally popular in the UK when they were young. Colin was older than Rose. He was born at the start of World War 2 while she was born after it ended, so he had vivid memories of those dark years in the UK. He even recounted how his house had almost been struck by a doodle bug, with himself, his sister, and his Mum at home. He also had terrors occasionally from the nights spent in the Anderson shelter which his Dad had built, like many others, in the back garden, and where the family had tried to sleep during air raids. Despite the age gap, they often had similar recollections from their childhood, which never failed to amuse them. Laughing about drinks like Milo, Tizer, Dandelion and Burdock, they climbed back into the Mitsubishi.

After a couple more hours they found themselves in the Hutt Valley, just north of Wellington. The roads were very busy. The complex of motorways was difficult to negotiate and Rose began to panic as co-driver and map-reader. Colin was never patient when the map-reader made mistakes. Finally, they glimpsed the sea. They were just above the port and the ferry terminal. They parked the car in the requisite lane for boarding the ferry, checked their tickets and realised they had quite a wait before departure. They were trapped in the car, now, so lunch would have to be delayed until then. As they waited a call came in on Rose's mobile phone from a former colleague in Bahrein.

'It's Melissa - do you remember her? Did you know her or her husband?' Rose asked Colin, who had known some of the same GPC staff.

'I think so. Not too sure.'

'Well, she wants to meet up. But I don't know how we can do that. We are rather stuck here in this queue, aren't we?'

'Mm. It's a pity we didn't just park up before getting in line here.'

'Never mind. At least we know we will get on the boat OK.'

With cars lined up all around them there was no escaping the ferry boarding queue, so a brief phone conversation was all that could be managed. So many things to do at the same time was a scenario Rose had grown accustomed to all her life. She hoped that one day she would be able to either move more slowly or even settle down. She aspired to boredom, or at least a less hectic existence.

'See you in Farmerston, perhaps, Mel? It would be great to catch up properly.'

The huge ship tooted its horn and they were off. The ferry maneouvred its way out of port and into the Foveaux Straits. This journey could be treacherous, as the *Wahine* disaster of April, 1968 had proven. If the weather was even slightly inclement, the crossing could be unpleasant. Fortunately for them, it was calm if cool. Wellington itself had been windy, far more so than either of them had expected. But here on board it was refreshing to breathe the sea air and view the amazingly blue sea. The two coasts offered broad vistas with many enticing inlets and coves, giving an impression of an exciting seascape. Overhead seagulls and the occasional albatross steered their way through the skies, looking for any titbits in the ship's wake.

'Shall we go down and get some lunch? Are you hungry?'

'We might as well - how long will the ride be?'

'About two and a half hours I think. If we eat now, then we can drive straight on to Nelson when we disembark.'

The fare on board was attractively presented. They chose a light meal and avoided any alcohol as they needed to drive on arrival in Picton.

'I should have had a look at the map to see where we will be going.'

'Oh, don't worry. Just relax. It can't be that difficult, can it?'

In fact, it wasn't quite as easy as they had hoped. On disembarking at Picton it appeared that all the other drivers were very familiar with the route. They found themselves in a queue to get onto State Highway 1 heading south towards Blenheim. Once they were on the road, there was no exit to get off.

'I didn't really want to come this way. It's taking us off course. We should have gone towards Nelson much earlier.'

'Well, we didn't get much choice, did we? I'll try to get us off this road. We can turn around and go back.'

'Yes, it seems mad, but I think that's the best thing to do.'

After several kilometres racing with the pack southwards, Colin managed to take a slip road which enabled them to do a U-turn. As they pulled into Picton once again, this time in a more leisurely fashion, they could easily see the coastal road towards Nelson on the outskirts of the town. They filled up with petrol then set off down what seemed at times to be a cart-track rather than a road. Luckily there was very little other traffic, so they could pull in to view the wonderful Queen Charlotte Sounds seascapes as they travelled from east to west across the northern coast of the South Island. Some of the hamlets they went through were delightfully reminiscent of the south coast of England, and the sun shone warmly as they wended their way towards Nelson. They wished they had more time to enjoy a walk in the area.

On the edge of this seaside resort there was a proliferation of motels and bed and breakfast signs. Eventually they came to a quiet, broad street, with a medium-sized motel which offered off-street parking. After checking in they set off with a street map to explore this well-known artists' colony. As it was already after 6pm they did not expect to find anything open, but a taste of the town was all they wanted. Rose had purchased a couple of garden statues by a Nelson artist from that year's Farmerston home show so had the impression that Nelson would be chockfull of lovely artists' studios. After a couple of kilometres walking through wide, tree-lined avenues, they realised that there was very little of interest they could find on foot.

Disappointed but now tired, hungry and unwilling to drive around after their long day, they welcomed the sight of a takeaway shop. With deep-fried prawns, chips, and a pottle of tartare sauce, plus a couple of bottles of beer from a nearby liquor shop they made their way back to the motel. After eating, they climbed into bed to watch TV but Colin was soon fast asleep. Rose managed to catch up with the headlines on CNN before she fell asleep too. No news from Iraq tonight. Touring was fun but tiring.

CHAPTER 26

Romance in Hong Kong

October 1991

At the end of September, around my 44th birthday, Neil and Alice injected some glamour into my social life by inviting me to their wedding party for those friends and colleagues who hadn't been able to get to their summer vacation wedding in Edinburgh. The party was a glamorous affair held in the University Chapel Hall and I was glad to be able to wear new green leather high heels with a matching clutch handbag, found on a foray to a well known Western shoe shop. Chinese shoe shops didn't usually carry sizes suitable for Western women. The designer shops had Western sizes, but my budget didn't allow for Christian Dior shoes, though I'd once owned a Charles Jourdan pair purchased second hand from my Uni buddy, Marie. As the party was informal, I wore a green day dress purchased that summer in the UK, so it fitted me sleekly. I was pleased to note that I was almost as slim as the Chinese girls I saw around me on a daily basis, and my green shoes and bag went perfectly with my dress. This was going to be a night to remember, dressing up, even though unescorted. I wondered if Nabeel would mind. I decided I wouldn't tell him about the party to avoid any possible jealousy.

The Hall was right next door to the Hong Kong Towers blocks, so I could walk round to the venue as dusk fell that Saturday night. There was a bring your own bar, so I placed my bottle of white wine on the table and accepted a glass of fizz from Neil as he and Alice greeted me. I'd taken them a wedding present on their big day in Edinburgh, so nothing more was expected of me. I looked around and seeing a few of my Language Centre colleagues, went over to join them. After a few drinks people began dancing, and although I had no partner, I was asked to dance by several of the men at the function, including Neil. I loved dancing, so was very happy. In no time it seemed the party was over, with only a few guests remaining. The live band played a romantic last dance, and I picked up my clutch to leave.

As I made my way to say goodbye to my hosts a young but prematurely balding Chinese man stopped me. We had danced earlier and had talked a little. He was an engineer, a faculty member, and his incipient baldness and serious demeanour made him appear older. With a Ph.D. in Engineering and five years experience in University teaching he must have been over 30 years old but younger than me. We danced the slow dance and the music, the physical contact, and admittedly the wine I had drunk began to work on my emotions. After the slow dance I felt I should leave, but Chong urged me to stay. Since the band played on and Neil and Alice were still on the floor it seemed appropriate to continue. After that I said I really must go and Chong said he would escort me home. As it was midnight I felt that would be a good idea, not being used to walking around at night.

We said good night to our hosts and left together despite potentially prying eyes. We had no reason to feel ashamed of walking home together as colleagues.

'Where do you live, Rose?'

'I'm in Hong Kong Towers.'

'Me too! In block 3.'

'I'm in block 2.'

'That's great. Take my arm. The walkways around here can be uneven.'

Arm in arm we walked the short distance back to the Towers. I wondered if it was polite to invite Chong for a nightcap or if it would be considered 'fast'. Uncertain what to do, but erring on the side of politeness, I offered him coffee as we came to the midpoint between our buildings.

'Well, I don't drink coffee at night, but brandy would be good.'

I knew that Chinese men believe that brandy allows for better yin/yang balance. Luckily I always kept my drinks cupboard stocked, even when in dire straits financially.

'OK. I've got brandy. I'm on the 7th floor.'

We took the lift and I took a deep breath. I had just invited a man into my home. I knew he was a bachelor but I couldn't remember if I'd said I was married or not. Whatever, it was only a drink invitation after all. As Chong followed me into my flat he looked around.

'Oh, just like mine.'

'Really? I guess all the apartments are similar at first. I haven't had time to introduce any soft furnishings yet.'

He sat down on one of the large clunky armchairs, upholstered in 'university green', the standard colour for the basic sofa and two armchairs which came with the flat. I went into the kitchen for the brandy and two wine glasses.

'Sorry I haven't got brandy balloons yet. I've only just started shopping.'

'Oh. Do you like shopping?'

'Yes, it's fun everywhere, but here it's more exciting.'

'Yes, Hong Kong Chinese love to shop. It's our major pastime.'

'I see. But do men enjoy shopping as much as women?'

'Indeed. We could go shopping one day. I know where there are better bargains, away from the tourists.'

'That would be great. Thanks for the offer.'

'I'll take you to the best place for Chinese food too.'

I hesitated to say anything which might firm up this offer in case it was 'late night madness' talking but Chong pursued the matter himself.

'How about next weekend?'

'Yes, great, but could we go on Sunday? I like to get some work done on Saturday.'

'That's fine. I usually go into work on Saturdays to get ahead for the week.'

'Great. Thanks very much. That's very kind of you.'

As he sipped his drink he seemed to relax a bit more, and did not seem ready to leave.

I wondered if he was going to make a move. After all, we had danced well together and I was looking my best. What would I do if faced with intimacy?

'Well, I'd better be going now. It's late.'

'OK. It was a great evening. Thanks for walking me home safely.'

'Thanks for the cognac. It was a good one.'

We stood up and walked to the front door, where he turned and kissed me. As he felt me reciprocate, he snapped off the lights and held me close. The kiss lasted long enough to sway my logical mind and ignite my latent erogenous zones. With our arms wrapped around each other, he led me to my bedroom. There was enough light from the uncurtained windows to see our way without impediment. What happened next was both unexpected and new to me. I felt more ardour for this man than I had ever felt for my husband. Feeling Chong's smooth, hairless skin next to mine was like handling expensive Chinese silk. Our love-making was passionate and renewed throughout the night till at dawn Chong whispered in my ear as I dozed.

'I have to go. Can I use the backstairs?'

'Of course.'

It suited me very well that he was keen to keep the lid on our lust. Mindful of the Hong Kong goldfish bowl effect, I slipped out of bed and pulled on a robe as he got into his clothes. As he left by the maid's entrance, he whispered,

'Have a good Sunday.'

'You too.'

'And see you next Sunday, OK?'

My heart leaped with joy. This wasn't a one night stand. He was willing to see me again. Even if he hadn't meant the date seriously, I didn't really care. One night would have been enough to save me from the sexual wilderness I had been in during my marriage.

'OK. Have a good week.'

I moved to kiss him on the cheek to say goodbye, but he kissed me warmly on the mouth instead. My body thrilled again but tiredness made me glad that he turned and ran down the stairs. Oh what a night! As I climbed back into bed I reran the events. I would never forget the flame that burned through me during those hours. Guilt began to edge into my mind as I remembered that the next day I would have to call Nabeel. It was easy to push the thought away as I climbed back into bed and wrapped the crumpled sheets around me, a physical reminder of a night of bliss such as I had never had before. Tomorrow was in fact today, but I needed to sleep for a few hours before I got my senses together to call Kuwait. The implications of what had happened could be handled later. For now, I was happier than I had been for a long time.

On Sunday my call to Nabeel in Kuwait was prosaic. I described the party briefly and felt no guilt about my omissions. What happens in Hong Kong stays in Hong Kong, I hoped. I knew the affair was temporary, but its effect would be permanent. Back at work on Monday, I met up with Vicky for lunch. My former colleague from Kuwait was a reliable ally, sharing as we did the experience of moving from teaching in the Middle East to the Far East. Both teaching locations were monolingual, i.e. the students all shared a common mother tongue, but our profession entailed using only the target language, English, to extend our students' knowledge and skills in English. Even though we didn't need to speak the students' mother tongues, a knowledge of them was a valuable asset.

During my years in Kuwait I'd learned Arabic despite the unwillingness of my in-laws to speak Arabic to me. My husband and his family were happy to have a language in which they could keep secrets but I was a good language learner and taught myself, practising with the students and staff at work. I decided I would try to learn some Chinese while I was in

Hong Kong, though which of the two dominant Chinese languages to learn was an issue. Hong Kong Chinese speak Cantonese, which has nine tones, while the predominant language, Mandarin has only four. In the end, this simplicity decided me. I attended classes in *putonghua*.

In Kuwait I had regularly presented papers based on my practical work experience and knowledge of ESOL and teacher education, but real research had not been possible in my working situation previously. Now I was able to join a group of teachers, as Neil had suggested, who were investigating independent learning. My new colleagues were open, inviting and encouraging as they led our little group in our similarly focussed, but each slightly different research studies. Our research group utilised the optimum blend of teamwork and individual freedom: We met once a month to share our feedback and keep up our motivation for our individual projects, which had to be accomplished in addition to our teaching workload.

As well as my teaching and my research, I was able to get involved in editing the Language Centre Newsletter. I had worked with Neil in Kuwait on the *English for Medical and Paramedical Purposes Newsletter* he had founded and circulated internationally with financial support from the University for this small, free, publication. With my full time teaching load, my Extra Mural evening classes teaching Master's Degree level Economics students and some British Council teaching, plus the editing and 'A' level test writing, I felt fully engaged in my professional life.

To this mix, of course, I had to add my secret romantic involvement. Our only 'date', which took place the week following our first 'hook up', did not go well. To cope with the heat I wore loose trousers and a cotton shirt. In the broad light of day I didn't feel as glamorous as I had on our midnight hook up. In addition, I think Chong felt rather exposed, out in public with a Western woman. Out shopping we attracted some attention from the usually reticent Chinese population. Conducting a relationship so visibly across cultures would not be easy. From then on we only met in my flat but our trysts became purely physical and not very satisfying to me. About three weeks later I noticed a beautiful young Chinese female staff member sitting with Chong and his colleagues at lunch. Our relationship was at an end. I had guarded my heart and hidden the brief affair, given my marital status and my age, so all was well.

By Thanksgiving, the fourth Thursday in November, I was ready to offer some traditional roast turkey hospitality to my group of friends. I had new Chinese crockery and cutlery for the table. My lavish drapes for the huge French windows were in impressionist hues of pink, blue, green and white. My new rattan furniture was covered in pink watershot silk. The standard hard furniture was covered in pale blue cotton with cushion covers matching the drapes. The colour palette of the sitting room picked up the tones of the sea and sky especially at sunset. I felt proud of how far I had come in such a short time. I had spent everything I earned so far on making my apartment comfortable and as beautiful as my Libran nature could desire. I enjoyed my work and I looked forward to continuing it. If Nabeel insisted on staying in Kuwait, then I needed to rethink our future together.

A week or so later I was invited to a colleague's lunch party where I met Harold, an American visiting professor. He was handsome, with a designer beard and a heavy physique. The American accent and well modulated deep voice attracted me and his first question amused me: 'What's your emotional geography?'

I laughed outright, wondering at the same time if this line was taken from some famous writer I had not read.

'Well, I'm flying solo but I'm married. It's a long story.'

I was reluctant to go into the details of Kuwait at this point. It was too complicated and telling the story always made me sad afterwards. 'What about you?'

'Flying solo and divorced, with a grown up daughter back in New York. Have you got any kids?'

'No, again, a very long story for another day.'

'What do you do here?'

'I'm in the Language Centre. I teach English, language not literature.'

'Wow. I admire the life you language teachers have, trotting around the world, having fun.'

'Yes, we have fun, but we don't get paid much, you know. We are quite low on the tertiary career ladder.'

'I didn't know that. You could make some money writing a book though.'

'Yes, I suppose I could, if I had time. We teach 20 hours a week, you know.'

'Wow. Our load is 12, with reductions for responsibility.'

'Exactly. But you have to do research. We don't. Enough of work. How do you like Hong Kong?'

'I find it interesting. I've explored a fair bit, but there's more to do. What about you?'

'Well, in my two months here I've been settling in, setting up my apartment.'

'We should explore together. What about concerts? Would you like to come along one evening?'

'I really would. That would be great.'

And so began a valued friendship which lasted the rest of the academic year. On most Saturday evenings we would go to concerts together. Harold dressed well and looked like an influential banker. I was enjoying wearing my new up to the minute clothes. We made a smart pair, but our relationship was purely platonic. Over our musical dates I gradually shared some of my story as best I understood it myself at the time. The dialogue we were having about my life inhibited any involvement of a sexual nature. Ours was the life of the mind.

As well as enriching my life with concerts I began to go dancing with a girlfriend who was married to the University Registrar, so we could chaperone each other at nightclubs. The overall effect of the development of my social life on me was like breaking one's fast after Ramadan. I felt happy, excited and fulfilled both at work and socially. I shared very little of my social life with Nabeel in our weekly phone conversations. I was only in my 40s, but living in Kuwait had restricted my life so greatly that I felt old before my time. I had taken a huge risk with my Chinese lover but it was worth it. I had learned a lot about the weaknesses in my marital sex life.

CHAPTER 27

The West Coast, South Island

Xmas 2003

The next morning after cups of tea Rose and Colin headed off to their next destination, Greymouth, a former mining town on the West Coast of the South Island. As they drove along the Coast Road the stunning views were accompanied by much wilder weather. They made a stop at Westport to visit Cape Foulwind, aptly named by Captain Cook in 1770. They enjoyed the broad seascapes and endless horizons, as well as watching the local seal colony. 50 kilometres further south the cliffs and water spouts at *Punakaiki*, Pancake Rocks, were amazing. The drive along the coast was thrilling but they were glad to reach their destination, where they had pre-booked a motel room with seaviews.

After checking in Rose and Colin went in search of an evening meal. They found a fish and chip takeaway that offered battered Green Lip mussels at prices cheaper than in the North Island but they tussled with their order for two scoops of chips. It seemed that even very hungry people did not usually order two scoops! Succumbing to local advice, they found that one scoop with two fish portions and half a dozen huge fried mussels provided a plentiful meal. As the evening was still warm and sunny, they settled themselves at an outdoor table and ate their food. It was delicious enough without any wine but they picked up a bottle of chilled New Zealand *Riesling* at a liquor store to enjoy in their room afterwards.

They set off promptly the next morning to start the southern West Coast drive. They drove along enjoying the coastal views till they reached Hokitika where they indulged in *pounamu* shopping. They found a small craft shop with genuine New Zealand jade which was being carved *in situ* into traditional Maori designs. Rose chose a *taiaha* for herself and one for Heather. A fighting stick might originally have been a male prerogative but this was the 21st century and new customs prevailed. They stopped for lunch in Pukekura, famous for its Possum Pie cafe. Colin was intrigued but unwilling to risk his stomach opted for steak and cheese with potato topping. As they drove further south down the West Coast the landscape became visibly more rugged. In the distance there were mountain peaks glistening with snow in the summer sunlight. As they finally pulled into the small town of Franz Josef they had the impression they were arriving in a Swiss village. There were brightly decorated shops along the main street selling souvenirs as well as walking and climbing equipment. First, however, they needed to find a motel. As they drove slowly along the main street, they spotted a Swiss Chalet facade with a Vacancy sign. They booked in, dumped their bags, then walked around the village to find some dinner.

There was a wide selection of cafes, but in the warm late afternoon sunshine they selected a pub where they could sit outside. The food was delicious, washed down with a 'handle' of cold lager. At times like these, when the two of them seemed so completely in sync and could enjoy each other's company without stress, Rose wondered why their relationship had broken down in rows so often. They were compatible in so many ways. After their meal they strolled along the main street. Rose didn't need to shop so sat in the sunshine outside a gift shop. Colin moved rather purposefully around inside. Then a thought struck Rose like a dart to her heart. Had he taken this opportunity to look around on his own because he was choosing a post card or a souvenir for someone back home? Trust was still absent from her side of the relationship and unlikely to return without great effort on her part and reassurance on his. Reluctant to spoil the moment she said nothing.

'Ready to roll?'

'Sure. Let's go back and work out how to access the Glacier tomorrow.'

Despite their best efforts to plan for the next day they quickly found themselves asleep. The next morning they were up early to find the car park close to the Franz Josef Glacier. From there it was an easy but long hike to the ice, which was retreating every year. As they walked they avoided the puddles and pools being filled by the melting ice stream. When they finally arrived at the Glacier, and began to climb higher to where the ice was cleaner Rose was amazed to see the streaks of vivid blue in the rather dingy white ice. Colin had visited Iceland as part of his science degree in the '60s, so he was more familiar with this landscape. Rose was curious.

'How long did you stay in the camp? Did you sleep in cabins or tents?'

'We had tents.'

'And who did you go with? The girl you later married?'

'No, the trip was well before then.'

Rose could see from the small smile which played around Colin's lips that he hadn't forgotten his experiences even so long ago. She couldn't be jealous of those, could she? That would be crazy.

'Do you wish you'd spent longer teaching science?'

'Not really. The kids weren't too bad, but some of them were unteachable. That's why I moved into educational management.'

'I see. I felt the same. I didn't want to discipline kids. That's their parents' job. I just wanted to teach French. So I moved into tertiary teaching.'

After coming to an area where spiked boots were necessary, they turned around and retraced their steps. Back at the car park they were sweating under the hot sun.

'That was such fun. My first glacier.' Rose laughed. 'But isn't it amazing how much of the Glacier has melted. Look at this map on the signboard. This car park is where the Glacier ended previously. Now it's a good kilometre's walk to the ice.'

'Yup. Global warming isn't a figment of the imagination when you come here, is it?'

They drove back to the motel for a shower and change of clothes after the long walk. Then they sought out a different cafe for an early dinner and an early night ready for the next leg of their journey in the morning to the Fox Glacier.

The weather was wet and grey as they set off the next day. The sea pounded onto the shores of the West Coast, and dark clouds were gathered and threatening over the Land of the Long White Cloud. The journey to the Fox Glacier was short but they decided to visit Lake Mathieson instead of walking up a glacial valley in bad weather. The walk around the Lake was beautiful and sheltered. They heard bell birds and took photographs of the trees reflected in the still clear water before heading back on SH 6 south towards Haast where they decided to rest up for the night. The motel was clean and tidy and memorable for its pub food. The next day they set off at dawn for the long drive to Queenstown. The topography as they travelled was more open and less dramatic. Then as SH6 reached Lake Wanaka and Lake Hawea the scenery became more impressive, with vivid blue water in deep ravines next to the road.

'Shall we stop for a look-see in Wanaka?' Colin asked.

'Cool. It's very pretty here, isn't it?'

The car park was right on the Lake, so they could take a short walk and get a coffee and sandwich at the same time. The weather was bright and sunny again, and they enjoyed the resort feeling of the town but they weren't inclined to linger.

'Come on, let's push on to be sure to find a motel in Queenstown. It'll be Xmas Eve tomorrow, do you realise? It's the school holidays so I don't know how crowded hotels will be.' Rose was anxious to enjoy Xmas with Colin.

'I wonder if it will snow and give us a white Xmas!'

'I hope not. I prefer snow in pictures only!'

The rest of the journey to Queenstown was terrifying as they chose the high road, 1121 metres in places along the Cardrona River, which was almost deserted. As they drove through Arrowtown, the former gold rush settlement, the road became busier.

'At last! Some other travellers.'

'Yes, look! The world hasn't ended then.'

As there was no snow, the ski slopes were not open yet, so the town was fairly quiet. Not far from the centre of town they noticed a large hotel facing Lake Wakatipu, so pulled in to check on rooms and prices. It was more expensive than other places they'd stayed in so far but it was Xmas after all. They could push the boat out a little. They even booked themselves into the Xmas Special Dinner as they checked in. While they unpacked, showered and changed ready for their evening drinks and meal, they discussed the revised schedule.

'We could spend tomorrow, Xmas Eve, doing the fiords, then have a quiet Xmas Day resting up, ready for the journey to Mount Cook on Boxing Day,' Rose suggested.

'Sounds good. Let's do that,' Colin agreed readily.

As so often, they were in unison, and Rose felt the pang of longing deep in her heart for a steady, quiet relationship based on trust. She'd given Colin a heart of gold one Xmas, a pretty tree decoration, but she didn't now believe that she had given it to the right person. How did the pop song go? *'Last Xmas I gave you my heart, but the very next day you gave it away.'* Pop songs often expressed sentiments which Rose felt were right on target with her life. This year she hadn't prepared any gifts and she hoped Colin hadn't either. That evening they dined at a cafe a short walk from their hotel.

'You are lucky to have such a range of wine at these prices in restaurants. In London there'd be a huge mark up.'

'Yes, but we Kiwis don't earn that much, you know. Prices can't go sky high. And it's wonderful that I don't need a liquor licence to buy wine any more!'

'Indeed. Those were the bad old days, weren't they?'

'In some ways... But you know, I had a strange experience at Easter.'

'Really? ...with wine?'

'Yes, I went over to the Bay of Plenty to look at sections and houses, and I stayed in a motel for Friday night. I didn't carry any wine from Farmerston - rather like taking coals to Newcastle, hey? So when I arrived I stopped in a dairy - you know, a little shop, or superette as they call them here, to get some food and wine, and guess what?'

'What?'

'Shops can't sell wine on Good Friday. And the same is true on Easter Sunday.'

'Amazing. Culture shock! Do you think that will happen tomorrow?'

'Probably not tomorrow, but Xmas Day for sure.'

'Let's buy some wine then to take us through the religious holiday, shall we?!'

They wandered back to the hotel, taking in a liquor store *en route,* and went back to the room for a glass of the Extra Reserve ready-chilled *pinot gris* they had bought.

The next morning bright and early Rose and Colin were on the road south and west to Te Anau. Lupins were colourful and prolific on the sides of the road. The forest on either side was thick in places and there were very few other travellers. The tunnel through the mountains was a surprise and a little scary, then suddenly they were at the port, with its huge car and coach park. They were early enough to find a good boat to tour Milford Sound and excellent seats on deck. They observed the many waterfalls gushing from high cliffs into the fiord but retreated under cover when the captain pushed the prow right under one of the falls for a good-humoured passenger 'baptism'.

'I'm glad we did this, aren't you?' asked Colin.

'Yes, it's great. A long drive, but well worth doing.'

'When we get off, let's try to be near the front, so that we can get to the car park quickly and exit before the others. There will be a huge traffic jam I reckon.'

As many of the passengers were on tour buses there was no need to worry about traffic. The high spot of the drive back to Queenstown was a brief stop in the car park near the tunnel where the alpine parrots, the *kea*, were noted for their cheekiness and daring, with a proclivity for eating windscreen wipers on tourists' cars!

That evening they had dinner in the room, tired after so much driving. Rose missed the traditions she had established over the years in Kuwait: a huge Xmas party with carols around the piano on Xmas Eve, then a family gathering with a splendid turkey on Xmas Day. This was the first Xmas she had ever spent in a hotel. Feeling a little melancholy, she turned on the TV and noted that a world away Saddam was being given health checks after spending six months in a tunnel. Rose felt strangely sorry for his humiliation, photographed in his underwear. On the other hand she was relieved to learn that a US Library of Congress team had visited Iraq's National Library and found that the stacks sealed by Iraqi librarians in April had survived the bombs. However, before fleeing, Saddam had ordered the archives of his Government from 1979 to be burned so as to hide the details of his cruel reign of terror. *Blue on blue* for his own people, who would take their own revenge later.

CHAPTER 28

Return to Beirut, Kuwait, UK

Xmas 1991, Easter, Summer and Xmas 1992

By Xmas 1991 I'd re-established myself as an independent woman in Hong Kong so the journey to Beirut to meet up with Nabeel put a brake on my rapid development. I'd been asked to buy some Chinese upholstery silk to renovate the sitting room furniture in the family's Kuwait villa. They had two eight-piece Chinese sitting room suites so needed a large quantity of silk which would be heavy to transport as well as expensive. But the price of silk in Hong Kong was cheaper than in the Middle East and there was more choice available so I paid for it myself as well as my air ticket to Beirut. I wondered if I would be reimbursed or whether this was Nabeel's way of ensuring I didn't build up any savings to try to make a getaway from the marriage. I hadn't told him what I was earning from my fulltime and part-time jobs and he hadn't asked. On the way back to Beirut for Christmas I had to overnight in Dubai. It was strange to be alone in the hotel observing others at dinner and wondering what their 'backstory' was. I had to admit I felt lonely and began to examine my motives in trying to keep my marriage going. I'd been unfaithful and enjoyed the brief fling. Was I trying to fix something which was completely broken or merely cracked by the Invasion and subsequent war?

My first visit to Beirut had been in 1973 when we'd scandalised the family by turning up as an unmarried couple. This was possible in Beirut, the Paris of the Middle East, but certainly not in the Gulf. We'd had fun meeting Nabeel's friends and his sister's family then and I hoped we'd have fun again. The Lebanese are known for their party-minded spirit and their 'never say die' attitude. The Civil War which began in 1975 had scarred but not changed them. Henri, Asma, and Adel had gone back to Beirut permanently, leaving only Edouard in Kuwait working with Nabeel on the commercial side of their company.

I was thrilled to see the things that Nabeel had retrieved from our home in Kuwait, especially my gold and silver jewellery. But most of the clothes he'd saved were not only unfashionable but too big for my Hong Kong figure. I'd reduced without trying to the girlish frame I had when I married. So Nabeel took me shopping for a new outfit for the New Year's Eve party in a nightclub in downtown Beirut, now peaceful after six years of fighting.

'Buy anything you like. I want you to look good. We'll have a great life here when you come back from Hong Kong. I'm going to look for a flat with a sea view. It will be better than you've got in Hong Kong.'

I was dubious about that, but in fact, the party was fun and I felt happy for the family that Beirut seemed to be returning to how it used to be, the Paris of the Middle East.

Next day we enjoyed being up in the mountains with Nabeel's sister's family, this time without the sound of shelling as when we had gone to Beirut for Nabeel's nephew's funeral in 1980. Nabeel had helped the young man to study medicine in France, but the boy had failed anatomy twice and been dismissed. While working for the Red Cross during the Lebanese Civil War he had become depressed and finally had killed himself. The memory of that sad occasion came back clearly. Given the local traditions of mourning, I had realised then that I did not want to sit around my own husband's open coffin for days. I had to face up to my feelings. After living away from him I knew I couldn't keep my marriage vows. I did not want to stay with him till death parted us.

I had every reason to reflect on Nabeel's mortality when he told me that a recent chest X-ray had revealed a shadow on one lung. The cause could be lung cancer or tuberculosis (TB). My own health was now in question. If Nabeel had TB, then during this Xmas/New Year holiday I might have contracted it too. Some Xmas present! Although my health checks for my new job had shown a clear chest X-ray I was advised by Nabeel's doctor to have another check up when I got back to Hong Kong. If Nabeel had cancer as a result of his heavy smoking, then I might be susceptible after years of breathing secondary smoke. To calm my nerves I played my piano brought over from Kuwait. Asma's piano from Kuwait was standing beside it, like a twin! Everything seemed strange, especially the shock of discovering handwriting on our framed photo, which Nabeel had retrieved from our trashed home. On the back someone had scrawled a sinister message: 'I know you but I do not love you'. After one week in wartorn Beirut I was ready to return to my new life in the Far

East, which after only three months seemed more like home than the Middle East where I'd lived for the past 15 years.

First, however, I had to visit Nabeel's new flat in Kuwait, changing the stopover on my air ticket. He wanted to show me his fully furnished apartment. Two items from our former home were in pride of place on the coffee table in the lounge, a small jade lion, the only one remaining of a pair, and one solitary *cloisonne* chopstick. The whole of our married life in Kuwait was summed up in those two items. The brothers' office on the Sheraton Roundabout was functioning normally but a Philippina secretary was at work as Nabeel's personal assistant. She seemed to have taken on some extremely personal duties, such as giving him a pedicure. His chronic back problems meant that he could not bend forward to cut his own toenails. I commented that she must be very dedicated and wondered to myself just how far duty was involved or some other sentiment? The scent of money might make this tall, skinny, balding, big-nosed man attractive I supposed. I was used to his appearance having changed myself over time but Nabeel had certainly not won the lottery of good looks his brothers enjoyed. They were all much more handsome in Omar Sharif style. Our time together was thankfully short as we bickered about small things, about buying a flat in Lebanon, as well as arguing about politics again.

Back in Hong Kong my chest X-ray came back negative and I thankfully resumed my single life and busy work. Easter holidays were coming but I really did not want to go back to Kuwait again even though I had to keep up appearances and I still felt some loyalty to Nabeel. In my weaker moments, afraid of upsetting the status quo, I somehow hoped to rekindle our marriage. Saddam Hussein wasn't going to be allowed to ruin my marriage, I told myself. However, the Easter break found me flying to Seoul to assess the Teaching Diploma for English language teachers in South Korea. I was glad to be back in my professional assessor capacity and it was fun to be in a new country, with old friends and former colleagues from Kuwait. The question uppermost in my mind, however, was where I would spend the next summer holidays. Could I face another return to Kuwait?

As it happened, my younger brother John provided me with the perfect excuse not to return to Kuwait for the whole of summer. He'd recently separated from his wife and his three children were experiencing the difficulties of living with their Mum during the week and their Dad at the weekend. I wanted to give them a holiday to remember. Nabeel agreed to my travelling back to the UK first, but wanted me to visit him too to discuss the future. In September I was to present my research paper to a university conference and I made an appointment to visit my MA tutor in Birmingham. I had a lot of preparation to do, completing my research and teaching duties and planning a trip for myself, Mum, John and three children, aged 3, 5 and 8 to Paris Disneyworld. We would travel by car from Mossfield, and spend a week in one of the themed hotels. We all began to get excited as the plan developed. As John was a qualified and experienced bus driver he would do the driving, with Mum riding comfortably in the front passenger seat. I would sit in the back with the three small children.

Our plan worked out perfectly. We had a safe, easy trip to the Channel Ferry at Dover, a calm sailing across the English Channel, and a first night in a motel at Boulogne. My older niece stayed in a room with me and Mum, causing her to muse out loud, 'We're just like the Golden Girls, aren't we?' Indeed we were. The youngest child amused us all with her attempts to speak French. Although she hadn't been able to grasp the concept of 'country' she realised the waiters couldn't understand English and used French to order *pommes frites*. Next day after negotiating some tricky ring roads in Paris we checked into the Wild West Hotel. We had chosen very well since the beds were high enough for Mum to get herself unassisted onto and off the bed. The weather was good so we could enjoy the rides and stroll around the park in the bright sunshine. It was a welcome break for all of us.

Reluctantly I spent a week in Kuwait, discussing future possibilities.

'I know it seems strange to you, but I'm not willing to break my three year contract after only one year. I've made great progress at work, and I don't want to give up these opportunities to come back here.'

'What about going back to Beirut?'

'Are you ready to leave Kuwait now? I thought you wanted to be back here.'

'Well, not yet, things are going very well, I didn't lose any capital and it's good for me again.'

'Yes, but remember, it's not the same for me. I've finally got some research opportunities and here there's only teaching. I can't go backwards.'

'OK. I'll leave it for now. I understand your position.'

Thankfully I left him to his happy days in his old office and returned to the UK to spend time with Mum and prepare for my conference presentation at Aston University. I was not so happy realising how much emotional distance now separated me from my husband. The sympathy I'd felt for him after learning about his life as a Palestinian with no right to return to his native land had not faded, but my motivation to stay with him had declined as a result of our constant quarrels and the putdowns I was subjected to, together with the restrictions of life in Kuwait.

After spending the rest of summer in the UK I returned to Hong Kong looking forward to meeting up again with old and new friends. Harold had spent the summer travelling and would be completing his sabbatical year before Xmas. He introduced me to his replacement, Kyle, an Emily Dickenson scholar. Kyle's manner and appearance belied his professorial status back home. He was short and stocky, with a full head of curly hair and twinkling green eyes, like an oversized leprechaun. With Irish ancestry he certainly had the gift of the blarney and an obvious eye for the ladies. We became a threesome on our trips to concerts, enjoying each other's company till the day he made a pass at me.

It was late evening after a party. We went home together in a taxi, dropping Harold off first while Kyle offered to see me to my apartment safely. I didn't refuse. We'd all had a few drinks and the night was young. I was in the mood for more research to confirm my hypothesis that my marriage was over. If Harold had made the right move, things could have gone his way, but he was a true gentleman so I had to be a lady. Kyle's move was passionate, and it moved us to another level in our friendship which we had to keep secret from Harold so that he would not judge us. He eventually found us out and was very angry. As friends we'd betrayed his trust. As a potential lover he'd been ignored. As a Jew, he may have felt that he was contributing to better Palestinian

Israeli relationships by respecting the wife of a Palestinian Christian. The problem was that Kyle couldn't care less about any of those issues, while I was happy to take whatever opportunities presented themselves at this investigative stage in my emotional development. I wanted some fun.

I liked Kyle's humour, conversation, and though baptised a Catholic, his lack of concern about religion. His experience of world travel was similar to mine though his social class was superior. He'd experienced schooling overseas and his retired parents lived in comfort and style near Washington, D.C. But like me he had emotional baggage. He'd met and married a Russian beauty despite the challenges of the Cold War. That wife had left him for someone with more money after getting to the USA. He owned a small ranch in Texas where he'd lived with his second wife. That relationship too had ended. His potential for fidelity was not his strong suit. In his work with adult students teaching poetry there was scope for flights of fancy plus the temptation to act on some of them.

We had various impromptu trysts in his office but we managed to keep our relationship low key so as not to pique outside interest. No one really knew the full complexity of my life as I had various strands involving different friends. My Chinese friend, Carrie, worked in the General Office but spoke hardly any English. I began teaching her twice a week in my office at lunch time, so stopped going to the Dining Room every day. Another friend in the Law Department was completing her PhD dissertation on taxation laws in UK offshore territories. We went for walks on the Outer Islands and to parties where she played her trumpet. I edited parts of her thesis and I helped my friend June with her

PhD dissertation by contributing to her surveys. Lucy and I made regular forays to Chinese markets. My full time job was challenging and I had three nights of evening classes. I was a busy lady.

As my second Xmas in Hong Kong drew closer the issue of where to spend it arose. Surprisingly Nabeel agreed to meet on neutral ground. I had had an operation for superficial leg veins, so didn't want to travel far by air. We arranged to meet up in Jakarta. We'd already been to Bali and Lombok earlier in our married life so this time sight-seeing was not our main objective. We would simply spend some time trying to get to know each other again during a relaxing holiday. We had a wonderful New Year's Eve, dining and dancing in our four star hotel discotheque but the next morning, over breakfast in bed, the happy atmosphere was ruined by Nabeel's suspicious questions about details of my life in Hong Kong. I was surprised and enraged. I was a virgin when I met him and had not had any point of comparison to assess his lovemaking. Upset that he should take such a positive moment to start an inquisition I became angry. He had touched on the truth but this was not the moment to reveal it.

'What do you think I've been doing in Hong Kong?' I shouted. 'I've been living a normal life for once. I've escaped from the cage you dragged me into. As for 'I'll marry you one day', why don't you find someone else to marry in the Church? There's no point in hanging on to me if you don't trust me!'

I stormed into the bathroom to cool down, staring at my red face in the mirror. I wasn't ready to introduce the idea of separation and divorce myself yet I wanted out of a marriage I hadn't wanted to enter into. He should have let me be. He may have got what he wanted in the short term, but I'd finally escaped after spending so many years putting up with my circumstances. Kuwait was liberated and returning to normalcy but my life there had ended. I saw no future in returning. However, we had to get through this holiday somehow, so I got into the shower to cool down physically and emotionally. I went back into the bedroom and apologised.

'Look, our lives in Kuwait are limited to work. You know why, and I hope I don't have to remind you. The Invasion has shattered my work prospects, but Hong Kong has given my career back to me. I can see a way to achieving my doctorate and that's not something I want to give up. Can you understand?'

'Yes, I know you like your pieces of paper. Donkeys laden with knowledge is what I think of doctors. Remember when they called me doctor because I was wearing glasses?'

I couldn't help laughing at the memory. 'Yes, but perhaps it was because you were with me, you know.' Nabeel looked at me sceptically. 'It was my picture in the paper, remember? Not yours.'

'OK. Whatever. I'm sorry I upset you. I know you work hard. I'll come and see you at Easter, shall I?'

'Yes, come and see my lovely flat, my office and my friends. Maybe you'll change YOUR mind.'

And so our Christmas holiday ended amicably, though my mind was uneasy still. How could I get out of this marriage without damaging my husband of 16 years?

CHAPTER 29

Fiords, Mount Cook, Wellington, Napier

Xmas 2003, New Year 2004

Xmas morning dawned bright and sunny but not warm.

'Good morning, darling. Merry Xmas!'

Colin slipped a card and a small present under her pillow. So he had planned a gift.

Rose smiled her thanks.

'I'm sorry, darling, I didn't think we'd be doing gifts. Let mine be tonight's special dinner and an excellent wine.'

Colin's family had a tradition of sharing all costs at Xmas as Rose had found out when she visited the family one holiday. Colin's sister and brother-in-law owned a large detached house with extensive, manicured grounds, but everything spent on the Xmas lunch was accounted for and divided by the number of people attending. Rose had found this very strange. In her family food was there to be shared generously. On this trip, however, they were sharing costs, so she could record that night's expenses to her account, rather than the 'kitty' they were keeping jointly for shared expenses.

'That's OK. I didn't expect anything. After all, you've bought the tickets to Tonga. I thought you might like this. I got it in that souvenir shop.'

Colin's gift was a pretty silver and *paua* shell kiwi bird.

'It's delightful. Thank you so much.'

So that was why he had been sneaking around in the shop. Rose felt guilty about mistrusting him. The card's message was sentimental and indicated that Colin might be thinking long term. Rose decided not to broach the subject and risk ruining the moment.

'Come back to bed. We don't have to get up yet. Would you like a mimosa?'

'That sounds great.' Colin slid back between the crisp linen sheets. 'Mm... champagne and orange juice... my favourite breakfast.'

Later after croissants and coffee they decided to drive to Glenorchy along Lake Wakatipu, New Zealand's third largest lake at 84 kms long. The drive was spectacular but there was nowhere open to get a drink, so they drove back to bathe and change before the festive dinner. The six course meal was pleasant but not gourmet standard. There was traditional roast turkey with all the trimmings, including brussels sprouts, one of their favourite vegetables, and crackers and decorations on the table. A live band played Christmas carols, then pop music for dancing, but Colin was unwilling to take to the floor, so they watched some children amusing themselves, running around and sliding on the parquet as their parents danced.

'Can you see it's still light outside? The days are getting longer,' Rose remarked.

'Yes, it's so strange to be celebrating Xmas for the first time in this upside down world. It's a pity it's not warm enough to swim yet!'

'Maybe it's a good thing we've got the tropics to look forward to!'

'Absolutely. This is different, but it doesn't really compare to Xmas in Bahrein, does it?'

'I think we've been spoiled by 5 star hotel dinners in the Gulf, don't you?'

Rose couldn't push the old memory out of her mind of their first Xmas dinner and dance, when she had left early in tears. The next Christmas had repaired that memory with a quiet Xmas at her house, with her Canadian friend, when they'd sung carols around Rose's keyboard. In their three years together at the GPC they had had lots of good times, mostly on island holidays in Thailand and the Philippines. She especially remembered Boracay: a wonderful location, very new on the tourist scene, arriving by boat and riding bicycles around the island. But she knew that for every moment of happiness with Colin she had endured pain at other times. Now she wanted to stay in the moment.

'Come on. If you don't want to dance, let's take a walk, shall we?'

They strolled around the hotel grounds for a few moments, but then withdrew as the evening air turned colder. The rest of the evening was more intimate and soon turned to night. The delightful gift had restored her faith in Colin and raised a hope that all might be well in the future. The gamble of the visit might still pay off.

The next day they checked out early. Colin drove along the twisty road through the Kawarau Gorge to Cromwell and along the Lindis River, then Rose drove along the more sedate stretch of SH8 to Twizel, where they found a motel for the night. After checking in and leaving their bags they pushed on to Mount Cook, the 3,754 metre mountain known in *te reo* as *Aoraki,* 'cloud piercer'. The drive along Lake Pukaki was beautiful and after finding a parking space they headed to the iconic Heritage Hotel which hosts an Alpine Centre.

'I think we need a coffee and some food, don't we?' asked Rose.

'Yeah. I'm hungry. Look at the bronze statue. It's Edmund Hillary. You know, the first man to climb Mt Everest. In 1953, wasn't it?'

'Oh yes, I've read a little about him in the local materials we use for teaching visiting student groups. He's on one of our bank notes too.'

'Which one?'

'Sorry, can't remember. We must look it up in the cafe.'

The young 'Sir Ed' in the statue was gazing towards the summit Aoraki, Mt Cook, a mountain he never in fact climbed himself. Strange that he should persist in the achievement of a lifetime yet never achieve the mountain on his doorstep. After his success with Sherpa Norgay Tensing, Sir Ed had invested a lot of time and money in improving the lot of the Nepalese Sherpa people. He had built schools and hospitals, visiting the place frequently despite the loss of his wife and daughter when their plane crashed on landing for a visit to him. A sacrifice of a lifetime, Rose supposed.

'And we've just celebrated the 50th year of his ascent. It turns out the news was received at the time of Queen Elizabeth's coronation. Do you remember that?'

'Not really. Do you?'

'Well, yes, I was only little, six, I think, but it was like a fairy tale. I can still visualise the gilded coach and immaculately harnessed horses and the wonderful crown and flowing gown she wore. She was so beautiful, and her two little children looked angelic. We had one of the first TVs in our little coal mining village. Surprising really, considering my Dad was a strong socialist, almost a communist. He still enjoyed his TV though.'

'I don't think we had a TV at that time, but we got souvenir coronation mugs, Petra and I.'

'Have you kept them? They might be worth something now.'

'No, long gone.'

'Ours too. My Mum wasn't into keeping things. Pity really.'

'Now, come on, let's get coffee and something to eat.'

After a snack in the crowded cafe the pair walked on in what had become bright sunshine over walkways and bridges, around curving paths and some steeper terrain until it became clear that only serious climbers could go further towards the summit.

'I think we should turn back. Can you feel the change in the wind?'

'Yes. There's a front coming in over there - see the dark sky?' Colin the geographer knew his weather forecasts.

'OK. Let's beat a retreat. Climbers sometimes misjudge the weather, and we're not wearing enough or carrying anything to protect us.'

They hurried back to the car park. They had a long drive ahead, another 80 kms back to Twizel but they were glad to have made this side trip to visit the iconic mountain.

The next day Christchurch was on their agenda, but first they headed for the stunningly turquoise Lake Tekapo and visited the small stone Church of the Good Shepherd, with the dog statue commemorating hardworking sheep dogs. They were not particularly keen on visiting Christchurch itself, billed as a very English city, but they enjoyed the drive away from the mountains, through the verdant coastal agricultural lands. Otago countryside famous for its soft fruits and vineyards stretched endlessly around them, with the peaks of the mountains rising high far away in the distance. They stopped in Geraldine for lunch, a pretty market town, sweltering in the heat of midday and bought homemade jam for breakfast next day. They then took the ring road around Christchurch towards a motel and camping ground on the edge of the city. This place positioned them well for an early start to Kaikoura the next day. They found a fish and chip shop open and enjoyed the meal with a couple of cans of beer. Afterwards they took a walk down to the river, through pine forest.

They saw kingfishers sitting quietly in the trees and egrets/ibis wading in the water. Sitting by the water they relished the peace and solitude. They wished they had more time to take in the beauty of New Zealand, but their Interisland ferry schedule pushed them onwards.

The east coast town of Kaikoura was famous for its whale-watching but they hadn't been able to book a boat trip in advance so they wanted to arrive there early to get a chance of a ride. When they arrived the boat ticket offices in Kaikoura were already buzzing with tourists snapping up the last seats on whale-watching boats. The next best thing was an albatross viewing boat ride. The trip turned out to be extremely interesting. The huge birds were amazingly beautiful and soaringly graceful. All too soon Rose and Colin were eating a seafood evening meal then turning in early so as to catch the Picton ferry in the morning. They awoke in the early hours and drove away from their motel in the dark.

The journey was scary as the narrow winding road paralleled the railway with oncoming trains very close to them in the darkness. Their eventual arrival at the ferry port was a great relief. After departure they settled down for a rest, expecting to have breakfast in Wellington. They had booked a hotel downtown but the Novotel didn't have its own parking. Parking elsewhere was a minor but annoying inconvenience of the kind they were getting used to. After the lifestyle in the Gulf, with the luxury of valet parking or multi-storey car parks in all hotels the somewhat simpler lifestyle in New Zealand took a little getting used to. The famously pioneering Kiwis didn't mind such petty challenges.

They toured Te Papa, the National Museum, and walked around Lambton Quay to window shop, then visited the Beehive, the Parliament Building, and the docksides. There was to be a free New Year's Eve concert outdoors and a ticketed event which they planned to attend even though the names of the Kiwi bands were not known to them. Earlier in the evening, they were able to get tickets to the first week screening of *King Kong,* the new Peter Jackson movie which was drawing crowds. It was showing in a refurbished traditional old cinema with Art Deco style. It was fun to dress up and watch the movie with like-minded, well-dressed people. After that, there was the question of where to have dinner. The evening was warm and some restaurants were advertising expensive set menus but Colin was reluctant to spend more than necessary. So they had a cocktail in one bar then moved to another for some food. Disappointed Rose would have preferred a more scintillating dinner.

As the clock drew near to midnight and the New Year they walked to the public concert area full of families and young children, then moved on to the ticketed venue, where the music from the unfamiliar bands was new to them. Colin, an amateur but skilled drummer, was ill at ease with the uneven sound quality. They were alternately deafened or unable to hear the lyrics depending on their position in the concreted site. It was nothing like the wonderful concerts they had attended together on the beach in the Gulf given by the likes of Tom Jones, Simply Red, or UB40. They were both slightly disappointed that the whole occasion went off like a damp squib, despite the fireworks display at midnight. They kissed at midnight, but felt uncomfortable standing in the ugly urban surroundings amongst strangers much younger than themselves. They were out of time and place it seemed.

All in all Rose felt that the evening had been pleasant, but not pleasurable. The gloss had gone off their holiday somehow. She had even found herself irritated with Colin when he chose a Subway Sandwich for lunch earlier that day. After taking the cable car up to the Botanical Garden and then walking around and back down to the city for a couple of hours Rose would have sat down at any cafe and eaten anything as she was hungry but Colin wanted to take a sandwich back to the room. It was trivial but it reminded her that they were not as in sync as she had thought previously.

However, Rose knew she was notoriously bad-tempered when hungry, so she blamed herself for the *contretemps*.

The last leg of their journey was extended to include a visit to Napier, the town almost levelled by an earthquake in the 1920s and rebuilt in Art Deco style. To celebrate the beauty of the architecture and painting of public and private buildings an annual weekend of festivities is held each Spring/ Summer. Because of the special nature of the town, there was a tourist hum about the place. Cafes and restaurants were full and the streets and beach had more people than Rose and Colin had seen while in the South Island. They found a small motel on the edge of town which had a clean spacious room with kitchenette, but they took the opportunity to savour a feast of fish at a specialty restaurant by the seaside. A crisp *pinot gris* washed down the snapper and scallops they chose for their meal. Afterwards they walked on the beach as the sun set, passing the little mermaid statue, Pania of the Reef, a figure from Maori legend.

Although reluctant to break the peaceful mood of the evening, Rose insisted on checking world news as usual when they got back to their motel room. Colin got ready for bed while Rose sat glued to the TV. The atrocious murders in Fallujah at the end of November had awakened the world to the worsening situation in Iraq, as well as the presence of hundreds of Private Contractors, civilians, who were working alongside the coalition forces with very little physical protection in their vehicles from the growing number of roadside attacks with IEDs.

Expecting more such attacks over the Christian holiday period the US army launched a campaign of pre-emptive strikes against suspected fighters just before Xmas. *Operation*

Iron Grip was one of many campaigns in the theatre of war involving artillery and aircraft to destroy hideouts and kill potential rebel fighters in and around Baghdad. Nevertheless, the Sheraton Hotel, where many foreign journalists stayed, was the target of a rocket attack on Xmas Day and three US soldiers were killed in roadside attacks.

The news item mentioned the presence in Iraq of former Kiwi soldiers who had taken the opportunity to earn some cash by joining the 'contractors'. Their families would be especially worried at this time, Rose knew. She switched off the TV thanking her lucky stars once again that she was in New Zealand. Her own future was not yet clear, but she was safe and well, *elhamdulillah*. She had successfully avoided Gulf War 2 and the threat on her life from Nabeel was slowly receding from her consciousness. Her new, independent life suited her, and as Kyle had warned her, she could only play tennis on one side of the net. If Colin was willing to renew their relationship and give it some permanency, then he would surely tell her that, before he left. She would be willing to give it another go, but only if he promised monogamy!

C H A P T E R 30

Promises

April - November 1993

Back in Hong Kong after New Year in Jakarta I focussed on editing my research paper. My report was to be published in the conference proceedings. I felt a glow of satisfaction at my achievement but once again this experience made me realise how constrained my professional as well as my personal life had been in Kuwait.

True to his promise Nabeel decided to come over and spend Easter in Hong Kong. I was pleased that I would not have to go to Kuwait or Beirut and was looking forward to showing him around. He took the opportunity to buy dozens of silk shirts for himself and his brothers in the street markets. However, he had come to see me with an ultimatum. He detailed his current financial status, writing currencies and figures down to illustrate the renewal of his fortune. He surprised me by announcing he'd also bought two flats in the Christian area of Beirut, one for Asma and one for us. But his persuasion was based on money, not emotion. He did not stress his great love for me. He had simply got to save face by getting me back by his side.

I was extremely reluctant to agree to go back, but to save his face as well as my own I set some parameters for my return. We had to purchase a flat in London in case of future disaster. Nabeel agreed. I would be able to live in the flat while pursuing a lifetime's ambition, a doctoral degree. In this way I created some distance between us. I hoped to introduce the idea of divorce again in the future. Nabeel might be willing to separate if he could obtain a British passport as a result of my study residence in the UK. So, after reluctantly submitting my resignation, we embarked on the purchase of some Chinese furniture for what would be our flat in London. All these new items were to be packed into a container for shipment to London. My new keyboard, personal computer and clothes were packed for shipment to Kuwait, where I'd be returning after I found a London flat.

My friends were dismayed at my decision to leave after only two years, as was my boss. Lucy and I launched on some last minute shopping excursions but most of my remaining time was spent completing my teaching duties. Kyle had introduced me to the US poetess Emily Dickinson and I was still writing materials for independent learning based on her work. I hid the poetry book under my bed so that the packers would not take it away, but they found it and it disappeared into the container. Kyle would be leaving in summer too. He invited me to stay with him in the USA at any time I wished, but there was no long term commitment from him, so I was cautious.

Carefully I explained that I would be happy to take up the invitation if my attempt to rejoin my husband failed. I was so busy at work that when the time came to leave I still had packing to do. Thanks to Lucy's help, frantically stuffing things into cases, I made it into the taxi to the airport, and onto the Emirates flight to Dubai. As soon as the plane took off I burst into tears to the amazement of the stewardesses who brought me a whole box of tissues to absorb the incessant flow. The sound of the aircraft wheels being folded away resembled a prison door closing on me again. I knew in that moment that I had taken the wrong turning again in my life. Just as when I first arrived in Kuwait my grandmother's words came back to me. *You've made your bed and now you must lie in it.*

This time my reaction was different. I was beginning to challenge the idea of putting up with a bad choice. Very slowly, thanks to two years of independence in Hong Kong, somewhere in the back of my mind I was beginning to be the person I might have been had I not married in the first place. I had no clear idea, at that moment, of how I would remedy the situation I was in. I was set on the path of finding a flat in London to which my shipping container and its contents could be delivered. Then, in September I would be returning to Kuwait, to work at the University or at the British Council. Gradually my sobs abated, thanks to multiple whisky and sodas served to me by the friendly service staff. I would have to grin and bear it, I decided. At least, I thought, I might have an escape route to Texas if things became impossible for me, provided Kyle could be trusted.

At Heathrow my brother Bill met me and I was able to relax into the family atmosphere of their home as I began a month of visiting estate agents and searching through property listings. My six year old nephew, Rupert, showed he was a chip off the old block, reading the descriptions for the prices, and informing me which I could afford for my budget.

The latter was steadily increasing as I gave Nabeel feedback over the phone on what was available, for a price of around 50,000 pounds sterling. This would buy a studio in the centre of London, typically a former council, state-owned property. The location would be superb for a student, but this did not appeal to Nabeel's pretensions to grandeur, so he urged me to look for larger places at around 150 thousand sterling. In August he came over to check on the findings, when he increased the budget to 250 thousand British pounds. He then returned to Kuwait.

In September I called him when a decision needed to be made on a smart flat near High St Kensington versus a larger one in West Kensington. A deposit was required to secure either of these properties.

'You decide. They both seem OK to me.'

'OK. I'll go for the smarter address.'

'Good.'

'When can you transfer the deposit?'

'Oh, I'll have to ask Edouard about that. He has the signature on all our money.'

'But you told me you had all those funds when you were in Hong Kong.'

'Yes, but you've got access to the Isle of Man money. You can buy the flat with that.'

'But that would use up the total 250k we have there. How would I pay for the annual service charge on an apartment? What if something happened to you? We would lose the place.'

'Nothing will happen.' As usual, he had no sense of the precariousness of life.

My temper flared.

'Actually you are right. Nothing will happen. If you go back on your promise, I won't buy the flat and I won't come back to Kuwait.'

'What do you mean?'

'I mean what I say.'

I slammed the phone down and burst into tears. So this was his plan, to use the money set aside for me to inherit in case of his sudden death instead of transferring additional money to the UK for the purchase. He had used his current financial standing to persuade me to return to him. I was furious at his trickery. I had not expected this of him, despite my knowledge of his wheeling and dealing. I was regretting my lack of foresight. The money in the Isle of Man had been my insurance policy against his sudden demise and the application of Lebanese law on his wealth. Of course, having married in London according to English law I was entitled to full inheritance but I didn't want to enter into a future contest with Nabeel's family. It was ironic that not having married in the Catholic Church in Lebanon had given Nabeel the opening for another regular putdown. His backhanded compliment to me was 'I'll marry you one day.' Of course living together outside marriage was illegal in Kuwait. But as a baptised Catholic, Nabeel was unmarried in the Church's eyes and I'd refused to marry in the Catholic Church. As a consequence, if he wished, he was free to marry again. I went to my bedroom to think things over. My shock and disappointment turned to frustration and then anger as I went over our history.

I had been with Nabeel for 23 years at this point, having left my family, my country, and my burgeoning career in Adult Education in London after marrying him. I had accepted not having children, putting my own biological urges on the back burner to comply with his wishes. I had just given up my second chance of a flourishing career with research possibilities in Hong Kong and now was being denied a secure financial future with a home in London. I was not prepared to go back to war-torn Kuwait, working as a teacher, with a home life I no longer wanted. All my earnings in Kuwait had gone into our joint account there. Nabeel had bought two apartments in Beirut without considering me, but now he was not willing to invest any more in a future with me. My cards were on the table. 'Keep your promises or I am out.' I guessed he had watched me spend the money on the furniture in Hong Kong expecting that I would be financially needy as a result and would have to go back to him.

Knowing my feelings for him were based on pity and a sense of loyalty rather than true love, it suddenly seemed ridiculous to waste any more time on what was a lost cause. What was the point of trying to save his face? I knew how I felt and this latest development had simply confirmed my innermost thoughts. That night I decided that I would never go back. Instead I might take up Kyle's offer to visit him in Texas. I had long entertained thoughts of living in the USA ever since my happy time in a US Summer Camp in 1970. I told my brother the next morning that there had been a change of plan and that I was not going back to Kuwait. I explained the problem briefly, without tears. Bill was happy to back me. 'You'll always have a home here.'

Katie reassured me, 'You can stay here as long as you like. You'll be our permanent baby sitter.'

Of course, I had a plan of my own for a new life, but I wanted to check out whether Kyle had changed his mind or not. After all, he might just be a player. I didn't want to jump out of the frying pan into the fire. Staying with my brother or mother would be a better option than that. The phone rang after Bill had gone to work. I was having breakfast. It was afternoon in Kuwait and Nabeel wanted to speak to me. He opened the conversation calmly. 'Why are you so upset about the money for the flat?'

'Because I've been pounding the streets of London for four weeks and we had a plan to buy a flat.'

'Yes, but you have the money there to buy it.'

'If I buy with that money I lose my financial security and I won't be able to pay the service charges. If the flat was cheaper, that wouldn't be a problem. But I'm buying a big flat for you and your family and to impress your business associates. I can't do that with the only money I have after working in Kuwait for 14 years.'

'Oh, I see. Well, I told you I have to check with Edouard first.'

'You didn't have to check with Edouard when you were trying to persuade me to come back to Kuwait, did you?'

'No, but I didn't think it was a business deal. Are you trying to take me to the cleaners?'

'Oh, so you are chewing that old bone again now. If I was trying to take you to the cleaners I would have done it while I was in Hong Kong and I'd have stayed where I had a wonderful job, flat and friends. The boot is on the other foot I'm afraid. You think I am a doormat and you can just walk all over me as you've been doing since I married you.'

'Well, if you feel like that I guess there's nothing I can do.'

'Too right. Nothing. The worm has turned. I've had enough. I'm going to stay here and we can sort things out legally.'

I couldn't help crying again as I spoke, so I said goodbye and put down the phone.

It rang again immediately.

'Please don't take this as the end. I'm sure we can work something out.'

'Well, tell me how. If you stick to your promise, perhaps we can talk again. If not, then I'm out.'

'OK. I'll talk to Edouard.'

'Goodbye.'

I felt a headache starting as I went back to the breakfast table. I was sick to my stomach with this momentous decision which had come out of the blue. All the conflicts which had been bubbling under the surface of our marriage suddenly erupted in one moment, like molten lava flowing from a volcanic eruption. One thing was certain, I couldn't saddle myself with a huge flat with annual outgoings, and even a small flat would be pointless without a job. After all, work was going to be the only way I could manage financially on my own. Quite the contrary to Nabeel's fears about being 'taken to the cleaners' I was the fairest person I knew with regard to money. I was honest. If anyone was 'taken to the cleaners' it was me.

Nabeel on the other hand was a 'wheeler dealer' by profession and possibly by nature. I had warned him at the start of our marriage not to give me details of the bribery which was the norm in Middle Eastern commercial dealings when he began bringing business visitors to our home in Kuwait. Visitors preferred eating take away pizza with my home made wine and beer to five star cuisine accompanied by Pepsi in the hotels they stayed in. I had been brought up to be meticulously honest, and I disliked the potential for corruption in business. I kept my professional integrity and left him to his. His own family had called him a liar, a coward and a cheat in an argument after we had been belatedly welcomed into the family as a newly married couple in Kuwait. I had defended him then, but now I could see that they were probably right.

Over the month of September the phone calls from Nabeel in Kuwait continued to come in to my brother's home, culminating with the most awful birthday I'd had in years. Slowly I regained the strength in myself and my hope for a new beginning and decided to ignore the calls. I warned Katie to say I was out if she took a call from him. Mum was upset about the whole affair but told me she was not surprised. She'd had plenty of evidence that all was not well when she stayed with us in Kuwait the last time. I wished she'd told me some of the things she now felt free to reveal. Most tellingly, when I'd travelled to Baghdad during the Iran-Iraq war to assess Margaret Hassan's Teaching Diploma lessons Nabeel had insisted that he wouldn't allow me to come back. How strange to hear that! I wished I hadn't left Mum with him during that three day trip. She warned me not to go back to him now that I had upset him. I guessed Nabeel would try to contact her, but now I knew how she really felt about my marriage I knew she would be on my 'side'. I began to blame the Tarot cards at that point. If Mum hadn't read them as 'domestic bliss' I would never have married. Now how stupid is that? I let my life go down the tubes because of a Tarot card reading.

With this new perception of my own role in the current drama, I began to worry that Nabeel might come over to London to try to persuade or even force me to go back. Fear and depression began to gnaw at me as I realised I'd been the architect of my own defeat. Peter Berger was right: We build our own Alcatraz. Eventually I developed acute back pain which severely limited my movements. My body was paralysed by the fear in my mind. I crossed London to visit a chiropractor lying in the back of a taxi. Gradually these treatments helped me to cope with driving so I went home to see Mum. She told me she'd noticed that my whole personality had changed since my marriage. I didn't blame Nabeel completely for this as the religious and cultural constraints of living in Kuwait had played some part in the modifications in my behaviour. But my personality had been affected by the continual putdowns from my supposedly loving husband. Many friends told me how highly he spoke of me when I wasn't there. But face to face he'd been at worst cruel and at best insensitive. I began to think his taunts stemmed from his aggressive defense of his own ego. As I had constantly pursued excellence in my career and continued to improve my qualifications, he may well have felt threatened and worried that I might leave him. Well, here I was, leaving him despite his best efforts to denigrate and disempower me, and perhaps ultimately destroy me.

I told Mum about Kyle and his offer of hospitality. She thought it was a good idea to get completely away from Nabeel's sphere of influence. After all, he could visit the UK at any time for business reasons. Although his actions were potentially criminal he could not be pursued in the courts without me incurring huge costs. Doubting Kyle's sincerity even more as a result of the recent developments with Nabeel, I decided to make a short trip first, taking only hand luggage, to assess whether I would be able to start a real relationship with Kyle. I didn't want a fling. I wanted to settle down in the USA. Kyle was overjoyed, or so it seemed, when I rang him.

'When are you coming over?'

'Well, whenever it suits you. I'm a free woman now.'

I wondered if that admission might take the edge off the 'chase' in Kyle's game playing mind. I dared to hope for the best, but stuck to my 'toe in the water' plan.

'Well, I've got a break in teaching for Thanksgiving. It's a long weekend. Why don't you arrive then?'

And so on the fourth Thursday in November 1993, I landed in Texas and was met at the airport by Kyle in his little white Honda. I was emotional at the big step I was taking, but he had enough exuberance for two.

'Hey! Great to see you! Let me look at you! Wow. So glad you're here.'

He hugged me in a warm embrace.

'Thanks for having me. Things have taken an unexpected turn, haven't they?'

He interrupted me,

'...but it's for the better, isn't it?'

'Yes, I hope so. Are you sure I won't be in the way here?'

'Not at all. In fact, you can do a bit of teaching with me if you like.'

'Wow. That's a surprise. Tell me more!'

As we drove the winding country roads back to his place in the country, Kyle explained his teaching program. His students were mainly mature, postgraduates, and I suspected, mainly women too. A small doubt began to wriggle like a worm in the back of my mind. He continued.

'Anyway, we have class on Tuesday and Thursday evening. Today's class was cancelled for the holiday. So you can come along next time.'

'OK. I'm just staying for ten days you know. I'll be leaving soon.'

'That's fine. I'm SO glad to see you.'

On arrival at the single storey, wooden ranch style house which Kyle called home, his large dog bounded up to me and licked my hands frantically. I loved dogs. The shabby chic comfort of Kyle's simple but charming home was welcoming. I felt so glad I had made this trip. A seed of hope began to grow inside me. Perhaps this would be MY new home?

Kyle made coffee for us and it smelled delicious. I'd never had such aromatic and tasty coffee. It was surprising and pleasing that he was so domesticated. We took our cups out into the garden where dusk was falling and dew beginning to settle on the grass. We leant against the fence and sipped our coffee.

'Look out there. It's all mine. There's a pond down the hill where we can row my little boat.'

'It's absolutely beautiful, so peaceful out here. I'm so happy. Thanks for inviting me.'

'Well, I hope you're going to like it enough to come back.'

My heart bounded in my chest and hope began to grow. He seemed to be right on target, ready to start a new relationship with me. I found my pyjamas, ready for bed.

'Wow - you certainly aren't staying long this time! I've never seen such a small bag.'

'Well, I didn't want to outstay my welcome so I packed light.'

'No chance of that. Come over here.'

He led me into a country style bedroom with a high wooden bedstead and colourful patchwork quilt. I tried not to think of who else had slept with him there. It was easy enough to do as he kissed me gently. In moments we resumed what we had started in Hong Kong. I was blissfully happy and sleep came readily after my long journey and the month of stressful phone calls from Nabeel. I had found a peaceful rural haven.

CHAPTER 31

Tonga and Closure

January - February 2004

Back home in Farmerston Colin and Rose started packing for their trip to Tonga and the guaranteed sun. Mosquito spray, sunscreen, sunhats, jandals, 'togs', shorts and tops were the bare necessities. They were staying at a resort on the coast, in a bamboo *whare* by the sea. The downside was the neighbouring basket ball court which was floodlit and used late at night by the local teenagers. Romantic evenings sitting outside, sipping drinks, were ruined by raucous shouting and the risk of balls bouncing around them. Even inside the *whare* the sound of voices and the bouncing ball penetrated clearly. But they did not complain to the management or ask to be moved, keen on not upsetting the local people in their own environment.

The island was beautiful. They took long walks along the coast, visiting secluded coves for skinny dipping. After one such walk, young children approached them as they neared the hotel. During the garbled conversation, with many gesticulations to increase comprehension, Rose dropped a jandal. She had to return to pick it up, much to the annoyance of Colin, who refused to wait for her, and walked on to the pool. No doubt he was hot and thirsty, but Rose recalled how angry he had been with a young boy who had asked permission to play on his drumset after an amateur concert in Bahrein. If looks could kill the child would no longer draw breath. Colin was not generous where children were concerned. He gave of his time in strict rations and of his possessions according to need. Right from the start Rose had realised that Colin was not easy-going, though his liberal approach to sex and to making loud music at any time of day or night suggested otherwise. He alternated between controlling repression and creative expression. He was very hard to 'read', Rose realised.

The week in Tonga sped by. They visited the capital, an island hotel, the city markets, the yacht club and another distant boutique hotel which had a free shuttle bus. They swam in the infinity pool and met a small number of other guests on holiday. But the *coup de grace* was administered by the hotel chef. The food had been good so they had eaten in the hotel restaurant each night, until two nights before departure when they were stricken by food poisoning after eating fish. The first night was terrible. As soon as one of them got back in bed, the other had to get up to use the toilet. It was unbelievable. But worse than the pain and discomfort was Colin's attitude. Each time she got up, he groaned, as if she was causing him discomfort. Whether he did this consciously or not, Rose could not tell. 'You have the blackest heart ever,' she muttered at one low point in that terrible night. If he heard, he said nothing. But Rose knew at that moment, that there was no future unless things took a radical turn for the better in their relationship. She needed reciprocal support and kindness, not just romantic love and sex.

Colin's state of health was better on the second day whereas Rose remained in bed for a further day. She could not eat but Colin went to the restaurant for toast and scrambled eggs. Fortunately they had another day to recover before taking the plane home. Alone in the room Rose mulled over the way the island holiday had gone. They had had no discussion of the future, the place was beautiful but not inspiring, and finally they had suffered *gyppy* tummy which had revealed, she felt, an inner lack of compassion on Colin's side. She was able to get on the plane, but immediately on being seated in the cramped airliner she felt griping pains again and had to scramble into the toilet. She managed to get out of the tiny cubicle in time for takeoff, but once again, Colin offered no support for her physical condition, instead appearing to panic. Rose realised that she had to accept his lack of concern for her if she wanted to continue the relationship with him. The investment of time and money in bringing him over to sample her new home had been worth it, for she finally had to face up to his failings, just as she had had to confront the fissures in her marriage ten years previously. At least she had enjoyed the travel and touring with a companion.

Back home in Farmerston and at work again after the romantic, tropical holiday which had ended with something of an anti-climax if not in complete disaster, Rose wondered if Colin would raise the issue of their future before he left for the UK. There was only one more weekend together before he went back home and she returned to Dubai for a check up on her mouth operation. She decided that she would give him this last chance to bring some stability to their rocky ten year relationship. She discussed with Colin what he would like to do for the final weekend.

'Well, we've been dashing around quite a lot. Why don't we take it easy on Sunday at least? You need to pack for your trip to Dubai too, don't you?'

'OK, but Saturday we could drive down to Kawhia on the West coast. It's not too far and I haven't been there either. Captain Cook was there in 1769 I think. You could look it up in the guide book and be my guide.'

'All right. It looks as if the weather will be good.'

Saturday dawned bright and sunny as they set off with a picnic lunch. The road was 'metal' and quite a slow drive, but they visited the West coast black sand beach at Raglan first, to see the world famous surf beach. When they eventually got to the small but beautiful village of Kawhia they walked to the beach and settled down for lunch and a swim. The beach was almost empty and the sea and sky were azure blue. Rose wondered if this idyllic spot would be where they might discuss the future. Alas, no. Their conversation was as mundane as usual. Sunday passed equally pleasantly but again no discussion. On Monday at work Rose decided she would have to call the shots. Both she and Colin were leaving on Wednesday, so it would be best to open the discussion that night. Back at the house she found Colin looking pale and strained.

'What's wrong, sweetheart?'

Colin stammered his reply. 'I've had some bad news.'

'Really? from home? ...about Mum?'

Colin's Mum was in her nineties, but in the best of health as far as we knew.

'No. It's Petra.'

As he spoke his sister's name his face crumpled and he began to weep.

'Petra? Has there been an accident?'

Petra was a games teacher at a secondary school. She was as fit as a fiddle.

'No. Well, yes. She had a massive coronary. She's dead.'

Rose screamed in anguish. 'No! It can't be true.'

The two clung to each other and both sobbed uncontrollably. Then Rose grabbed the scotch bottle and poured two stiff drinks.

'When did you hear? Why didn't you ring me?'

'Mum rang this morning after you'd gone to work. I didn't want to upset you there.'

'Oh my God. This is so terrible. How are Alex and Amelia?'

'In a bad way, of course.'

'What about you? Will you go back tonight?'

'No, it's not worth changing the flights now. I'll be back in time for the funeral.'

'Will there be an autopsy? She was sporty. What could have been wrong?'

'I've no idea. It's too terrible to think of.'

'Let's go and lie down. I need another drink.'

They lay on the huge bed, glasses in hand, and sipped and cried together, refilling their glasses as fast as they emptied them.

After half an hour, they both fell into a shallow sleep. On awakening, it was dusk.

'Have you eaten today, Colin?'

'No. I couldn't face anything after I got the phone call.'

'Shall we get a takeaway? I had thought we might go out but we can't do that now.'

'Yes, a takeaway's good.'

Rose rang for pizza and fries to be delivered. Comfort food was what they needed. They ate in silence, overwhelmed by the sense of loss, but hungry after a day without much, if any food. They drank more whisky as they watched TV afterwards. The distance separating Colin from his family on the opposite side of the world seemed immense. There was no point in talking about their personal relationship. A close-knit, loving family had just been torn apart by a sudden death. And so, the last chance for a discussion of their future together was lost. They were close, she felt his pain and tried to console him, but the rest would have to be silence for now.

On Wednesday morning Rose had hired a shuttle service to drive them both to the airport. Colin was heading to the UK, while Rose was heading to Dubai. They went together through passport control, then said their goodbyes before walking to their different departure lounges, but their pervading sadness made this parting unimportant. Colin was heading towards a very difficult time. A widower and a motherless child awaited him. His widowed mother had lost one of her two children. Perhaps this tragedy would awaken him to the need for permanence in their relationship while they still had a chance to spend the rest of their lives together, Rose thought as she waited in the departure lounge. If not, she wondered what would become of the two of them. Ten years had gone by since they first met, and as she thought, fallen deeply in love.

She had made the decisive step to move away from the UK after her Mum's sudden death, as much to be away from Colin's philandering as to escape her grief. Now she knew they could still be 'in love' in a transient, romantic, fashion but did Colin really love her enough to want to be faithful and to be able to offer her support in bad times, such as illness? Rose understood in retrospect that she had married Nabeel in order to have a family with someone who was a hard worker like herself, not really because she loved him for himself. She had felt sorry for him and his family as refugees. She could have lived without him that much was sure. Having their own babies had been out of the question and Nabeel had refused to adopt. As a result, though she had tried to keep the relationship going, the disaster of the Invasion and the increasingly gaping gulf between their political leanings had cracked the structure of their relationship. In the end she had succumbed to physical temptation while away from him and Nabeel had not managed to hold onto her. She needed more than a nominal or occasional relationship, which did not seem possible with Colin.

In Dubai the warm sunshine and Hinewai welcomed her. Rose had an appointment for a check up with the American doctor at the Dental Clinic in Dubai. Her original palate operation had been in their branch in Abu Dhabi, but Dubai was more convenient now that Hinewai had moved there. An X-ray later, the oral surgeon confirmed that the gum had healed well, and, as she knew, the plastic 'flipper' that she had been wearing for a year now, was no longer a good fit. He recommended a porcelain tooth on a Maryland bridge, which he would prepare. It would be the only possible solution. Implants would not be possible since the filler, plastic and human cadaver, was not stable enough. With a sigh, Rose hoped for the best and took herself and Hinewai off to the Lemon Tree for lunch. Another appointment and she'd be able to return to New Zealand. She was relieved to have a permanent replacement for the temporary plastic 'flipper' she had been wearing for a year. Rose knew her confidence would be boosted by no longer having the flipper. Perhaps she would be able to find herself a permanent romantic partner, she mused, if Colin 'failed'.

Back in New Zealand work kept Rose fully occupied as usual until she heard from Colin. His sister's funeral was arranged and she asked him to buy a wreath of flowers on her behalf. She wrote a card of condolences for Alex and Amelia and Colin's Mum. That was all she could do. She certainly couldn't travel to the UK as she had no annual leave left and since she was not in a formal relationship it would be hard to ask for familial compassionate leave. Anyway, perhaps Colin did not want her there? Tillie or Sue or any one of the other old flames could be at his side now. Negative thoughts like these crept into her mind unbidden. Their past was strewn with so many rows and so much suspicion that even now, after a month spent happily together, the absence of discussion had thrown her attitude back into negativity. She wasn't depressed, or anguished, she was simply unsettled and very sad for Colin.

Rose was not yet ready to start the separation process, however. In a secret part of her heart she was waiting to see if Colin would like her to go back to the UK to be with him. She doubted that he would want to come over to be with her in New Zealand. He hadn't waxed lyrical about the place, and admittedly, New Zealand did not offer everything that the UK did. He had a lovely home, with new friends and hobbies. But Rose needed someone by her side who could share her happiness and sadness as she moved towards retirement. With Colin there would always be the shadows of past sadness and disappointments in her memory. She wanted to give her new life a fighting chance. One way to do that would be to find a new partner. But she couldn't do that unless she closed the door once and for all on Colin as a partner. She needed to see what he had been feeling while he was out in New Zealand with her.

In February it wasn't easy writing the Dear Colin letter so soon after his bereavement, but it had to be done. Rose explained that she had hoped for some discussion and closure over the Xmas/New Year holiday. She apologised for bringing more sadness so soon after the grief of Petra's death, but she had to be free to move on if he wasn't able to commit to any more permanent relationship than before. For two weeks she had no response to her email. Then came a simple one liner:

> If that's what you want, then please feel free to
> move on.

Once again he had put the onus for their relationship on her. She was to be the decision maker. Rose controlled her anger and calmly wrote back:

> I want a permanent, committed relationship with
> someone who loves me more than anyone else and
> wants to be with me all the time, not occasionally.
> Just confirming that's not what you want?

After another wait, shorter this time, came the reply:

> You must do what suits you. You never really loved
> me anyway. I always felt I wasn't perfect for you.
> So, goodbye.

Rose stared at the message in astonishment. After ten years of Colin refusing to commit to her, now he was self-identifying as the victim. Could this be just a game? Whatever it was, Rose couldn't cope with it any longer. Nor, it seemed could Colin. Tears were useless, so she refused to shed them. It was the end of the relationship, for sure. The die was cast. She would console herself by searching for a new partner in her new home, New Zealand.

Rose's problems, she knew, were as nothing compared with those of the citizens of Iraq in January and February 2004. Despite the UN decision to hold direct elections of a new Iraqi Head of State in July there was so much disorder in the country that they were not considered practicable. Iraqi Heads of Government were still being appointed on a monthly basis but to date none of them had managed to win confidence and make a difference to the state of lawlessness in the country. The resentment of the now unemployed army officers had caused continuing unrest amongst the Sunni, former Ba'athist soldiers. Paul Bremer failed to understand that anyone who wanted to succeed in Saddam's time in power had to follow Ba'athist policies. As a consequence of former soldiers not being paid, their children were dying of malnutrition and disease.

The discontent escalated in January when a suicide bomber killed 20 and injured about 60 Iraqis who were queuing for jobs outside the US Coalition HQ. It seemed impossible for those in charge to prevent these attacks yet to Rose it seemed that simple security measures could have been put in place to do so. Meanwhile Saddam Hussein was still in prison and on 21 February a Red Cross visitor was permitted to visit him for the first time. Rose wondered whether that delay breached the Geneva Convention. It probably did, but the so-called liberation of Iraq was patently not intended to replace Saddam's regime with the dawn of human rights and the rule of international law.

CHAPTER 32

Kyle in Texas

November 1993

The next morning Kyle and I could sleep in. After a leisurely breakfast, with the fragrant aroma of good coffee filling the country kitchen, we took the dog out to look at the land. There were empty stables for two horses in the first paddock.

'Have you kept horses here?' I asked, intrigued.

'Yes, my second wife, Sandra, loves horses. She's a child of nature. I bought this place so that she could keep her horses here.'

'Do you ride?'

'Not really. I tried to learn but I was no good at it.'

'Can I ask why you broke up with Sandra?'

'Well, as always, it's complicated, but I think she thought I was having other relationships.'

'Mm...I see. And you couldn't persuade her otherwise? Because it was true?'

'Well, I suppose it might have been.'

'Are you still in touch with her?'

'From time to time. She went back to her home state. She's a school teacher.'

My suspicions about Kyle's potential as a philanderer confirmed, but not wanting to turn our lovely morning into the Spanish Inquisition, I changed the subject.

'Where's the lake you told me about yesterday?'

'Down here, behind those trees. Come on.'

We walked on through another paddock and past some graceful willows which had lost almost all their leaves. Their leafless branches looked like ballerinas gracefully performing an arabesque, raising their arms above their heads. As we stepped through the trees, lying in front of us was a small but magical expanse of water, with a tiny island in the centre. It was the landscape of the imagination come to life. The leafless, fragile, dark branches silhouetted against the cool grey of the sky resembled an etching of the lake.

'Wow. That doesn't seem an adequate comment, so wow again.'

'Yes, double wow is how I feel about it.'

'You are so lucky to have this.'

'Well, you know, I haven't felt like that for a long time. This place is a long way from my work and I've been alone here since Sandra left me.'

'I thought writers liked having their own space and time to write?'

'You know, that's another thing about me. I haven't really felt like writing for quite a while. I went to Hong Kong hoping to get some inspiration.'

'What kind of writing do you want to do? Research or creative?'

'I should do both really. Scholarship, publishing papers, is the only way I'll get a better job, but creative writing could make me some real money.'

'Don't you find that as you're teaching poetry, the creative urge is stronger than the research mode? I am inspired to write by my work in teaching.'

'You're right. I wish I could show my students some excellent published work of mine. I suppose I'm a bit lazy.'

'I understand. The daily grind gets you down sometimes. If I came out to stay, would you be able to settle into a writing routine, do you think?'

'Yes, that would be great. We could work alongside each other.'

'That would be good for me but I don't want to push you into anything. Let's see how our time together goes.'

'OK. Now what shall we do about lunch? Out or in?'

As we walked back to the house with the dog hunting in the long grass beside us, we decided to go into the local town to explore and have lunch. Leaving the dog behind we set off on the ten minute car ride. This small town of almost ten thousand people was enchanting, with wide tree-lined avenues in old world provincial North American style, edged by weatherboard or stone built houses with 'stoops', broad wooden steps leading up to the houses, mosquito netted front doors, and swings on the porches. In the downtown area the large brick built public buildings signalled their origins in the Victorian era. As it was a holiday there were quite a few people out for lunch. In a ranch styled country restaurant we enjoyed a buffet meal of baked ham with fresh vegetables, and a broccoli cheese soup starter that was a meal in itself.

'You remember I'm a vegetarian, don't you, Kyle?'

'Yes, one who eats pork,' he commented drily.

'Full marks for memory! I occasionally eat a little ham, or bacon, after all those years in Kuwait, where pork is *haraam*, forbidden, in Islam.'

'I would find not eating bacon quite difficult.'

'Which is why I'm enjoying this meal!'

After lunch we went back and took a nap, another opportunity for us to renew our emotional connection. We were comfortable together, Kyle was relaxed and so was I, which looked very promising for a future together. Later that evening as we sipped a scotch and soda - my duty free offering - Kyle showed me his study which was more of a store, filled with packing cases, some open, some untouched.

Kyle explained the mess. 'I haven't been able to tidy up all this stuff since I moved here.'

'How long ago was that?' I laughed. I knew how quickly I could create chaos with all my paraphernalia for teaching. I hated to throw things away in case they came in useful for my writing or research.

'I suppose it's been ten years now.'

'Well, would you like me to help you sort through some stuff?'

'Perhaps. For now, here's the PC for you to do email if you like.'

'There's no need really, but if you're switching on, I might just send a message to my brother to let him know I'm safe.'

We spent a convivial few hours writing and reading together. I loved the atmosphere of calm purposefulness, both of us happy doing our own thing quietly. Nabeel had always been on the go and always smoking. I had only been tranquil when he was out of the house, I reflected. The next day, Saturday, we drove into Austin where I admired the huge public buildings, open spaces and the beautiful Colorado River. The grand scale of the streets was amazing. Such vision and symmetry of town planning for a London resident accustomed to a city which had grown in random style. We picked up some food to cook dinner at home and enjoyed a simple meal in the evening with some inexpensive Californian wine. On Sunday we visited Kyle's friends who owned a working ranch. We took drinks and dessert for lunch, which was a casual, friendly, open air affair in their huge barn of a home. These friends were delightful and I hoped to see them all again.

All too soon it was Monday and I went into work with Kyle to meet some of his colleagues in the University town. The rest of my short stay we established a routine of going into the University each morning, reading and writing for me and marking for Kyle, with the highlight being teaching with Kyle on Tuesday and Thursday evening, then going for drinks with his students. I noticed one woman in particular, petite, blonde with a short pixie haircut, watching me closely. I dismissed it as unimportant. After all, it was likely that several of the women might be jealous of Kyle's new girlfriend.

By the end of the week we'd decided that I should come back to stay for a while as we both felt happy with this new living situation. So I went back to the UK, gave positive feedback to Mum and Bill about my new relationship, then packed two large cases for the coming winter and returned to the USA within two weeks glad to escape the phone calls still coming from Nabeel. He had told Mum that he thought I was under some kind of spell. I was, indeed. It was the spell of freedom and happiness while spending time with someone who was compatible, in a location which was charming and unrestricted by culture and traditions I found difficult to accept.

Nevertheless, my welcome on returning to Texas was not as joyous as I had anticipated. I attributed it to the inconvenience of the large heavy luggage Kyle had to manipulate into his small hatchback. I guessed that the bags represented a permanence this time that was not there on my first visit but I wondered if there were other reasons too, perhaps related to other relationships. As half expected, they popped up soon enough.

The first discovery was that Kyle had had a girlfriend waiting for him while he was in Hong Kong on his sabbatical year. He had let her know about me, sending her photos which she had rightly guessed included a new sexual encounter. As a result, she had split up with him and was now living in San Francisco. She had been hurt by Kyle's cheating, but he proclaimed himself solo when I met him, so I felt no guilt, though I felt sorry for the other young woman.

Next, I found a trail of messages on the computer and photos which Kyle had either made no attempt to hide or didn't know how to hide. They were to a former student, with whom he had also indulged in office sex. She had a boyfriend now, so she was off the radar, but available when the time was right, i.e. when she was free and lonely. I wondered what part these ladies might play in Kyle's future.

We had developed a routine in which I stayed home most days, going into the University with him only to help individual students with language problems, to hand over some articles I edited for publication for a History Professor, or to meet up with various colleagues and friends for lunch and chat. I had made myself a reading list and was busy taking notes for my own personal and professional future plans. I was eager to complete a doctoral research project, so I spent this 'time out' in the USA scoping my research topic. On the days I stayed home to read and study I cooked, cleaned, spent occasional hours hiding in the tornado shelter after radio warnings and took walks with the dog.

During this 'escape hatch' period I wrote to Nabeel, attempting to restore communication in a positive, adult manner. Ours was not the first broken marriage in the world and I had given him several clues to the puzzle he believed me to be. We had almost broken up when I first arrived in Kuwait, and then again when I was completing my Master's degree in the mid '80s and coming to terms with our childless marriage. I had told him many times how unhappy I was with the amount of time we had to spend with his family. As for his business, I hated the bribery. Then, in our post Invasion phase, I had been unwilling to leave my Hong Kong job and new home, only breaking my three year contract after he persuaded me to continue my longed for doctoral studies in London. How much more evidence did he need to know his wife was not a happy woman?

It was obvious to me now that I had stayed with Nabeel out of pity despite my personal unhappiness. Saving him or saving his face had always been more important than saving myself, which is why I hadn't walked out of the marriage in those very early days. I had no idea whether he had found someone else to take my place, but I sincerely hoped he had. As a wealthy man he could easily find a new wife. But first he had to get rid of me, by fair means or foul, as it turned out.

CHAPTER 33

Internet Dating: Ward

March 2004

Rose knew she had to take matters of the heart into her own hands now. One of her single female colleagues had told her about various online dating sites, so Rose began the process of describing herself in her online profile. Was she a social butterfly, or the life and soul of the party? How old should she say she was, she wondered, as the truth might be off-putting? As for choosing a photograph to illustrate her charms, there was no way she was getting a glamour portrait done. Instead, she posted a couple of photos of her 'country' self, walking round Farmerston in the winter wearing a beanie and a waterproof jacket, and on the beach, with her long, wavy, chestnut-tinted hair flowing. She gave her age as 51, just five years younger than reality. She didn't want to push her luck by decreasing it too much. After posting her own profile, she read several men's profiles and contacted some who met her essential criteria, non smokers, and at least 5'8" tall. On her own site she set herself a radius of 150 miles, which would include Auckland.

Several responses came in but no one interested her until she saw a message from an American scientist working at a local environmental station. They arranged to meet on St Patrick's Day in a Farmerston pub after work. Ward had not posted a photo, but said he had light coloured hair and wore glasses. At 6pm the pub was buzzing with Irish festival revellers. When Rose arrived she looked around but couldn't spot anyone who fitted the description. She ordered a drink at the bar, wondering about the green beer, the festival special. As she was being served her date tapped her on the shoulder, smiling delightedly.

'I thought you'd be at least 10 kilos more than you are!' was his first, rather surprising comment.

Rose laughed out loud. 'Hi, Ward. Nice to meet you!' What had he expected? A loser, probably, in the dating game.

It was difficult to find a quiet place to talk with the live music playing for St Patrick's Day. So, after finishing their drinks they walked down to the nearby Waikato river bank. Rose was tired after work as usual so they arranged to meet up another night for a meal. Ward was a visiting US ecology specialist, living close to his office, so had not bought a car. Rose arranged to pick him up at his accommodation on Friday evening. Surprisingly, he pulled her close for a warm embrace and a kiss as they said their goodbyes. There was no doubting the attraction they both felt.

'Wow. That was a nice surprise,' Rose whispered.

'Good. I hope we can follow up next time. I'll walk home to cool down now. My place is just over the river.'

Rose walked to her car, shivering inside, smiling outside. This was a turn up for the books. Ward had billed himself in his online profile as a social butterfly, so Rose hardened her heart in advance. She wasn't about to fall in love. Her body was ready, but her heart was on guard. She would take this one slowly for a change, she promised herself. But Friday was a different matter. The evening was warm and balmy. On arrival at Ward's address he invited her in and showed her around the lovely house, with wooden floors and big windows making it bright and airy.

Ward explained: 'My homestay hostess is away. She spends most weekends in Auckland, which is nice for me. I can have the place to myself. Would you like a glass of cold white wine outside?'

'Yes, that would be lovely. Can I help you?'

'No, don't worry. Take a seat on the deck.'

Rose enjoyed a relaxing drink in the evening but she'd have to be careful driving without eating. The New Zealand police were trigger happy with their breathalysers on weekends.

'Where would you like to eat? I'm a vegetarian,' she told him.

'I'm easy with food. I don't mind anything.'

'How about an Indian meal?'

'That would be great.'

'OK. There's a nice place in the centre of town. We probably don't need to book if we arrive early enough.'

They had an early dinner with a beer to accompany the spicy food, divided the bill between them and afterwards Rose drove Ward back home.

'What about a nightcap? Or another glass of wine?' he asked with a smile.

As she'd eaten and hadn't drunk too much, Rose thought she might risk the traffic police patrols. But Ward had other ideas.

'I have a promise to follow up on, you know?' he murmured.

'I think I know what you mean...'

Some people can eat a spicy meal together and still enjoy a kiss afterwards. Rose and Ward were that kind. Their kisses were delightful and led to reactions Rose had not expected. They retreated to Ward's bedroom upstairs for the rest of the night.

In the morning, Rose was glad she had no commitments. On the other hand, Ward probably had places to go and other people to meet so she steeled herself not to react if so. She did not want to give the impression that she was needy. Sure enough he told her, 'I've got a lunch date with a colleague and then we're going to play tennis.'

The invitation obviously didn't include her.

'That's nice. Thanks for breakfast. Bye for now.' Rose intended to play it cool.

Their occasional trysts continued but usually involved a meal out, then bed and 'bye'. Rose was happy with this level of connection. She enjoyed her time alone as she was so busy in the daytime. However, one Friday evening after dinner, Ward decided to stay the night. The next morning, Rose found herself making tea for two. She wondered if they were becoming a couple. Ward broke into her thoughts.

'Can I come into town with you?'

'Of course. I'm looking forward to investigating a new bookshop.'

Once there she was looking through the sheet music when Ward suggested they have coffee before he left for a prior lunch engagement. As they chatted over coffee Rose was looking forward to going back into the bookshop, quite unsuspecting of an ulterior motive.

'Have you noticed anything unusual about me recently?' he asked with a serious face.

She giggled and responded teasingly, 'Not more than usual, no. Why, what's up Doc?'

The joking reference didn't seem to register with Ward. He had a serious intent.

'Haven't you noticed I'm changing colour?'

'No, I haven't. What colour are you changing to? Purple?' Rose couldn't resist the humorous response.

Once again, Ward refused to acknowledge the joke.

'No, I've been having sunbed sessions. I'm trying to get a tan.'

'Really? Why? Medical reasons? Psoriasis?'

'No, I'm going to Hawaii for a couple of weeks.'

'OK. Is that for work or vacation?' Rose reacted calmly. His travel plans were not her business, so why was he making such a big deal about them?

'Vacation.'

'Cool. I've always wanted to go to Hawaii.'

'Well, that's the thing.'

Rose wondered if she was about to get an invitation.

'I'm not going alone.'

So there would be an invitation. She waited, holding her breath.

'I'm going with another woman.'

'OK. Fine. It's a free world.'

'Yes. You do realise that you are not my dream woman, don't you?'

'Well, it hadn't crossed my mind really. I don't think dream women exist do they?'

'Well, I'm sorry to tell you that you are not.'

'And I'm sorry to tell you that that means I will start looking for someone who might classify me higher up the species,' Rose retorted.

'OK.' Somewhat taken aback, Ward lapsed into silence. 'OK. Bye then.'

With a casual wave Rose walked out of the cafe. It had been a roller coaster morning.

Even more surprising was Ward's email after his trip. Intrigued, Rose met him in a bar. She was not angry. She had had few expectations, even though she liked him.

'So how did the vacation go?' Rose asked with a smile.

'Well, there were ups and downs.'

'So your companion wasn't your dream girl either?'

'No, not really.'

'Look, Ward, are you married?'

'Yes. I suppose I am.'

'Well, in that case, you are not my dream man. I don't like dating married men.'

'OK. I get it,' he stuttered.

So that was that. She did not intend to waste any more time with a player.

March was not a good month in Iraq either. After the approval of the new Constitution, there had been suicide bombs on the Shia festival of Ashourah which had killed hundreds of worshippers in Kerbala and Baghdad. Sunni rebels were blamed. Then, at the end of the month, in Fallujah four American civilian contractors in unarmed vehicles were ambushed, killed, and burned by jubilant insurgents. The Sunni Triangle west of Baghdad became a 'no go' area for US personnel when five GIs were killed by an IED on the same day. *Heartache on heartache.*

CHAPTER 34

Kyle's Problem

Xmas 1993

As time went on I noticed that Kyle was bad-tempered and drank more when he got home from work. After long experience at hiding my own feelings I put up with his moodiness for quite a while until one evening I felt compelled to ask if something was wrong. In response, he handed me a sheaf of papers pulled from his briefcase. They were affidavits, the basis of a legal case against him, an accusation of sexual harassment, brought by the attractive mature female student I had met a few weeks earlier. I read them quickly with growing horror as Kyle, sipping a Jack Daniels, watched me closely.

'Can this be real, Kyle? What happened between you to cause this anger?'

'Well, it's a long story. Are you ready for it?'

He was visibly emotional, red in the face, but not blustering. He told me his story. It sounded like the synopsis of a Steven King novel, but this was reality.

'Donna is one of my students, as you know. Two semesters ago she got an A+ for the course, then last semester she only got an A-. She thinks I am being unfair.'

'But how does that relate to this accusation of harassment?'

'Well, in that first semester of study I used to have drinks with students after our course, as we all did with you, remember?'

'Yes, I do. And then?'

'Well, on 4 July I decided to have a BBQ at home and they all came out in the afternoon and we had a late lunch. The party continued into the evening. Donna had no car, so after the others left I suggested she could stay over if she liked. She agreed, so I thought she might be interested in me. I took a blanket outside into the moonlight and we lay there talking. Then I made a pass at her, and she responded. We continued caressing, kissing, you know..., but suddenly she sprang up as I attempted to fondle her breasts. She told me she had to tell me something.'

I listened, amazed at the close detail he was recalling.

'It seems she had had a double mastectomy, but she hadn't had replacement surgery, so she felt very insecure. I was her first 'contact' sexually since that huge operation.'

'Wow. A tricky situation.'

'Yes, so I wanted to reassure her that she was a pretty woman still, and I did what seemed natural to me, I continued my caresses and sweet talk.'

'Oh dear. Did she relax?'

'Not at all. She leapt up and said something like 'No way, Jose. I want to go home.'

Now, I'd been drinking all afternoon and evening, and wasn't expecting to have to get in the car and drive my guest home. But I fixed myself a coffee, put the dog in the back, and we set off down the road. The thing is I don't remember the rest very clearly... perhaps I was babbling nervously or drunkenly, but she has taken offence at what I said during the car ride. She alleges that I asked her for a blow job while I was driving.'

'It seems crazy to say that seriously. After all you'd have been risking a car crash!'

'Just so. I was trying to lighten the scenario. I'd been blown away by what she told me, for sure. But it's a 'he says' 'she says' scenario according to my lawyer.'

'OMG. Do you think it has blown up, sorry, because she realised that you and I had got together back in Hong Kong and now that I'm out here she's jealous?'

'Could be. I guess so. Whatever the reason I'm in deep shit. Our Uni has got harassment guidelines and I'm subject to their policies as well as the legal system. I could lose my job, which is as serious for me as a court case. It's been brewing for a while, and I'm sorry you have to know about it.'

'Well, in a way it's a relief. I began to think you hated having me here.'

'No, I've been wondering whether to tell you or not. She could settle out of court, but there's still the Uni to consider.'

'Perhaps I could be a character witness for you?'

'Well, if it comes to that, thanks for the offer. Meanwhile, don't let it bother you.'

'Easy to say, but hard to do. I care about you, you know.'

'And I for you. I'm sorry about all this hassle. Hey, what's for dinner tonight? Another of your specialties I hope!'

Kyle seemed to be cheered up by sharing his story. We ate dinner and watched TV as usual before turning in for the night. Both of us had plenty on our minds. My initial instinct had been to get out of this complicated situation, but on reflection, I couldn't leave Kyle in such a mess after he'd helped me by providing me with an escape route from my marriage. I was in this situation for a while and I needed to stay calm and offer support as and when needed.

From then on the ongoing case was our nightly topic of discussion, with Kyle continuing to stress about the lack of resolution and continued aggression on Donna's part. She had definitely been affected by that night's events, but it was also possible that she had suffered emotional damage after her surgery which Kyle could not be responsible for. Fortunately I was busy with my teaching, editing jobs and my own research so that during the day I could free my mind. I kept in touch with my Mum and brother and from time to time I also wrote to Nabeel, though still without any response. I had enough worries of my own about my future, so Kyle and I were both sometimes preoccupied. The mood of our relationship had changed irrevocably. It was darker and more complex now.

We went to Kyle's parents near Washington D.C. for Xmas, staying in a hotel so as not to bother them in their old age. Kyle's Mum was an elegant and beautiful senior citizen, while his father was a distinguished elder statesman type. Visiting their house for Xmas dinner was a treat, as their home was luxurious. In our conversations it was clear that Kyle's parents had a sophisticated and wise attitude to life. It was also patent that their son's career, which had started so well with his acknowledged scholarship, had been something of a disappointment thereafter for them. It was no doubt so for Kyle too, though he hid it well with his *bonhomie*. What was fun was seeing how adaptable Kyle was in any circumstances. In the hotel there was no guest kettle, so if he wanted hot water to make instant coffee, he used the bathroom tap, unconcerned about the cleanliness of the hotel's hot water tanks. I could see that my experiences in both war-torn and developing countries had sensitized me to such things. I could no more drink from a bathroom hot water tap than I could from a rain puddle in the street. We visited museums, including the Freer Gallery and enjoyed meals out. But in the back of both our minds were our individual problems and how to resolve them.

We spent New Year in Texas, inviting friends for supper on New Year's Day, after a quiet New Year's Eve at home. The dog disappointed us all by licking the almond-coated cheese log placed on a low coffee table with crackers as *hors d'oeuvre*. We had to throw it out even though he only licked the crushed nuts! Luckily my roast turkey with all the trimmings went down well and satisfied everyone's appetite, washed down with plenty of wine, and followed with a fruit crumble and cream prepared from apples grown on the ranch. Kyle's guests included a high flying theatrical producer and his partner, one of Kyle's former students. Other invitees came from the University and the local community. One of the young women, a school teacher, showed me the small pistol she kept tucked into her skirt waistband, in case of trouble on the roads. According to her, hold ups, robberies and carjacking were frequent occurrences. Texas was not a 'down home', relaxed and friendly place but an economically and socially challenged environment, not quite as attractive as I had first thought when I arrived.

At Easter I took myself off to the International TESOL Convention in Baltimore, where I met up with old friends, caught up with trends in the field, and looked at job opportunities worldwide including one in Bahrein at a new

Polytechnic system. I shed a few tears with two friends as we reminisced about the past. Both women had suffered major disappointments in their love lives as I had. Away from Kyle, I realised that my work had been the one constant which I could rely on and which could enable me to live the life I wanted to achieve, especially if I continued my studies as I so desired.

The question was, would I find a job in the USA and stay with Kyle? If we married, I would be on a better footing to find a job. Despite the setback with his situation, I felt optimistic about our future. I could buy a house in my own right, as I still had the money from Nabeel's and my joint account, half of which was mine incontrovertibly. There were large villas and luxurious condominiums all well within my budget, assuming I used only the half of the 250k sterling which was rightfully mine. I decided to push the issue of divorce with Nabeel, amicably divide up the assets I had moved for security and get myself my own home, job and future in the USA.

CHAPTER 35

Internet Dating: Ronald

August 2004

Rose had hoped that finding a partner so far from the Middle East would help her put thoughts of war behind her, but once again she found herself obsessed with the increasingly tragic events in Iraq. Not only the disenfranchised Sunni population but also some Shiites following Maqtada Al Sadr, a cleric from Fallujah, had begun to oppose the US troops. On 2 April Al Sadr incited riot with a sermon which resulted in the formation of his Mahdi Army. Two days later the US forces, in revenge for the March attacks on soldiers and civilian contractors, began an attack named *Vigilant Resolve* on Fallujah which was successfully defended by the Mahdi Army. On 9 April another ambush attack was made on civilian contractors in a fuel convoy *en route* to Baghdad International Airport in which both US soldiers and Iraqi civilians were killed. It was clear that a violent game of chess was in play, with no winners. But worse was to follow.

Abu Ghraib Prison in Baghdad had been notorious in Saddam's reign for the abuse and torture of prisoners but under US control the Geneva Convention was assumed to apply. But back in November 2003 an Associated Press report had described torture and humiliation tactics there. US General Taguba was brought in from Kuwait in December that year to investigate. In late April 2004 CBS News broadcast details from the Taguba report. The details were as damning as the full report revealed in May in the *New Yorker*. Although six soldiers were punished, and the Head of Prisons in Iraq, Janis Karpinski, was demoted, Donald Rumsfeld as Secretary of Defence ultimately blamed Taguba for revealing the extent of the Guantanamo procedures introduced to extract information from detainees.

In May a video emerged showing the beheading of US contractor Nick Berg in Iraq, attributing his murder as retaliation for the Abu Ghraib abuses. Thus began the terrible saga of what soldiers termed 'the Baghdad haircut', beheading, more feared than injury or death by IED. Finally, aware of the hatred for the US forces on the ground as a result of their harsh treatment of Iraqi civilians, on June 28 Paul Bremer left Iraq, handing control and sovereignty over to Iyad Allawi as interim Prime Minister of Iraq. In July Saddam Hussein went on trial for war crimes. The list of horrors and heartaches continued.

To counteract her despair Rose decided to continue her internet search for love. She was surprised at how many responses she received. Some men wanted to chat, others wanted to meet up. After honesty check questions weeded out some of the cheats, Rose agreed to meet up with a British expatriate resident in Oz who was coming to Auckland on business in mid-August. By supreme coincidence at that time Rose would be working in Auckland on a Distance Training orientation course. Ronald's posted picture showed a young man in a tuxedo cavorting among the lion statues and the pigeons of London's Trafalgar Square. Rose realised that the photo was by no means current. Another photo showed a sea fishing boat. As Rose preferred *terra firma* this was not particularly enticing but it suggested Ronald could afford fairly expensive leisure pursuits. Although Rose was not searching for a millionaire she needed an independently wealthy partner, having left her marriage with no financial assets. Despite the obvious age of the personal photo, she hoped that Ronald in the flesh would not be too much of a let-down!

With both work and play on her mind, Rose packed carefully for the first week of the course. She was staying in a four star hotel, and would need winter work clothes, but for her potential blind date she packed some black stockings, nice underwear, smart shoes and a long suede skirt to wear with a slinky jersey top. She hoped her sartorial efforts would be rewarded with a pleasant evening out at least. Work on the course was demanding, so for the first two evenings Rose was pleased to be able to go back to the hotel, kick off her shoes, and make herself some soup. Then, on Wednesday evening came the phone call she had been half expecting, half dreading.

'Hi. Is that Rose?'

'Yes, Ronald?'

'Indeed. I'm staying at the Sky Tower Hotel. Would you like to join me for dinner?'

'When were you thinking of?'

'Tonight? Have you eaten?'

'Well, no. I'm a little tired as the course is quite hard work, but it would be nice to go out for a change.'

'That's great. I'm in Room 625. Just come on up.'

'OK. See you in an hour.'

Rose showered and changed speedily. She applied a little make up, which she normally didn't wear in the daytime. She brushed her hair and applied her lipstick. Well, she certainly looked better than her *au naturel* photo, so on with the show. She walked briskly over to the hotel which was only two blocks away. The winter evening was dark but not too cold, so her smart shoes and sheer black stockings were warm enough. Arriving at the hotel she felt a little 'smutty' going up to the room of a man she had never met before. Of course, they had chatted online for a month or so, but this was a bold step, especially in light of the code she had lived by in Kuwait. Rose had not told anyone what she was doing, as she was rather ashamed of herself. But having stayed in plenty of five star hotels herself she knew she could use the phone to get herself out of trouble if necessary. She was up for the challenge. Her social life had been pretty boring since Ward. She knocked on the door.

Ronald opened it, giving Rose a moment's pause. Was that really him? The short, balding man who stood there smiling at her certainly was not threatening, but he wasn't the reasonably good-looking young man in the photo. He might have been so 30 to 40 years earlier though. Hiding her disappointment, Rose smiled and held out her hand to shake his. Taking her hand Ronald pulled her gently inside and wrapped his arms around her to give her a kiss on both cheeks. Oh dear, would things work out all right, she wondered? Drawing away from him after this rather familiar greeting, she walked into the room and sat on the armchair between the twin beds.

'Are you ready to go down for dinner?' she asked.

'Yes, all but my shoes, but would you like a drink first?'

'OK. That sounds relaxing. What have you got?'

'What would you like? The minibar is extensive here.'

'Thanks. A scotch and soda would be perfect.'

'Ice?'

'No, thanks.'

Ronald busied himself with the drinks, then came over and sat on the bed.

'Well, it's nice to see you. Cheers! I wasn't sure that you'd come.'

'I said I would, and I keep my promises.'

'I can see that. You look marvellous.'

'Mm. Thanks. You look smart in your suit.'

Rose avoided returning the compliment too effusively as it just wouldn't ring true.

She felt it necessary to get the conversation going.

'How is your trip going? Are you busy? I'm run off my feet with the course I'm teaching.'

'Well, I come over here quite frequently, but I've got a tricky deal going down at the moment. It's a takeover which keeps changing its plan, so it's a bit frustrating.'

'I see.' Rose really didn't like discussing business. It reminded her of her ex-husband. She changed the subject.

'How do you like Auckland? Do you know New Zealand well?'

'Not too much. I have only really visited Auckland. How about you?'

'Well, I haven't seen much yet. I've only been here for seventeen months, so I'm no expert.'

'How about internet dating? Have you done much before?'

'No, never. This is my first foray into that world. How about you?'

'Well, I've tried before, but I've not been as lucky as I am tonight.'

'Thanks for the compliment! First of all, tell me the truth, are you married?'

Out came the old excuse Rose had heard before.

'Yes, but I'm separated.'

'Do you still live together?'

'Well, yes, but only until we sell the house and go our separate ways.'

'Mm. That's a rather ambiguous situation. I prefer not to date married men. Shall we go for dinner?'

Disappointed both by Ronald's appearance and his marital status Rose tried to keep the conversation light during dinner, but Ronald kept turning on the charm and the sexual innuendo. They ate in one of the hotel's restaurants and drank some excellent Gisborne *pinot gris*. After the meal came the moment of decision as Ronald asked her,

'Would you like to have a night cap upstairs?'

Rose thought about making an excuse, but the wine and the scotch had mellowed her. Taking a chance, she agreed to the nightcap.

'OK. Just one. I have to work tomorrow, so I won't linger.'

Back in the room the dim lights, soft music, the smooth cognac Ronald offered and the promisingly sweet kisses led on to a brief, semi-clad connection. As Rose freshened up in the bathroom she looked at herself in surprise. She had hooked up, as Facebook described it. It wasn't something she wanted to do again. Ronald, on the other hand, seemed delighted. He hugged her warmly and asked if he could see her the following day. Rose demurred as she was very busy with her course. The next week Ronald called repeatedly until she finally agreed to have dinner again, but arranged this time to meet in public. Ronald limped into the hotel foyer, suffering from gout. Because of his painful foot they took a taxi down to the Viaduct Harbour, where he regaled her with champagne and seafood. At the end of the evening Rose took a taxi back to her own hotel. With a firm handshake she said goodbye. Although she promised to email, she knew in her heart that was the end of Ronald.

CHAPTER 36

Fraud

April 1994

On my return from Baltimore Kyle met me at Texas' Will Rogers Airport with an international telegram from my friend in Kuwait, Patti, a physiotherapy teacher. She had returned to Kuwait University after Gulf War 1 and resumed work there. She'd been in touch with Nabeel intermittently and had news for me. He was out to defraud me and was boasting about it. Patti gave me her phone number so that she could give me more details. I could hardly believe my eyes. I turned to Kyle as we drove away.

'Well, honey, we are both in the proverbial now. I've got no money it seems.'

'I did think you should have spent it all on Day 1 of departure. He's a wily bastard.'

'Bastard is the right word. And naive was the right word for me. But I'm not used to wheeling and dealing. I'm too honest for my own good.'

On following up with Patti on the phone, it seemed that my attempts at an amicable separation had fallen on deaf ears. Nabeel was furious and my honesty about moving the money out of his reach had made him angrier than ever. He had managed to extract the money from my account in Hong Kong and move it to Kuwait. I was penniless. Although I was white with anger about the defrauding, I realised that now more than ever I needed to get a job. I should probably not rely on Kyle either financially or emotionally given his pending legal situation. I decided to follow up some of the job leads from the TESOL conference I'd attended. My CV was easily refreshed and sent off to Arabian Gulf universities with vacancies. I spoke Arabic and I had relevant experience, so why not capitalise on it? Plus, the Gulf countries did not tax the income they paid employees and the health care systems were good, should I need them, after the operation in Hong Kong.

The next month was busy with communications to my bank in Hong Kong. My case was reported to the Hong Kong Commercial Crime Bureau, who invited me to report to them in person as soon as possible. At the same time I was called for interview in Washington by a new and growing Polytechnic system in Bahrein. The job advertised was in a Supervisory capacity and well within my capabilities. Once again I flew to Washington D.C. from Texas. Kyle had said very little about my plans. I assumed this was because he was fully occupied with his own troubles. He took me to the airport again and wished me luck. In Washington I took the shuttle bus downtown. I was staying in a hotel near the infamous Waterhouse Complex. I only had one night, and I was keen to make a good impression so I did very little other than take a stroll around the block. I needed a good night's sleep.

My interview for the Bahrein position was in the Embassy. I made sure I arrived early. I was interviewed by two male Americans, both PhDs, one more friendly than the other.

It was fortunate for me that the friendly one was looking to fill a vacancy in his own Department. Having completed the rigorous interview, and admitting, honestly if unwisely, that I really needed this job as I had just been defrauded by my ex-husband, another job description was placed in front of me.

'Do you think you could do that?' the friendly American asked.

The job description was an even better fit for me than the job I had just interviewed for. I elaborated on the training expertise I had, including my work in language testing and teacher development. In next to no time, the interview was over. I felt reasonably confident that I would get one job or the other.

Back in Texas, both Kyle and I were playing waiting games: me for the job, Kyle for the sexual harassment case. Kyle seemed rather subdued, but I was not prepared for the real reason why. One morning while tidying papers in the bedroom I came across a manila envelope, half A4 size. In it were photos of Kyle and Virginia, one of his students, having a picnic in a park. The intimacy of the photos suggested that there had been something going on while I was out of town first for the Conference and then for the interview. I was seething with anger and placed them on the table ready for Kyle's return.

'So this is what you were up to while I was away?'

'What? Having a picnic? Is that illegal?'

'You know what it is better than me. It's a sign that you can't be alone for three days.'

'Well, I needed someone to talk to about the case. Virginia supports me. She's a married woman, you know.'

'She may be now, but she won't be for long if these pictures tell the story.'

'You know I gave up all the others for you - why would I cheat on you?'

'I don't know, and really, I don't care.'

'But I thought we might get married before you started applying for jobs so as to leave me.'

The words struck my heart like daggers.

'Get married? Really? Why would you? And why would I, other than to get a job here?'

'Well, that would be a start. We could work on things. We get on so well together.'

'Yes, we do, but only because I'm here temporarily. I can't trust you, and I need trust in a relationship. Let's see what happens to the job offer and discuss again. Enough for now. But thanks for the proposal.'

I was tired of this pointless argument. I got a response to my application the following week: I was given a managerial position. The salary was excellent, the perks were good, and I could start in August. My plans were quickly made. I would leave the USA in May, go home to see Mum and leave my heavy suitcases, then travel to Hong Kong to report the criminal act of fraud. Back in the UK I would pack and leave for my new job in Bahrein.

Kyle was upset. 'So you are leaving me. I knew I was your rebound lover.'

'Well, you made yourself the rebound. Let me sum up my experience with you. First you cheated on Amy when you were in Hong Kong with me, then I came here and you were still in touch with your student lover, after that was the court case, and now Virginia. It's a bit much in a short time, Kyle.'

'OK, OK. I get it. But can I see you again? What about my coming over to the UK this summer?'

'Well, if you can get over before I leave in early August, that's no problem. You've been a good friend to me, and I'm not going to take all this too seriously, though I am disappointed.'

'OK, I could come to London and we'd do some sightseeing together. I'd love to meet your Mum and brothers.'

'All right. We'll do that. I don't want to lose your friendship, Kyle. We've had some good times together. You've helped me reinvent myself.'

'Great. I'm sorry to cause you so much grief. I'm needy I suppose.'

'Yes, and spoilt,' I thought to myself, but I said: 'Yes, and I'm insecure. Let's see how we feel about each other when we meet up again.'

Although I didn't stress the case, I was so hurt that before leaving I searched Kyle's packing boxes for photos of me. I felt he didn't deserve these intimate souvenirs of our time together. My trust in him had gone.

I left the USA in early May, and stayed briefly in London and then Mossfield. While there I received one of the phone calls Nabeel had been assailing my family with. I challenged him about the defrauding and told him that I was reporting the fraud to the authorities. I reminded him of our agreement that the funds in the term deposit in the Isle of Man were ours jointly, so I was entitled to half of the 250,000 GBP I had moved to Hong Kong to keep the money out of his reach, till our divorce was final. I felt entitled to 125,000 GBP given the fact that I'd worked all my married life and had sacrificed having children on his account.

'You know, it would be cheaper to have you killed,' Nabeel said in response.

'Those are the last words you will ever speak to me. Never call me again. The rest of our discussions will be through my solicitor.'

I put the phone down abruptly, chilled by his venom and warned Mum and Bill to ignore his calls in future. I then flew to Hong Kong, where the mysteries of the Far East in the shape of the Hong Kong Commercial Crime Bureau were to unfold before my eyes. Despite the excitement I always felt in Hong Kong it was strange for me to return to the place in which the cracked vessel of my marriage had started to break apart. I had always cherished the sensation of being a resident worker in this magical place but now I was merely a visitor. I stayed with my friend, Lucy. It was fun to be back with her and her mynah bird, Bugsie, who made us laugh with his chatter. He wished visitors a firm 'goodbye' when he was ready to see them go, and referred to breakfast Weetabix in milk as, 'nice wormies', his own favourite food.

When I kept my appointment in the Police Headquarters building in Wan Chai Roger Fong led me to the basement floor and a small, dark, wooden framed interview cubicle. Under his watchful gaze I began to feel wary, like a suspect, as I gave my tale of the fraud.

'So, start from the beginning, Madam.'

'Well, I had an account in Hong Kong when I worked here. My branch was at the University where the personnel knew me. I opened a savings account, in September 1993 and I was in communication with the Branch Manager by letter about that.'

'What was in this account?'

'I moved 250,000 sterling from an account in the Isle of Man.'

'Why did you move the money?'

'Because I had decided to divorce my husband after two years of separation, and I was afraid that he would remove this money without my permission. It was a joint account, but with a single signature needed to move the money. I didn't trust him.'

'So you moved it without his permission?'

'Yes, but I wrote and told him about my action. I told him I wanted this to be subject to our divorce settlement, after 23 years together and 17 years of marriage.'

'So how did he react to this information?'

'He gave me no response at all, so I assumed we would move into the next stage of the divorce at some time in the future. I never dreamed he would do what he did.'

'What did he do?'

'He sent a forged letter, full of typing errors and English language mistakes, asking to have the money transferred to his brother's account in Kuwait. That brother has the same first name initial and family name as mine.'

'Did you challenge him about this?'

'Yes, I rang him and told him that I would pursue him through the law.'

'What was his response?'

'He threatened to have me killed.'

'Did you believe him?'

'Yes. After seeing what he is capable of with this theft, I would believe anything about him now.'

'This is a difficult situation.'

'Yes, I know. Where do I stand according to the law in Hong Kong? Can I sue the bank? Can I sue the perpetrator of the offence?'

'Well, I'm sure you feel like suing them both, but in fact, the complexity is compounded by the fact that this is a civil case between two people who are married.

In addition, we have had the letter which asked for the transfer checked by our forgery experts and they have affirmed that the signature on the letter is indeed yours.'

'I thought as much. I have been extremely honest, naive and trusting.'

'How did he get your signature on the letter?'

'He didn't. I gave him two or even three pieces of blank A4 paper at the start of our marriage with my signature on. I was a fool but he said they were for visas.'

'Well, I'm afraid it puts a very different perspective on things. The bank received a letter with your signature on. Despite the spelling and grammar errors, they were obliged to fulfil the request for a transfer of funds.'

'So you don't think I will get any satisfaction from the Bank?'

'Well, you can try, but legally they are not bound to help you.'

I did my best not to burst into tears at this point.

'Well, what about my legal rights with regard to my estranged husband?'

'The question for the bank is, whose money is it?'

'Well, half of it was mine and half was his. That was our agreement.'

'So why did you move all of it?'

'Because he had enticed me to leave my job here, saying he had plenty of money, and would buy a flat for us in London. When he reneged on that I felt entitled to more of the total sum, but was willing to wait for jurisdiction on that issue.'

'You know, if you had spent the money, he wouldn't have been able to do anything.'

'So, are you saying that now he has moved the money, he has pre-empted me? I can do nothing?'

'Madam, let me give you an example. Imagine you borrow your neighbour's lawn mower and leave it in your shed overnight.'

'Yes?'

'That night someone steals it. Who has lost the lawnmower?'

'Well, my neighbour has. But I was involved because it was my shed.'

'Yes, but the law cannot pursue YOU if you locked the shed, just as you cannot pursue the bank in this case. Nor can we pursue him for moving money which was his as well as yours. It's up to you to sort it out in your divorce settlement.'

'Right. Thank you for your time. As a language teacher I feel affronted because it was so obviously not my letter, but it was my signature, so I contributed to my own downfall.'

'That is the sad side of it. But Confucius says, we live and learn.'

'We do indeed. And we can live to tell the tale.'

'I hope you will be able to do so. Your signature is a precious thing and should not be given away to anyone.'

'You are so right. I have been a fool.'

That night I reported the day's events back to Lucy and we drank a farewell to what I might have done with my half of the quarter million pounds. If I had bought a small flat I would have been able to complete my PhD in the UK. Now I was left with what remained of my 20,000 sterling pounds savings, all I had in the world. But at least those pounds were all mine, and thank goodness I had a job to go to. This now had to become my focus. The friendly fire from my husband had shot me right in the heart, but not in the head. *Blue on blue* once again. Friendly fire.

CHAPTER 37

A Dream and a Nightmare

September - December 2004

On Rose's return to Farmerston her workload continued to increase in quantity and pace due to her own initiatives. She was spending more and more time in the office collecting and compiling data from students to revise the writing descriptors in use in the Centre. She was leading in-house professional development workshops as well as the commercially marketed courses for training new language teachers. She was also writing new listening and reading tests for the advanced level students' achievement tests. Then there was a new training course for overseas teachers starting in September for which she had to prepare materials and prepare her training team. In addition to that she was interviewing teachers for her own research paper and typing up the scripts steadily after work hours. No work-life balance was as yet in sight!

At weekends she was still researching plans and considering budgets for her future home at the beach. She had bought the creek section despite her concerns about mosquitoes and potential nuisance from passersby because the price seemed right for her budget but she still didn't feel ready to commit to building on it. Although she had seen a much more expensive section with potential sea views she had not heard from the agent as promised when the sections were released for sale. She had built up quite a portfolio of house features she liked, such as sliding doors, so she felt she should start to build before the end of September, but something was holding her back. She wanted to stay in New Zealand, so why couldn't she take the plunge and build her dream home?

In early September Rose booked into a seaside motel for what she considered a final time before signing up to build. She took a last ride around the Paloa Beach area. She drove by the sections with potential sea views and noticed a *Private Sale* sign on one of them with a phone number which she noted down. She spent the rest of the day doing what had become her beach routine, viewing houses, taking a beach walk with an ice cream, having a take away evening meal and again, watching CNN and BBC TV to catch up on the Middle East where the horrors continued. The 'Baghdad haircuts' were increasing, with a mass beheading in August of twelve Nepalese workers in orange jumpsuits, and the kidnapping of six Egyptian workers and three civilian contractors, two Americans and one British man who pleaded for their lives in a video intended to drive the coalition forces out of Iraq. Rose wondered with sadness if their voices would be heard by Bush and Blair, the political leaders who had started this trail of violence.

While she absorbed the terrible news, her mind kept returning to the section she had seen with the Private for

Sale notice. What should she do about the phone number? Was it a complicating factor she should ignore or a sign that she should pay attention to? Rose's inability to make a decision caused her a couple of sleepless nights. At work the following Monday morning her friend Heather asked her how the building process was going.

'I haven't signed the contract yet,' Rose told her.

'Why not? Not sure about it?'

'Not so much the design as the location. I'm still not sure about the creek. And you know what? I came across a Private Sale notice for one of the sea view sections I was interested in.'

'Really? How much do they want?'

'I haven't rung the number.'

'Why not? What are you waiting for?'

'Do you think I should?'

'Of course.'

There and then Rose picked up the phone and spoke to the owner. He wanted 220 thousand NZ Dollars after paying only 140 thousand for it. It was typical of the current huge resale profit taking. She discussed it with Heather.

'You know, if you sell your section, then you will probably make the same gain.'

'Do you think so?'

'Yes, you have to be determined. If you got 160 thousand, then the difference between the creek and the sea view sections would be exactly the same as it was when you were originally interested.'

'You're right. What shall I do? I want to be able to see the sea if I buy it.'

'Then book a cherry picker and we'll go over and have a look at it.'

'Great idea. Wow. You know what to do. Thanks!'

Within 24 hours Rose had organised a viewing with the seller and the builder. The following Saturday the two friends were loaded into the cherry picker bucket, and raised to the height that a second storey would be. Heather pointed out the 180 degree sea vista that would be possible. Rose was ready! By chance and with her friend's help she had found her dream property. However, the financial situation weighed heavily on Rose's mind during September. Her savings were in sterling pounds and the exchange rate was decreasing so she was losing money. She was also committed to the design process now, though rather baffled by the expectation that she would know what she wanted. Top of the list was double glazing, which was derided by the builders. 'No one has that here.'

'Well, I guessed that, and I'm freezing in my house in Farmerston. I have to wear a beanie in bed.'

'OK. If you insist, but you'll have to pay separately for that.'

'And what about insect screens?'

'We don't do those. You can put them in afterwards.'

'And central heating?'

'No, no such thing here. But heat pumps do the job. They are new but they are becoming popular. Separate charge for those too.'

'OK. What about bookshelves? I have to have those integral to the house.'

'OK. We can do that. Where do you want them? Up or downstairs?'

'Both please.'

Slightly stunned at such extravagance, the designer made a note on the plan.

'And, I really like the sliding door in the show home here. Can I have one in the study/fourth bedroom?'

'Of course. And there's one in the entrance to the walk in wardrobe. With a mirror.'

'Perfect.'

The contract was finally signed at the end of September, with a six month build period and staged payments mapped out. With relief she achieved a profitable sale of her original section in October. Her finances were falling into place satisfactorily but Rose was still cautious. She monitored the build every weekend, driving over for the day only as she was now inordinately busy with work and study as well.

In her limited free time Rose was still keeping up with events in Iraq. The two Americans and the Englishman, Ken Bigley, had finally been beheaded in front of the video camera in September. Then, on 20 October a familiar face and name appeared on BBC News, another kidnap victim in Iraq, but for the first time, a female Westerner. Margaret Hassan, whose Diploma examination lesson Rose had assessed back in 1988 in Baghdad, was an Irish woman married to an Iraqi. Like Rose, she had met her husband in London. They had lived in Iraq since 1972. Margaret had worked at the British Council, Baghdad, just as Rose had worked at the British Council, Kuwait from 1976. Nabeel had forbidden Rose to travel to Iraq during the Iran Iraq war but Rose had defied his wishes to help Margaret and another colleague. The British Council, Baghdad had closed as of the invasion of Kuwait and Margaret had become head of the local branch of an international charity organisation, Care.

In horror Rose watched tear-drenched Margaret plead with Tony Blair for her life by freeing some imprisoned Iraqis.

At one point Margaret appeared to faint, and her hooded captors threw a bucket of water over her. Rose sobbed as the news item moved on. No one knew who had kidnapped Margaret as she was being driven to her office. Local women who had benefited from her charity work had marched in public on her behalf, protesting at the kidnapping and asking for her release. In vain. Days later Margaret was declared missing, presumed dead. No one could have expected this in a society where women are protected. The unimaginable was becoming the norm in war-torn Iraq. Life was cheap, death common. Rose shuddered. Thank goodness she had got out of the Middle East before these terrible events took place.

In December, Rose realised that her Farmerston house would need to be sold so as to make the final payments on the new build. She had enjoyed her first house in New Zealand but was not sad at the thought of leaving it. She engaged a real estate agent to manage the sale while Rose was over at the beach checking on the progress of the new house. Despite all the checking her lack of expertise with interpreting building plans meant that her coveted sliding fourth bedroom/study door was omitted. She was grateful to the electrician for pointing it out to her so that she could discuss a Plan B with her builder. Disappointed at this error she began to worry about how many more things might go wrong with her 'dream home'.

The continuing bad news coming out of Iraq convinced Rose that all her problems were little ones. Bush had declared on 2 May, 2003 that 'The Battle of Iraq is one victory in a war on terror that began on 11 September 2001, and still goes on.' Unfortunately, the Americans brought chaos and terror to innocent victims in Iraq that may have equalled what Saddam Hussein had done to his country and it was by no means over. Margaret had paid the ultimate price despite working for the local people. *Blue on blue* indeed. Rose found it hard to sleep at night, thinking of how Margaret's husband and family were coping with this tragedy.

CHAPTER 38

Moving to Bahrein

August 1994

I had told the family only a little about my emotional ups and downs with Kyle in the USA. To them he was just a friend who had offered me a place to hide away from Nabeel. So, when Kyle came to London as my friend, he stayed at my brother's in a separate bedroom, since my niece and nephew were old enough to understand that Uncle Nabeel had gone and someone else was taking his place. I didn't want that to happen. We stayed only a couple of nights in London for some sightseeing and a theatre trip. Then we drove up to Mossfield, where I showed Kyle around some local beauty spots. Mum didn't say much. I know she disapproved of my finding a replacement man. She wrote in my birthday card in September that year, 'Why do you need a man in your life?' 'Mum, you weren't the best role model,' I whispered under my breath. I suppose she was trying to protect me from further heartache.

To get away for a while we went up to the Lake District. We visited the site of Wordsworth's famous *Daffodils* poem and his home, Dove Cottage. We wandered lonely as the clouds and had a happy time together but I felt once again the disappointment of a relationship that was so close to what I wanted, yet so far away from perfection in terms of trust. I knew I had to go on with my own plans. Being financially independent was my major goal at this point in my life.

On returning to Mossfield, Kyle tried to charm Mum, but only managed to get a smile from her on the morning he left to catch a train up to Scotland to visit family. On the platform he repeated his earlier proposal: 'Will you marry me and come back to the USA?'

'Perhaps, but not yet,' I said, just as I had to Nabeel almost twenty years earlier. 'Ask me again in six months time.'

Obligations of return hospitality completed I had to prepare myself for the new job in Bahrein. I needed smart clothes suitable for the Muslim world, with longish skirts, or loose trousers and long sleeved, torso covering jackets, for my new role. My flight from London to Bahrein with Gulf Air was uneventful. After my experience in Hong Kong I was chastened, but not depressed. I felt positive and strong. The only thing that surprised me was the strength of emotion I felt on hearing Arabic spoken around me on the plane. I had transferred my new hatred of my husband to all those who spoke his native tongue. I had no control over my feelings whatsoever. On arrival Jack, a former colleague in Kuwait, met me at the huge, modern airport. He drove me to my hotel in his large American car and as we approached the capital the illuminated skyline of Manama arose like New York from the desert.

'Wow. This is a surprise,' I commented. 'I visited Bahrein in the '80s when I was in Kuwait, but this is so different, so amazing.'

'Yes, the Bahreinis have made huge strides since they discovered oil. Even though their oil was found later than Kuwait's, they've caught them up in next to no time.'

'So do you find it much easier living here than in Kuwait, Jack?

'Yes, there's no comparison. Not having to brew wine and beer helps a lot, you know!'

'Gosh, yes. Will I be able to buy booze?'

'Yes, as soon as you get your liquor licence. That might take a couple of weeks.'

'Interesting!'

'You're allowed to buy booze according to a fixed percentage of your salary, no more, but you can buy less of course.'

'Well, I can look forward to that. What else can I expect to be different?'

'Well, the job is a bit tricky. The colleges are like the legs of a spider - and we are the eyes in the head, trying to watch the legs and cajole them all to go in the same direction. Our job is really Quality Control and leadership, but each College wants to do its own thing at some time or other. You'll find out soon enough.'

'What's my boss like? He seemed a very nice chap at my interview.'

'Yes, he's great. He's very hands off if you are doing a good job, but he'll get on your case if things start to go wrong.'

'So what advice can you give me?'

'Keep your sense of humour ready. Don't let things get you down. And ask me anything you like, any time.'

'What happened, can I ask, to you and your wife? Why isn't she here with you as she was in Kuwait?'

'The Invasion upset her. She was traumatised when I was taken prisoner. She doesn't want to live in the Arab World again.'

'Funny, that's one of the feelings I had on the plane coming over - I hope it won't last. Do you think she'll change her mind? Have you been here long?'

'I've been here for just one year. She's going to visit, so we'll see. There's lots to do here. She can teach, there's the theatre, she'd be fine.'

'Yes, she loved amateur dramatics in Kuwait, didn't she?'

'Yes, but our son is in boarding school in the UK and she likes to see him in the holidays.'

'Gosh, I'd almost forgotten your son. He was only little in Kuwait, wasn't he?'

'Yes, he was born there!'

By now we were pulling into the downtown Holiday Inn, where Jack checked me in and told me who would pick me up in the morning.

'Be ready for 8 o'clock. There's a lot to do. You'll be in a group, getting blood tests, chest X-rays, etcetera.'

'OK. Thanks, Jack. See you soon.'

I was tired. I unpacked my toiletries, took a shower and slid into bed. Tomorrow I would learn more. For now, memories of Kuwait were mixed with the first impressions of Bahrein. 'Here I go again,' I thought. 'A new job, a new country, and a new life to build.'

The next morning I went down early to the marble-floored, coolly air-conditioned lobby. There I found a tall, blonde young woman and two young men, as well as a couple who had been on the plane with me from London. The six of us were ushered into a small minibus and driven to the

Health Centre where we had blood taken for AIDS testing. Workers with AIDS would be deported. We worried that our samples might be wrongly labelled but tried to joke the fear away. Then came the chest X-rays. Queueing with other workers, including labourers in overalls, and Pakistanis in their *shalwar kameez* and a sprinkling of Philippina or Sri Lankan maids was amusing. The men from societies where women were in purdah could not take their eyes off the range of beauties presented unveiled to their eyes. After our check ups we were taken back to the hotel for a well earned rest.

I took a walk in the afternoon, despite the heat. I popped into shopping malls and stores for respite from the heat along the main street. I managed to get as far as the Porsche showroom without needing a drink. Sweating, red in the face, and desperately thirsty, I showed unfeigned interest in a purple Porsche. I declined the invitation to sit inside on the pristine leather but I accepted the traditional Arab hospitality of a cold drink, then coffee, while discussing the various models and their prices. Having cooled down in the air conditioned showroom, I made my way in the dusk back to the hotel. My negative reaction to Arabic heard on the plane had completely disappeared. I could still read the illuminated Arabic script on shop frontages even after two years in Hong Kong. I wondered if the Mandarin Chinese I'd learned there would last as long. I remembered how free and easy I had felt in Hong Kong. Here in Bahrein I felt that my every move was observed closely. The cage I had experienced in Kuwait was closing in again, but at least I had newfound confidence. I was now almost a single woman again, though the divorce was not yet finalised.

Back at the hotel the others had returned from their College experiences. We had dinner together in the coffee shop, chatting about our future accommodation. We were allowed only one week in the security and companionship of the hotel. Then we were to move out to our permanent housing. Only a few of us were moving into flats which other GPC staff had furnished. I paid the previous tenant for the curtains, carpet and cooker in my flat. The first week flew by in a frenzy of getting to know the ropes at work, meeting colleagues, and shopping for a TV, fridge and a bed. I was planning to send for my Hong Kong shipping, in storage at the docks in London. I was also eager to get my own liquor licence. Jack had promised he would help me but loaned me a bottle of whisky in the meantime.

Watching TV in my new flat one evening I heard a knock on the door. I found an unfamiliar European male standing there. Surprised, I could only say, 'Yes?'

He appeared a little taken aback by my reaction but he smiled as he spoke.

'My name's Colin and I work for GPC like you. I live in this building, just below you and we earn the same salary! I'm a 'manager' too.'

Now it was my turn to be taken aback. I didn't even know my own salary, so how did this stranger? 'Curiouser and curiouser' as Alice in Wonderland said.

'Really?'

'Yes, we met this morning at the staff meeting and I wondered if you needed any booze.'

I didn't like to admit that I hadn't even noticed him that morning! I could tell from his accent and vocabulary that he was a Brit like me. So, ignoring the strange fact he had produced about our equal salary status, I took the stance that he was trying to help me, even if he wasn't very good at choosing his words.

'That's very kind. I haven't got my licence yet.'

'Well, what would you like? Some gin? Some wine or beer?'

'A bottle of gin would be marvellous if you can spare it. Would you like to come in?'

'I'll go and bring the gin for you, OK? Back in a mo.'

Colin sprinted downstairs and soon reappeared with the liquid silver.

'It's a good one, Bombay Gin.'

'Thanks very much. I'll replace it as soon as I can. Would you like to come in?'

'No, I won't, thanks. I guess you are busy.'

'Yes, and I don't have any furniture yet, just a bean bag and a TV.'

'OK. Well, nice to talk to you.'

'See you again when I get my licence!'

'Sing out if you need more - I'm downstairs, 507.'

'Thanks a lot. I appreciate this. Bye for now.'

As I closed the door, my impressions of Colin were pleasant but confused. He appeared strikingly handsome, with sky-blue eyes. His sudden appearance had been a surprise, as was the bottle of gin. Colin's office was downtown, whereas I worked in a block near to my apartment building. So I didn't think I'd be seeing very much of him even though we were neighbours. The next day, to my surprise, he turned up again, with a case of beer.

'Wow, that's wonderful. You must come in and have one.'

'OK. Have you seen the whole building yet?'

'Well, two days haven't been long enough to even map out where I'll put my furniture when my shipping comes. I've no idea about the building, except that the boys who are on the front desk are very kind.'

'Well, there's a small pool on the roof. It's handy for a swim after work, but the beaches are better on weekends. Then there are some hotel resorts, with club facilities.'

'OK - but I guess they are expensive?'

'It depends what you want to do. The gyms are good but we have a small one here on the ninth floor. Next door to it is a pool table. And, there's a squash court.'

'Great. I don't play pool or squash but I'd like to learn. For now, would you like a beer?'

'Yes, please. Have you been here before?'

'No, I was in Kuwait for 15 years. It's a long story.'

'OK. No need for history right now.'

'What about you?'

'Well, let's keep it for another night. But I've been here for a year already and I've got two more on my contract.'

'I see. Well, I feel very much the new girl. I still have to get a fridge, and work seems quite hectic. I don't know if I'll need a car or not.'

'The only time you really need a car is when you pick up your booze. The taxi drivers recognise the carrier bags and they don't like carrying these *haraam*, forbidden, goods.'

'I see. Wow.'

'But I'll be happy to take you along when I go booze shopping. Just let me know when you get your licence.'

'OK - that could be next week.'

Our drinks finished, Colin stood up to go. As he reached the door, he turned and kissed me briefly and unexpectedly on the lips. I felt a surge of electricity through me as he did so, and my eyes opened wide. I don't know if he felt the same, but it was a shock to me to experience such a chemical reaction. I closed the door on him, and leaned against it in shock. Wow. What next, I wondered?

CHAPTER 39

Heart of Gold?

December 2004

By the end of the year the second storey of the house frame was up, and the weatherboard cladding was being installed on the first floor but the progress hadn't been as fast as Rose expected. The builder was moaning about the intensive labour that the concrete weatherboard cladding required. This wasn't Rose's problem. She suspected the franchisee had not been totally honest when he sub-contracted the build out. On her weekly inspections she had noted the ladder up to the second floor but she hadn't dared to go up it as she had no head for heights. The sea was only 500 metres away but was tantalisingly out of sight behind the sand dunes. She needed someone to help her enjoy this ambitious step in her life but so far she hadn't found that elusive special someone. It was not for lack of trying, however.

Rose had renewed her subscription to the online dating service and was chatting intermittently to some respondents though she had not had time to meet anyone. She was reluctant to move to the face to face status given the disappointments in March and August. She had invitations from colleagues for Christmas Day and decided to offer her own Christmas hospitality on Christmas Eve. She invited one of her online 'chatters' to dinner along with her other friends. Ben was recently widowed with adult children. He fitted in with everyone and Rose was pleased to have made the effort to cook. Having friends round for dinner meant that she had no time to dwell on her memories of Christmas 2003 spent in the South Island with Colin. Nor did she dwell on distant Christmases past, when she had friends round for a turkey buffet with illicit homemade wine, beer and carols round the piano every Christmas Eve in Kuwait. All that was missing was a special someone she could make new memories with.

Left alone after dinner with Ben she realised that his passion was WW2 aeroplanes. The topic did not grip Rose quite as much. To bring the evening to a close, she asked him what he was doing for New Year's Eve. They said goodnight with a promise to get in touch during the week. Rose prevaricated because there was another person in her sight lines. She had been chatting online to Jed, a three times married man, now free, but with shared custody of two school age children. He had been honest, as far as she could tell from a distance, and amusing about his status. He too had expressed interest in meeting up over Christmas, but Rose had the first two days already covered. She had promised to ring him on Boxing Day. She hoped he would be more compatible with her than Ben.

On Boxing Day Rose decided to ring Jed as soon as she finished cleaning the house. But at 4pm the phone rang. It was Jed. He was coming over from wherever he lived, no excuses accepted! She would just have time to shower and wash her hair before he arrived at 6pm. When she opened the door to him, promptly at 6pm, the handsome smiling face she saw appealed to her instantly. She felt a forgotten tingle down her spine at the touch of his hand, and wondered briefly what he thought of her, a 'Pommy bastard' as some put it. Jed's thick, white hair and his suntanned complexion were striking. Was he Maori, she wondered? First impressions on her side were excellent! Ben was fading from the picture by the instant.

After pouring some chilled bubbles they sat outside on the swing on the deck and talked for hours. Evidently Jed had had as much of a rough ride as she had with relationships, tougher in fact, since all three wives had produced children he had had custody of. As a father he hadn't had it easy. All in all they had a lot of emotional baggage to share, but no secrets, she hoped, to ruin that immediate chemistry on meeting. Drinks led to dinner eaten inside as the evening was cooling. They dined on warmed up leftovers, which seemed to suit Jed well enough. He wasn't interested in going out and neither was she, with drink driving legislation adding tension to dining out. After a day cleaning her house, Rose began to feel tired, so suggested they move to the sitting area. Jed appraised the formal, uncomfortable looking Chinese sitting room suite with a critical glance.

'That doesn't look very cosy to me.'

'Well, if you want cosy, and a bit of TV news, there's the master bedroom if you like,' she said with a laugh. 'I'm a world news addict.'

'Let me see,' he grinned. 'Wow, that bed's huge, but the TV's small.'

'Big enough to keep up with world affairs,' she told him, still laughing.

They took their shoes off, put their glasses on the bedside cabinets, and Rose switched on the 10.30pm news. To their horror they saw the havoc wreaked by the Boxing Day tsunami on South East Asia. The tragedy affected them both emotionally and they turned to hug each other in consolation. Then their personal fireworks began and lasted till they fell asleep, with Rose silently counting her blessings.

The next morning Rose wondered whether Jed would leave after such a sudden and unexpected acceleration of events. She made him breakfast, which he ate silently after showering and dressing.

'How are the scrambled eggs?' she asked diffidently to break the unusual silence.

'I make them with parsley,' he told her. She wondered if that meant he didn't like hers. Perhaps he was tired after their night together. A moment later he reassured her.

'Would you like to see where I spent my childhood?' he asked as he put down his knife and fork. Perhaps he'd been wondering whether to ask her out.

'Well, yes, if it's not too far away, I suppose,' Rose replied.

'It's Ngaruawahia. Have you been there?'

'No, I haven't. I can't say that name either. Can you repeat it slowly for me?'

After repeating the name a few times, Rose asked where it was.

'Not far from here, just up the highway.'

'Cool. I'll get ready. Won't be long.'

Their visit to the small town where Jed explained the Maori King lived was extremely interesting. The two rivers, the Waipa and the Waikato, the longest river in New Zealand, met there and Jed described how he had rowed there as a young man. Jed was certainly more interesting than Ben. She hoped he would be interested enough in her to suggest they do something for New Year's Eve together. The lonely New Year's Eve in Dubai when Norman had rejected her still resonated in a melancholy way in her memory. *Blue on blue.*

The next three days blended into each other without a moment of boredom. Jed even took Rose to visit one of his family members in their home, which reassured her that he was serious about keeping her in his life, for the time being at least. Finally, one morning he declared that he had to leave, as Rose had been expecting.

'But what about New Year's Eve?' he asked. 'What are you doing?'

'Nothing special,' she told him happily.

'Well, I've got an idea,' he told her, 'how would you like to camp out at your house?'

Surprised and puzzled, Rose said she'd love it.

'But is it legal? The house isn't finished yet. Would we be trespassing?'

'It's your house, isn't it? I bet all your neighbours have been up that ladder you told me about. Now it's your turn to admire the view.'

Rose laughed. 'I'd love that. What do I need to do?'

'Well, you pack a picnic for the evening and some breakfast. I'll look after the rest.'

Smiling, they said goodbye. Rose rang Ben immediately.

'I'm sorry, Ben, but something has come up. I'm not free on New Year's Eve.'

Ben may have been disappointed, but he didn't comment. Without recriminations, he accepted that their relationship was a non-starter, and Rose looked forward to her surprisingly different New Year's Eve celebration.

When she arrived at the house on a pleasantly warm and sunny afternoon, she found Jed there already. He was a technical and gadget whizz. He had planned the camping experience at the semi-constructed new house in detail. They had a BBQ, TV, music, lights and a pump up bed. Rose laid out pate, cheese, ham and smoked salmon for their evening meal, with their guests, a couple who would be soon be Rose's neighbours. Joe grilled some French bread slices to make *bruschetta* with black olive *tappenade*, then produced some fresh fish which he grilled and they ate with a lemony *tabbouleh* salad Rose had made. The friends left before midnight to get home to their girls, while Jed and Rose saw in the New Year with more bubbles. The stars in the sky shone brightly over their heads, as they settled down to sleep. The deep dark velvet of the sky was amazing. The experience of the dawning New Year's Day creeping across the sky, the first country in the world to experience the New Year, was equally wonderful. Rose was in awe. What a novel New Year she had had with her new man. Was he the heart of gold she had crossed the ocean for, as Paul Young put it? She hoped so.

Over just a few days Rose had shared a lot of her past heartaches and her current concerns with Jed. She had been surprised at how much of her back story he empathised with. Many people didn't even know where Palestine was. Others had never noticed the invasion of Kuwait. Some people couldn't care less about Iraq. Jed understood why Rose's eyes filled with tears while watching TV news. The kidnapping and beheading of civilians, the IEDs and the suicide bombs killing and injuring soldiers and civilians created *heartache on heartache* for Rose, as surely as if she was still in a war zone. Perhaps now she could make a fresh start with Jed at her side to give her strength and turn her focus forwards rather than backwards. She was alive and she was grateful to have a future. *Blue on blue* might be fading away.

CHAPTER 40

Falling in Love Again

August 1994

Work became more and more demanding over the next days. My office was next door to my apartment building so it was extraordinarily convenient to work overtime. One new work friend was the strikingly red-haired Michelle. We had something in common. Her brother had been the only British expatriate to be killed during the attempt to escape across the desert to Saudi Arabia during the invasion of Kuwait. We shared the sense of past tragedy whose shadow over our lives we had to push away constantly. *Blue on blue*, indeed. Michelle's boyfriend sailed Lasers with Colin. I didn't want to appear too interested in Colin, so asked no questions. I might have been wiser to do so.

After two weeks, as promised, Jack escorted me and a male colleague to get our liquor licences at the Ministry of the Interior offices, large white cement buildings on a huge campus in the city. We sat in armchairs in a huge office with small glasses of sweet hot tea, *istakaan*, on coffee tables beside our seats while the big chief, in full military uniform, but with his peaked cap on the table, perused our completed documentation and photos. He gazed at each photo thoughtfully then matched it to the Westerners in front of him. I was glad I was wearing a long skirt and long sleeved jacket as I modestly raised my eyes and met his gaze. He spoke at last, in good English.

'Welcome to our country, dear friends.'

'Thank you very much,' we responded in polite chorus.

'Your licences are being prepared right now. They will take a few moments.

Now, Rose, I hope you will drink alcohol slowly and not too much.'

'Of course, your Excellency.'

It seemed appropriate to flatter this man with the politest of titles since he held power over our drinking habits.

'You will see that you do not have as much on your licence as your male colleague.'

I was impressed by his use of English but not by his message.

'Why is that, your Excellency? We have the same salaries, I believe?'

'Yes, but I must take care of ladies. Their livers are not so strong as those of men. You can only buy half of what men can buy.'

'I see,' I said with a polite smile. There was indeed some truth in this medically, so I felt ill-equipped and unwilling to argue the case. It seemed wiser to show that I appreciated this thoughtfulness. 'I am grateful to you for your care and attention to ladies. You are most kind.'

The other two men could barely hide their smiles. We said our farewells and walked across the Military compound to Jack's car, then we all collapsed into laughter.

'Well, I hope I don't ever get caught drunk and disorderly. He'll be on my case and ladies' liquor licences will be reduced even more!' I giggled.

That evening I boldly knocked on Colin's door.

'I've got my licence at last!'

'Great. When would you like to go booze shopping?'

'Tomorrow? After work?' I suggested.

'Fine. See you after 5pm.'

The next afternoon we went off to an area of downtown I had never seen: the booze shop. The people leaving the shop all had big plastic bags in their arms, or were followed by porters who manhandled cases of beverages into their cars. Inside, I was bemused by the variety and range of prices.

'Start small,' he suggested. 'Just buy a few items.'

'I need to replace your gin and Jack's whisky so I'll focus on spirits and beer today I think.'

'Good idea, anyway, for future reference, the French wine doesn't travel too well - too much heat on the ships/docks I guess. But the Ozzy stuff is good.'

I chose a few bottles, then at the checkout I paid my bill and kept back some change for a porter.

'You don't need a porter. I'll carry your stuff.'

'OK, thanks. But I'm used to porters - in Kuwait I always used them at the Coops for my weekly food shopping. It helps them to live.'

'I suppose so. It doesn't appeal to my Yorkshire pocket to spend money on something unnecessary.'

I took a little hint here and stored it away in my mind. As we drove away I suddenly remembered something.

'OMG, I forgot to get some sherry for a trifle.'

His response was sharp and revealed limits to his kindness.

'Well, I'm not going back to the shop now. It's the rush hour. You'll have to get it another time.'

Once again, I stashed this in my memory bank, but on a very high shelf. I hadn't asked him to go back, but he made it clear he wasn't willing to do so. Colin's generosity went so far and no more but I was grateful. After all, how would I have done this booze shop without his help? And wasn't he drop dead gorgeous? Back at our apartment building our door porters sprang into action and took our packages upstairs to our separate homes. I threw a quick 'thanks very much' in Colin's direction as the boys from the front desk rushed us off with our booty. I was unpacking the loot from the booze shop when I was interrupted by the doorbell.

'Hi, Colin. Glad you came up - I need to give you your bottle of gin replacement.'

'OK, thanks. That's great.'

'Would you like a drink?'

'Well, I need a shower after that sweaty trip - why don't I pop back in half an hour?'

'Great. Me too - it's so sticky out there.'

As I took my shower I wondered why he'd come to see me, then what we would do about dinner. I didn't have much in the fridge. Perhaps Colin had eaten, or maybe he was thinking of popping out somewhere. Whatever he wanted to do, if it was with me, I was ready to do it. The bell rang again as I pulled on a cotton maxi dress and sprayed my hair with perfume as there was no time for a shampoo.

'Hiya. You were quick.'

'Well, I was looking forward to seeing you.'

'Nice! What would you like to drink?'

'I brought two cold beers up with me, would you like one?'

'Great, thanks. It's thirsty work booze shopping. Glass?'

I tried to reconcile this considerate Colin with the one who would not go the extra yard. It was too much for the moment. I left the analysis till later.

'I think you said you were in Kuwait before this, Rose?'

'Yes, and Hong Kong and the USA most recently.'

'Could you get booze in Kuwait?'

'No, not at all, except through the black market. But that was so expensive it was like drinking liquid gold. But of course, everyone made beer and wine!'

I began to feel hungry as we drank our beers.

'Have you eaten yet, Colin?'

'No. What about you?'

'Me neither. I could make us an omelette if you like?'

'Mm. I love omelettes, especially cheese ones.'

'Well, you are in luck. I've got cheese!'

As I cooked our food, Colin stood in the kitchen and chatted about his experiences over the last year. I got the impression that he enjoyed his life, but I didn't dare ask if he was single. We ate sitting on the bean bags I had in the lounge. A fruity *Riesling* went very well with the rich cheese dish. We ate by the light of the TV, watching the news. It was dark outside and the shadowy sitting room seemed romantic as we sat companionably together on the floor. The plates returned to the kitchen sink, we sank on to the cushions and poured some more wine. Suddenly, the mood changed. My temperature soared as Colin leaned towards me, and kissed me, more fully than the previous embrace. This time it was serious. I didn't stop to think, I just reciprocated. In no time we were in each other's arms, and time flew by. When we eventually took a breath we smiled at each other. I tried to lighten the moment.

'Well, if that's what happens after a booze shopping trip, there's no wonder it's a Government licensed activity.'

Colin chuckled. 'Indeed. It needs to be strictly controlled.'

We drank another glass of wine and then, acknowledging the hour, Colin left. We made no promises. It was an interlude, an extremely pleasant one. But I did wonder if it would be repeated, or if this was a one off. There was no contact the next day, no roses on the door mat, nor email in the inbox. I reconciled myself to the inevitable: Man wants sex, girl wants love. For a few days I was content with this. Then my mind began to play tricks with me. I started remembering the joy I felt in Colin's arms, and the memory of that first electric shock from his kiss replayed itself over and over in my body. I shivered whenever I recalled it. Surely he felt the same? So, a week or so after our hook up I went down to knock on Colin's door. He seemed surprised to see me, but invited me into his well-furnished flat.

'Sorry to drop in on you but I wondered if you could help me with the gym equipment when you have time? I can use some of it, but other bits are a mystery to me.'

'No problem. But not right now. I've got some people coming round.'

'That's fine. Let me know when is good.'

'Tomorrow? After work?'

'OK. Knock on the door when you are ready. I'll be there after 5pm.'

Colin showed me out and made no attempt to kiss me. I felt a little let down, but at least I had tested the water. I wondered what the story was. All that day I kept wondering about Colin but didn't dare ask any questions about him as sexual relations between unmarried people were illegal in the Gulf. As a married woman, not yet divorced, I could even be accused of adultery. The last thing I wanted was a truckful of stones dumping on me in a public square, the modern way of public stoning. Next day at 5pm I rushed home, showered and changed into lycra. When the knock came on the door I opened it rather breathlessly. There stood Colin in his workout gear. I smiled happily at him.

'I thought we could do a work out together, OK?'

'That's great. I feel a bit wary in there on my own. I never go in if there's a man in there, either.'

'Yes, be careful. No one could hear you if there was a problem up there and you look very fetching in that outfit, if I may say so.'

'Thank you, kind sir!' I laughed.

'Come on then - bring a towel! It's best to wipe down any sweaty surfaces.'

We found the gym empty and Colin talked me through the equipment I was unsure of. He demonstrated how to use the weighted apparatus and the pull down wires, then we began our personal work outs. It was reassuring to be in the gym with someone I knew. After 30 minutes I was hot and sweaty. Unused to regular workouts I didn't want to push it too far.

'Well, I'm going to call it a day. What about you?'

'I'll give it another 30 minutes. I like to keep fit.'

'Mm. I can see that.'

I smiled, wondering if I should suggest a drink, but deciding to let him make the running from then on. I'd opened the door, but he had to decide whether to take the next step in.

How about getting together again tomorrow?' he asked on cue.

'Fine. In the gym?'

'Would you like to try squash?'

'Yes, that would be great. 5.30 or 6pm?'

'6 is good. See you then.'

I ran downstairs, gleeful. So he did want to meet up again, but he probably wanted to move slowly. That suited me. I realised I would have been greatly disappointed if he hadn't wanted to. I couldn't wait for the next day to come.

Our squash encounter was fun. Colin was very good, certainly too good for me to give him any kind of game, but he was more patient than I expected and I did my best to put up a good fight. My cheeks flamed red with the heat of the exercise and after an hour I was ready to stop. This time he took the lead.

'Have you got a cold beer in the fridge now?'

'Yes, several. Welcome!'

We went down to my flat and downed the first beer quickly. I felt uncomfortably hot and in desperate need of a shower. I wondered if he would leave and head for his shower. Instead, he made a surprising suggestion.

'Do you think your bath can take two of us?'

'Well, I don't know. I suppose we can try.'

We took a refreshing shower together, then lazed in a bubble bath with another cold beer each. We laughed and chatted easily in this new context. Secretly I wondered what next? That night Colin went back to his own flat, but on many more evenings we either worked out or played squash, often sharing bath and bed. I was happy but my bubble was about to burst.

Jack invited me out for dinner one night to catch up. He told me that the staff member who had occupied my flat prior to me had had her heart broken.

'She fell for Colin, the ladies' man.'

'Colin? The ladies' man?'

My heart fell into my shoes and icy waves snaked down my spine.

'Yes. He's a real misogynist. He takes what he wants from the ladies and then dumps them.'

'Really? How long were they together?'

'Most of last year - for both of them it was their first year on contract. They were quite an item.'

I was mortified, but determined to keep my own secret. I managed to speak.

'So what broke them up?'

'I'm not sure. I suppose he wanted something on tap and when she was moving, it didn't suit him.'

'Oh dear. Is she OK about it?'

'Well, not really. She fell pretty heavily. She'll find someone else I'm sure, though you have to be careful here. Don't fall into the hands of an Arab!'

'I won't be doing that. I've had enough of that menu.'

'Yes, I suppose so. How's the divorce going?'

'Early days yet. Lots of affidavits from the ex which are nothing but lies. It gets me down, arriving home to sheets and sheets of fax paper on my hall floor.'

I kept my cool but my heart was breaking. Was this the explanation for Colin's initial random behaviour? As I went to sleep that night I asked myself if it was worth starting another relationship? Was I strong enough to take a risk again? As Kyle used to say, you can't play tennis on both sides of the net. I would play my own strokes and respond to those of the other person. There was no point in trying to anticipate what they would be. I had to confess to Kyle that I had fallen in love. He was upset but as he had suggested earlier he had been the rebound guy. *Blue on blue.*

I asked Colin about the other woman when he next came over. He had the grace to look ashamed.

'You know, whatever Jack says, we were not really an item. I just wanted a fling.'

'Did she know that?'

'I thought so. I didn't want her to think it was going to be anything more than sex.'

'I see. Dare I ask about us?'

'Well, right now, I think we have something stronger, but it's early days yet, isn't it?'

'Yes, and I am married still, so we have to be careful.'

'Good. That's cleared that up then, hasn't it?'

'Yes, but sooner or later people will find out about us. So what shall we say?'

'As the saying goes, we are just good friends. That should do it.'

'OK. Subject closed.'

I was glad that this had come up and we'd handled it in an adult fashion. I remained besotted with Colin. I did not anticipate the heartache to come.

Epilogue

Gulf War 1 1991

My divorce proceeded slowly as I strove for a settlement of half of the stolen 250k sterling. Despite the heartlessness of the fraud, I was unprepared for the lies which Nabeel presented as 'evidence' in his divorce case. His friendly fire was embedded in his affidavits. First, he denied enticing me from my job in Hong Kong. Even when I produced the piece of paper on which he had handwritten his assets, he maintained that he was a humble shipping clerk, earning next to nothing. One of his putdowns had been that a wife is nothing more than an expensive prostitute. Now he complained that I had wasted his money with my profligate spending habits. In fact, I topped up my wardrobe in the summer sales in the UK on visits to my family. And apart from two years when I worked part time because I was trying to get pregnant, I had worked full time for twelve years with no direct access to my own salary.

I was fortunate to meet a female lawyer with international experience who cut through the complexity of my divorce like a knife through butter. Over lunch she listened to my story, then drafted a letter on a paper napkin for me to write to my lawyers, instructing them to give Nabeel a divorce provided he paid my legal costs and gave me full rights to any proceeds from the UN claim lodged with the British Government. In a few words she cut the Gordian knot I had been wrestling with. Nabeel didn't want to be 'taken to the cleaners' but I wanted my rights.

After three years the story was over, except for the threat Nabeel had made against my life. I lived in fear for years. It was too late for me to have children, but I had my career and my integrity. I could honestly say that everything I owned I had earned by myself. I was an independent, educated woman, who wanted to make her way in the world on merit. In my quest for happiness after divorce I had had a proposal of marriage which I had turned down. Then I had fallen madly in love with someone new who perhaps didn't deserve my love. What else would life throw at me?

Gulf War 2 2003-4

Ten years have gone by since Rose went to her new job in Bahrein and met Colin. She has lost her mother without saying a final goodbye. She has reluctantly ended the romantic relationship but maintained a friendship with Colin which had been impossible with her ex-husband. She has established a new life in peaceful New Zealand. Comparing her fate with that of others she knows she is lucky to have avoided Gulf War 2 and the terrible repercussions of the mismanagement of the occupation of Iraq. With a happy heart she hopes she has found, at last, a heart of gold and the quiet, calm life she longs for.

Questions for Book Club Readers

1. What is the purpose of the two 'voices' in alternate chapters of the novel?

2. What does the phrase 'blue on blue' mean? (Look for Bobby Vinton's song or Maureen McGovern's cover of the song *Blue on blue* on **You Tube**.)

3. What were the effects of Gulf War 1 on Rose?

4. What were the effects of Gulf War 2 on Rose?

5. Do you think Jed will bring 'true love' to Rose?

6. To what extent is Rose's story typical of every woman's search for love?

7. Why does the reader have to travel around New Zealand with Colin and Rose?

8. What did Rose learn from her several relationships?

9. How important in Rose's life was her relationship with her mother?

10. How important in Rose's life is her pursuit of education and her career?

Suggested answers for Book Club Readers

1. What is the purpose of the two 'voices' in alternate chapters of the novel?

   To tell the two stories, of how the two Gulf Wars impacted on one person, interweaving the threads together.

2. What does the phrase 'blue on blue' mean?

   Blue on blue can mean heartache on heartache, or friendly fire in army terminology. In either case it is about heartbreak.

3. What were the effects of Gulf War 1 on Rose?

   She never forgot how her husband turned against her after spending 20 plus years together.

4. What were the effects of Gulf War 2 on Rose?

   Having avoided a war zone, she was determined to move forward and finish building her new life in New Zealand by finding a life partner.

5. Do you think Jed will bring 'true love' to Rose?

   Time will tell.

6. To what extent is Rose's story typical of every woman's search for love?

    Love is the driving force of life, and Rose, like every woman, seeks to find someone with whom she can feel serene.

7. Why does the reader have to travel around New Zealand with Colin and Rose?

    Rose wanted to give the relationship with Colin one last chance. The journey was a test of their potential for togetherness and a reminder of the good times.

8. What did Rose learn from her several relationships?

    She realised that she needed to share her life with a partner. She had missed a lot of physical joy in her marriage, which she had stuck to out of sympathy and adherence to principles but she could not enter into another relationship which lacked trust.

9. How important in Rose's life was her relationship with her Mother?

    Rose's Mother's life was an example of how hard work can give you independence, but also a warning of the danger of relying on a man rather than on oneself.

10. How important in Rose's life is her pursuit of education and her career?

    They are the mainstay of her identity and the props of her independence.

Select Bibliography

Since 1970 I have learned a lot about the Middle East, by reading and from personal experience. These are some titles that I found valuable.

Barr, J., 2011, *A Line in the Sand: Britain, France and the struggle that shaped the Middle East,* Simon & Schuster UK Ltd.

Bhatia, S. & McGrory, D., 2002, *Saddam's Bomb: The Iraqi Race for Nuclear Weapons,* Time Warner Paperbacks, London, UK.

Blix, H., 2004, *Disarming Iraq: The search for weapons of mass destruction,* Bloomsbury Publishing. London, UK.

Chomsky, N. 1983, *The Fateful Triangle: The United States, Israel and the Palestinians,* South End Press, Boston, MA.

Fisk, R., 2006, *The Great War for Civilisation: The conquest of the Middle East,* Harper Perennial, London, UK.

Hamza, K. 2000, *Saddam's Bombmaker,* Touchstone, Simon & Schuster, New York.

Karmi, G., 2009, *In Search of Fatima: A Palestinian story,* Verso, London, UK.

Karsh, E. & I. Rautsi, 2002, *Saddam Hussein: A Political Biography,* Grove Press, New York.

Khalidi, R., 2013, *Brokers of Deceit: How the US has undermined peace in the Middle East,* Beacon Press, Massachusetts.

Lewis, T.R. & J. Brookes, 1991, *The Human Shield,* Leomansley Press, Lichfield, Staffordshire, UK.

Low, S. 2008, *The Boys from Baghdad: From the Foreign Legion to the killing fields of Iraq,* Mainstream Publishing Co. Ltd., Edinburgh, UK.

Rajab, J.S., 1993, *Invasion Kuwait: An Englishwoman's Tale,* Radcliffe Press, London, UK.

Said, E.W., 1995, *The Politics of Dispossession: The struggle for Palestinian self-determination 1969-1994,* Vintage, London, UK.